THE

SHENANDOAH VALLEY

THE

SHENANDOAH VALLEY

In 1864

BY

GEORGE E. POND,

ASSOCIATE EDITOR OF THE ARMY AND NAVY JOURNAL

NEW YORK
CHARLES SCRIBNER'S SONS

PREFACE.

THE Author desires to acknowledge his indebtedness to Colonel R. N. Scott, U. S. A., for the facilities furnished him at the War Records Office, in studying the official documents relating to the events described in the present volume.

In making free use of field despatches, many of which have never hitherto been published, it has not been deemed desirable to strike out occasional errors of statement, arising from imperfect information; since, in order to profitably study and rightly understand the military operations herein described, it is necessary to know the views on which they were based, and to recall, in 1883, the facts as they appeared in 1864.

NEW YORK, January, 1883.

CONTENTS.

CHAPTER VII.

CHAPTER VIII.

CHAPTER IX.

CHAPTER X.

CHAPTER XI.

CHAPTER XII.

CHAPTER XIII.

CHAPTER XIV.

APPENDIX A.

APPENDIX B.

APPENDIX C.

APPENDIX D.

LIST OF MAPS.

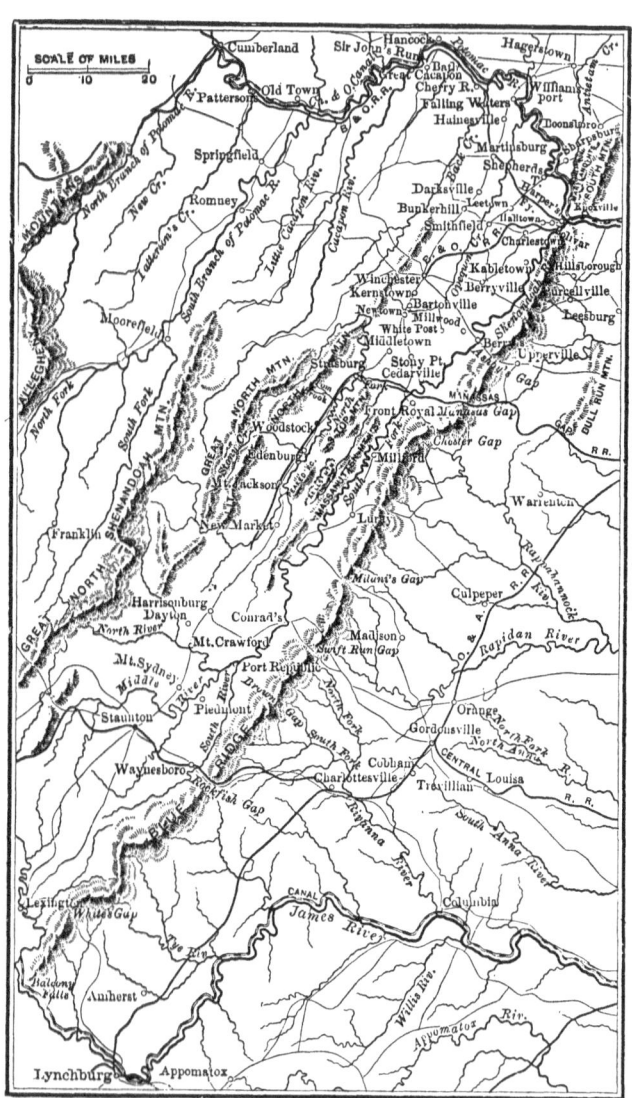

The Shenandoah Valley.

THE SHENANDOAH VALLEY.

CHAPTER I.

THE VALLEY OF VIRGINIA.

THE mountain region of Virginia, from the beginning of
the war, held a close military relation to the broad plain
that stretches from the foot of the Blue Ridge to the sea,
and it eventually became the theatre of a series of campaigns at once picturesque and decisive. The State was like
a vast fortress or intrenched camp, thrown out above the
line of the other ten Confederate commonwealths to guard
their capital. Its parallel rivers, flowing to the Atlantic,
were water-barriers against attack from the north, while
upreared to shield its western front were the rampart ridges
of its highland domain. The valleys between these ridges
furnished well-sheltered avenues for invading Northern territory.

Of these avenues the most commanding was the Valley
of Virginia, called also, from the chief river that drains it,
the Valley of the Shenandoah. Its eastern wall is the
lofty Blue Ridge; its western, the North Mountains, a part
of the main chain of the Alleghanies. Since its course
is southwesterly, a Confederate army moving northward

XI.—1

through it would at the same time draw nearer Washington, whereas a Union advance southward would diverge from the straight course to Richmond. The Potomac running at right angles to the line of the Ridge, a Confederate force crossing this border stream at the mouth of the Valley, as at Williamsport, would already be sixty miles north or in rear of Washington. State lines there are not determined by the highland configuration—what is known in Virginia as the Valley of the Shenandoah continues unbroken north of the Potomac, taking there the name of Cumberland Valley, while its protecting wall is also prolonged with a simple change of appellation from Blue Ridge to South Mountain ; and one day's march through the Cumberland Valley would carry a body of Confederate horsemen among the peaceful farm lands of Pennsylvania.

Beautiful to look upon, and so fertile that it was styled the granary of Virginia, rich in its well-filled barns, its cattle, its busy mills, the Valley furnished from its abundant crops much of the subsistence of Lee's army. When Confederate forces occupied it, their horses fattened on its forage, and in quitting it to invade the North, the commissaries filled their wagons from its storehouses and farms. While a few of the people of the lower Valley shared the sentiments of loyalty which animated West Virginia, the inhabitants as a whole became bitterly hostile to the Union. There was, however, a large population of Dunkards, with whom nonresistance was an article of religious faith, and who were accordingly exempt from conscription on payment of a specified sum, even when the Confederate need of troops was sore. These became, in time, of hardly less military value than an equal number of combatants, for they raised the crops on which the Confederate armies depended for sustenance, and often, also, cared for the families of absent soldiers. At last their whirring mills and golden wheat-fields ceased to be at the service of the South; for the Valley felt the fury of war, and its fatal wealth of resources was laid waste.

Looking at the Shenandoah Valley in history, we observe that it was the scene of constant Confederate manœuvring, whether on a large scale, under Jackson, Ewell, and Early, or on a smaller one, under Ashby, Mosby, Imboden, and Gilmor. From the first it was a tempting field for the strategists of both armies. The initial campaign of the war turned on the use made of the Valley by the forces which General J. E. Johnston posted at its outlet under the name of "The Army of the Shenandoah." There, too, Jackson began the campaign of 1862 by sustaining a check from Shields, for which he fully indemnified himself when, a few months later, he fell upon Shields at Fort Republic, defeated Fremont at Cross Keys, captured the garrison of Front Royal, drove Banks across the Potomac, and, by alarming Washington, broke up the impending junction of McDowell and McClellan, and the threatened capture of Richmond. It was from the Valley that Jackson, repeating on a bolder circuit the Manassas device of 1861, hurried to turn the Union right on the Peninsula. Lee found in the Valley a line of communications for his Maryland campaign, and captured at Harper's Ferry 11,000 men, seventy-three guns, and thirteen thousand small arms; there, too, he sought rest and refreshment on retreating from the Antietam. The Valley was Lee's route of invasion after defeating Hooker at Chancellorsville; Ewell, entering it at Chester Gap, took several thousand men and a score or more of guns from Milroy; and thither again Lee fell back after Gettysburg, pitching his camps along the Opequon.

These events, described in preceding volumes of the pres-

ent series, show that, though subordinate to the main scene
of operations east of the Blue Ridge, the Valley of Virginia
had always played an important part in the drama of the
war. It had yielded so many captures of Union garrisons
and so many disasters in the field, as to be called the Valley
of Humiliation; and not until it was wrested from Confederate control did the problem of the Richmond campaign
find a successful solution.

To set forth the manner in which Confederate power in
the Shenandoah Valley was overthrown during 1864 is the
purpose of the present volume. But before entering upon
this narrative it is well to describe the *terrain* in detail.

The Shenandoah River rises a little south of the 38th parallel; but military operations extended nearly to the border of North Carolina. From this boundary northward to
where, in latitude 37° 30', the James crosses the Blue Ridge,
the surface is broken by tumultuous upheavals, spurs pushing out from the main ranges in all directions; still, everywhere can be traced the familiar double chain of mountains,
which becomes, indeed, a triple chain south of Floyd County,
where the Blue Ridge forks. The landscape is now of
surpassing beauty and again of savage grandeur; but though
there are practicable passages in the mountains for all
three arms, deep chasms being threaded by narrow roads
that climb the sides of the precipitous bluffs, yet the region
is hostile to campaigning. The chief strategic importance
of the rugged southwestern angle of Virginia was an artifi-
cial one, contributed by the East Tennessee Railroad, which
connected Lynchburg with Knoxville, and hence Richmond
with the South and West. Southern Virginia, through
which this road ran, was rich in minerals and grains, and
full of supplies and manufactured products of many sorts,

important to Lee's army. The principal stations in Virginia, starting westward from Lynchburg, were Liberty, Salem, Christiansburg, Newbern, Wytheville, and Abingdon. All these became intimately connected with one of the Shenandoah campaigns of 1864; and though the latter three properly came within the scope of operations that have the Kanawha as a base, they held direct relations with the Richmond campaign, since at Newbern the railroad crossed New River, an affluent of the Kanawha, offering an important bridge for destruction, while the lead works of Wytheville and the salt works at Saltville, near Abingdon, furnished to the Confederacy valuable military stores.

In the mountainous country above and beyond the Shenandoah Valley proper, the rivers run to all points of the compass. The Roanoke and the New diverge from opposite slopes of the same range; the Kanawha and the James, from neighboring headwaters, take their several ways, after many turnings, the one to the Mississippi and the other to the Atlantic. A little south of where the James rushes through the Blue Ridge at Balcony Falls, the range also breaks apart at the Peaks of Otter. On a branch of the James, called North River, is Lexington, the seat of Rockbridge County. We are now in the Valley itself; for below Lexington the Shenandoah takes its rise in a multitude of streams that combine in three, called North, Middle, and South, these uniting in turn lower down, near Port Republic. From Lexington to Harper's Ferry, at the foot of the Valley, the distance is one hundred and fifty-five miles; and at Staunton, thirty-five miles below Lexington, we strike upon the Valley turnpike that runs northward through Harrisonburg, New Market, Woodstock, Strasburg, and Winchester to Martinsburg — a fine, macadamized road, well worn by Northern and Southern troops and trains. West of the pike is the Back Road, with a Middle Road in some places between the two. Here at Staunton the Virginia Central Railroad crosses the Valley on its way to Charlottesville, Gordonsville, and Richmond, traversing the Blue Ridge at Rockfish Gap, near the village of Waynesboro.

Five-and-twenty miles north of Staunton, near Harrisonburg, an isolated chain, called Massanutten, rising abruptly to a height equal to that of the Blue Ridge, divides the Valley for a distance of more than forty miles, until, at Strasburg, this beautiful range suddenly falls again into the plain. The Massanutten Mountains are presently seen to follow the prevailing type of the Appalachian system, by breaking into two parallel ridges, Massanutten proper and Kell's Mountain, leaving between them Powell's Fort Valley, or the "The Fort," a narrow, picturesque vale, through which winds Passage Creek to the Shenandoah below; while west of Kell's is another parallel sub-range, Peaked Ridge and Three Top, allowing space between them and Kell's for a Little Fort Valley. Massanutten was crossed by a good road, connecting New Market and Luray, which had military importance; but in other respects, since its enclosed valley was only the scene of minor cavalry operations, it may be remembered simply *en bloc*.

The larger branch of the Shenandoah, the South Fork, flows through the easternmost of the two valleys created by Massanutten—called Page or Luray Valley—while the main or Strasburg Valley, west of the range, is drained by the other affluent, the North Fork, which, rising in the North Mountains, winds along the west flank of Massanutten, until, escaping around the base, at Strasburg, it joins the South Fork near Front Royal; and the main river thus formed skirts thenceforth the foot of the Blue Ridge, till it swells the Potomac at Harper's Ferry.

At Strasburg, the Valley, relieved of the Massanutten, re-
covers its usual breadth of twenty miles. Here we observe an historically important stream, Cedar Creek, which,
having taken its rise and its early course behind Little
North Mountain, has found its opportunity at Sydnor Gap
to enter the Valley proper, where, flowing southerly, it joins
the North Fork at Strasburg. Following down the pike, we
leave the river on the right, and, crossing Cedar Creek, pass
through Middletown, Newtown, and Kernstown to Winchester, a place of consequence, from which the Winchester and
Potomac Railroad had run to Harper's Ferry until torn up,
like the Manassas Gap road, by the Confederates, in 1862.
From Winchester the pike proceeds through Bunker Hill to
Martinsburg, the chief city of the lower Valley, on the Baltimore and Ohio Railroad. A good macadamized road leads
from Winchester to Harper's Ferry through Berryville, and
one from Martinsburg strikes the Potomac opposite Williamsport, at the extreme north end of the Valley. Another
road, proceeding easterly from Martinsburg, reaches the
river at Shepherdstown, after crossing Opequon Creek—a
stream, which, rising south of Winchester, drains in its exceedingly tortuous course the western portion of the lower
Valley, being separated from the Shenandoah by Limestone
Ridge. The picturesque town of Harper's Ferry, at the
junction of the Shenandoah with the Potomac, is dominated
both by the lofty Loudoun Heights on the south bank of the
Potomac and by the towering and precipitous Maryland
Heights on the other.

Military operations were aided by the fine roads that connected all the important towns with each other and, through
the leading gaps, with those of Eastern Virginia. The Valley
was also so largely cleared and cultivated that troops could
march almost where they liked through the fields, on both

sides of the roads, leaving these for the guns and wagons, the whole column thereby advancing very rapidly. The creeks and rivers could be waded nearly everywhere during the summer and autumn, the military significance of the fords being in most instances simply that of levelled approaches to the crossing-places; for often even small streams ran between high and precipitous banks.

In the Blue Ridge there are practicable gaps all the way from the James to the Potomac, that connect the Valley with Eastern Virginia. Beginning with Rockfish, the outlet of Staunton, and passing Jaman's, Brown's, Semons, Powell's, and High Top, which give access from Port Republic to Charlottesville, we come to Swift Run Gap, through which a turnpike leads from Conrad's Store to Stannardsville, and there branches to Orange and Gordonsville. A little farther north two more turnpikes cross the Ridge through Milani's and Thornton Gaps, one leading from New Market, across the Massanutten to Madison, and the other diverging from it by way of Luray to Culpepper. From Luray a very good road runs northward between the Ridge and the South Fork to Front Royal, where another pike gives access to the country east of the Ridge by Thoroughfare and Chester Gaps. A few miles farther on, through Manassas Gap, ran the railroad of that name. From Winchester turnpikes led through Ashby's and Snicker's Gaps to Aldie, while Gregory's and Keyes Gaps are nearer Harper's Ferry. Doorways in plenty, therefore, opened through the Ridge. The best single point for commanding these passes was Gordonsville.

CHAPTER II.

CLOYD'S MOUNTAIN AND NEW MARKET.

In the spring of 1864, the Department of West Virginia, which included the Shenandoah Valley, was under the command of Major-General Franz Sigel. A large portion of his forces was in the Kanawha region, under Brigadier-General George Crook; the remainder, distributed near the Potomac line, and in the lower part of the Valley, where were his headquarters. Apart from its physical configuration, the chief feature of this Department was its lines of railroad. Traversing its northern section was the main route of Union communication between Washington and the West, the Baltimore and Ohio road, constantly used in the transfer of troops and supplies—there were more northerly lines which could take its place if needful, but its military value was indisputable. Just beyond the southern boundary of West Virginia ran a very important Confederate line, the Virginia and Tennessee Railroad, which directly connected Richmond and the West. Between these the Virginia Central, also a Confederate railway line, crossed the Shenandoah Valley at Staunton, and, penetrating the Blue Ridge at Rockfish Gap, led through Charlottesville and Gordonsville to Richmond.

It is therefore apparent that the military problem in this region was of the same nature for the Kanawha and the Shenandoah forces of General Sigel—its defensive factor, the protection of the Union railway, and therewith Maryland and

1*

Pennsylvania; its aggressive, the destruction of the two Confederate lines of supply. Hence, in opening his Virginia campaign, Lieutenant-General Grant directed Sigel to form two columns, whereof one, under Crook, should break the Virginia and Tennessee Railroad at the New River bridge, and should also, if possible, destroy the salt works at Saltville; while the other column, under Sigel himself, proceeding up the Shenandoah Valley, was to distract attention from Crook by menacing the Virginia Central Railroad at Staunton. Sigel's was primarily a defensive department, designed to secure the North from invasion, but such advancing columns, thought General Grant, would "give a better protection than if lying idle in garrison;" while, in threatening important lines of supply, they might detain troops that otherwise would reinforce Lee's army.

Crook, learning what was expected of him, divided his task into two portions, assigning to the cavalry, under Brigadier-General W. W. Averell, the attempt against Saltville, while for the burning of the New River bridge he reserved the infantry, under his own command. The West Virginia movements were timed to the march of the Lieutenant-General from Culpepper.

Averell, with 2,079 officers and men, the brigades of General Duffié and Colonel Schoonmaker, left Charleston, W. Va., May 1st, and Logan, May 5th, wretchedly supplied with transportation, and marched through Wyoming and Tazewell, there capturing some Confederate pickets. Such accounts were given him of the enemy's defences at Saltville that, being without artillery, Averell determined not to attempt this place, but to advance instead against the lead works of Wytheville. Yet Wytheville proved every whit as difficult of approach; for the Saltville forces of General John Morgan, with three guns, rapidly transferred themselves thither. Averell moved forward Schoonmaker, with the Fourteenth Pennsylvania and the First Virginia cavalry, to open the attack, while the main line was Duffié, with the Second and Third Virginia and a part of the Thirty-fourth Ohio. But the enemy assailed him with vigor and pressed heavily upon both flanks, Averell resisting until night, when he made off eastward, with a loss in killed and wounded of 123. His hard ride,

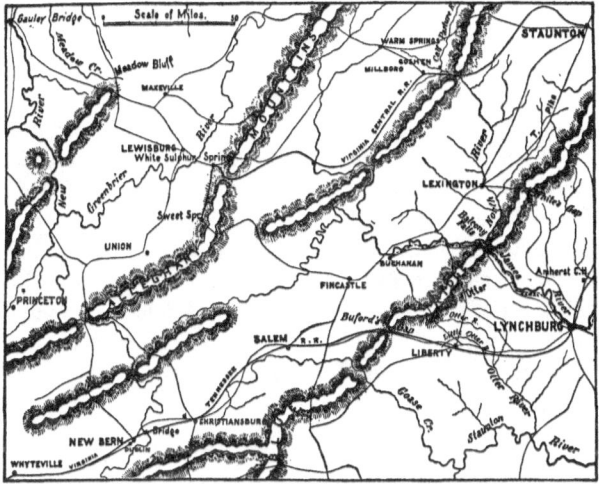

The Region Around Newbern.

however, was not wholly fruitless, for he destroyed a part of the railroad near Christiansburg, with its station and repair shops, and found some 3-inch guns which the enemy had left in the town. He then drew off to join Crook at Union.

Crook meanwhile had met with better fortune. His force included eleven infantry regiments. The First Brigade

Colonel R. B. Hayes, comprised the Twenty-third, Thirty-fourth, and Thirty-sixth Ohio; the Second, Colonel C. B. White, the Twelfth and Ninety-first Ohio and the Ninth and Fourteenth Virginia; the Third, Colonel Sickel, the Third and Fourth Pennsylvania and the Eleventh and Fifteenth Virginia. To these were joined two battalions of artillery, besides four hundred cavalry under Colonel Oley, the whole force being about six thousand strong. Leaving Fayette May 3d, the column proceeded southeastward for three days without opposition, and then, near Princeton, the enemy's skirmishers were encountered and driven away. Entering this town, General Crook destroyed the tents of McCausland's cavalry, which had been incautiously left there. The night of the 8th he reached Shannon's, seven miles from Dublin, where he found the enemy posted two miles ahead, on Cloyd's Mountain, commanding the road: Daybreak revealed several thousand men, under Generals W. E. Jones and Jenkins, intrenched on a wooded spur behind rail breastworks, with their guns so placed as to sweep a broad field that fronted the works, while a knee-deep brook wound around the foot of the steep slope crowned by the rifle-pits. " The enemy is in force, and in strong position," said Crook, lowering his field-glass; " he may whip us, but I guess not."

Forming under cover of the thick timber, the Union commander sent White, with his own brigade and two regiments of Sickel's, to turn the enemy's right, and the moment they were engaged moved the rest of his forces directly against the works. His men were received with a hot fire as they struggled across the open, but, after a hard contest, carried the intrenchments at all points. Crook's loss was 600, Colonel Woolworth, Fourth Pennsylvania, being among the killed. More than half the casualties fell upon White's brigade, while Duval's Ninth Virginia regiment alone had 45 killed and 125 wounded, out of the 450 men engaged. The enemy's loss must have been heavy, judging by the dead left on the field; among his mortally wounded was General Jenkins. Had Averell's cavalry been with him, Crook might have made his victory still more marked; but he had only Oley's command to aid him in the pursuit. Nevertheless, he captured 230 unwounded prisoners and two guns.

The enemy fled to Dublin, where, two miles in front of the town, reinforcements of Morgan's men, having arrived on the cars from Saltville too late to take part in the main action, covered the retreat. These troops Crook promptly put to flight, and then, entering Dublin, destroyed sundry military stores which had been abandoned there. The next morning he marched on to Newbern, whither the forces from Cloyd's Mountain had retreated for the purpose of protecting the bridge over New River. After an artillery duel of two hours, with a Union loss of but 11 men, Crook took possession of this important structure, and burned it. His main purpose being now accomplished he began his homeward march, by way of Union, where he had given rendezvous to Averell. He left behind, with surgeons and drugs, 200 of his wounded, who could not have borne the long journey in that rugged region. Indeed, what was to have been a four days' march consumed nine, a prolonged storm making the roads heavy and toilsome. This delay, in turn, caused not only rations but forage to run short, so that some of the wagons had to be abandoned, the mules being too weak to drag them. The enemy's cavalry endeavored to harass the march, but was driven off, and the 19th of May Crook and Averell ended their weary tramp at Meadow Bluff.

This campaign of the Kanawha forces must be set down as achieving a good measure of success. It is true that Saltville and Wytheville were not reached, and that Averell, on approaching them, was roughly handled by John Morgan's troopers, as the importance of these places to the Confederacy caused them to be resolutely defended; still, the destruction of New River bridge was the main object of the expedition, and this was accomplished.

It is perhaps worth observing that Sigel hardly expected Averell's part of the project to succeed. Crook having reported to him what he proposed to do, Sigel forwarded a copy of the despatch to General Grant, with these remarks : "This plan of General Crook's may prove successful, and may have very important results, but it is not in accordance with my views, because it brings General Averell too far west, and out of reach of General Crook. His cavalry will be used up, and therefore cannot assist General Crook in future operations. Secondly, because this movement will allow the enemy to concentrate nearly all his forces which are between Staunton and Lewisburg at Staunton. Thirdly, because it makes all co-operation of forces here with those of General Crook impossible. My understanding was that all the forces of General Crook should operate between the James and New Rivers, and that the movements should end with a demonstration against Staunton, with all the forces under Crook—the cavalry included ; but I may be wrong, and it is too late to interfere. I will therefore say nothing to General Crook, but wish him success, which he so well deserves." General Grant, however, was pleased with the boldness of Crook's proposed march : " To cut New River bridge," he replied, "and the road ten or twenty miles east from there, would be the most important work Crook could do." As for Sigel's suggested movement of Crook to Staunton, in co-operation with a force to march up the Valley, this was shortly after carried out, but under another commander.

Crook's losses in this expedition were 109 killed and 513

wounded ; Averell's, 17 killed, 72 wounded, 34 missing—the aggregate, 745. Crook's and Averell's prisoners numbered nearly 300, and the enemy's killed and wounded may have made his total loss equal to that of the Union commanders.

In the twofold campaign assigned to Sigel, the portion set apart for the Kanawha column had been obviously the more definite as well as the more important ; in fact, after guard· ing even scantily the supply depots of the lower Valley and the Baltimore and Ohio Railroad, Sigel, for a movement co-operating with Crook, would have a field force at most of six or seven thousand men. However, toward the end of April, he gathered the available troops from his garrisons, and the 30th started up the Valley. The next day he notified General Grant that he was occupying Winchester with all his available forces, " consisting of about four thousand in-fantry, one thousand cavalry and three batteries, and would push his advance toward Cedar Creek." The following day he asked for more specific instructions. " I would very much like to know what your expectations are. I under-stand that I am to occupy the line at Cedar Creek, and to advance up the Shenandoah Valley if circumstances will allow me to do so. To advance beyond Strasburg with my present force is hardly possible, if I cannot at the same time have a pretty strong force opposite Front Royal to prevent the enemy from marching into my rear or cutting off my line of communication with cavalry. I have only a very vague idea about the position of the Army of the Potomac, and do not know whether there is any force of ours at or near Luray. If I am expected to make energetic and decisive movements, I should have at least five thousand more of good infantry, with which I could march up the Shenandoah Valley. The few troops I have here are excellent, with the exception of the cav·

alry." It was certainly clear that, with so small a number of
men at command, in order to reach Staunton, if the march
were seriously resisted, there needed to be a co-operative
movement from the Kanawha forces upon the same point—
yet Crook was starting for Newbern. "I do not want you,"
replied Grant, the next day, "to move farther south than
Cedar River, to watch any movement the enemy may attempt
by way of the Shenandoah Valley. The Army of the Potomac
occupies nothing between the Blue Ridge and Orange and
Alexandria Railroad. It is to be hoped that efforts making
for raising troops will enable us to send any reinforcements
you may require, should the enemy move down the Valley."

It chanced that, a few days later, May 5th, a hundred of
McNeil's horsemen rode to the Baltimore and Ohio Railroad
at Piedmont, in West Virginia, captured the guard, and there
and at Bloomington burned a few loaded cars and engines.
Secretary Stanton called upon Governor Brough, of Ohio,
to send some troops to defend the railroad. "Sigel's advance has exposed the Baltimore and Ohio Road," he said.
Governor Brough promptly furnished four hundred-days
regiments for Charleston, three for Parkersburg, three for
New Creek, three for Harper's Ferry, and two for Cumberland, so that the railroad was reasonably guarded; and General Kelley took command at Cumberland, with orders to
watch the road west of the Monocacy, while Sigel sent five
hundred cavalry to Moorefield to try to cut off the retreat of
the raiders. This force was quickly defeated, with a loss of
fifty men, near Wardensville, and driven to Romney; but
meanwhile the railroad had been put in running order.
The chief importance of the incident was in calling to the
railroad and the Potomac line the Ohio hundred-days men.

On the 9th Sigel, with Sullivan's division of infantry and
Stahel's cavalry, moved up the Valley pike to Cedar Creek,

and the 11th pushed through Strasburg to Woodstock, whence the cavalry advanced to Mount Pleasant or Jackson. At Woodstock he sent to the Adjutant-General this message: "My principal object in advancing up the Shenandoah Valley was to threaten Staunton, to divide the forces of Breckenridge, and to assist by these means General Crook, whose object is to destroy New River bridge. My forces are insufficient for offensive operations in this country, where the cavalry is continually on my flank and rear. My intention, therefore, is not to advance farther than this place with my main force, but have sent out strong parties in every direction. Skirmishing is going on every day. If Breckenridge should advance against us, I will resist him at some convenient position."

On the 14th he moved Colonel Moor with infantry to Mount Jackson; and there Boyd's First New York Cavalry, which had been prudently sent three days before to scout through Luray Valley, so as to guard the left flank, under orders to rejoin the main body through Massanutten Gap at New Market, reported the enemy to be in force at the latter point. On Moor advancing thither from Rude's Hill, which is a few miles beyond Mount Jackson, east of the North Fork, the roar of hostile guns confirmed the tidings that the unchallenged stage of Sigel's march was over.

The Confederate presence thus disclosed was the advance of General Breckenridge, who, having been intrusted with the command of the Valley, and observing Sigel's arrival at Strasburg, was marching rapidly from his post at Staunton to oppose him, with a force of nearly 5,000 men. Moor had, besides cavalry and artillery, two regiments of his own brigade and two of the other, Thoburn's. General Stahel came up next morning and took command.

New Market is on the Valley pike, about eight miles

above Mount Jackson. At the latter point, the road, after having followed the left bank of the North Fork all the way up from Strasburg, crosses the river and passes about half-way between its right bank and a nearly parallel little stream known as Smith's Creek. At New Market the Valley pike is joined by the turnpike which comes up from Front Royal to Luray, and thence traverses the Massanutten Mountains by Massanutten Gap; hence this was one of the points in the Valley possessing a certain degree of military importance,

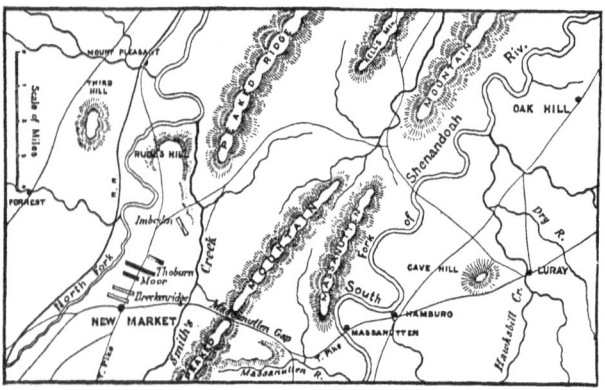

The Battle of New Market.

and as good a place as any for Breckenridge to execute his purpose of attacking Sigel.

It is obvious that the Union general was not prepared for battle, his forces being scattered along the pike. But Moor, having established himself on an elevation north-west of New Market, remained there through the stormy night of the 14th, and sent out his skirmishers at daylight; and, a few hours later, Sigel came up with the remainder of his small army to accept battle. The arrangement of the line under these hurried circumstances gave some of the troops an exhausting tramp back and forth through the sticky mud of fields of young wheat. Moor was left in advance to break the enemy's onset, drawn back, however, a considerable distance to the rear of the position he had at first reached. His troops consisted of the Eighteenth Connecticut and One Hundred and Twenty-third Ohio infantry, with a small body of cavalry, the two regiments which had reinforced him being returned to their proper brigade, Thoburn's. This latter was formed as the main line of battle, under Sigel's personal direction. The artillery was carefully disposed. On the left of the guns at the right was the Thirty-fourth Massachusetts, except one company, detached and thrown out as skirmishers in the woods of the river bank; then came the First Virginia and Fifty-fourth Pennsylvania. A few companies of the Twelfth West Virginia supported the artillery on the right, the others being formed in double column in rear of the Thirty-fourth. The cavalry was behind the centre, and on the left flank. The line extended across the pike on rising ground, while another slope in front was held by Moor.

Breckenridge moved to the attack with the veteran brigades of Echols and Wharton and some local forces, while McLaughlin's artillery went into action on a sharp ridge that ran parallel with the pike. Overlapping Moor, Breckenridge drove him in confusion to the rear, and, with hardly a pause, came in excellent order across the intervening depression, against Thoburn. The shouts of his attack were answered by a handsome charge from the Union right that promptly checked him. But the left was already in difficulty. Imboden, who commanded Breckenridge's cavalry, galloping down Smith's Creek, along the eastern bank, to the bridge on the Luray road, had there recrossed, and come up on the west side, the manœuvre being such as to bring him upon Sigel's left flank. He had taken two guns with him, and running these up to short range, opened on the cavalry there and routed it. Pressing his advantage, he se-cured a flank and almost rear fire against Sigel's left, while Breckenridge, charging heavily in front, compelled the en-tire force to retreat. Yet the Union troops contested the ground; and one of Sigel's batteries was ill rewarded for its good service and reluctant withdrawal by falling into the enemy's hands.[1]

At Rude's Hill a new line was formed, Moor's troops having rallied, and the Twenty-eighth and One Hundred and Sixteenth Ohio being brought up from the charge of the wagons. But after a brief halt Sigel resumed his re-treat along the turnpike, bringing off all his train. He crossed the Shenandoah to Mount Jackson on the narrow bridge, which he burned behind him. Breckenridge followed only to Rude's Hill, but Sigel marched on till he had en-camped his forces behind Cedar Creek. His losses in this engagement were as follows: killed, 93; wounded, 482; missing, 256—total, 831. The Confederate loss was also severe: killed, 34; wounded, 484; missing, 13—total, 531.[2] Sigel's dead and his badly wounded were left in the enemy's hands.

---

[1] Imboden's official report employs the following language: "Sigel's entire line retired slowly. His artillery was especially damaging, and he (Breckenridge) de-termined to silence at least one, and the most mischievous battery, directly in front of the centre of his line; and Colonel Smith, of the Sixty-second Virginia, and Colonel Skip, with his Cadets, were ordered to charge and take it. . . . The battery was taken, but with fearful loss on both sides." Sigel's despatches speak of losing five guns; other accounts give the number as six. He made no official report of the battle.

[2] "The Sixty-second Regiment alone," says Imboden, "reported 241 killed and wounded, including seven of the ten captains, three of whom were killed in

The reason assigned by General Sigel for his defeat was that the Confederate forces outnumbered him, and that in consequence of the long trains he had to guard, " he could not bring more than six regiments into the fight, besides the artillery and cavalry, and the enemy had about seven thousand infantry, besides other arms." In a previous despatch he said that "the battle was fought on our side by 5,500 in all, against 8,000 to 9,000 of the enemy." But even if we deduct from Sigel's 5,500 the two regiments that did not participate in the battle, there was little disparity in numbers.[1] While his force, almost wholly composed of troops taken from garrison, was much too small, yet it is palpable that the battle was fought hurriedly, and that Moor's line was too weak to check the enemy, yet too important a fraction of the command to be left where it could be made useless by an overwhelming attack. The indefinite character of Sigel's task seems to have left him without a clear objective, and, as a consequence, without a precise idea of what he might be called upon to meet. But it is due to him to say that he spared no personal exertions to redeem the day.

---

the charge of the captured battery. The corps of Cadets lost 8 killed and 4 officers and 57 privates wounded, out of a total force of 250 engaged. General Echols's casualties were nearly 300, including the Cadets, mostly wounded. The artillery did not lose over eight or ten killed and wounded."

[1] In the Appendix will be found the documents of the War Records office on this subject. In addition, General W. S. Lincoln, in "The Thirty-fourth Massachusetts Infantry in the War of the Rebellion," has made a special study of the rosters, from which it appears that the official report of Breckenridge's strength the day after the battle shows the following aggregate then present: Wharton's brigade, 1,309 ; Echols's, 1,488 ; Northwest, 983 ; Cadet battalion, 221 ; Engineer Corps, 46 ; McLaughlin's artillery, 235—total of infantry and artillery, 4,282. Imboden, in his report, gives the cavalry at 800, which would make the total of the three arms over 5,000. He also puts the infantry actually engaged at 3,440 and the artillery at 350, with 18 guns, making a total of 4,590 men. The report after the battle presumably excludes the killed and missing ; and we may, therefore, safely set down the Confederate strength in the engagement at from 4,600 to 5,000 men.

Sigel telegraphed to Washington, the day after the battle, that the troops were in good spirits, and would make a good fight if the enemy should advance ; and sending his cavalry to Woodstock, he moved his infantry across the creek through Strasburg, and with his advance occupied Fisher's Hill. But Grant, not regarding Sigel's operations as satisfactory, had asked for his removal immediately on hearing of his defeat ; for he had so little expected this event that an hour before receiving news of it he had asked Halleck if Sigel could not go up to Staunton, and destroy the road there. Halleck answered that "the Secretary of War directs me to say that the President will appoint General Hunter to command the Department of West Virginia if you desire it." Grant accordingly welcomed the opportunity of placing Hunter in command, in Sigel's stead.

CHAPTER III.

GENERAL HUNTER'S LYNCHBURG CAMPAIGN.

THE Virginia and Tennessee road being broken at New River, the Shenandoah problem was narrowed and simplified. The 20th of May, the day before Hunter took command in the Valley, the Lieutenant-General expressed through Halleck his opinion of what should be done next, inclining to pursue the plan for which Sigel had already given instructions. "In regard to the operations," he said, "it is better for General Hunter to engage in, with the disposable forces at his command, I am a little in doubt. It is evident that he can move South, covering the road he has to guard, with a larger force than he can spare to be removed to reinforce armies elsewhere. Then, too, under the instructions of General Sigel,[1] Crook was to get through to the Virginia and Tennessee Railroad, at New River Bridge, and move eastward to Lynchburg, if he could; if not, to Fincastle, Staunton, and down the Shenandoah Valley. Sigel was to collect what force he could spare from the railroad, and move up the Valley with a supply-train, to meet him. The enemy are evidently relying for supplies greatly on such as are brought over the branch road running through

---

[1] "On my arrival at Meadow Bluffs, May 19th, from the New River expedition, I received a despatch from Major-General Sigel, then commanding the Department, to make a demonstration on Staunton as soon as possible" (General Crook's Report, July 7th).

Staunton. On the whole, therefore, I think it would be better for General Hunter to move in that direction, and reach
Staunton and Gordonsville or Charlottesville, if he does not
meet with too much opposition. If he can hold at bay a
force equal to his own, he will be doing good service."
Hunter, therefore, vigorously pushed his preparations for a
very long march. He left Sigel in charge of the reserve
troops and the railroad, Kelley and Weber reporting to him.

The 26th of May Hunter broke camp at Cedar Creek and
marched up the pike to Woodstock. He had with him
Sigel's former troops, reinforced so that they now amounted
to 8,500 men of all arms, with twenty-one guns, the infantry
under Sullivan and the cavalry under Stahel. At Woodstock
he halted for shoes to come up, and wrote Halleck that he
should " depend entirely on the country [for food] and hope
to form a junction with Crook at Staunton, and then move
immediately on Lynchburg." Halleck that same day had
sent him word where Grant was, adding, " he wishes you to
push on, if possible, to Charlottesville and Lynchburg, and
destroy the railroad and canal beyond possibility of repair
for weeks ; then, either return to your original base or join
Grant, via Gordonsville. In your movements live as much
as possible on the country." Grant had, in fact, just given
to Halleck these instructions. From Woodstock Hunter
marched past Mount Jackson and Rude's Hill to New Market, the scene of Sigel's defeat, there remaining a few days,
while sending out his foragers for beeves, sheep, grain, and
flour, under the following orders :

III. Brigade and all other Commanders will be held strictly responsible that their commands are supplied from the country. Cattle, sheep,
and hogs, and, if necessary, horses and mules must be taken, and
slaughtered. These supplies will be seized under the direction of
officers duly authorized, and upon a system which will hereafter be

regulated. No straggling or pillaging will be allowed. Brigade and other commanders will be held responsible that there is no waste; and that there is a proper and orderly division amongst their men, of the supplies taken for our use.

At Woodstock he had ordered Stahel to send out foraging parties, "under command of reliable and just officers, who will collect such subsistence and forage as the army needs, allowing no waste nor pillage, and giving such of the residents as claim to be and are commonly reputed to be loyal, certificates of the amount of stores taken for the use of the United States Government. You will charge the officers detailed for this duty to hold their men well in hand, and to allow no plundering or oppression of the inhabitants; nothing being seized except by order of the officers in charge of such party." Three days later, at Rude's Hill, he called Stahel's attention to "the numerous and grave complaints against soldiers of this command for unauthorized pillaging," and insisted that they should cease. "Many of the residents of this neighborhood," he said, "have been very kind to our wounded, and it is neither just nor politic to allow wanton outrage and injuries to be inflicted upon any people." Hunter's foraging soon proved useful, as a supply train moving to him from Martinsburg was seized and burned by Gilmor's horsemen at Newtown. Its escort consisted of 83 men of the Fifteenth and Twenty-first New York cavalry, under Lieutenant-Colonel Root, of the former, who in the engagement lost 10 killed and wounded and 9 prisoners.

From New Market Hunter proceeded to Harrisonburg, where, June 2d, he found Imboden posted about seven miles ahead on the pike, at Mount Crawford, his right at Rockland Mills and his left at Bridgewater, the line of defence being the North River. After examining this

XI.—2

position, he moved by a side road southeastward to Port
Republic, where he crossed the South Fork of the Shenandoah, flanking the Mount Crawford position. A large supply train was overhauled and in part captured by Stahel's
cavalry.

The morning of the 5th he advanced toward Staunton, and
found that the enemy, under General W. E. Jones, had
brought up his forces from Lynchburg to Piedmont, to resist the Union march. This little village is four miles east

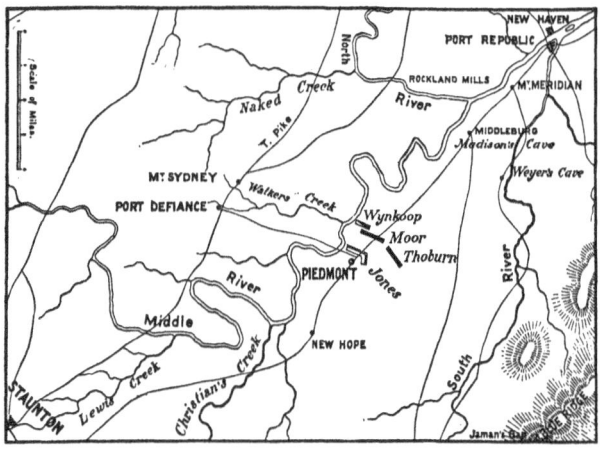

The Battle-field of Piedmont.

of the Valley pike, and seven southwest of Port Republic, on
a road which farther south forks to Staunton and Waynesboro. Stahel having driven back Jones's pickets, Hunter
drew up in front of the Piedmont line, Moor's brigade on
the right and Thoburn's on the left, Wynkoop's brigade of
Stahel's cavalry massed in rear of Moor. After an artillery
fire of two hours, the enemy's guns slackened.

Soon after noon, Moor attacked the Confederate left. The Eighteenth Connecticut held his extreme right, with the Fifth New York Heavy Artillery on its left. An advance across the open drove the enemy through the woods to his main works, which were on a curving range of thickly timbered hills ; but these Moor could not carry, and he fell back. The enemy then attempted in turn to crush Hunter's right, but was checked by Moor, aided by Von Kleyser's battery, with a cross-fire from Morton's and Carlin's on the left. While Jones was concentrating for this attack, Thoburn had been moved across a ravine to gain the enemy's weakened right flank. There he made a very gallant charge on the woods and heights, and Moor and Wynkoop promptly co-operating, the enemy abandoned the entire position, a portion of his men rushing over the steep bank into the river which covered his left.

Over one thousand of the enemy, including sixty officers, were captured on the field, and among the killed was the Confederate commander. The next day Hunter captured 400 sick and wounded. The total number of prisoners was about 1,500, and to these losses of the enemy must be added his killed and stragglers.[1] Three guns and many small arms fell into the hands of Hunter, whose loss was but 420. Secretary Stanton sent thanks for this victory, expressing the hope that, " led on by the courage and guided by the experienced skill of its commander, the Army of the Shenandoah will rival our other gallant armies in the successful blows against the rebels."

The remnant of Jones's troops, under Vaughan, fled to Waynesboro, abandoning Staunton, where Hunter estab-

---

[1] "Went in the fight yesterday with an aggregate of 5,600. I have not over 3,000 effectives, including Imboden's cavalry, 800." (Vaughan to Bragg, June 6th.)

lished himself the next day. Here, the 8th, he was joined
by the troops of Crook and Averell, who had marched from
West Virginia, by way of Callaghan's, Warm Springs, and
Goshen. Crook, on returning to Meadow Bluff, had found
Sigel's orders to proceed to Staunton, but had been delayed,
" owing to the miserable transportation," and was at last
compelled "to leave on the 30th with many of my men barefoot and scantily supplied with rations." During his march
Crook burned the Virginia Central Railroad bridge over
Calf Pasture River at Goshen Springs, and destroyed several
miles of the track. Averell had skirmished most of the way
with the cavalry of McCausland and Jackson, who, however,
rapidly retreated when they learned the fate that had befallen Jones. Averell brought with him 4,400 men, and
these with Crook's infantry made a total of about 10,000,
with two batteries.

Hunter was now about 18,000 strong, with thirty guns, and
well able to make his way to Lynchburg ; meanwhile he destroyed at Staunton the enemy's factories and completed
stocks of saddles, harness, military clothing, and shoes.
The Virginia Central Railroad, which runs through the town,
was well broken for several miles, east and west, the stations,
repair shops, and warehouses being burned, the culverts
blown up and trestle-work demolished. Perhaps the most
conclusive testimony to the thoroughness of Hunter's work
is a despatch of June 17th from Colonel E. G. Lee, commanding the post at Staunton, to Adjutant-General S. Cooper,
at Richmond : "The depot, woollen factory, government
stables, steam mill, wagon shops, and storehouses for tax in
kind, were burned. The railroad was effectually destroyed
for three miles and partially for three more. The bridge
at Christian's Creek, about fifty feet long, was burned ; the
telegraph destroyed for six miles—that I have repaired. The

hands are slowly at work on the railroad. At the rate they are moving, it will take a month or more to repair it. Our sick and wounded at the hospital, with attendants, were paroled by the enemy. They left 300 wounded and 40 nurses here, of their own, with one assistant surgeon. Upon arriving on the 12th I had no guard, and did not know whether we would hold the place or not, so, to be at least even with the Yankees, I paroled all of them." This officer also gives a very long list of commissary stores, horse equipments, and ordnance, the latter including a thousand small arms, three howitzers and a 12-pounder Napoleon, destroyed by Hunter, and a "quantity of provisions belonging to or intended for the Ordnance Department in Richmond. The agent in charge of them estimates their value at $400,000."

At Staunton, Crook and Averell got shoes for their barefoot men ; while Hunter sent back, under Colonel Moor, a convoy of prisoners, negroes, and refugees by way of Buffalo Gap and Beverly, escorted by 800 men whose enlistments had nearly expired. He also relieved Stahel, in consequence of a wound received while gallantly leading his command at Piedmont, instructing him to collect a strong escort of spare troops at the foot of the Valley, and to bring it forward in charge of an important train of supplies. Stahel proceeded to fulfil his instructions, but succeeding events prevented the sending of this train.

The morning of June 10th, the combined army moved forward toward Lynchburg on four nearly parallel roads. Two steady marches, through a charming country, abounding in broad fields of luxuriant wheat, that half hid from view the battalions trampling through them, compassed the thirty-six miles between Staunton and Lexington. McCausland's troopers retreated before Crook's advance on the right, burning the bridge over the North River, on which Lexington is

situated, and then posting their sharpshooters and artillery
among the buildings of the town. Hunter desiring to avoid
opening fire on Lexington, as he might have done, sent
Averell to flank it, and Crook despatched White's brigade of
infantry for the same purpose; whereupon the enemy hastily
withdrew. Lexington contained several public buildings
of consequence, notably the Virginia Military Institute,
which had furnished to the battle of New Market a large
share of its cadets, under their principal, Colonel Smith;
from this building a few defiant shots had been fired at Hunter's forces. The institute was burned, as also several iron
mills. A misguided sense of exclusive proprietorship in the
fame of the First President led some of the troops to seize
his statue from the hall of Washington College, load it in
their wagons, and carry it to Wheeling, so as to "rescue it,"
as Colonel Cathcart explained, "from the degenerate sons of
worthy sires." At Lexington Hunter found, he says, "a
violent and inflammatory proclamation from John Letcher,
lately Governor of Virginia, inciting the population of the
country to rise and wage a guerilla warfare on my troops;
and ascertaining that after having advised his fellow-citizens
to this cause the ex-governor had himself ignominiously
taken to flight, I ordered his property to be burned, under
my Orders, published May 24th, against persons practising
or abetting such unlawful and uncivilized warfare." A few
prisoners were taken in Lexington, and some small arms
and cartridges, while six canal barges, laden with commissary stores, and containing about half a dozen cannon and
their ammunition, were also captured and destroyed.

In setting out from Staunton the First (Stahel's) division
of cavalry, now under Duffié, moving to the left, had demonstrated against the enemy at Waynesboro, and finding him
in strong force there, had crossed the Blue Ridge further

south, at Tye River Gap, whence he moved to Amherst
Court House, and broke the Charlottesville and Lynchburg
Railroad at Arrington Station.   Imboden followed him,
but was repulsed with loss.   Duffié captured about 100
prisoners, including 17 officers, together with 400 horses,
and destroyed two iron furnaces, large quantities of commissary supplies, and a part of Imboden's train, returning
by White's Gap without serious loss.   While this expedition
was enterprising, it must be adjudged, on the whole, unfortunate ; for General Hunter had already made a long delay
at Staunton, awaiting Crook and refitting his command, so
that to reach Lynchburg before it should be reinforced he
needed to leave Lexington the day after he entered it.   Yet
he seems to have felt constrained to wait for Duffié, perhaps
fearing he was lost, while that officer, pleased with his new
command, went on raiding until Hunter's couriers at last
found him and hurried him back ; but he did not arrive till
after noon of June 13th.   This delay at Lexington was enough
to prove the salvation of Lynchburg ; and, after all, Duffié's
breaking of the railroad was not sufficient, as we shall presently observe, to prevent its use in forwarding troops to
Lynchburg by the time Hunter arrived there.   Here, perhaps, a mistake was committed ; for Duffié, with a cavalry
command, ought to have been able, at that season, at least
to take care of himself, if he could do nothing more.   Probably, instead of waiting for him, Hunter might have safely
allowed him to go on, and even to make a circuit around
Lynchburg, and then join the main body west of that city
at Liberty, for an excursion like this was soon after effected
with success by a much smaller body of Hunter's horsemen.

There was another cause of delay at Lexington, which perhaps had as much influence as the absence of Duffié, whose
return was hourly expected.   A train of two hundred wagons

came up, guarded by two regiments, and loaded with rations, clothing, and ammunition—all very acceptable, and the latter a necessity, for the supply was running short. Hunter had learned that this train was on its way up the Valley, and "I delayed one day in Lexington," he says, "to allow it to overtake us." While anxiously awaiting Duffié, Hunter, the morning of the 13th, sent Averell to Buchanan to dislodge McCausland, and to secure the use of the bridge over the James. Meanwhile Averell had detached 200 picked men to ride completely around Lynchburg, cut its communications, and get news of the enemy. That day Hunter learned positively that Breckenridge had taken command at Rockfish Gap, and Duffié's prisoners brought "rumors that a formidable rebel force was hastening toward the Valley from Richmond, and that Sheridan had met with a reverse near Louisa Court House," while other information represented Lynchburg to be weakly defended. These tidings suggested the possible success of a rapid advance against the city by the comparatively open route through the Peaks of Otter, whereas the effort to first dislodge Breckenridge in Rockfish Gap might cause a fatal delay.

The 14th, Hunter moved his army by a hard march of twenty-five miles to Buchanan, which Averell had already approached, driving off McCausland, and capturing some loaded canal barges and prisoners. The river was easily fordable here, but McCausland zealously burned the bridge, to the regret of the people, and eleven buildings took fire from it, Hunter's troops helping to check the flames. The Blue Ridge was crossed next day at the Peaks of Otter, McCausland felling the trees behind him, in a vain effort to obstruct the Union march. Powell's brigade, riding in advance, occupied Liberty, the county town of Bedford, on the Virginia and Tennessee Railroad, twenty-four miles west of Lynchburg. There Averell's picked men reported. They had struck and broken the Charlottesville Railroad near Amherst, crossed the James below Lynchburg, injured the Southside Railroad, burned two trains at Concordia Station, and thence had moved westward to Liberty; still they brought no trustworthy news of the enemy's strength. Of the prisoners captured, "some reported that Sheridan had been defeated near Louisa Court House, while others said that he was already in Lynchburg."

Giving little heed to these stories, Hunter, the 16th, moved through Liberty toward Lynchburg, sending Duffié north to Balcony Falls to see if the enemy was there, and Crook along the railroad, to destroy it as he marched. Averell, followed by Sullivan's division, the reserve artillery and the trains, advanced on the Bedford pike, and drove back McCausland, but with increasing difficulty, indicating that he had now been reinforced by Imboden. At night Hunter encamped seven miles east of Liberty, and then sent through Lewisburg to Charleston the two hundred wagons which had reached him at Lexington, together with many refugees, under guard of Colonel Putnam's regiment of Ohio hundred-days men. Crook had destroyed the railroad from Liberty to Big Otter Creek, burning the ties and bending the rails.

The next day Averell came upon the enemy at Quaker church, five miles from Lynchburg, and, aided by Duffié, charged his intrenchments. The infantry, hastening forward, carried the works, capturing 70 prisoners and one cannon. The troops encamped on the field.

Thus far Hunter's campaign had been not only vigorous, but brilliantly successful; while his penetration of a vital part of the enemy's country was something new after the

2*

mortifying experiences of Union campaigning in the Valley
of Virginia. Nevertheless, events showed that in one respect
his plan might have been more fortunate. Instead of marching to Lynchburg from Staunton by way of Lexington and
Buchanan, which had seemed the most expedient course,
from such facts as were known to him, a better route might
have been through Rockfish Gap to Charlottesville. Intrin-
sically, the occupation of this town would have been as
important as that of Lexington, and would have formed a satisfactory close of the campaign, even had it then proved impossible to visit Lynchburg. For Charlottesville was more
closely connected than Lexington with the general scheme
of military operations in Virginia, and its capture was the
most natural forerunner of a serious attempt on Lynchburg.
Not only would a force established there threaten Gordonsville as well as Lynchburg, thus dividing the enemy's preparations for defence, but it would break the railroad connecting them, and cut off Lynchburg from reinforcement. That
General Lee would succor the latter city unless Richmond
itself were on the point of capture, was obvious, since, as a
seat of manufactures and the key of a region of plenty, it
was to him the most important town in Virginia west of the
capital, and its occupation would cut his chief line of railroad supply. The reinforcements for this purpose would
naturally go by way of Charlottesville by rail, there being
no troops to come from the region west of the Blue Ridge.
At Charlottesville, Hunter, learning whether these reinforcements had already gone forward, would also have known
whether he could wisely move to Lynchburg. Vaughan's
troops that retreated from Piedmont had themselves broadly
suggested the line they wished to secure, by escaping to
Waynesboro instead of Staunton—this movement making
them available for the defence of Charlottesville and Gor-

donsville as well as Lynchburg. Finally, at Charlottesville
Hunter would have covered his line of retreat down the
Shenandoah Valley, whereas a column sent through Charlottesville, while he was far south, might force him to drift
off along the distant line of the Kanawha; and this form of
withdrawal in fact occurred.

To explain how Lynchburg was relieved, we must go back
a little. After Sigel's defeat at New Market, Lee at once
summoned the infantry of Breckenridge to reinforce him
against Grant. Experience justified this step, because a
Union repulse in the Valley had usually been followed by a
period of dazed inaction. But in repeating this manœuvre
with a commander whose policy was that of "hammering
continuously," Lee committed an error. The two brigades
of Breckenridge, Wharton's and Echols's, were transferred
to the North Anna and were of service there; but meanwhile the defeat at Piedmont more than counterbalanced
any service they had rendered Lee, and they were hastily
sent back to the Valley, reaching Rockfish Gap in season to
have reinforced Vaughan, had Hunter moved from Staunton
to Waynesboro. Breckenridge pushed on to Lynchburg by a
forced march, and long before Hunter's arrival had placed
his troops and Vaughan's behind the intrenchments, being
able to add to them a considerable array of home guards
and convalescents; for Lynchburg contained not a few of
the sick and wounded of Lee's army, and Generals D. H.
Hill and Hays, who were among them, aided in the defence.

Lee took further precautions. He directed his Second
Corps, Ewell's, now under Early, to withdraw from Cold
Harbor, June 13th, and to proceed by Louisa and Charlottes-
ville through either Brown's or Swift Run Gap, across the
Blue Ridge, so as to strike the rear of Hunter, then sup-
posed to be still at Staunton—for Hunter's men had cut the

railroad and telegraph lines, "so that there was no communication with Breckenridge." Early crossed the Chickahominy, and reached Trevillian's Station, June 15th, in a
march of a little over two days ; and the Rivanna, near Charlottesville, the day after, having marched eighty miles in
four days. His was Stonewall Jackson's old corps, famous
for quick marches—Jackson's "foot cavalry."

Breckenridge, at Lynchburg, had scanty information of
Hunter's progress. The 11th, he telegraphed Imboden that
Hunter's cavalry was passing through Tye River Gap: "Overtake, engage and whip him. You have the force to do it."
Four days later, both to Bragg, at Richmond, and to Imboden himself he telegraphed bitterly in regard to the latter's inactivity. But the 16th Early was at Charlottesville,
where the railroad, already repaired, could bring forward
his troops to Lynchburg, and then Breckenridge's anxiety
was over. "My fear is that the enemy will go away," he
telegraphed Early on that day ; and he encouraged General
Vaughan by this assurance : "There is no occasion for any
disorder. The enemy is advancing slowly. We will have
General Early and large reinforcements to-morrow morning,
and if the enemy comes in earnest, he will be destroyed."
In truth, the next day, the 17th, brought to the city half
of Early's corps and Hunter's main body.

It has been seen that Crook and Averell promptly attacked
the outworks of Lynchburg, the evening of the 17th ; they
had shut up the enemy within a redoubt only two miles
from the city. Early at that time threw two brigades of
Ramseur's division into this redoubt, and placed the third
and a part of Gordon's division in support.

Throughout the night Hunter heard trains moving, drums
beating, and constant cheering, which indicated that Lynchburg had been succored ; but he still felt confident of tak-

ing it, provided this succor was not a corps from Richmond. The next morning he drove in the enemy's skir-mishers to the toll-gate on the Bedford pike, two miles from the town, and vigorously demonstrated with infantry, cavalry, and artillery against the strong works—redoubts protected by abatis. During the afternoon Hunter attacked in force, bringing into action his two divisions of infantry and his artillery in the centre, on and near the Bedford turnpike, Duffié along the Forest road on the left, and a part of Averell along the Campbell road on the right. Early's infantry sallied from their works on the Bedford road to meet this attack, but were gallantly driven back by Sullivan, aided by Crook, and the One Hundred and Sixteenth Ohio even planted its colors on Early's breastworks. The Union losses were about two hundred, and the Confederate must have been severe. Assured now from many sources that Early's corps had arrived, and that Lynchburg could not be carried, Hunter withdrew at night along the turnpike toward Liberty, bivouacking seven miles east of this town, and thence the following day, July 19th, marching on Buford's Gap.

When Early discovered that Hunter had disappeared, he put all his forces in pursuit, Elzey receiving the command of Breckenridge's troops during the latter's illness, while Ransom, having arrived from Richmond, assumed general charge of the cavalry. By hard marching Early's advance, at 4 P.M., came up with Hunter's rear guard, under Averell, and drove it through Liberty after an engagement of two hours. Averell's loss was 122 men, chiefly in Schoonmaker's brigade.

Now the infelicity of General Hunter's position became manifest. With the Charlottesville and Lynchburg Railroad repaired, and in the enemy's possession, he could not

well return by the Peaks of Otter to Lexington and Staunton, for Early, sending a part of his forces by rail, might
enter Rockfish Gap in season to plant himself on his opponent's line of retreat and supply, or to attack him in flank.
Hunter could perhaps have fought his way through, but he
no longer had ammunition for a pitched battle, or series of
battles, against a force like Early's. His rations, too, were
nearly gone, and he was 200 miles from his base. He resolved to retreat, not by his Shenandoah line, but through
Buford's Gap to Charleston, in the Kanawha Valley—a route
which would be in great part unmolested, while Crook had
left ample supplies under guard at Meadow Bluff, and the
question of rations was imperative.[1]

At midnight the retreat was resumed, and Buford's Gap
was reached the morning of the 20th. Duffié, who had gone
forward to secure this pass, employed his whole force in destroying the railroad. Thence the march was continued
through Bonsack's Station, on the Tennessee Railroad, to
Salem ; and it is worthy of note that, on the way, as if this
were still a destroying expedition instead of a retreat, all
bridges, water-tanks, and railroad stations were wrecked, and
the enemy was repulsed wherever he attacked. Even the
19th, the day when Hunter withdrew from Lynchburg, he
had actually issued orders to Averell to break the Richmond and Danville Railroad where it crosses the Staunton
River, far south of Lynchburg, and to return to "rejoin the

---

[1] At Sweet Springs there was a possibility of an intermediate route, nearer the
Shenandoah Valley, but, as General Hunter's report says, it was rejected for
sound reasons : "From this point it was suggested that we should move northward by the Warm Springs and the Valley of the South Branch of the Potomac, a
route lying west of and running parallel to the Valley of the Shenandoah. By
this route the army would have reached the Baltimore and Ohio Railroad at
New Creek and Cumberland. It was objected that by this road the troops would
find it impossible to collect necessary supplies and run risks of being cut off by
the enemy coming in by way of Staunton and Harrisonburg."

column moving in the direction of Lewisburg." The next day, the 20th, General Sullivan was directed, as soon as his men were "somewhat rested," to "turn out as many of them as possible to tear up the railroad and destroy as much of it as possible; also, the telegraph line." Such orders indicate that while at Washington Hunter's westward withdrawal was soon after viewed simply as an escape, it was for him a feasible method of completing a successful expedition.

Salem was reached the 21st. That morning Early's advance was repulsed by Crook and Averell, holding Buford's Gap in the rear. The trains and reserve artillery continued along the New Castle road, but through inadvertence the proper guard did not go with them, so that McCausland, dashing in on the guns, rapidly carried off or shot the horses, and began to destroy the caissons and limbers. At once, troops hastened up from the rear, and drove him away with a loss of about thirty men; but he made off with three guns, and five others were abandoned for want of horses to drag them, while the wrecked caissons and limbers were also, of course, left behind. A sharp repulse of the enemy's cavalry the following morning ended the pursuit; for Early, having no mind to be drawn into the Kanawha Valley on a wild-goose chase, through a desolate and waterless region, returned to Lynchburg.

Still the retreat was continued through New Castle with the same headlong speed, not through fear of the enemy, but through the necessity of reaching supplies. During the week that elapsed before these were obtained, the troops had no hard bread, and only one issue of six ounces of flour per man. But there was beef on the hoof, the cattle being driven by day, and eaten the same night. Many horses and mules died for want of fodder and rest, and not a few wagons were burned for lack of animals to draw them.

The night of June 24th, having passed Sweet Springs, the column reached White Sulphur Springs, and there had delicious water and a good rest. But suitable food was still wanting, and the army pressed on to Meadow Bluff. Here the supplies were expected; but the officer in charge of them, with 400 men, being alarmed at guerilla demonstrations, had fallen back with all his stores to Gauley Bridge. At last, the 27th, a train with seventy thousand rations of hard-tack, sugar, coffee, and bacon reached the hungry troops, a day's march short of Gauley Bridge, and the sufferings of the retreat were over.

Here a brief account may properly be given of a movement made by Grant to co-operate with Hunter: for the reader will have surmised that since Lee, in his strait for troops, found a corps and a division of infantry to spare for checking this officer, the Lieutenant-General may have taken some steps to aid him in his important enterprise. In his despatch to Halleck, of May 25th, from Jericho Ford, Grant used the following language: "If Hunter can possibly get to Charlottesville and Lynchburg, he should do so, living on the country. The railroads and canals should be destroyed beyond possibility of repairs for weeks. Completing this, he could find his way back to his original base, or from about Gordonsville join this army." While Hunter was moving to Staunton, Grant directed Major-General P. H. Sheridan, commanding the cavalry of the Army of the Potomac, to proceed with two divisions to Charlottesville, destroy the railroad, and thence accompany Hunter's command, if found there, to the Army of the Potomac. Crossing the Pamunkey, June 7th, with Torbert's and Gregg's divisions, General Sheridan marched by Aylett's, Dunkirk, Polecat Station, Childsburg, New Market, and Andrews's Tavern, and, after four days, reached the Virginia Central Railroad at Trevillian Station the morning of June 11th. He found that the enemy's cavalry had stolen around in his front, and had constructed breastworks in dense timber at Trevillian, anticipating that he would strike that point. In a brilliant and severe engagement, Sheridan drove the enemy's cavalry, consisting of Fitz Lee's and Hampton's divisions, back to and beyond the station, where he camped. The next day, the 12th, after breaking the railroad back to Louisa Court House, he made a vigorous effort, using both Torbert's division and one brigade of Gregg's, to move toward Gordonsville; but he found the enemy there in too great force. He had hoped and intended to reach the Orange and Alexandria Railroad at Cobham's Station, and to break it in a march toward Charlottesville; but this plan had to be given up, while to reach Gordonsville had become apparently no less difficult. In his two days' engagements, he had lost 735 men in killed, wounded, and captured, but had severely retaliated on the enemy, bringing off 377 prisoners. It seemed improbable that Hunter could be anywhere around Gordonsville, when such a force of the enemy was left free at Trevillian to oppose Sheridan; and captured prisoners reported that Hunter had not, up to that time, been near Charlottesville. Sheridan skilfully and rapidly withdrew under cover of the night, and a brief pursuit by the enemy was easily repulsed by General Davies. A field telegram of June 16th, from General R. E. Lee's headquarters at Drewry's Bluff to Hampton at Polecat Station, shows that the Confederate general made an unsuccessful effort to cut off Sheridan's withdrawal, by means of the cavalry forces which he had retained on both sides of the Chickahominy when despatching Hampton to foil the attack on Gordonsville and Charlottesville: "Our cavalry north and south of

Chickahominy have been advised of movements by bearer of despatches; also to endeavor to ascertain movements of Sheridan, and to unite with you when practicable to crush him." But Sheridan succeeded in carrying his command safely through to White House. His subsequent adventures at that point do not come within the scope of the present volume.

General Halleck had sent word to Hunter, June 12th, "that General Grant is about to move his army to the James River, at or near City Point, and that he will continue to hold the bridge across the Pamunkey, at the White House, to facilitate the junction of yourself and General Sheridan with the Army of the Potomac;" but this despatch doubtless reached Hunter only on his return from Lynchburg. Several days earlier, June 6th, Grant had written Hunter the following letter, to be delivered by Sheridan:

General Sheridan leaves to-morrow morning with instructions to proceed to Charlottesville, Va., and to commence there the destruction of the Virginia Central Railroad, destroying this way as much as possible. The complete destruction of this road and of the canal on James River is of great importance to us. According to the instructions I sent General Halleck for your guidance, you were to proceed to Lynchburg for a single day. But that point is of so much importance to the enemy, that in attempting to get it, such resistance may be met as to defeat your getting on to the road or canal at all. I see, in looking over my letter to General Halleck on the subject of your instructions, that it rather indicates that your route should be from Staunton *via* Charlottesville. If you have so understood it, you will be doing just what I want. The direction I would now give is, that if this letter reaches you in the Valley between Staunton and Lynchburg, you immediately turn east by the most practicable road until you strike the Lynchburg branch of the Virginia Central road. From there move eastward along the line of the road, destroying it completely and thoroughly until you join General Sheridan. After the work laid out for General Sheridan and yourself is thoroughly done, proceed to join the

Army of the Potomac by the route laid out in General Sheridan's instructions. If any portion of your force, especially of your cavalry, is needed back in your department, you are authorized to send it back. If on receipt of this you should be near to Lynchburg, and deem it practicable to reach that point, you will exercise your judgment about going there. If you should be on the railroad between Charlottesville and Lynchburg, it may be practicable to detach a cavalry force to destroy the canal. Lose no opportunity to destroy the canal.

This letter of course did not reach Hunter. The 19th, Secretary Stanton wrote to Stahel as follows: "General Sheridan, who was sent by General Grant to open communication with General Hunter, by way of Charlottesville, has just returned to York River without effecting his object. It is therefore very probable that General Hunter will be compelled to fall back into West Virginia." A despatch of Grant to Meade, at City Point, June 21st, is also noteworthy. "The only word I would send Hunter," he said, "would be verbal, and simply to let him know where we are, and tell him to save his army in the way he thinks best, either by getting back into his own department or by joining us. If we had the enemy driven north of the Appomattox, I think he would have no difficulty in joining us by taking a wide sweep south."

Thus two campaigns in the Shenandoah Valley, Sigel's and Hunter's, had ended. Grant's plan in regard to them has been pronounced faulty, on the ground that it unduly scattered his forces, rendering them liable to be beaten in detail. This criticism seems strained, since when he crossed the Rapidan Grant had provided for his main army all the troops it needed at that time, and all that could be handled to advantage. The alternative instruction to Hunter to join the Army of the Potomac from Gordonsville, after a specific work, shows that this outlying force was looked on as a reserve, to be used for watching a dangerous flank and for menacing the enemy's communications till needed in the main army. Lee, on his part, so highly appreciated the importance of the Valley, that he held it at first with a large force. Even the temporary detention of the division of Breckenridge from him had made easier the first stage of Grant's Virginia task. Hunter's movement in turn forced Lee to strip his Richmond intrenchments to avoid a fatal disaster at Lynchburg.

General Hunter had relieved his command with address from a critical position, and his campaign throughout had been one of exceptional audacity and vigor, even though the great effort made by Lee checked its final stage. That there was no precise understanding between Grant and Hunter as to the latter's course has been made apparent; but as the Lieutenant-General had expressly made it optional with Hunter in all the despatches that ever reached him, to end his campaign either by joining the Army of the Potomac or by returning to his own department, and as the results achieved surpassed any that Grant had expected, since he had doubted whether this expedition could remain at Lynchburg, "for a single day," or be able to reach the Tennessee Railroad at all, he lauded his subordinate's energy.

Hunter's own view of his campaign was given in a despatch from Loup Creek, near Gauley Bridge, June 28th, in which he declared that the expedition had been "extremely successful, inflicting great injury upon the enemy," going forward until short of ammunition, and until the hostile army had been so strongly reinforced that he could no longer collect subsistence. "The command," he added, "is in excellent heart and health." Mr. Stanton, in replying, referred to "the great satisfaction your operations have given." Jefferson Davis told the people of Georgia, after the fall of Atlanta, that "an audacious movement of the enemy up to the very walls of Lynchburg had rendered it necessary that the Government should send a formidable body of troops to cover that vital point, which had otherwise been intended for the relief of Atlanta." Colonel Strother, General Hunter's chief of staff, in his report of the expedition, sets forth these results: "About fifty miles of the Virginia Central Railroad had been effectually destroyed; the Virginia and Tennessee road had been destroyed to some extent for the same distance; an incredible amount of public property had been burned, including canal-boats and railroad trains loaded with ordnance and commissary stores, numerous extensive iron works, manufactories of saltpetre, musket-stocks, shoes, saddles and artillery-harness, woollen cloths, and grain mills. About three thousand muskets and twenty pieces of cannon, with quantities of shells and gunpowder, fell into our hands, while immense quantities of provisions, cattle, and horses were captured and used by the army." Colonel Strother also claims the infliction of a loss of 2,000 killed and wounded on the enemy, besides the taking of 2,000 prisoners, with a total loss of only 1,500 men and eight guns in Hunter's command.

Nevertheless, it turned out that Hunter's success eliminated the defensive factor from the Valley more effectually than his predecessor's failure.

CHAPTER IV.

EARLY MENACES WASHINGTON.

WHEN Lee saw that Hunter's erratic line of retreat had uncovered the Shenandoah Valley, he turned this advantage to account by a manœuvre which had been serviceable to him in former campaigns, and for the repetition of which unexpected facilities were now furnished. Instead of recalling Early and Breckenridge to his side, he despatched them into Maryland, correctly assuming that this stroke, by terrifying Washington, would cause troops to be sent to its protection from the Army of the Potomac, and so relieve his own stress.

The scheme of invading the North was made a part of Early's instructions when he marched to relieve Lynchburg; for since it was necessary to detach troops to save that city from capture, Lee determined to send a force large enough to execute a decisive counter-stroke; but as Hunter, instead of being defeated, had retreated into the Kanawha Valley, Lee desired his subordinate, under the changed circumstances, to judge whether to carry out the original project or to abandon it; and Early's adventurous temperament led him to choose the former course.

The army assembled for the march into Maryland consisted of the four infantry divisions of Rodes, Gordon, Ramseur, and Echols; Ransom's division of cavalry, including the brigades of Bradley T. Johnson (formerly W.

E. Jones's), Imboden, W. L. Jackson, and McCausland, for the brigade of Vaughan served as infantry till its return from the expedition, when it was remounted; and Long's three battalions of artillery, comprising the batteries of Nelson, King, Braxton, and McLaughlin, whose guns numbered about forty, many being 12-pounder Napoleons. The cavalry had additional pieces. The division ascribed to Echols was Breckenridge's old command, temporarily given to Elzey at Lynchburg, and afterward, at Staunton, temporarily to Vaughan; but Echols received it in, Maryland. Breckenridge was assigned something resembling a corps command, having under him the two divisions of Gordon and Echols; while the other two infantry divisions and the cavalry reported directly to Early. The army numbered apparently about 17,000 officers and men.[1]

The 27th of June Early's army arrived at Staunton, where a brief halt was made to fill his wagons with provisions brought through Rockfish Gap, and to reduce his transportation, even regimental officers being obliged to carry with them all the underclothing they might need. The next day the Confederate commander moved down the pike, sending Imboden ahead with his brigade and a battery through Brock's Gap, in the North Mountain, to destroy the railroad bridges west of Martinsburg. Early reached Winchester the 2d of July, there receiving instructions from Lee to remain in the Lower Valley until fully prepared to cross the Potomac, and meanwhile to wreck the Baltimore and Ohio road and the canal.

McCausland was detached to burn the railroad bridge at

---

[1] See Appendix. Partisan cavalry forces were also active coadjutors of Early. June 29th, a force of about 500 cavalry and two guns plundered and ravaged at Duffield's, five miles northwest of Harper's Ferry, burning the storehouses and capturing 25 men.

Back Creek, and, after accomplishing this, and capturing
the small guard at North Mountain Station, he proceeded to
Hainesville, between Martinsburg and Williamsport. At
Martinsburg, an important city and depot of supplies, Sigel
had established himself when Hunter moved up the Valley
in May; while Brigadier-General Max Weber commanded at
Harper's Ferry. The morning of July 3d, Bradley Johnson
was sent forward with directions to proceed through Smithfield and Leetown, to cross the railroad at Kearneysville,
east of Martinsburg, and, passing north of the town, to unite
with McCausland at Hainesville, so as to cut off Sigel's retreat. Early followed close upon Johnson, with Rodes's and
Ramseur's divisions, while Breckenridge moved directly to
Martinsburg on the pike, driving before him Stahel, who
held an outpost on the road thither at Darksville. But Sigel,
the moment his pickets warned him of Early's approach, had
begun sending off the Government stores, telegraphing for
empty trains. Much of this property was thus saved, and
the remainder having been mostly destroyed, Sigel retreated
to Shepherdstown; while Johnson, arriving at Leetown the
same morning, was checked by Colonel Mulligan, and driven
back, after severe fighting, upon the infantry of Rodes and
Ramseur. Mulligan then slowly withdrew, having foiled
Early's project of capturing Sigel's forces, as Ewell had
captured Milroy's, with these same troops, near Winchester,
the year before. Sigel, joined by his small garrisons of
Leetown and Darksville, withdrew that night, July 3d,
across the Potomac at Shepherdstown, bringing off his Leetown wounded, and established his command on Maryland
Heights. There he had a force of two veteran regiments,
four of Ohio militia, 2,500 dismounted cavalry, two battalions
of heavy artillery, and twenty-six field guns; while hard by,
in Pleasant Valley, were Stahel's cavalry, from 1,000 to 1,500

strong, two companies of artillery acting as infantry, and four guns. Breckenridge, after burning the bridges at Martinsburg and on the Opequon, broke the railroad along to Duffield's, five miles from Harper's Ferry, and then followed Sigel across the river, Gordon during the two subsequent days moving down the Antietam, driving back Stahel, and confining Sigel within the works on Maryland Heights.

The 4th of July, therefore, found Early master of the Valley; yet his plan had not wholly succeeded, for he had neither captured Sigel nor driven him northward. In moving to Maryland Heights, this officer had gone precisely where Early did not want him to be, since the Confederate general had purposed to seize Harper's Ferry, and to make that his point of departure for Washington. When, with Rodes and Ramseur, he pressed Weber from Bolivar back to the bank of the river, this officer was protected by the heavy guns on the Heights, to which point he crossed at night, taking up the pontoon bridge. Mr. Garrett, the president of the railroad company, had urged Weber to exert himself to save the trestle bridge,[1] but Weber sought rather to destroy it.

Early found himself unable to occupy Harper's Ferry, save

---

[1] Mr. Garrett, in informing Secretary Stanton and General Halleck that Weber had reported to him that he must retreat to the Heights, sternly reminded them that "a want of firmness is to be found at Harper's Ferry. Your further communication to the commandant may aid in its [the railroad's] preservation." Halleck quickly told Weber to defend his works, "and the first man who proposes a surrender, or retreats, should be hung." Garrett, on getting a request from Weber for empty cars, asked "whether this meant evacuation," but directed Weber's attention to "fully covering and protecting from the Maryland Heights," in case he must abandon Harper's Ferry, "the trestle-work from the bridge a mile west. With Sigel's large force," he added, "I judge the enemy can be driven entirely from the road." Weber, however, thought it more important to prevent the enemy's use of the bridge, and so destroyed the two western spans, leaving the rest intact. Four trains loaded with Government supplies were saved from Harper's Ferry, and then Weber, having only 400 men in his command, and not knowing where Sigel was, retreated to the Heights.

by skirmishers, so thoroughly was it commanded by Sigel's artillery and sharpshooters. Accordingly, after demonstrating there with Rodes and Ramseur through the 5th, he crossed the Potomac at Shepherdstown. Breckenridge continued to demonstrate against Maryland Heights, cannonading going on through the night of July 6th and sharp fighting the next day. Finding his lines shelled for a long distance by Sigel's batteries, which prevented his own from getting into position, Early at length drew off across South Mountain toward Frederick. A brigade left at Harper's Ferry joined him, after burning such captured stores as the Confederate wagons had not taken away. Working parties had meanwhile been employed in destroying the aqueduct of the Chesapeake and Ohio Canal over the Antietam, and the locks and boats there. Boonsboro had been occupied by Johnson, while, July 6th, McCausland entered Hagerstown and levied a requisition of $20,000; here much hay and grain were burned. As for Imboden, the 3d of July he had partly destroyed the railroad bridge that crosses the South Branch of the Potomac, but was checked in some of his purposes by the guard in the block-house there; he had also had only partial success with the Patterson's Creek bridge. Big Cacapon had been unsuccessfully attacked, July 6th, the bridge being saved; the station-houses on St. John's Run were burned. Imboden had been ill, and his brigade, under Colonel Smith, now rejoined Early.

When it became known that a Confederate army was in Maryland, a natural terror seized on the farmers. Men, women, and children, accompanied by droves of cattle and by wagons laden with household goods, or carrying their portable property on their backs, thronged the roads to the east and to the north. Early had issued orders forbidding pillage, and reminding his army that "they are engaged in

no marauding expedition and are not making war upon the
defenceless and unresisting. Such supplies as are needed for
the army will be taken by or under the direction of the
chiefs of the various departments, and payment made there-
for, or certificate given, as the owner may prefer; and any
officer or man found committing depredations of any sort will
be at once arrested and summarily punished." But such
orders are apt, in military expeditions, to be either forgotten
by some troops, or taken with a liberal allowance, so that even
had Early's commands been known to the people of Maryland they would scarcely have allayed apprehension. Hence
the fugitives encumbered themselves with articles which the
most rapacious trooper might have been puzzled to use.

Startled by these events, President Lincoln called on the
Governors of Pennsylvania, New York, and Massachusetts for
hundred-day volunteers, to aid in repelling the invaders, and
Hunter was notified to move back to the Valley. This officer was already, of course, on the way, surmising that the
enemy would seize the occasion of his absence to march
North. Our account left him near Gauley Bridge. There
remaining two days to rest his troops, he had moved them,
June 30th, to Charleston. Whatever the urgency, neither
men nor animals were fit to march, and transportation by
water promised not only to save time but to rest the troops.
Hunter therefore seized all available light-draught boats—
for the low water in the rivers made others useless—and began sending his troops down the Kanawha to Point Pleasant,
and thence up the Ohio to Parkersburg. Here he received
despatches from the War Department telling him of Early's
march, and urging haste. Unhappily, owing to an unusual
drought, the shallowness of the rivers repeatedly required
the men to disembark at shoals and march around them, so
that the boats might float over, and often resort had to be

made to smaller boats. Thus the delays were great. From
Parkersburg the Baltimore and Ohio Railroad took the
troops to New Creek and Cumberland, some time being lost
on this route until temporary repairs could be made to the
bridge at Green Spring, broken by Early's cavalry. Hun-

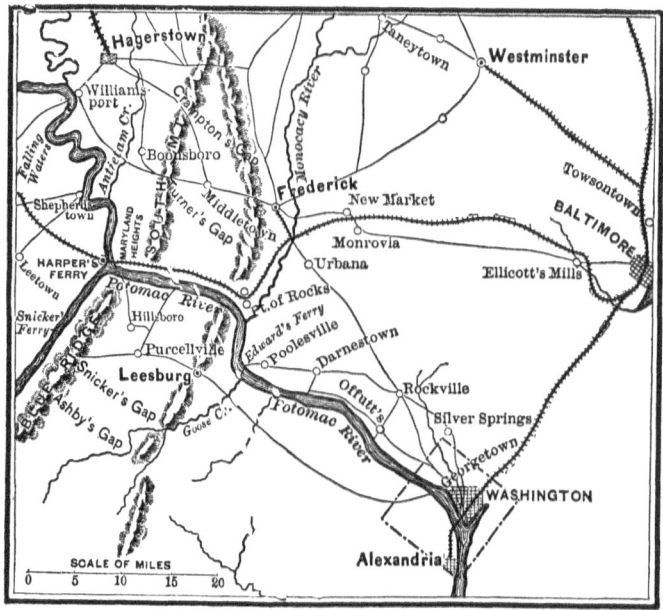

Early's Maryland Campaign.

ter's advance, Sullivan's division, reached Cumberland July
8th, concentrated at Cherry Run the 9th, and at noon of the
11th had marched to Martinsburg.

Meanwhile Early continued his eastward course to Frederick. The morning of the 8th Breckenridge moved through
Fox's Gap and Ramseur through Boonsboro, both camping

near Middletown; Rodes, who had marched by Rohrers-
ville, entered Crampton's Gap, and crossing Catoctin Creek
camped near Jefferson. Ransom was busy with the Union
cavalry between Middletown and Frederick; and McCausland set out toward Monocacy to cut the railroad and the
wires.

Thus far Early had met little resistance since leaving
Lynchburg. Urgent appeals were made to General Grant
for troops; but the information brought him from his own front
at City Point was at first remarkably erroneous, so that he
could not know the real danger. Before Early's presence in
the Valley was discovered, Halleck had shrewdly suggested
to Grant that it " would be good policy for them [the Con-
federates], while Hunter's army is on the Kanawha, to destroy
the Baltimore and Ohio Railroad and make a raid in Maryland and Pennsylvania: Sigel has very little besides militia
at Harper's Ferry and on the railroad;" but Grant replied
that " Ewell's [Early's] corps has returned here." Even the
night of July 3d, when Early held Martinsburg, having
fought Sigel that day at Leetown, Grant wrote that "Early's
corps is now here; there are no troops that can now be
threatening Hunter's department, except the remnant of the
force W. E. Jones had, and possibly Breckenridge." Secretary Stanton became much impressed with this view, and
wrote as late even as July 5th to Governor Curtin that " it
seems to be a raiding expedition by some of the partisan
robbers that infest that region." The truth is that slender
faith was reposed, at Washington, in the military perspi-
cacity of the generals collected around Harper's Ferry,
although they were now remarkably accurate in their reports. "The three principal officers on the line of the road,"
wrote Halleck, somewhat cynically, to Grant, " are Sigel,
Stahel, and Max Weber. You can therefore judge what prob-

ability there is of a good defence if the enemy should attack the line in force." [1]

By the 5th Grant, convinced of Early's presence on the Maryland border, offered Halleck an army corps to repel invasion. Halleck answered that Grant's dismounted cavalry might be sufficient; but since he added that "we have almost nothing in Baltimore or Washington except militia," Grant decided to send both the dismounted cavalry and a division of infantry, "which will be followed by the balance of the corps, if necessary. We want now to crush out and destroy any force the enemy dares send North. Force enough can be spared from here to do it." He directed General Meade to "send in one good division," with "all the dismounted cavalry," and Meade sent Ricketts's of the Sixth Corps, which embarked at City Point, the 6th, for Harper's Ferry by way of Baltimore. But Grant afterward learned that the dismounted cavalry which had been sent were odds and ends, the larger part sick or otherwise unfit for good service, instead of organized regiments, as he had intended; and this mistake proved costly, in the conduct of the month's operations.

Union forces from other quarters were gathering in Early's front. Major-General Lew Wallace, whose headquarters were in Baltimore, reinforcing the spare men of his garrison with home guards and hundred-day militia, moved them forward, under Brigadier-General E. B. Tyler, to Monocacy Junction near Frederick. The map will show the importance of this position, the salient of the triangle on whose base, at either end, equally distant, are Washington and

---

[1] "Sigel has been removed from Harper's Ferry and Howe sent to take his place till Hunter arrives. Of Couch, Ord, and Gillmore I think the latter the best, and have sent for him to-night." (Halleck to Grant, July 6th). "Won't General Couch do well to command until Hunter reaches?" (Grant to Halleck, July 7th).

Baltimore. Frederick itself was not defensible, the line of resistance being about three miles south, where the Baltimore and Ohio Railroad crosses the Monocacy. As the stream was everywhere fordable, this position could be easily turned on either flank. Mosby, a few days before, had dashed across the Potomac at Point of Rocks, with about six score men, there plundering the stores, and Lieutenant-Colonel Clendenin, Eighth Illinois Cavalry, 230 strong, had been sent from Washington to drive him off; this force Wallace called to Monocacy. It was still doubtful whether Early was aiming at Baltimore or at Washington, but Wallace's position within the space of three miles covered the turnpikes from Frederick to both cities and therewith the railroad.

The position and purposes of the enemy remaining hidden, Wallace, the 7th of July, despatched Clendenin on a reconnoissance five miles west of Frederick, toward Middletown. There this officer ran against B. T. Johnson's skirmishers, including the First Maryland, mostly armed with the Spencer rifle, and though his two light guns did good execution at first, when the full brigade came up he was driven back to Frederick, whither his assailants followed, yet only to retreat behind the mountains at nightfall,[1] when Gilpin came up and attacked them with his regiment and Alexander's battery. Apprised by Sigel, the next day, that the enemy's forces had quitted the neighborhood of Maryland Heights, Wallace concluded that they must be in force just beyond the Catoctin Mountains; and having

---

[1] General Wallace was at first inclined to attribute to this action a greater importance than it really had. "A battle now taking place at Frederick," he wrote Colonel Lawrence, of his staff, "with fair chance to whip the enemy. I shall hold the bridge. Inform Mr. Garrett of my purpose as to the bridge;" and a little later, to the same officer, thus: "Think I have had the best little battle of the war."

also heard a rumor that Breckenridge had moved past his
left flank toward Urbana, which is south of Frederick on
the Washington pike, he sent to the rear, by highway and
rail, the surplus Government stores, and moved his advance
at night back from Frederick to Monocacy Junction, Clendenin, whose cavalry was now about 450 strong, withdrawing from the Catoctins, where he had skirmished all day.
At dawn Early was in the town, levying a contribution of
$200,000, which was paid, and supplying himself with gar-
ments, shoes, bacon and flour. Johnson's brigade and a
battery were sent to threaten Baltimore, and to cut the railroads running thence to Washington, Philadelphia, and Harrisburg, with instructions also to release, if practicable, the
Confederate prisoners at Point Lookout. With his main
force Early girded himself to dislodge Wallace from his
position outside the town on the left bank of the Monocacy.

The troops originally at the Union general's command
consisted, as has been said, of companies from the Baltimore garrison, under General Tyler, organized as the first
separate brigade, Eighth Corps, and strengthened by hundred-days men and others. But during the evening of the
7th, Ricketts's division of the Sixth Corps began to arrive at
Baltimore from City Point, and was hurried by Halleck to
aid Wallace. This officer placed Ricketts on his left, the
main point of attack, covering the Washington pike and its
wooden bridge, while the miscellaneous forces of Tyler held
the right, covering the railroad and the Baltimore pike,
with its stone pier bridge. Three companies of Gilpin held
Crum's ford, above the bridges, and Clendenin also posted
there Captain Leib's mounted infantry, while on the other
flank he watched the lower fords and occupied the Washington pike. Skirmishers were deployed on the western
bank. To oppose Early's powerful artillery Wallace had

only one 24-pounder howitzer, planted near the block-house, one mountain howitzer, and six 3-inch rifles. Three of these were given to Ricketts and three to Tyler.

Early moved out of Frederick, with Rodes on the left, along the Baltimore pike, and Ramseur in the centre, on the Washington road, driving Wallace's pickets to the river, while Gordon, preceded by McCausland's cavalry, was inclined to the right so as to reach the fords a mile below the Union left. These movements were covered by Long's artillery, consisting of the batteries of Nelson, Braxton, King, and McLaughlin, which crowned the heights near the river, and exchanged shots with the little Union battery on the opposite bank. It need hardly be said that Wallace, with his single division of 3,350 veterans and his 2,500 troops under Tyler, many of whom had never been in action, was greatly inferior to Early. Nevertheless, the Confederate advance was stubbornly resisted. Rodes was called upon to do little but demonstrate, not even driving the Union skirmishers across the stream, while Gordon and the cavalry should turn the left under Breckenridge's direction. This was accomplished about noon, after the morning hours had been occupied with artillery fire and skirmishing. McCausland, dismounting his men, forded the river and advanced against the works, but was speedily driven back. Gordon, crossing, then reinforced the cavalry. Ricketts partly changed front to the left to face this strong column marching up the river, but he had also to hold firmly by his right, lest Ramseur should cross. King's battery was run through the river, and Nelson's from the opposite bank was turned on Ricketts. Wallace sent him two more guns, and burnt the wooden bridge and block-house, in order to release the forces defending them. But Ricketts was overwhelmed by the combined infantry and artillery fire, and Wallace di-

3*

rected him to withdraw toward the Baltimore pike, after a gallant resistance, prolonged till the middle of the afternoon. Tyler had meanwhile held on to his stone pier bridge through a series of skirmishes, Brown's Ohio troops being posted there, on the Frederick side of the stream, with Lieb's horsemen, and its retention was warmly urged by Wallace, so as to secure an orderly retreat on the Baltimore pike. But the enemy, pressing up from the south on the heels of Ricketts, struck the road before the bridge guard could all get away, and captured several hundred prisoners, General Tyler and his staff putting spurs to their horses barely in season to escape.

Wallace fell back on the Baltimore turnpike, while Ramseur and Rodes, crossing the river, made a show of pursuit. At New Market, the three remaining regiments of Ricketts's division came over from Monrovia, where, six miles from the battle-field, they had halted several hours for rations; and they covered the retreat, which continued but four miles farther. Early, too intent on going to Washington to think much about Wallace, drew back his forces at sunset. Clendenin had been cut off on the left, by Breckenridge's move, and was forced back by McCausland to Urbana, where he charged his pursuers and captured a flag. Two companies were driven toward Washington; the rest reached Monrovia and Wallace's rear.

Wallace's loss in this battle was 98 killed, 579 wounded, and 1,282 missing; total, 1,959. A train containing a part of the wounded was brought off. As Early only claimed "between 600 and 700 unwounded prisoners," some portion of the Union missing must have been stragglers. By far the greater part of the loss in killed, 84, and in wounded, 511, was in the division of the Sixth Corps; yet also, contrary to what is generally supposed, the greater part of the missing, 1,054, is also attributable to it. Ricketts's losses were thus 1,649, or nearly half his force engaged. Wallace suggests that Tyler's reports were somewhat imperfect, as his regiments were moved off soon after the battle, so that the total losses may have been over 2,000; but on the other hand, the return of stragglers may have eventually reduced it even to 1,500. Early's loss in killed and wounded was given by him as "about 700"—an evidence of the good fight made by Wallace; and 435 of his wounded, mostly such as could not be moved, were found in the Frederick hospitals and country houses when Sigel's cavalry reoccupied the town. Colonel Lamar and Lieutenant-Colonel Taverner were among his killed, and General Evans among the wounded.

Hours counted in the rescue of the national capital; and apart from the delay caused to the invading army, Wallace's merit is that he went to the right place at the right time, and did the best he could with such force as he had, not seeking to postpone the task of planting an obstacle in the enemy's path. He inflicted no little loss on Early, and brought off his stores and guns, Alexander saving even the two howitzers. "I did as I promised—held the bridge to the last," he reported to Garrett; and to Halleck he telegraphed that he was "retreating with a foot-sore, battered, and half-demoralized column. I think the troops of the Sixth Corps fought magnificently."

Wallace withdrew to Ellicott's Mills, where the Frederick turnpike crosses the Patapsco; but Early's selection of flank attack had already indicated that he had chosen Washington for his objective, and his troops were moving in that direction, while Wallace was still retrograding to Baltimore. That night Early brought his trains across the Monocacy, and began burying his dead and placing his wounded in the hospitals of Frederick; and next morning, July 10th, he was

afoot by daylight. Moving unopposed along the Georgetown turnpike, he camped that night four miles north of
Rockville, having made twenty miles for all his troops,
while some had marched thirty-four during the two days
that included the battle. McCausland encountered near
Rockville the Union cavalry, consisting of Major Fry's
Sixteenth Pennsylvania, 500 strong, and Wells's and Wing's
companies, Eighth Illinois, 120 strong, which had been cut
off from Clendenin's regiment at Monocacy, and in a sharp
conflict, drove it beyond the town. Ramseur, remaining at
Monocacy to insure the destruction of the railroad bridge,
was attacked by Sigel's cavalry, and arrived at the Rockville camp only after midnight. Sigel had reoccupied Harper's Ferry and Bolivar Heights the night of the 8th, and
Stahel had possessed himself of Sharpsburg, Boonsboro,
and Crampton's Gap, skirmishing with the enemy's rear-
guard. Couch's cavalry duly moved into Hagerstown, and
Stahel, the 10th, occupied Frederick.

The defeat of Wallace, followed by this swift swoop upon
the capital, created a profound sensation throughout the
North. People who had stoutly maintained that the whole
affair was the irruption of a gang of horse-thieves now gave
way as oracles to those who computed the invading army at
50,000 strong; and some who had suspected Harry Gilmor
of being its presiding genius discerned in its marks of far-
reaching strategy the direction of General Robert Lee.
Preceding summers had witnessed invasions, but as not one
of them had come so near the capital, it was natural to attribute to Early's movement an exaggerated strength.

In Baltimore the bells that rang that Sunday morning,
July 10th, were not calls to matins, but the summons of citi-
zens to line the trenches in the suburbs. Wallace instructed
Ricketts to withdraw from Ellicott's Mills. The 2,500 dis-

mounted cavalry from Sheridan's corps had arrived, under
charge of Major Beaumont, but were ordered to Washington;
authority, however, was given to stop and use Veteran Reserve Corps regiments, Governor Seymour's militia, and all
other troops on the way from the North.   One hundred convalescents were sent from Washington to protect the ferry
and railroad at Havre de Grace, where Major Judd caused
notices to be read in all the churches, and repeated by the
city's crier in the streets, for the assembly of men, of whom
he raised a thirty-day regiment.   Martial law was proclaimed
by Colonel Root, in Annapolis, and General E. O. C. Ord
was sent from City Point to command at Baltimore, Grant
saying, "I would give more for him as a commander in the
field than for most of the generals now in Maryland."   The
12th, Ord reported the force at Baltimore to be Ricketts's,
2,488 ; 3,000 hundred-day men and armed citizens ; 200 sailors and 500 Africans.   Governor Bradford, at his request,
called for 10,000 militia.

Meanwhile the Confederate cavalry gathered up grain,
bacon, horses, hogs, cattle, sheep, shoes, and clothing, sending the live stock back to the Potomac, whose fords they
held by small cavalry squads.   At Frederick, Johnson's cavalry brigade had been detached for Baltimore.   It occupied
Westminster, Towsontown, and Reisterstown, and tore up the
Northern Central Railroad at Cockeysville.   At Belleville
several hundred mules were captured, and wires were cut
at many points.   The damage would have been more serious
in this region, save that some of the bridges were protected
by gunboats.   Gilmor struck the Philadelphia, Wilmington
and Baltimore Railroad at Magnolia Station, and stopping
two passenger trains near the bridge where it crosses the
Gunpowder River, burned them ; then he backed one of the
trains upon this bridge, and the flaming mass soon set fire

to the important structure. A force of a few score hundred-day men were dispersed, and a Government steamer,
near by, stationed expressly to guard the bridge, lacked
steam at the critical moment.[1] General Franklin chanced to
be a passenger on one of the trains and was captured, but
afterward made his escape. This raid severed railroad and
telegraphic communication with the North, thus reducing
Early's danger of an attack upon his left and rear. As for
the attempt upon Point Lookout, where many thousand
Confederate prisoners were confined, it was imperfectly arranged, and abandoned; it could not have succeeded, for
the place was attainable only over ground commanded by
gunboats. The dwelling of Governor Bradford, four miles
from Baltimore, was burned, and a score of Union cavalry
pickets were captured at Camp Bradford.

At dawn of Monday, July 11th, Early pushed forward
from Rockville; McCausland, in advance, moved toward
Tenallytown, arriving by eight or nine o'clock north of
Georgetown, where he held Early's right. The main force
took the Seventh Street road, preceded by Imboden's brigade, under Smith, while Jackson moved on the left flank ;
the Union cavalry of Lowell, Fry, and Wing were driven
back to the works.

The day was intensely hot, the night had been oppressive ;
a prolonged drought had laid the roads in dust, and men
who had sturdily tramped from Cold Harbor to Lynchburg,

---

[1] Gilmor, in Four Years in the Saddle, narrates that a few months earlier he
ran a passenger train off the track, by means of fence rails and logs, near
Duffield's Station, in the Valley, and burned it. "The Northern papers made
such an outcry against me," he says, "that General Robert E. Lee ordered me to
be tried by court-martial." The Court acquitted him, as he testified that the robbing of the passengers, which occurred while he was burning the train, had been
done against his orders. Fortunately for the trains stopped at Gunpowder Bridge,
Gilmor did not experiment on them with his device of logs and rails—they might
not have glided off so easily as at Duffield's.

and from Lynchburg to Frederick, fell by the wayside, exhausted and half suffocated. But, between eleven o'clock and noon, Early's advance approached within eyesight of the capital, Frazee's One Hundred and Fiftieth Ohio and the Twenty-fifth New York cavalry retiring to the works. Early's leading division, Rodes's, having marched by the flank, was ordered into line, and when his skirmishers were within range, about 1.30 P.M., the forts opened a rapid shelling, under which his sharpshooters drew back, and the

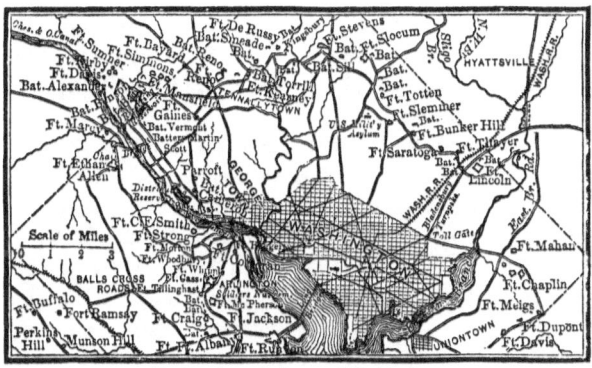

The Northern Defences of Washington.

Union picket line was re-established by 600 dismounted cavalry, under Major Briggs, Seventh Michigan.

Early's position was near Silver Spring, due north of Washington, a little west of the Seventh Street road, with the dome of the Capitol in full view ; he had cavalry camps on his right and left flanks, but his infantry was mostly along this road, between the houses of Blair and Batchelor, the latter two miles north of the former. The defences of the city on that side consisted of a series of detached forts, generally connected by rifle-pits. They were regu-

larly built field works of strong profile, and provided with
ditches and abatis, the timber having been felled where it
stood, within cannon-range; while everywhere there was a
sweeping cross-fire of artillery. The forts mounted many
32-pounders, with some 30-pounder and 100-pounder Par-
rotts. The one in Early's front was Fort Stevens, with De
Russy on the west, and Slocum on the east. Between
Stevens and De Russy was a deep ravine, through which
ran Rock Creek, and this suggested shelter for a storming
party; but the hollow had been rendered difficult by level-
ling the woods on each slope, while the Georgetown pike,
beyond, was swept by the fire of Fort Reno. In this system
of works, the carrying of one fort would bring it under the
fire of its neighbors.

From his prisoners Early knew positively that troops
must have been sent from Grant's army, since a division of
the Sixth Corps was as far distant as Frederick several days
before. The newspapers in the towns through which he
passed told him of Hunter's return to the Valley, and of
the expected presence of large forces from the Army of
the Potomac to defend the capital. Hence, when his
field-glass revealed to him, immediately on arriving, bodies
of troops filing into the works in his front, he naturally
concluded that Washington had been succored by this
army.

General C. C. Augur, commanding the Department of
Washington, had collected heavy artillery, hundred-day
men, convalescents, invalid corps, marines and sailors from
the navy yard, militia, quartermaster's clerks and other
employees, and had placed them in and around the forts,
with General A. McD. McCook in command. The line
directly north of the city was garrisoned chiefly by the One
Hundred and Fiftieth and One Hundred and Fifty-first Ohio

hundred-day militia, two or three companies in each fort, and by detachments of volunteer heavy artillery, of Hardin's division of the Twenty-second Corps, whose two brigades, Warner's and Haskins's, held the whole line from the Potomac to the Eastern Branch.   Warner was reinforced, during the 10th, by five regiments of Veterans, the Seventh, under Lieutenant-Colonel Thomas, and Gile's brigade.   The cavalry consisted of the Second Massachusetts, Colonel Lowell, the Sixteenth Pennsylvania, Major Fry, and some smaller detachments.   The Second D. C. Volunteers, Colonel Alexander, the Ninth V. R. C., Colonel Johnson, Gibbs's Ohio Battery, and Bradbury's Maine Battery were in the rifle-pits on the 11th, and during the afternoon a body of the quartermaster's employees went to the front, with several hundred dismounted cavalry.[1]

Yet these troops would have proved a very inadequate defence against an army like Early's.   The chief source of safety came from another quarter.   The night of July 9th, a few hours after Wallace's defeat on the banks of the Monocacy, Major-General H. G. Wright was directed to march the First and Second divisions of the Sixth Corps from their camp at Petersburg to City Point, fourteen miles distant,

---

[1] "The effective forces were 1,819 infantry, 1,834 artillery, and 63 cavalry north of the Potomac, and 4,064 infantry, 1,772 artillery, and 51 cavalry south thereof. There were besides, in Washington and Alexandria, about 3,900 effectives . . . and about 4,400 (six regiments) of Veteran Reserves. . . . The foregoing constitute a total of about 20,400 men. Of that number, however, but 9,600, mostly perfectly raw troops, constituted the *garrison* of the defences. Of the other troops, a considerable portion were unavailable, and the whole would form but an inefficient force for service on the lines." (Barnard's Defences of Washington.) This was the available force, of course, exclusive of the Sixth and Nineteenth Corps. Behind strong works, some of those troops who did not belong to the garrisons might have proved effective, for the 4,400 Veteran Reserves, presumably, were old soldiers, as were many of the quartermaster's men, nearly 2,000 of whom were reported by General Meigs for duty the night before Early's arrival.

where, arriving at daylight, they took transports, and were soon steaming to Fort Monroe. Before 2 P.M. of the 11th, the vessels touched the wharves of Washington, and there found, also just arriving, an ocean-going steamer, bringing a portion, 800 men, of Emory's division of the Nineteenth Corps, which, having reached Hampton Roads from New Orleans, had been sent directly to the capital. President Lincoln stood on the Sixth Street wharf to greet the troops, the gaunt figure as welcome a sight to them as they to him. Quickly landing, they marched up Seventh Street, amidst the acclaims of the people who thronged the foot-ways, and to whom the Greek cross seemed an emblem of rescue. Wright had at first been ordered to Fort Sumner on the Potomac, but at Early's approach he was directed instead to Fort Stevens. As his troops neared the northern outskirts, the sound of artillery quickened their footsteps, as it is wont to do with reinforcements arriving at need.

About the same time, therefore, that Early was arriving in front of Fort Stevens, Wright was approaching the other end of the city at the river piers; and while Rodes, after a brief halt for his parched and panting men, was deploying his columns into line of battle to test the strength of the works, Augur's provisional levies were filing into Stevens and De Russy.

From this coincidence of events has resulted a diversity of opinion as to whether Early could have seized Washington by a bold assault delivered the moment he reached the city. A fair judgment seems to be that Lieutenant-General Grant cannot be brought under the imputation of neglect which an affirmative view of this question would necessarily imply. Were the safety of Washington dependent on the fact that though Early might have carried it, yet for lack of enterprise he failed to do so, its preservation would be due rather to the good fortune than to the vigilance of Grant. Early had been swift in his later movements, having brought his troops and trains from the Catoctin Mountains, between morning of June 9th and noon of June 11th, in extraordinary heat and dust, but the reinforcements from Petersburg had also come quickly. There was no time to spare; but even could Early have carried Stevens or De Russy, by an immediate assault, as very likely he might have done, had he been regardless of loss, he would have afterward met the two divisions of the Sixth Corps and a portion of the Nineteenth between the works and the city itself; and unless we are to suppose that he could both have taken one of these forts and beaten all the troops in the city, his assault would have involved him in no little peril. While McCausland's cavalry was near Fort De Russy at nine o'clock, and Rodes near Fort Stevens soon after noon, yet the rear did not reach its encampment at Batchelor's, two miles from Silver Spring, until 6 P.M. In a despatch to Lee from Leesburg, three days later, Early gives this account of his actions and motives after leaving Frederick :

" The day [the 10th] was very hot, and the roads exceedingly dusty, but we marched thirty miles. On the morning of the 11th we continued the march, but the day was so excessively hot, even at a very early hour in the morning, and the dust was so dense, that many of the men fell by the way, and it became necessary to slacken our pace. Nevertheless, when we reached the enemy's fortifications, the men were completely exhausted, and not in a condition to make an attack. . . . I determined to make an assault, but before it could be made it became apparent that the enemy had been strongly reinforced. . . . After consultation with my division commanders, I became satisfied that the assault, even if successful, would be attended with such great sacrifice as would insure the destruction of my whole force, before the victory could have been made available, and if unsuccessful would necessarily have resulted in the loss of the whole force."

At 4.10 o'clock that Monday afternoon, Wright, from Fort
Stevens, addressed this note to Augur : "The head of my
column has nearly reached the front, and at the suggestion
of Major-General McCook I have directed them to bivouac
at Crystal Spring, about half mile in rear. The enemy
has been close to Fort Stevens, and although driven back
is still not far distant. I believe it to be only a very
light skirmish line, and with your permission will send a
brigade out against it, and try to clear it out. General Mc-
Cook's men are not as good as mine for this purpose." He
added that he held his corps in reserve, subject to McCook's
orders. Augur replied that he did not consider it advisable
to make any advance " until our lines are better established
—perhaps to-morrow." However, that night the Sixth Corps
relieved the provisional forces on picket, with 900 men, and,
in Virginia fashion, promptly intrenched the line. At nine
o'clock, Quartermaster General Meigs reported for duty with
1,500 of his employees, armed and equipped, under immediate command of General Rucker, and these were placed in
position in the rifle pits on the right and left of Fort Slocum,
while an hour later Colonel Price reported with his provisional brigade of 2,800 convalescents.[1]

Dawn of Tuesday, the 12th, showed the enemy in possession of the Rives house, on the right of the Silver Spring
road; it stood on rising ground, surrounded by shade trees,
with an orchard hard by, affording cover for his sharpshooters, who commanded the Union skirmish line from this
point and from Mrs. Lay's house, on the left of the road.
Wheaton's brigade of the Second (Getty's) Division, Sixth

---

[1] Augur's telegraphic order to McCook read thus : Doubleday to command south
of Eastern Branch ; Gillmore north of Eastern Branch to include Fort Slemmer ;
Meigs from Fort Totten to Forts De Russy and Kearney, including dependent
batteries ; Hardin from Fort Reno, inclusive, to the Potomac.

Corps, was thrown out on picket in front of Fort Stevens, and instantly puffs of white smoke and the whiz of bullets from the opposite lines told that the Confederate sharpshooters were at work. Skirmishing continued through the day; by the middle of the afternoon General Wright pushed out a strong reconnoissance, with the Third Brigade of the same (Getty's) division, which in these operations was under charge of General Wheaton, during Getty's absence. This brigade, Bidwell's, was formed in two lines, with the Seventy-seventh New York, Seventh Maine, and Forty-ninth New York in the first, and the Forty-third New York, Sixty-first Pennsylvania and One Hundred and Twenty-second New York in the second. The central point of attack was the Rives house, about midway of the open. The guns of Fort Stevens having cleared the way, Bidwell, at a sign from Wright, who stood on the parapet, advanced in good alignment, passing through the First Brigade's line and over a slight acclivity, beyond the orchard and grove to the house, from which Early's skirmishers were soon expelled. On a farther crest, a stout resistance was made, but after gallant fighting the position was swept, and Early's pickets were driven back a mile.

Rarely did a minor engagement present so clear an opportunity for viewing its progress, and rarely for such a scene was a more memorable group of spectators assembled. On the parapet of Fort Stevens stood the tall form of Abraham Lincoln, by the side of General Wright, who in vain warned the eager President that his position was swept by the bullets of sharpshooters, until an officer was shot down within three feet of him, when he reluctantly stepped below. Sheltered from the line of fire, Cabinet officers and a group of citizens and ladies, breathless with excitement, watched the fortunes of the fight. Strange as was this spectacle at the gates of the national capital, it would have seemed stranger still to the onlookers, could they have known that in the camp yonder, as if in typical contrast to the figure on the parapet, stood one who four years before had been the Vice-President of the United States.

It was no mock battle that these spectators witnessed. Stretchers soon came from the field by scores, with their ghastly loads; the hospitals in the rear of the fort were astir; and here and there, dotting the meadow, the orchard and the dusty highway, lay many a lad for whom the wild cheers of the crowd fell on deaf ears. Colonel Visscher was dead, Lieutenant-Colonel Johnson mortally wounded, Major Jones dead, Major Crosby with his left arm gone—in brief, every regimental commander of the Third Brigade killed or wounded, with a loss of 250 in the brigade and a total loss of 280 out of the force engaged. The enemy must also have suffered severely, as about 30 of his dead and 70 of his most seriously wounded were left on the field and at Blair's house with surgeons and attendants. Hardin's division lost 73 killed and wounded during the two days of Early's presence, and other casualties made the total Union loss in this demonstration against Washington between 400 and 500. A monument on the slope fronting Fort Stevens preserves the memory of the Union dead.

Early was quick to read the warning that it was time for him to be away. That night he fell back through Rockville, his soldiers having first set fire to the house of Montgomery Blair near his camp; he marched all night, and halted near Darnestown.

CHAPTER V.

IN THE VALLEY AGAIN.

THE one want now was a field commander. The 12th of July, Early being still before Washington, Assistant Secretary C. A. Dana telegraphed Grant as follows: "Nothing can possibly be done here toward pursuing or cutting off the enemy, for want of a commander. Augur commands the defences of Washington, with McCook and a lot of brigadiers under him, but he is not allowed to go outside; Wright commands his own corps; Gillmore has been assigned to the temporary command of those troops of the Nineteenth Corps in the city of Washington; Ord to command the Eighth Corps and all other troops in the Middle Department, leaving Wallace to command the city of Baltimore alone; but there is no head to the whole, and it seems indispensable that you should at once appoint one. . . . General Halleck will not give orders, except as he receives them. The President will give none; and until you direct positively and explicitly what is to be done, everything will go on in the deplorable and fatal way in which it has gone on for the past week."

Grant at midnight sent this message to Halleck: "Give orders assigning Major-General H. G. Wright to supreme command of all troops moving out against the enemy, regardless of the rank of other commanders. He should get outside of the trenches with all the force he possibly can, and should push him [Early] to the last moment." To Dana "Boldness is all," he said, "that is needed to drive the enemy out of Maryland in confusion. I hope and believe Wright is the man to assure that."

The morning of July 13th having disclosed that Early had vanished from Silver Spring, Wright, with the two divisions of the Sixth Corps, at noon drew out of the trenches for the chase, Emory's division of the Nineteenth being directed to follow. Lowell's cavalry, riding to Rock-ville, was there driven back by McCausland, losing about 30 killed and wounded, but bringing off 38 prisoners.

Grant was so anxious to have Early pursued and attacked, after his audacious foray, that he had at first even contemplated undertaking this task in person; and an ingenious speculation could be spun on what might have happened had he carried this project into effect. "Forces enough," he telegraphed to Halleck, July 9th, "to defeat all that Early has with him should get in his rear, south of him, and follow him up sharply, leaving him to go north, defending depots, towns, etc., with small garrisons and the militia. If the President thinks it advisable that I should go to Washington in person, I can start in an hour after receiving notice, leaving everything here on the defensive." Mr. Lincoln caught at the hint. "What I think is," he answered, "that you should provide to retain your hold where you are certainly, and bring the rest with you personally, and make a vigorous effort to defeat the enemy's force in this vicinity. I think there is really a fair chance to do this, if the movement is prompt. This is what I think upon your suggestion, and is not an order." Early was then approaching Washington from Frederick, his force unknown, and the President's project was based on the premise that " General Halleck says we have absolutely no force here

fit to go to the field;" but Grant saw that there might be
an outcry that this was the campaign of 1862 repeated. " I
have sent from here," he wrote to Mr. Lincoln, " a whole
corps, commanded by an excellent officer, besides over 3,000
other troops. One division of the Nineteenth Corps, 6,000
strong, is now on its way to Washington, one steamer loaded
with these troops having passed Fort Monroe to-day. They
will probably reach Washington to-morrow night. This
force under Wright will be able to compete with the whole
force under Early. . . . I think, on reflection, it would
have a bad effect for me to leave here, and with General
Ord at Baltimore, and Hunter and Wright with the forces
following the enemy up, could do no good. I have great
faith that the enemy will never be able to get back with
much of his force." To Halleck he wrote that " a force
should be collected in rear of the enemy, at Edward's Ferry,
and follow him up and cut off retreat, if possible ; " whereupon Halleck, at his direction, gave Hunter a rendezvous
with Wright at that point. To Meade at that time—that
Sunday of panic in Washington and Baltimore—Grant had
said with characteristic equipoise, " Taking all together,
everything looks favorable to me."

About noon of July 13th, Halleck notified Augur that
General Wright's forces ought to " immediately move out
on the river road from Tenallytown, and Gillmore follow as
soon as possible." Stanton, in a despatch directed to
Wright " on march," declared that " 4,600 of the Nineteenth
Corps in all have arrived ; about 1,500 more are on the river
coming up ; " and added that he need not delay for want
of support. Everybody had welcomed Wright's oncoming,
and all were as feverish to speed his parting. At 5 P.M. his
head of column had reached Fort Reno, and he sent back
word to Stanton that the troops would be " pushed to the

XI.—4

limits of the endurance of the men. I can assure yourself and the President that there will be no delay on my part to head off the enemy." At 6.30 P.M. he had reached Offutt's Cross Roads, with his cavalry, and an hour later with the head of his infantry, and there camped for the night. He had with him Lowell's cavalry, 750 strong, about 10,000 effective of the Sixth Corps and 650 of the Nineteenth, while about 3,500 of the latter were toiling up in the rear. Gillmore having sprained his foot at Offutt's, Emory, who had reported that day, went forward with his (First) division of the Nineteenth, and in time received charge of the corps. During the day and the night previous, 1,689 men of the Sixth and 3,560 of the Nineteenth had debarked at Washington.

The next day, the 14th, Wright had reached Seneca Creek, when, his scouts reporting the enemy in force at Darnestown, he halted and sent out an infantry reconnoissance. "I believe," he wrote back to Halleck, "that the bulk of the enemy's force has already crossed the river at Edward's Ferry. This fact will be shortly developed, and if they have left Darnestown, I shall continue the march to Edward's Ferry." It was true that Early was now across the Potomac, with his trains, his prisoners captured at Monocacy, a large number of beef cattle, and many horses for his cavalry and artillery; and he had been safely rejoined by the foraging parties that were spread over Eastern Maryland. He had marched from Washington to Rockville during the night of the 12th, had rested during a part of the 13th, at night had gone forward to Poolesville, and the morning of the 14th crossed the Potomac at White's Ford, camping at Leesburg.

Wright reached Poolesville, twenty-six miles from Fort Stevens, the evening of the same day, July 14th, most of Getty's infantry and a part of the artillery arriving at 6 P.M.,

while the train was stretched along the road in the rear.
The cavalry had overtaken the enemy's rear-guard at Poolesville earlier that day, demonstrating against it as it crossed
White's Ford behind the infantry, and during the afternoon
there was artillery firing across the river against Early's
pickets, who held the fords. At Poolesville Wright remained till the morning of the 16th, meanwhile, on the
14th, informing the War Department that the enemy had
crossed.[1] Early, on his part, remained at Leesburg, on the
south side of the Potomac, as long as Wright was at Poolesville, on the north side, namely, from the evening of the
14th to the morning of the 16th. To Lee he reported, the
14th, that he had brought off over 1,000 horses, adding, "I
shall rest here a day or two, and then move to the Valley,
and drive from Martinsburg a body of cavalry which has returned there, and then send the cavalry to destroy effectually the Baltimore and Ohio Railroad westward, and also
to destroy the coal mines and furnaces around Cumberland,
unless I get different orders. I will start for the Valley in
the morning. . . . I will retreat in forced marches by
land toward Richmond."

To Wright's message that he would halt for instructions
before going south of the Potomac, Halleck replied :

---

[1] "The main body of the enemy, with his trains, had crossed before we reached
this place. I have sent the cavalry forward to see whether anything can be done
against the rear-guard, but presume it will be too late. The enemy had and kept
about twenty-four hours the start of us, which gave him full time to secure his
crossing of the river. I have not been able to get any intelligence from General
Hunter's command, and have, therefore, for further operations only the two divisions of my corps, numbering, perhaps, 10,000, and some 500 possibly of the
Nineteenth Corps, which, unless I overrate the enemy's strength, is wholly insufficient to justify the following up of the enemy on the other side of the Potomac.
I presume this will not be the policy of the War Department, and I shall therefore wait instructions before proceeding farther, which I hope to receive by the
time the Nineteenth Corps arrives." (Wright to Halleck, Poolesville, Md., July
14, 1864, 6 P.M.)

" General Grant directed that a junction of your forces and that of General Hunter be made in the vicinity of Edward's Ferry, to cut off the enemy's retreat, if possible ; if not, to pursue him South, doing him all the damage you can. He further says that you must live mainly upon the country. He does not say how far South you are to pursue, but I will get his instructions on that point and communicate them to you. You will therefore continue the pursuit till you receive further orders. In giving you the supreme command with only general indications as to what you are to do, General Grant probably intended to leave you free to exercise your own judgment. As your force, until Hunter or the Nineteenth Corps reaches you, will be inferior to the enemy, you will move with caution. Ricketts's division and Kenly's brigade, under General Ord, left this morning to join you. They number about 5,000. About 4,000 of the Nineteenth Corps, under General Emory, have also left."

This despatch illustrated the universal leaning on the word and judgment of Grant, who, at City Point, could not know, and did not pretend to know, the exact situation, from hour to hour, on the Potomac.

Grant, though so urgent to get a strong force " south of Early," and so confident that he could be crushed, was quick to perceive that Early had probably made good his escape, and turned to a new plan. He told Halleck that " the Sixth and Nineteenth Corps should be got here [City Point] without any delay, so that they may be used before the return of the troops sent into the Valley by the enemy. Hunter, moving up the Valley, will either hold a large force of the enemy, or he will be enabled to reach Gordonsville and Charlottesville. The utter destruction of the road at and between these two points will be of immense value to us. I do not intend this as an order to bring Wright back whilst he is in pursuit of the enemy with any prospect of punishing him, but to secure his return at the earliest possible moment after he ceases to be absolutely necessary where he is." This quiet, persistent return to ideas once fixed was characteristic of the Lieutenant-General, and the destruction of Confederate railroads was one of his fixed ideas ; while had any officer ever taken Gordonsville, starting from any quarter of the compass, there is probably no end of the hearty approval he would have had for him.

Nevertheless he did not precisely like to have the pursuit cease. "If the enemy has left Maryland," he continued, "he should have upon his heels veterans, militiamen, men on horseback, everything that can be got to follow, to eat out Virginia clear and clean, as far as they go, so that crows flying over it, for the balance of this season, will have to carry their provender with them." Still, so mixed a force might have been only food for Early's powder and statistics for Ould, the commissioner of prisoners. Grant, in a letter of the same day, expressed the view that "Hunter should make all the Valley south of the B. and O. road a desert, as high up as possible. I do not mean that houses should be burned, but every particle of provisions and stock should be removed, and the people notified to move out." The following day he renewed his two ideas, declaring to Halleck that "there can be no use in Wright's following the enemy, with the latter a day ahead, after he has passed entirely beyond [south of] all our communications. I want, if possible, to get the Sixth and Nineteenth Corps here, to use them here before the enemy can get Early back." Hunter, he said, could always hold the Valley and protect Washington, at least until aid should come from City Point, provided he did not allow himself to be "squeezed out to one side. I do not think," he added, "there is now any further danger of an attempt to invade Maryland. The position of the enemy in the West and here is such as to demand all the force they can get together to save vital points. . . . As soon as the rebel army is known to have passed Hunter's forces, recall Wright, and send him back here with all despatch ; and also send the Nineteenth Corps. If the enemy have any notion of returning, the fact will be developed before Wright can start back."

Early had not then "passed Hunter's forces," but nobody knowing exactly where he was, Halleck turned back all troops of the Sixth and Nineteenth Corps still north of the Potomac on their way to join Wright, and the same day, the 17th, notified both Hunter and Wright of the change of plan, telling the latter that he was to pursue the enemy only far enough to be certain that he was really in full retreat toward Richmond, and then to direct Crook and Sullivan " to continue the pursuit cautiously, under General Hunter's orders." The forces of Hunter [1] had now, in fact, come upon

---

[1] There had been a disposition at the War Office to regard Hunter as the cause of all the mischief culminating with the siege of Washington ; but a special grievance seemed to be his neglect to telegraph frequently to Halleck and Stanton. General Halleck, the 14th, suggested to him that "General Crook would be a suitable person for the immediate command" of such troops as he might send to form a junction with Wright, adding that "for the last two weeks little or nothing of a reliable character has been heard from you." Hunter replied in a spirited letter to Stanton, expressing regret for such an imputation on the ground that it must be the President's, conveyed through Halleck. He said that if any important events had occurred in his department, of which necessarily the War Office must not have learned earlier than he, they had not yet come to his knowledge ; that his first step on hearing of Sigel's retreat from Martinsburg had been to instruct him that he must report directly to Washington, as he himself would be too far distant and too much occupied ; it was true that he "could have telegraphed many alarming rumors every hour," but this was not his practice, and of reports without the elements of knowledge or credibility it seemed to him that there must be already more than enough in the vicinity of Baltimore and Washington ; moreover, he was too busy, n ght and day, in the task of hurrying forward his command against the enemy, to give time to any labors not of public benefit—probably it was forgotten that his Lynchburg expedition had exhausted the ammunition, provisions, and clothing of his tired troops ; that in coming up the Ohio they had to be disembarked at every shoal and marched around it till the steamers could be sparred over, and that, after all, they found the railroad broken by Early's raids. In short, as the interests of the service had been his

the scene ; and his advance, which arrived at Martinsburg July 10th and 11th, pausing two days to refit and to allow other troops to get up from Cumberland, proceeded to Duffield's the 13th, and next day through Harper's Ferry across the Potomac, on the pontoon bridge, camping at Knoxville, on the left bank. That night, the 14th, Hunter, having arrived at Harper's Ferry, received from Wright a notification to join him at Leesburg, and early the following morning started eastward the divisions of Sullivan and Mulligan, 7,000 strong, under the former, and Duffié's division of 2,000

---

highest aim, to be pursued at any personal sacrifice, he most respectfully requested to be relieved from command by some officer more enjoying the confidence of the President. The same day, July 15th, he wrote to the Adjutant-General, requesting to be "relieved from the command of this Department, where my services can be of no further use," and then a second time to the same officer, reiterating this request; while Crook, arriving that day from West Virginia with two of his brigades, 3,400 strong, was ordered by him to relieve Sullivan and take command of all the forces in the field.

The very day, July 15th, that Hunter sent this letter from Harper's Ferry, where he had arrived from West Virginia the day before, he received the most powerful of all reinforcements for his cause. "I am sorry," wrote Grant to Dana, from City Point, "to see such a disposition to condemn as brave an old soldier as Hunter is known to be without a hearing. He is known to have advanced into the enemy's country toward their main army, inflicting a much greater damage upon them than they have inflicted upon us, with double his force, and moving directly away from our main army. Hunter acted, too, in a country where we had no friends. . . . Even the enemy give him credit for courage, and congratulate themselves that he will give them a chance of getting even with him." Two days later Hunter, hearing nothing from Washington, wrote a brief letter to President Lincoln, asking to be relieved from the command of his Department. "When an officer," he said, "is selected as the scapegoat to cover up the blunders of others, the best interests of the country require that he should at once be relieved from command." President Lincoln replied frankly: "You misconceive. The order you complain of was only nominally mine, and was framed by those who really made it with no thought of making you a scapegoat. It seemed to be General Grant's wish that the forces under General Wright and those under you should join, and drive at the enemy, under General Wright. Wright had the larger part of the force, but you had the rank. It was thought that you would prefer Crook's commanding your post to your serving in person under Wright. That is all of it. General Grant wishes you to remain in command of the Department, and I do not wish to order otherwise."

cavalry, which had only reached Martinsburg from Parkersburg about noon of the 14th. The column took the tow-
path of the Chesapeake and Ohio Canal to Berlin, and there
fording the river, nearly hip-deep, marched for the Leesburg pike, passing through Lovettsville, and thence southward; but instead of pressing forward to the pike, Sullivan,
when four miles short of it, turned to the west, going into
camp at Hillsboro.

Comparison of dates and places shows that these West
Virginia forces were now coming in directly and very fast
upon Early's right flank, and that, had it been wise to do so,
they might have been thrown exactly across his path; but
the night of the 15th, while Sullivan was at Hillsboro,
Wright was still at Poolesville, Md., north of the Potomac.
Had Wright and Sullivan possessed a common understanding for vigorous action in the best possible way, the former
close on Early's heels with 15,000 men, and Ricketts and
Kenly hurrying forward with several thousand more, Sullivan and Duffié might apparently have been able to use their
9,000 men with great effect against Early's line of march,
from Leesburg to Snicker's Gap. The 15th, on the way from
Lovettsville to Purcellsville, Sullivan's advance captured
a few of Jackson's cavalry, Early's forerunners.

The evening of the 15th, Wright, at Poolesville, had
received Halleck's despatch, ordering him to continue the
pursuit, but with caution, and about the same time had
learned, both from Hunter's staff officers and from his own
couriers, that Sullivan was moving by way of Hillsboro
toward Leesburg. The next morning, therefore, he crossed
at White's Ford for Leesburg, "fearing that he [Sullivan]
might meet the enemy in too strong force for his command." The troops of the Nineteenth Corps had reached him
the 15th. "The necessity for supporting General Sullivan's

movement," said Wright to Halleck, "renders it necessary
to move in advance of a portion of the trains not yet up;
but I think they will be sufficiently covered by the general
movement and the small force left for their protection."
Wright camped at Clark's Gap, three miles beyond Leesburg, reporting to Halleck that he had struck the rear-guard
of the enemy's cavalry at this place, but that the latter
retreated before the infantry could get up.

Sullivan, on his part, remained at Hillsboro from night
of the 15th till afternoon of the 16th; and at noon of the
latter day Crook came up and assumed command of all
Hunter's field forces. Four or five hours later he wrote to
Hunter that he had sent the cavalry out in different directions, immediately on arriving at Hillsboro, "and have lain
still until I could learn something definite of the enemy's
movements." Now, while Wright, that morning, leaving
Poolesville, had forded the Potomac and marched to Leesburg, Early, who had camped at Leesburg since the 14th,
marched through Hamilton and Purcellsville, to Snicker's
and Ashby's Gaps. Crook, hearing that there was a wagon
train near Waterford, ordered a brigade thither, to strike the
enemy's cavalry; and toward evening he marched his command forward and camped at Purcellsville, midway between
Leesburg and Snicker's Gap. A good part of Early's trains
and columns, therefore, must have been for many hours close
to Crook's command; but that officer, who only arrived at
Hillsboro at noon, did not know this, and when his cavalry
informed him, the infantry, he reported, could not be got
over from Hillsboro in season to attack Early's flank. But
Duffié had sent Tibbets's small brigade to fall on the trains,
and this it did near Purcellsville, capturing, without much
difficulty, one hundred and seventeen mules and horses,
eighty-two wagons, and 50 or 60 prisoners, Tibbets's own

4*

loss being but 20. This spirited attack by three small regiments, a few hundred strong, is worth commemorating, as
the only instance in which Early was forced to drop any of
his Maryland spoils. Troops from both Rodes's and Ramseur's divisions were hurried to repel this danger, and captured a gun and a caisson in doing so. Tibbets brought off
thirty-seven loaded wagons, and burned over forty more.

The forces of Hunter and Wright had now come together
just in season to allow Early to slip between them, grazing
the last of his trains and their guard. The night of the
16th, Crook, from his camp at Purcellsville, half a dozen
miles from Wright's, reported for orders, and was instructed
to move a force to Snicker's Gap. He despatched Duffié
and Mulligan for this purpose; but Early, who had crossed
the Shenandoah at Snicker's Ferry opposite the Gap, planted
two guns there, and checked farther approach, Duffié losing 17 men in the affair. Wright remained at Clark's Gap,
near Leesburg, and notified Halleck that he would verify
the enemy's retreat by sending a column ahead. The 18th,
he instructed Crook to move in force through Snicker's
Gap, where his advance was, and he put the Sixth Corps in
motion for the same point. Duffié was sent to Ashby's
Gap; but there he found, the next day, that the enemy was
in force, and after crossing the Shenandoah at Berry's Ferry,
was driven back with no little loss, about 50 of his troops being captured, and a considerable number killed and wounded.

Meanwhile, the afternoon of the 18th, from the summit
of the Blue Ridge the enemy could be seen on the heights
beyond the river. Early's force was around Berryville, and
Breckenridge had charge of the fords of the Shenandoah.
About two o'clock, Crook directed Thoburn to cross with
his own division and the Third Brigade of the Second, to dislodge the forces there, and to move for this purpose to Island

Ford, a mile or more below Snicker's Ferry. Here the enemy, who had a picket behind bushes, opened a hot fire ; but Wells's brigade found a good wading-place a few hundred yards below, and dashing across, carried the ford, capturing 15 skirmishers and the captain commanding them. From these it was learned that Early's whole force was not distant, and Gordon and Rodes only a mile or two away. Thoburn, on sending back this news to Crook, was directed not to attempt to move up to hold Snicker's Ferry for the passage of the army, as at first intended, but to await a division of the Sixth Corps which would cross for his support. Accordingly a position was selected, with the First, Wells's brigade, on the left, the Third, Frost's, in the centre, and the Second, commanded by Thoburn himself, on the right. Beyond the right flank was a force of about 1,000 dismounted cavalry, odds and ends of various regiments under Lieutenant-Colonel Young, Fourth Pennsylvania. Fully half an hour later, Breckenridge advanced against Thoburn's left and centre, with his two divisions, while Early sent Rodes to fall on the Union right. The dismounted cavalry on this flank was the first to break, under the fire of Rodes, and retreated across the river, despite the efforts of Young to rally it. Thoburn, who was in two lines, rapidly changed front to stem the tide, but at length the heavy impact of Rodes was too much for his force, which was driven into the stream. The left of his line, less sharply assailed, withdrew in good order, considering that its task was the trying one of retreating across a river under fire from the bank.[1] The dead and wounded were left on the

---

[1] " The head of the column of the Sixth Corps had reached the crossing of the river by this time, and as General Ricketts, commanding the corps, did not think it prudent under the circumstances to cross his men, and as the enemy were preparing for another attack on my lines, I gave the order to fall back, which was done in good order by the remaining troops " (Crook's Report, October 12, 1864).

field, and Thoburn's casualties in this engagement were 65 killed, 301 wounded, and 56 missing—total, 422. The enemy must also have suffered severely, for the troops of Rodes, who halted on the bank to fire at the fugitives, had exposed themselves to the Union batteries. Next day, the Confederates were busy burying their dead and removing their wounded.

In this affair no reproach can be applied to Thoburn's division, for it would have been preposterous to suppose that, unaided and in an unintrenched position, it could withstand the shock of all the force Early might choose to bring against it. The clue to what Thoburn's men considered an inexcusable lack of support may perhaps be found in a despatch of Wright to Halleck : " The attempt at crossing was resisted in strong force ; and believing it better to turn his position, I designed doing so by way of Keyes Gap, thus effecting a junction with some of the forces of General Hunter lower down the valley." But the repulse of Duffié at Ashby's Gap and other events induced him " to defer the movement by way of Keyes Gap, in the belief that a crossing might be effected where we were." Wright remained at Snicker's Gap through the 19th ; and that night Early retreated, taking the road to Strasburg.

Wright crossed the river next day, the 20th, to the battlefield, where were visible many Union dead, heads, arms and legs protruding from the slight heaps of earth hastily shovelled on them, while many Confederate graves also marked the field. He notified Hunter that he should move the same day " to Berryville, perhaps farther, toward Winchester," asking that supplies should be sent to the former point, and also all spare troops, " to swell my force, making it as large as possible to meet the enemy." Hunter had already, two days before, pushed all his available troops up the valley, in

co-operation, and now urged them forward again ; but Wright,
on more mature reflection, regarded his orders as contem-
plating his return, when he had verified the enemy's retreat ;
and accordingly, instead of moving to Winchester, he recrossed the Shenandoah, and marched back through Snicker's
Ferry to Leesburg. There, the 21st, he addressed Halleck,
saying, "Conceiving the object of the expedition to be accomplished, I at once started back, as directed in your orders, and to-night shall encamp on the east side of Goose
Creek, on the Leesburg Pike. Two days' easy march will
bring the command to Washington."

Lieutenant-General Grant, who had for several days been
pressed by Halleck in regard to the defencelessness of the
Maryland border, caused by the expiration of hundred-
days and other enlistments, at this time told him that he
might "retain Wright's command until the departure of
Early is assured, or other forces are collected to make his
presence unnecessary. If Early has halted about Berryville,
what is to prevent Wright and Hunter from attacking him?"
Wright, however, was already returning.

To comprehend Early's precipitate retreat from the line
of the Shenandoah, we must now turn our eyes to another
quarter. At Harper's Ferry Hunter, whose troops from the
Kanawha had continued to arrive by rail, had at command
a large body of men, in addition to those under Crook.
Amongst them was Averell's cavalry, whose advance reached
Martinsburg the 17th, and immediately moved up the valley
to find the enemy. The larger part of Crook's own infantry
division had also arrived, and when, the 18th, Hunter learned
that Crook was to attack at Snicker's and Ashby's Gaps, he directed Colonel R. B. Hayes to unite a portion of his brigade
to two of Duval's regiments then at Keyes Ferry, and to
march directly up the Shenandoah to Snicker's Ferry, there

to strike the enemy in conjunction with Crook, and then to join that officer.

Hayes failed to get through, and fell back to Keyes Ferry ; but Hunter pushed him forward again, and meantime called Averell's attention to Crook's purposes at Snicker's Ferry. "Perhaps by a prompt move in that direction," he said, "you can render General Crook great assistance, and capture a number of wagons. You must, however, exercise your own good judgment in the matter, and do as you think best under the circumstances." Averell with about 1,000 of his cavalry, consisting of the First and Third Virginia and Fourteenth Pennsylvania, with the First Virginia and First Ohio Batteries, aided by Duval's infantry brigade, Ninth and Fourteenth Virginia, and Ninety-first and Thirty-fourth Ohio, 1,350 strong, in all 2,350 men, moved up the pike from Martinsburg and drove the Confederate pickets from Darksville to Stephenson's Depot, half a dozen miles from Winchester. This vigorous stroke planted him on Early's rear, menacing his trains ; and that night the Confederate general, yielding the river whose passage he had shown a resolution to dispute, retreated through Berryville, Millwood, and White Post, then westward to Newtown and Middletown, thence along the valley pike southward toward Strasburg.

Meanwhile, to check Averell, he sent to Winchester Ramseur's division and two batteries ; [1] the cavalry of Jackson and of Vaughan, whose brigade had just been remounted, were already there, endeavoring to keep him back. But the 20th, Averell, who had received a reinforcement of 300 of the Second Virginia cavalry, making him about 2,700 strong, yet still numerically inferior to the enemy, moved up the pike toward the town in line of battle, a regiment of infantry

---

[1] Early says one battery was sent, but General A. L. Long, then his chief of artillery, says that two went.

on each side, with skirmishers out, another regiment on each side in column, in rear of the right and left flanks, artillery in the centre, and a regiment of cavalry on each flank. Three miles north of Winchester, on Carter's Farm, Ramseur was encountered, "moving by the flank," according to Early's account, with intent to capture Averell. At all events he rapidly formed, with Johnson's brigade on his right, Hoke's on his left, and Pegram's in reserve. Averell deployed the two infantry regiments which were in column, drew aside his cavalry skirmishers from the front to the flanks, and opened a hot fire from his twelve guns. Without pausing, he sent in all his cavalry and infantry. Duval's charge was across an open field, the two Ohio regiments east of the pike and the two Virginia regiments west. The vigorous assault broke Ramseur's left, which, followed by the remainder of the force, fled in confusion to Winchester, leaving in the Union general's hands four pieces of artillery, with 203 killed and wounded on the field, while the unwounded brought the list of captured up to 17 officers and 250 men.[1] The total Confederate loss was probably more than 400, including Generals Lewis and Lilly among the captured

---

[1] The Richmond Examiner of that period describes this action as "the deplorable affair in which Ramseur's division was humiliated in the dust." Ramseur was severely criticised for this defeat ; but Rodes, defending him in a letter to Ewell, September 12th, uses the following language : "Hoke's two left regiments broke and ran, behaving badly, as General Lewis himself said. Ramseur was on the right, or near Johnson's brigade—thought everything was going on finely till he saw this panic at the left. He immediately endeavored to restore the line by advancing Pegram's brigade, but it being embarrassed by Hoke's panic-stricken men became so itself ; broke and fled, as did the balance of Hoke's brigade, and finally Johnson's. Now, sir, this result would not occur one time in a hundred with these same troops under the same circumstances, and ought never to have occurred with old troops at all." Ramseur supposed, from Vaughan's reconnoissance the day before, that there were but two or three regiments in his front, which caused him to advance with too little precaution ; and thrown into confusion, the troops could not be rallied.

wounded, and Colonel Board, Fifty-eighth Virginia, among the killed. Averell's loss was 208 killed and wounded, and 6 missing—total 214; and his action of Carter's Farm was unusually creditable to the Union arms, while seldom has a Confederate defeat been so squarely acknowledged.

Averell refrained from endeavoring to occupy Winchester, and fortunately; for Early, who was at Newtown, on the way to Strasburg, hearing of Ramseur's mishap, hurried Rodes to his relief, and at sundown demonstrated against Averell. But knowing that his own rear and all his trains would now again be in danger should Wright and Crook move rapidly against them from Snicker's Ferry through Berryville, he contented himself with assuring Ramseur's safety, and then withdrew that night to Newtown, there halting his army while his trains moved south. The next day he went to Middletown, and the day after, July 22d, to Strasburg. Averell forthwith marched beyond Winchester to Kernstown, where, the 22d, he was joined by Crook from Berryville.

Here at Strasburg the retreat of Early came to an end; and accordingly, although, as we shall presently see, hostilities were resumed without a break between the two forces thus stationed less than twenty miles apart on the pike at Strasburg and Kernstown, yet this is a fitting stage at which to briefly review the campaign.

The pursuit of Early was a palpable failure, accentuated by the successes which followed the two minor attempts made against him by detachments—Tibbets's with a handful of cavalry near Purcellsville, and Averell's handsome victory at Winchester. But the fragmentary and extemporized character of the pursuing forces—drawn from many quarters, from the Army of the Potomac, from Louisiana, from the Kanawha and Shenandoah Valleys, and from the reserves of

Northern States—prevented them from being immediately moulded into a good weapon of offence. Looked at in retrospect, with the light of present knowledge of Early's strength and aims, the positions occupied by the various forces of Crook, Averell, and Sigel, not far from the enemy's prospective line of retreat, with Wright's army in his rear, are seen to have been favorable for endangering his march. Given the problem of places, times, and forces, after the event, it might be easy to show that Early could either have been engaged in front and flank by the Valley troops until those from Washington should attack his rear, or detained by the latter till Crook could draw near. Still, he would only have needed to go a little farther southward, in order to escape, crossing the Blue Ridge into the Valley by some gap higher up than Snicker's or Ashby's. But it is little wonder that there was not that systematic use of the pursuing forces which might have been made had they been parts of one army, under a single effective head. Wright's instructions to go only far enough to verify the enemy's retreat, and to be ready to return speedily to City Point, must also have embarrassed any purpose of vigorous pursuit.

Moreover, when the strength of Early is considered, the cry for " bagging " him, which arose from all quarters, was unreasonable ; but it was a frequent experience during the war that people whose most ardent prayers on one day were for simple relief from an invading army, though a bridge of gold should be built to entice it away, on the next, when the enemy had gone, clamored fiercely for his capture. Wright finally had a force at command much larger than Early's, but it only joined him by degrees, and his cavalry, at first, was not even a thousand strong.

Early, on the other hand, was sharply criticised at the South for lack of enterprise in not having captured Wash-

ington. Relying for its land defences on many forts, connected by rifle-pits, a large force would be needed by the
city to so man these defences as to guarantee that not one of
them should be carried by the sudden attack of a bold army.
Early, however, did not know, and could not wisely have
taken for granted, the condition of Washington prior to the
arrival of the transports. His expedition was based on the
opposite theory, that of drawing thither from Grant many
troops for its defence. He was prepared to believe that
20,000 or 30,000 veterans were concentrated there, because
that would have been the complete accomplishment and
vindication of his campaign. In the preceding chapter the
opinion has been expressed that Early acted prudently in
not assaulting the works, after arriving from Frederick.
But while his march from the Monocacy was as rapid as
possible, he had made halts at previous stages of his journey longer than simple rest required, and the omission of
either of these halts might have enabled him to seize
Washington, provided its reinforcements had arrived no
sooner than they actually did. The first of his delays was
in the lower Valley; his object was the breaking of the railroad and canal, for which very important task he seems to
have received special instructions from Lee; for perhaps
the Confederate chief [1] aimed to make sure an attainable advantage, before essaying a bolder enterprise that seemed too
doubtful of accomplishment to justify the sacrifice of genuine
gains to its mere possibilities. The second series of delays

---

[1] "Lee had been so crippled by his losses in the Wilderness that he could not
detach a force large enough to endanger Washington without risking his position
at Richmond; and when Early reached the capital he found troops assembled
there sufficient to repel him. . . . Lee could have had but little hope of capturing Washington, though he doubtless believed that Grant might be compelled
to weaken himself in front of Richmond, and perhaps to raise the siege" (Badeau's Military History of U. S. Grant).

occurred in and around Sharpsburg, where Early consumed
much time in minor operations, principally in demonstrating
against Sigel at Maryland Heights, a position, if not hopeless, at least needless to carry. That it would be folly to
essay a costly assault on the Heights for any resulting captures was the conclusion at length reached; and probably a
brief demonstration against Sigel by a division, while the
main body and the trains were passing as rapidly as possible from Shepherdstown to Frederick, would have accomplished all that Early needed.

The reasonable inference, therefore, from this fact, is that
Early did not fully expect, in setting out from Lynchburg,
to seize by a petty side-stroke the chief prize of the war. A
city girt with strong works,[1] on which much engineering
skill had been lavished, situated on a broad, navigable river,

---

[1] " Every prominent point, at intervals of eight hundred to one thousand yards,
was occupied by an inclosed field fort, every important approach or depression of
ground, unseen from the forts, swept by a battery for field-guns, and the whole
connected by rifle-trenches which were in fact lines of infantry parapet, furnish-
ing emplacement for two ranks of men, and affording covered communication
along the line, while roads were opened wherever necessary, so that troops and
artillery could be moved rapidly from one point of the immense periphery to
another, or, under cover, from point to point along the line. . . . The
counterscarps were surrounded by abatis; bomb-proofs were provided in nearly
all the forts; all guns not solely intended for distant fire, placed in embrasures
and well traversed. . . . All commanding points on which an enemy would
be likely to concentrate artillery to overpower that of one or two of our forts or
batteries were subjected not only to the fire, direct and cross, of many points
along the line, but also from heavy rifled guns from distant points unattainable
by the enemy's field guns. With all these developments the lines certainly ap-
proximated to the maximum degree of strength which can be attained from un-
revetted earth-works. . . . Bodies of hastily organized men, such as teamsters, quartermaster's men, citizen volunteers, etc., sent out to the lines, could
hardly go amiss. . . . The movable batteries of field-guns found, without a
moment's delay, the appropriate places where, covered from the enemy's fire, they
occupied the very best positions which the topography afforded. . . . Inade-
quately manned as they were, the fortifications compelled at least a concentration
and an arraying of force on the part of the assailants, and thus gave time for the
arrival of succor " (Barnard's Defences of Washington).

not fordable within thirty miles, and from which ships of
war had a fire along more than half the contour, should not
be had for the asking by a mere expeditionary column,
worn down by the prolonged tramp from Lynchburg,
especially when reinforcement was facile from the lines of
Petersburg. Early's campaign was based, we must conclude, not on anticipating but on compelling this reinforcement. Its real purpose may be fairly considered such a
demonstration against Washington as would break up the
campaign against Richmond. Hence Early was inclined to
impute greater strength than they possessed to Sigel's small
garrisons, which, eluding his clutch at Martinsburg and
Harper's Ferry, had taken post at Maryland Heights, as if
with a purpose to molest his march. Hence, also, when,
after reaching Frederick, and defeating Wallace, the awak-
ening possibility of really entering Washington caused him
to march thither at a very rapid rate, he was *prepared to
believe* that Washington was reinforced, since it would have
been inexcusable generalship to have left it undefended.
Though he had passed unchallenged, save at Monocacy, all
the way down the Valley to Harper's Ferry, and eastward to the great cities of Baltimore and Washington, it
was incredible that he should have outstripped a force
that could steam night and day from Fort Monroe.

The Lieutenant-General, on his part, presumably understood the effect of Early's circuitous course, and had calculated precisely the time required to suitably succor Washington, without merely trusting to possible ignorance or
timidity on the part of the enemy then marching upon it;
and his report definitely declares that his forces reached
Washington before Early's.

Still this, in some respects, was an opportunity for attacking Washington such as had not been offered to the Con-

federate arms since Bull Run. Could Lee have known
beforehand what he afterward learned, possibly the entire
portion of Early's march after reaching Winchester would
have assumed a different shape. With Hunter out of his
way, Early would perhaps have left Sigel and Harper's Ferry
to take care of each other, and, breaking the railroad with
cavalry, would have crossed the Blue Ridge, and hurried
through Loudoun, devising some plan for solving the hard
problem of supplies by that route, and fording the Potomac
at Edward's Ferry, would have reached the capital four days
earlier than he did.

Finally, while the Government was flattering itself that it
at last held Secession in an " anaconda coil," a discouraging
similitude to the campaigns of previous years had been
unexpectedly lent to the military situation by this invading
column, which camped in the suburbs of Baltimore and
knocked at the doors of Washington. So bold a march
revived for a time the failing fortunes of the South, which
was naturally elated that Confederate battalions had once
more, as in 1861, penned the Union forces in their capital.
It also enabled the enemy to harvest in peace a large part
of the year's crops in the Valley.

Yet, with this surface success accomplished, what lasting
advantage had been gained? The invasion had drawn a
corps from the Petersburg trenches, and was destined to aid
in prolonging the war to another year ; but it had not forced
off the clutch that was only to be loosened after Appomattox.

CHAPTER VI.

KERNSTOWN, CHAMBERSBURG, AND MOOREFIELD.

THE plan for disposing of the Sixth and Nineteenth Corps [1] took shape, July 23d, in an order from Grant to send him the Sixth, and to permit the Nineteenth, then at Washington, to remain there. Halleck feared a renewed invasion of

---

[1] This conclusion, if such it may be called, was abandoned within forty-eight hours, and had not been reached without some fluctuations:

"You may retain Wright's command until the departure of Early is assured." (Grant to Halleck, July 21st.)

"Acting on your previous orders, he had given up the pursuit, and would reach Washington to-day. He left the enemy retreating on Front Royal and Strasburg. In my opinion raids will be renewed as soon as he leaves." (Halleck to Grant, July 22d, 10 A.M.)

"Your despatch of 10 A.M. received. You need not send any troops back until the main force of the enemy are known to have left the Valley. Is Wright still where he can act in conjunction with Hunter? If the two can push the enemy back, and destroy the railroad from Charlottesville to Gordonsville, I would prefer that service to having them here." (Grant to Halleck, July 22d, 9 P.M.)

"If Wright has returned to Washington, send him immediately back here, retaining, however, the portion of the Nineteenth Corps now in Washington for further orders. Early is undoubtedly returning here to enable the enemy to detach troops to go to Georgia." (Grant to Halleck, July 23d.)

"General Wright in person arrived this morning, and most of his forces will encamp at an outer line to-night. The rebels generally said to the country people, that as soon as they secured their plunder, they would return to Maryland and Pennsylvania for more." (Halleck to Grant, July 23d, 1 P.M.)

"Your despatch of 1 P.M. just received. You can retain General Wright until I learn positively what has become of Early." (Grant to Halleck, July 24th, 12 M.)

"General Wright, in accordance with your orders, was about to embark for City Point. I have directed him to await your further orders. I shall exercise no further discretion in this matter, but shall carry out such orders as you may give." (Halleck to Grant, July 24th, 8 P.M.)

Maryland, whereas Grant believed that, should Early go
North again at all, he would march "through Western Virginia to Ohio, possibly taking Pittsburg by the way." Of the
Nineteenth Corps 263 officers and 5,320 men, under Emory,
were present for duty at Washington.

The apparent uncertainty on this subject was explicable.
Grant had always been eager to defeat Early; but he did not
want him simply escorted to Strasburg. When informed that
the enemy had regained the Valley, he sought to use Wright
and Emory for attacking Lee's lines, before Early could return to Richmond; but when the Confederate rear-guard
was found still waiting at the Blue Ridge, he paused in this
purpose; and when Duffié's little skirmish at Purcellville,
with a few wagons burned and a few provisions taken, and
Thoburn's attempt at Snicker's Ferry, gave faint signs of
breaking the spell of inaction, Grant's hopes so brightened
that he then repeatedly declared that he would rather have
Wright's forces engaged in destroying the Orange and Alexandria Railroad than helping him at Petersburg. In view
of his distance from the scene of Shenandoah operations,
and the necessity of instantly deciding whether to follow
Early up the Valley, in case he retreated, or to turn to account the Union advantage of rapid transportation by rail
and steam to Petersburg, his final decision for the latter
course was natural. For not only had the pursuit been a
hopeless failure, but it would have been in accordance with
Lee's methods to summon Early for a sudden attack in his
own front, as he had summoned Jackson in 1862. This
judgment of Grant, however, though founded on sound considerations, proved erroneous; for Lee had not recalled Early
when the Sixth Corps moved back from the Shenandoah,
having no immediate need of him, and probably desiring
that he should protect the gathering of the Valley harvests.

Accordingly when, July 23d, Early, who had halted at Strasburg, learned that the Sixth Corps had withdrawn to Washington, and that the forces occupying Kernstown, not twenty miles distant, on the turnpike, were only those of Crook and Averell, he resolved to attack them without delay. A reconnoissance resulted in deploying the whole Union force to resist it, the cavalry and artillery being sharply engaged.

Nature marks out strategic lines with her ridges and rivers, which successive generations attack and defend; battle after battle is repeated on the same ground. The military art is so precise in methods, that, with the face of the country unchanged, successive leaders adopt the same routes of march, the same positions, and the same manœuvres. To the catalogue of twice-fought fields that included Manassas and Chancellorsville, Corinth and Cold Harbor, was now to be added another, since Crook's ground, the morning of July 24th, was the same that Shields had occupied in his repulse of Jackson. Early's whole army advanced against Kernstown on the Valley pike, and at Bartonsville, a few miles south of the town, Ramseur's division was sent, in a detour, to turn Crook's right. The cavalry was divided into two columns, one proceeding to the east and the other to the west of Winchester, so as to unite north of the town and cut off Crook's retreat.

Crook's line covered the pike with the infantry divisions of Sullivan, Duval, and Mulligan, while the cavalry of Averell and Duffié was on his flanks. The country was open, a little broken with hollows to the east. Crook had directed Averell, who held his left, to pass around Early's right and attack his trains; and whether it was owing to this movement or to some other disposition of the line, Early, at all events, having driven in the Union skirmishers perceived Crook's left to be assailable, and hence, without depending upon Ramseur's turning movement on the other flank, directed Breckenridge to move Echols's division, now under Wharton, around and against the Union left. Wharton struck this flank in open ground, doubling it and throwing it into confusion.[1] Rodes, Gordon, and Ramseur at once pressing against Crook's centre and right, the whole line broke into retreat. The pike was quickly filled with trains and the fields with troops, striving for Winchester and beyond. Rodes pursued to Stephenson's Dépôt, six miles north of the town, where he halted, his division having marched twenty-seven miles that day. Early's cavalry fortunately proved somewhat inefficient, Ransom, who had been in bad health ever since leaving Lynchburg, being unable to take active command; and as the open fields and broad pike were favorable for rapid retreat, Crook brought off all his artillery and trains, till one of the flanking cavalry brigades at last struck the column on the pike, stampeding the teamsters, and causing many wagons and caissons to be abandoned and burned. One artillery officer cut loose his horses from four guns, but infantry brought them off. At dusk the fugitive troops reached Bunker Hill, and crossing Mill Creek, went into camp on the further bank.

---

[1] " I regret to say that the greater portion of my dismounted cavalry, along with some infantry, the whole numbering some 3,000 or 4,000, broke to the rear at the first fire, and all efforts to stop them proved of no avail. They mostly got into Martinsburg, circulating all manner of reports. A few of them were captured, endeavoring to escape my guards. I lost over one-third of my cavalry in this way " (Crook's Report, July 27, 1864). Hunter wrote to Halleck that " the cavalry and the dismounted men in the late fights behaved in the most disgraceful manner, their officers in many instances leading them off and starting all kinds of lying reports, tending to demoralize the whole command, and it was only owing to the steadiness and good conduct of the infantry which came with us from the Kanawha that the army was saved from utter annihilation. . . . The refuse force sent from Washington, representing twenty-seven different regiments, is said to have done more injury than service."

XI.--5

Crook's troops had campaigned too well at Cloyd's Mountain and during Hunter's bold march to Lynchburg to be
disgraced by this encounter; and while some of them, chiefly
the recent additions, had proved of little value, it must be
remembered that whatever efforts had been made to challenge Early's retreat from Washington were the work of this
command. Their defeat is not strange, for the force soon
after assembled in the Valley as needful to match Early
was thrice Crook's at Kernstown; and the chief criticism to
be passed on this action is that there had been little wari-
ness in confronting the enemy in an open position like this,
after most of the Union forces had been drawn away. Probably it would have been wiser to occupy the contracted lines
at Halltown, in front of Harper's Ferry. Yet it must not be
inferred that Crook had given insufficient thought to the
peril. A despatch of July 22d to Hunter furnishes the clue
to his purposes. "I want to remain here a day or two," he
said, "to give the enemy the impression we will not follow
them, so that they may send a good portion of their command to Richmond. I have not force sufficient to meet all
their force in this open Valley, and my only hope is for
them to divide their command." The President had asked
Hunter, the 23d, "Are you able to take care of the enemy,
when he turns back upon you, as he probably will, on finding that Wright has left?" and Hunter had answered, "My
force is not strong enough to hold the enemy, should he
return upon us with his whole force." But he added that
the information of Crook and the reconnoissances of Averell
tended to show that Early was falling back.

Crook's loss in this battle was somewhat uncertain, on
account of the number of fugitives, a part of whom afterward returned to their colors; but it could hardly have been
less than 1,200. Duval reported in the Second infantry divi-

sion alone 45 killed, 285 wounded, and 183 missing—total,
513. His Second Brigade, Johnson's (Ninth and Fourteenth
Virginia and Thirty-fourth and Ninety-first Ohio), holding
the extreme right, on the Romney pike, was not assailed
until the retreat; but the other, R. B. Hayes's (Fifth and
Thirteenth Virginia and Twenty-third and Thirty-sixth
Ohio), was on the left of the Third, Mulligan's division,
east of the pike, in the thick of the fray, and Hayes reported
a loss of 396 men—this officer claiming to have continued
east of the pike all the way up to Bunker Hill, thus keeping the road open for the trains. Colonel Campbell states
that the losses of the Third Division were 317, including
among the mortally wounded its commander, Mulligan,
known for his defence of Lexington in 1861. No field
officers were left in this division, which was brought off
by Captain Suter, and soon after consolidated as the Third
Brigade of the First Division. The Confederate loss was
light.

Between this engagement of Kernstown and the one
at Piedmont, six weeks earlier, there is a suggestive parallel, inasmuch as the result was in the one case partly due to
the withdrawal of Breckenridge by Lee, and in the other to
the withdrawal of the Sixth Corps by Grant, under a process
of reasoning that in each case seemed sound, but proved fal-
lacious. The parallel was immediately pushed further by
the prompt restoration of the Sixth and Nineteenth Corps to
the Valley, as Breckenridge had in like fashion been returned after Piedmont; while Grant, in addition, instead of
calling forces to City Point, now sent to Washington 4,600
more men of the Nineteenth Corps. He also insisted that,
since military conditions might wholly change while despatches were going to and from him, the events of July had
shown it to be "absolutely necessary that some one in

Washington should give orders and make dispositions of all the forces within reach of the line of the Potomac."

In a violent rain-storm, which came up the day after his Kernstown victory, Early followed Crook to Bunker Hill, twelve miles from Winchester, and there halted his infantry; while at Martinsburg the Union rear-guard, turning upon his cavalry, drove it back a mile. Then, after dusk, leaving many sick and wounded at Martinsburg, Crook retreated again along the Williamsport pike, and camped on the Po· tomac. The next morning, the 26th, having saved most of his trains—the enemy counting the lost portion as twelve caissons and seventy-two wagons—Crook crossed the river into Maryland, and marched through Boonesboro, ultimately taking post, by Hunter's direction, at Sharpsburg, to hold the South Mountain gaps. Averell was stationed at Hagerstown, his pickets guarding the Potomac fords.

Finding himself again in undisputed possession of the Valley, Early proceeded, with detachments of his infantry, to break afresh at Martinsburg the Baltimore and Ohio Railroad, which had been repaired since the beginning of the month, while at Back Creek he overpowered the guard, drove away the iron-clad cars, and burned the railroad bridge. Still, these exploits did not satisfy him. He coveted another dash into Union territory, and resolved to send the cavalry brigades of McCausland and Johnson, under command of the former, to burn sundry Northern towns, unless they should procure their safety by paying him a large money ransom. The first community on which McCausland was to direct himself was Chambersburg, the nearest town of importance in Pennsylvania; thence he was to move to Cumberland in Maryland, levying contributions upon that and other towns able to bear them, destroying the machinery of the Cumberland coal-pits, and the repair shops, stations, and bridges of the Baltimore Railroad.

July 29th, McCausland, with his two brigades and four guns, crossed the Potomac near Clear Spring, west of Williamsport, two infantry divisions covering the movement as far as the latter point, while Imboden and Jackson distracted attention by fording the river below and demonstrating against Harper's Ferry; and Vaughan, driving away the Union pickets at Williamsport, rode to Hagerstown.

The panic which had marked Early's previous incursion broke out afresh, and the people flew in all directions before McCausland's advance. Appeals for aid arose from the threatened region, but in the jumble of conflicting reports the Government at Washington could hardly tell at first why or against what its aid was demanded. It was evident at once that the tier of counties in Southern Pennsylvania could not be left to defend itself. "How could an agricultural people," pungently asked Governor Curtin, in a message to the Legislature, "in an open country, be expected to rise suddenly, and beat back hostile forces which had defeated organized veteran armies of the Government?" Though practically a border State, Pennsylvania had sent her troops to all the Union armies, retaining few or none for home defence.

Chambersburg lies about twenty-five miles northeast of Williamsport, and thither McCausland directed himself, driving back the pickets at McCoy's Ferry, which consisted of about thirty men from Carlisle barracks, under Lieutenant McLean, Sixth Cavalry. A few miles west of Clear Spring, Gilmor's two Maryland battalions, of Johnson's brigade, were repulsed with a loss of seventeen men; McCausland, however, marched on to Mercersburg.

At this time General Couch, commanding the Department

of the Susquehanna, was in Chambersburg with fewer than one hundred and fifty men. When McLean, who was under his orders, fell back, Couch notified Averell of the enemy's approach, collected and moved northward the horses in the Cumberland Valley, and early next morning, taking with him the Government stores, withdrew on the railroad toward Harrisburg. McCausland was then close to the town.

Averell, who had his headquarters at Hagerstown, with 2,600 men, many of whom were picketing the Potomac fords, had found his communication with the latter cut, about noon of the 29th; and perceiving that a force of unknown strength, with unknown purposes, had succeeded in crossing the river, and was rapidly marching north to Mercersburg, he withdrew on a parallel route to Greencastle, thus reprotecting his flanks, and covering the country east of his course. At Greencastle he reunited the brigade which had been picketing the Potomac, and was scattered by the enemy's crossing at several points. In leaving Hagerstown, Averell entrusted to the railroad authorities a train loaded with government stores; a blunder left it behind, so that when, a few hours later, Vaughan entered the place, he found and destroyed the train.

Couch had caused McLean, with about 60 men and a gun, to keep up the appearance of defending Chambersburg during the early morning of the 30th, about two miles from the town, being careful not to fire from within its limits. Soon after sunrise, leaving the greater part of his force at the Fair grounds, McCausland rode into Chambersburg with about 400 men. The chief burgess being absent, he arrested two score citizens and told them his errand. The announcement that he would burn the town unless $500,000 in currency or $100,000 in gold should be paid him, this being the ransom fixed by Early in a written order, was received with incredulity. Gold was out of the question, and he was told, also, that "there was probably not $50,000 in currency at hand." No time remained for haggling—his scouts brought news that Averell was not many miles away, pushing straight for the town, and the people seemed to be relying on this hope of succor. No sooner, therefore, had McCausland taken his breakfast at the hotel, than, summoning Major Gilmor, he directed him to burn the town. The torches were quickly applied, with a result best described in the language of the officer to whom the execution of this work was intrusted : "Deeply regretting that such a task should fall upon me, I had only to obey. . . . I felt more like weeping over Chambersburg, although the people covered me with reproaches, which all who know me will readily believe I felt hard to digest ; yet my pity was highly excited in behalf of these poor unfortunates, who were made to suffer for acts perpetrated by the officers of their own Government. The day was bright and intensely hot. The conflagration seemed to spring from one vast building. Dense clouds of smoke rose to the zenith, and hovered over the dark plain. At night it would have been a grand but terrible object to behold. How piteous the sight of those beautiful green meadows—groups of women and children exposed to the rays of a burning sun, hovering over the few articles they had saved, most of them wringing their hands, and with wild gesticulations bemoaning their ruined homes ! "

Leaving Chambersburg in flames, McCausland hastily marched westward to McConnellsburg and camped. Averell, who had received very tardily Couch's messages announcing the enemy's approach, put his command in the saddle, and aimed for Chambersburg. The burning town told its own story, and dashing through it, he was speedily away after McCausland, correctly surmising that repetitions of this

deed would be attempted elsewhere. It was a great mishap
that with Averell's strong force at the advantageous position
of Hagerstown, the disaster of Chambersburg was not
averted ; but the place had no strategic importance demanding special eagerness to converge troops there, and nobody
could have reasonably supposed that incendiarism was the
enemy's object. A few miles from McConnellsburg, Averell
struck McCausland's rear, forcing him to abandon a contemplated visit to Bedford, and to turn back to the Potomac,
which he reached by noon of July 31st, at Hancock.[1] The
Confederate commander was found in line of battle, having
already driven away with his guns an iron-clad car which
contested his crossing of the Potomac, and fired railroad
buildings on the Virginia side. Averell attacked him, and
whether it was that his artillery, controlling the ford, prevented McCausland from escaping there, or whether it was
that the latter wished to complete Early's programme, he
withdrew westward along the National road to Cumberland.
Probably, not only Hancock, but McConnellsburg and Bedford had been saved by Averell from the enemy's torch.

Reaching Cumberland August 1st, McCausland found
there Kelley, who had been notified by Halleck to block the
roads and destroy bridges to retard the enemy's advance.
Kelley had taken post at Folck's Mill, three miles from the

---

[1] "General McCausland," says Gilmor, " ordered a levy upon this place of
$30,000, which was so out of all reason that we Marylanders remonstrated, but to
no purpose. He told the principal men of the place that unless the money was
paid he would burn the town. To this I and all my men objected, saying that
too much Maryland blood had been shed in defence of the South for her towns to
be laid under contribution or burned. I perceived, too, that his men were inclined to plunder. After a consultation with General Johnson, I brought in my
whole command and stationed two men at each house and store for their protection. Before the money could be raised, Averell's troops arrived and attacked our
pickets and outposts, and a lively little fight occurred, chiefly in the streets and
on the high pine hills northeast of the town."

town, and was engaged by McCausland's battery. The
Confederate commander now found himself in a predica-
ment, having Kelley in front and Averell, as he supposed,
closing in upon his rear. About the middle of the afternoon he attacked Kelley, and continued to skirmish until
late at night, when he retreated, leaving 30 of his killed and
wounded on the field, with two caissons and some wagons
and ammunition. The point for which he made, with intent
to cross the Potomac, was Oldtown, near the junction of the
South Branch. Reaching the ford by an obscure mountain
road, at daylight, he found a garrison of Ohio hundred-days
men protecting it. His skirmishers were driven back ; but
the main body coming up, he dismounted three regiments,
and formed line of battle between the river and canal. The
Union troops thereupon withdrew across the river to Green
Spring Run Station, on the Baltimore and Ohio Railroad.
Here the defence was the customary one of a block-house
and an engine attached to a train of cars strengthened with
cross-ties, covering the ford and the bridge. After losing a
dozen men, a charge by one of Johnson's regiments being
repulsed, a flag was sent to the block-house demanding its
surrender, under the threat, as Gilmor narrates, that, if
taken by assault, no quarter would be given. As the troops
had nearly finished their term of enlistment, those in the
block-house, numbering about 80, surrendered on the
promise of being paroled, while the remainder escaped to
Cumberland. Destroying the cars, McCausland made good
his escape into West Virginia. The same afternoon he
moved to Springfield, nine miles distant, burning the wire
bridge, after passing over it, and proceeded the next day to
Romney, on the South Branch. From there, August 4th,
he sent an expedition to seize the railroad post at New
Creek. The garrison was under Colonels Stevenson and

5*

Hay and Major Simpson. A stubborn fight of several hours took place, when McCausland drew off repulsed, leaving his dead and wounded on the field. The loss of the garrison was about 75 killed and wounded, and that of the Confederates probably as severe. The Confederate general withdrew to Moorefield, where the South Fork joins the South Branch of the Potomac.

But he was not destined to rest in quiet here. August 2d, learning of McCausland's repulse at Cumberland, Halleck urged that Averell should be pushed to cut off his retreat; and Hunter gave reiterated orders to that effect. Averell crossed the Potomac at Hancock, the 4th, and after a forced march through Bath, Springfield, and Romney, at noon of the 6th drew near McCausland's camp. Before sunrise of the 7th, his advance brigade, Gibson, surprised Bradley Johnson, and drove him through the stream to the main position of the enemy on the opposite bank. Though McCausland had more warning, Powell's brigade, charging through the river, under a hot fire, routed him as quickly as Gibson had routed Johnson. The whole body was soon in disorderly retreat, and Major Work, Twenty-second Pennsylvania, who had been sent with a battalion, the day before, to co-operate on another road, also struck the flying forces, and picked up 35 prisoners and about one hundred horses. Averell captured four pieces of artillery—all that McCausland had—every caisson but one, nearly all his wagons, over four hundred horses, three battle-flags, many small arms, and 420 prisoners, including 38 officers. His own loss was given as 41 killed and wounded; but the killed included Major Conger and Captain Clark, Third West Virginia. Johnson was captured, and afterward escaped. The shattered relics of McCausland and Johnson fled in various directions to the shelter of the mountains, and made their way as best they could to the Shenandoah Valley. "This affair," says Early, "had a very damaging effect upon my cavalry for the rest of the campaign."

While these events were occurring in West Virginia, the excitement in Pennsylvania had not abated. Ignorance of the enemy's strength and position was always one of the most remarkable features in the conduct of the war, and led to strange results.[1] Mosby dashed across the Potomac, July 30th, at Cheek's Ford, where he overcame a picket of the Eighth Illinois Cavalry, who lost half a dozen killed and wounded, and perhaps as many prisoners; and this affair, so sensitive had public opinion become, increased the fears of an invasion. The people of Pittsburg, having been notified by General Couch that "it is believed Breckenridge is marching West" held a mass meeting for defence; while at urgent request that officer proceeded to the city, and enrolled the citizens for its protection. Indeed, an attack on Wheeling and Pittsburg was not at all impossible. Governor Curtin summoned the Legislature of Pennsylvania to meet in special session, and called out 30,000 militia.

We must now record the movements of the Union infantry during these events. The Sixth Corps, on receiving news of Crook's defeat, was hurriedly marched from its camp at Tenallytown, near Washington, to Harper's Ferry, whence it was ordered to Jefferson, and then, the 29th, drawn back through Harper's Ferry to Halltown, four miles beyond. Crook's command made a circuitous march from Sharpsburg to Harper's Ferry, and back across the Poto-

---

[1] "August 2d, information was received by telegraph from Washington that a heavy column of the enemy was moving on that city, *via* Rockville. Marching orders were promptly issued, and subsequently countermanded, when it was ascertained that the alarm had originated from the appearance of a squad of United States cavalry scouting near Rockville" (Report of Colonel Strother, Chief of Staff to General Hunter).

mac to Pleasant Valley, finally retracing its steps through
Harper's Ferry to the rendezvous at Halltown, which it
reached the same day as the Sixth. These movements had
in part resulted from directions sent by Halleck to Hunter,
which closed with the hope "that this time Wright's forces
will not be withdrawn." In these marches, men and horses
fell by hundreds from heat and lack of rest. "Our infantry
is suffering dreadfully," wrote Hunter to Halleck; "six fell
dead yesterday in one of our smallest brigades." Arriving
at the bivouac near midnight, the bugle would summon
the men before dawn to renew their tramp under the burning sun and in the stifling dust; when horses dropped the
riders struggled on afoot, under the extra load of the saddle, till they could procure another mount; if an unlucky
beast revived, some infantryman would get another mile out
of him bare-back, till he sank again. The casualties in this
expedition were all from sunstroke, for there was no enemy to
attack, Early's infantry being in camp south of the Potomac.

The day the commands of Wright and Hunter united at
Halltown, McCausland began his Chambersburg raid. Halleck directed Hunter to move all the forces east of South
Mountain, to guard against another invasion. Hunter acted
promptly, but found that "General Wright reports his corps
so much fatigued and scattered as to be unable to move this
morning." Halleck's rejoinder was that "Wright's and
Crook's forces should immediately move toward Emmetts-
burg—they must make a night march." Wright then occupied Crampton's and South Mountain Passes, and Halleck
forwarded Emory, 4,600 strong, to Frederick. Inquiring of
Couch whether the force that entered Chambersburg was
"a cavalry raid or the main army," Halleck received the reply that it was "about 1,000 cavalry and two pieces of artillery." However, as Wright and Crook were already afoot,

he determined to let them concentrate about Frederick, since there was a great and not ill-founded public fear of another invasion. Thus the troops trod again the familiar road through Sandy Hook to the line of the Monocacy. This was the first fruit of a new arrangement. For when Halleck, in despair over the prolonged uncertainty about what he should do with the Sixth and Nineteenth Corps, had notified Grant that he would "exercise no further discretion in the matter," but would "carry out such orders as you may give," the disaster at Kernstown, that very day, only strengthened the Lieutenant-General's conviction that, as he wrote the next morning, "despatches being so long between here [City Point] and Washington, orders must be given from there to meet pressing emergencies." This view he reiterated the following day, and "General Halleck," replied Stanton, "has been ordered to give, subject to your directions, such military orders as may be necessary in the present juncture, in accordance with the suggestion made in your telegram of yesterday." This is the explanation of Halleck's guidance of the operations that moved the Union forces from Halltown to Frederick.

In simply sensational effect, Early's second incursion had been as remarkable as the first, for he had caused almost as great a stir with two cavalry brigades and four guns as if he had used his entire army. He prevented the return of the Sixth and Nineteenth Corps to Petersburg, and broke more effectually than ever the railroad and canal which he was determined to keep useless; yet he had bought his success dearly, for Averell's victory at Moorefield had wrecked the raiding column.

The burning of Chambersburg, the central event of this incursion, was wholly indefensible. This was an open town, of no strategic value, and not amenable to the penalty a peaceful village sometimes incurs through being made the refuge of troops that use its dwellings for firing upon their assailants. Factories and granaries had been destroyed in the Valley by Union commanders; but to lay waste an enemy's subsistence in a mutual field of operations, whose crops furnish him the means of occupying it, is a different matter from putting the torch to a town with intent to lay it in ashes. Harboring and assisting guerillas may expose a community to destruction, but of this offence Chambersburg had never been guilty. Early's ground for his act was the recent burning of the houses of A. R. Boteler, E. I. Lee, and Andrew Hunter, in the lower Valley, "and a number of towns in the South." These towns he does not name; as for the individuals, they were prominent public men, whose residences ran a risk of destruction during the presence of armies, by the orders of generals or the ill-will of troops, as Hunter had burned Governor Letcher's house, and as some of Early's men, without his orders, burned Governor Bradford's near Baltimore, and Mr. Blair's near Washington. Such acts bore on their face an exceptional character, because thousands of other houses, equally within the power of the invading troops, had been spared. The conflagration of towns in pure retaliation would have devastated the border States without military gain; and such a bootless sacrifice was the holocaust of Chambersburg on the altar of revenge.

CHAPTER VII.

GENERAL SHERIDAN'S MARCH TO STRASBURG.

When Grant perceived that Early's success would probably cause him to be retained in the Valley as a permanent menace to the North, he resolved to accumulate against him an overwhelming force. Halleck having received by degrees, for the Potomac line, first the part of the Nineteenth Corps already there, then the Sixth, finally the remainder of the Nineteenth at City Point, next took the responsibility of retaining for Wright's use on the Monocacy the cavalry detachments that had been ordered back to the Army of the Potomac, and then urged "the importance of sending a force large enough to prevent his [Early's] again devastating Maryland and Pennsylvania." Coupled with this suggestion were complaints that the nominal force of 3,000 dismounted cavalry which had been sent North was of little value, whether on foot or in the saddle. Just then the flames of Chambersburg alarmed the North, and Grant notified Halleck that he should have a whole division of cavalry. "Will the division come armed, mounted, and ready for the field," asked Halleck sceptically, "or must they be mounted and fitted out here?" This was the 31st of July.

With two infantry corps and a third of his cavalry now on the Potomac, Grant determined that they must do something—either crush Early, or else so drive him back as to relieve the Richmond campaign of a constant hindrance;

and lest the Confederate commander, taking the alarm, should retreat just out of reach, with the view of returning when the Union force should be withdrawn, he purposed to so devastate the Valley that the enemy could no longer subsist there, and thus put an end to its availability as a highway to the North.

The first necessity was to concentrate under a single head several geographical commands : for there was a Department of West Virginia, including that State and Western Maryland ; a Department of the Susquehanna, including the State of Pennsylvania and three counties of Ohio ; a Department of Washington, including that city and parts of Virginia and Maryland ; and a Middle Department, including Delaware and a part of Maryland. The evil of this subdivision into co-ordinate provinces was aggravated by the distance of the Lieutenant-General's headquarters ; for, at critical moments, the wires might be cut by the enemy or thrown down by a storm, causing fatal delays in the transmission of the orders awaited by these various Departments. The disasters following his withdrawal of the Sixth Corps had only strengthened the determination of Grant that the Shenandoah campaign should not be conducted from City Point, except in a supervisory way, like other distant operations ; and already, July 18th, after finding that in the multiplicity of departments and commanders Early had escaped, he had notified Halleck that " to prevent a recurrence of what had just taken place in Maryland " he deemed it necessary to have those four departments merged into one. " What are now departments will be districts or corps. The one commander will then control all troops that co-operate in any movement of the enemy toward Maryland or Pennsylvania. I should name Major General W. B. Franklin for such commander." This nomination was received coldly.

Two days later Grant wrote that he had failed to hear what had been decided upon this subject, and Halleck replied that the telegram was in Stanton's hands. " I have no good reason," he said, " for removing or superseding General Augur. He is capable and efficient. General Franklin would not give satisfaction. The President ordered him to be tried for negligence and disobedience of orders when here before, but General McClellan assumed the responsibility of his reported delays in obeying orders." Grant next appealed to the President : " I do not insist," he said, " that the Departments should be broken up, nor do I insist upon General Franklin commanding. All I ask is that one general officer, in whom I and yourself have confidence, should command the whole. General Franklin was named because he was available, and I know him to be capable and believe him to be trustworthy. It would suit me equally as well to call the four departments referred to a ' Military Division,' and to have placed in command of it General Meade. In this case I would suggest General Hancock for command of the Army of the Potomac and General Gibbon for the command of the Second Corps. With General Meade in command of such a Division, I would have every confidence that all the troops within the Military Division would be used to the very best advantage, from a personal examination of the ground, and would adopt means of getting the earliest information of any advance of the enemy, and would prepare to meet it. During the last raid the wires happened to be down between here and Fort Monroe, and the cable broken [between] there and Cherrystone. This made it take from twelve to twenty-four hours each way for despatches to pass. Under such circumstances it was difficult for me to give positive orders or directions, because I could not tell how the conditions might change during the transit of despatches. Many reasons might be assigned for the changes here suggested, some of which I would not care to commit to paper, but would not hesitate to give verbally."

In its new form this proposition for the consolidation of commands was apparently not received with more warmth than the old—possibly because great changes would be involved by sending the commander of the Army of the Potomac into what then seemed to be a subordinate field. At all events, the President's reply was a request that Grant would name a time when they could meet at Fort Monroe. But just then, and for a week thereafter, operations of high importance were carried on—Hancock's attack at Deep Bottom and the explosion of the mine on Meade's Petersburg front ; while, perhaps inferring that, had the President approved his plan, he would have said so simply, Grant made a new and most fortunate nomination.

Early's second foray, wholly a cavalry affair, was now in progress, and to check it Grant had already ordered to the Valley one division of Army of the Potomac cavalry, and within three days was to send another ; to Meade, August 1st, he sent the following despatch : "I see the artillery belonging to the cavalry division is being shipped first ; my instructions were that the cavalry should be got off first. The enemy's cavalry is now in Pennsylvania, and it is important that we should get a mounted force after them. If Sheridan is able for duty, I wish you would send him to me in person. I shall send him to command all the forces against Early." Sheridan reported forthwith, and the next day was relieved temporarily of duty in the Army of the Potomac, and was ordered to report with his staff to Halleck. "I am sending General Sheridan," wrote Grant, "for temporary duty, whilst the army is being expelled from the border.   Unless General Hunter is in the field in person, I want Sheridan put in command of all the troops in the field, with instructions to put himself south of the enemy, and follow him to the death.   Wherever the enemy goes, let our troops go also.   Once started up the Valley, they ought to be followed till we get possession of the Virginia Central Railroad."   Halleck answered that "if Sheridan is *not* placed in general command, I think he should take all the cavalry, but not the Sixth Corps; to make that and the cavalry a single and separate command will, in my opinion, be a very bad arrangement.   If Sheridan *is* placed in general command, I presume Hunter will again ask to be relieved."   The President wrote to Grant that his language was, he thought, " exactly right as to how our troops should move ; but please look over the despatches you may have received from here even since you made that order, and discover, if you can, that there is any idea in the head of any one here of putting our army south of the enemy or of following him to the death in any direction.   I repeat to you, it will neither be done nor attempted, unless you watch it every day and hour, and force it."

The 3d of August Sheridan reached Washington, and Halleck wrote Grant as follows: "General Sheridan has just arrived.   He agrees with me about his command, and prefers the cavalry alone to that and the Sixth Corps.   How would it do to make a Military Division of Departments of Pennsylvania, Washington, Maryland, and West Virginia, and put Sheridan in general command, so far as military operations are concerned?   Only about three regiments of Sheridan's cavalry have arrived, and he thinks it will not all be here for several days.   It is important to hurry it up, for if the enemy should make a heavy cavalry raid toward Pittsburg or Harrisburg, it would have so much the start that it would do immense damage before Sheridan could possibly overtake it. He thinks that for operations in the open country of Pennsylvania, Maryland, and Northern Virginia, cavalry is much better than infantry, and that the cavalry arm can be much more effective there than about Richmond or south. He therefore suggests that another cavalry division be sent here, so that he can press the enemy clear down to the James River." Grant replied in a practical way by a despatch to Meade: "Send another division of cavalry to Washington at once."

The questions raised by Halleck as to commands requiring prompt decision, Grant determined to visit Hunter and confer with him.[1] He left City Point for this purpose August 4th, and arrived at Frederick, Hunter's headquarters, the next evening, not stopping at Washington on the way. The position selected by Hunter as the proper one for concentrating his forces in the Valley, just a week before, had been the admirable one of Halltown, four miles beyond Harper's Ferry. A very brief interchange of views between Grant and Hunter showed that there was no reason why the latter's Halltown position, the most impregnable in the Valley, with Maryland Heights in possession, should not be resumed at once, since the threatened peril under which Halleck had ordered the forces to Frederick no longer existed.

But Grant went further. With characteristic vigor, he directed Hunter, by an order dated "Headquarters in the Field, Monocacy Bridge, Md., August 5, 1864," first to concentrate all the forces, consisting thus far of the commands of Generals Wright, Emory, and Crook—Averell being then absent in pursuit of McCausland—in the vicinity

---

[1] "I can give no instructions to either [Hunter or Sheridan] till you decide upon their commands. I await your orders, and shall strictly carry them out whatever they may be" (Halleck to Grant, August 4th).

of Harper's Ferry, leaving in Maryland only such railroad guards and garrisons for public property as should be necessary; next, if it should be found that the enemy had moved north of the Potomac in large force, to follow and attack him, wherever he went; but should it be found that only a small force was north of the river, then Hunter was to move up the Valley and attack the main body, detaching "under a competent commander a sufficient force to look after the raiders and drive them to their homes. In detailing such a force," added General Grant, "the brigade of cavalry now *en route* from Washington *via* Rockville may be taken into account. There are now on the way to join you three other brigades of the best of cavalry, numbering at least 5,000 men and horses. These will be instructed, in the absence of further orders, to join you by the south side of the Potomac. One brigade will probably start to-morrow." The absence of nearly all the cavalry in pursuit of McCausland and the employment of the rest in guarding the Potomac line made it impossible to learn from Frederick Early's exact location and purposes; but Grant's instructions covered every contingency, as they amounted to an order to Hunter to attack the enemy wherever he might be, with an assurance of reinforcements enough to sustain him.

Hunter at once carried out these instructions, beginning by the re-establishment of his strong Halltown lines, as a basis for the proposed operations. That same night Crook's advance forded the Potomac and occupied Halltown, his left division extending to the Shenandoah; Emory, with his own division and the part of Grover's that had arrived, the next morning occupied the centre of the line on the right of Crook, with his right on the left of the pike; the Sixth Corps took position on the right of the line, the Second division, Getty, on the right of the pike, connecting with the Nineteenth, the Third, Ricketts, on the right of the Second, and the First, Russell, on the right and rear of the Third, extending almost to the Potomac, with the picket-line reaching that river.

One point in Hunter's instructions was of particular import, as the key-note of the subsequent campaign :

> In pushing up the Shenandoah Valley, as it is expected you will have to go, first or last, it is desirable that nothing should be left to invite the enemy to return. Take all provisions, forage, and stock wanted for the use of your command ; such as cannot be consumed, destroy. It is not desirable that buildings should be destroyed—they should rather be protected ; but the people should be informed that so long as an army can subsist among them, recurrences of these raids must be expected, and we are determined to stop them at all hazards.

> Bear in mind, the object is to drive the enemy south ; and to do this you want to keep him always in sight.   Be guided in your course by the course he takes.

> Make your own arrangements for supplies of all kinds, giving regular vouchers for such as may be taken from loyal citizens.

The emphatic words, "It is not desirable that buildings should be destroyed, they should rather be protected," coupled with the other phrase, "Take all provisions, forage, and stock wanted for the use of your command—such as cannot be consumed, destroy," indicate the extent and yet the limits of the campaign now authorized.

During the first three days of August, Early had remained quiet, with his main body at Bunker Hill ; but the 4th, he had moved in force toward the Potomac, camping six miles beyond Martinsburg, while his cavalry advance crossed the river at Shepherdstown, and drove the pickets from Antietam ford.   Rodes and Ramseur, the 5th, crossed at Williamsport, taking position at St. James's College, and Breckenridge crossed at Shepherdstown, occupying Sharpsburg, while Vaughan entered Hagerstown. Early's wagons accompanied the forces, and wheat was gathered into them from farms near Sharpsburg. Union cavalry from Maryland Heights attacked Jackson's brigade, which was with Breckenridge's command, till Gordon forced it to retire. Early says that his object in this movement was to protect McCausland's withdrawal from Maryland, and "to keep Hunter in a state of uncertainty." At all events, his whole army was hastily recalled to Martinsburg the morning of the 6th —a result possibly not disconnected with Hunter's advance from Frederick to Halltown, where he threatened Early's rear. It is very noteworthy that, though Early's crossing of the river in force produced some alarm, Grant, who was still at Frederick, did not recall his orders for massing the troops at Halltown. "From the despatches received by General Hunter, it appears to me evident," he wrote to Halleck, August 6th, from Monocacy, "there is no great force of the enemy, likely not more than 2,000 men, north of the Potomac, and they engaged in gathering and moving off stock and produce; I believe they will be gone before our troops can get near them." This latter belief was perfectly well-founded; Grant was in error in regard to the numbers north of the Potomac, for nearly all Early's army was there, but it was necessary that cavalry should arrive before he or Hunter could tell where the enemy really was.

The evening of the 5th, Grant, at Monocacy, had informed Halleck of the conclusion he had arrived at. "I have ordered," he said, "the concentration of all available forces under General Hunter—to be concentrated at once at Harper's Ferry, and to follow the enemy promptly wherever he may go; if it is found, as I suspect, nothing but a small raiding force is north of the Potomac, then he is to move up the Valley, detaching sufficient to attend [to] any force left north of him by the enemy." But Hunter was destined never again to move up the Valley; for very soon after, in the early hours of August 6th, Halleck received this memorable direction: " Send Sheridan by morning train to Harper's Ferry, calling here on his way to see if General Hunter has left. Give him orders to take general command of all the troops in the field within the Division. General Hunter will turn over to him my letter of instructions." During Grant's conference with Hunter, the fact had become developed that he had selected Sheridan to conduct the field operations against Early, and Hunter expressing his willingness to be relieved also from all command, Sheridan, who had been waiting at Washington, was summoned by the despatch just cited.

He arrived at Monocacy that day, August 6th, and everything now being arranged, Grant returned the same evening to Washington, while Sheridan crossed the Potomac, and entered his new field, the Shenandoah Valley. The next day an order was issued from the War Department, constituting the four Departments already spoken of as the Middle Military Division, under Sheridan's temporary command, and he formally assumed command at Harper's Ferry. Thus the famous campaign carried out by him in this new sphere dates from August 7, 1864.

The Army of the Shenandoah, as his force came to be called, and as it was afterward officially designated by Sheridan's order of November 17th, had at hand the Sixth Corps, three divisions; one division and a portion of another of the Nineteenth; Crook's Army of West Virginia, two divisions; Torbert's division of Army of the Potomac cavalry, and Lowell's provisional brigade of cavalry. In the Union army, as in the Confederate, most of the regiments had been largely reduced by casualty, for each side had inflicted great slaughter on the other; and the terms brigade, division, and corps rarely meant as much numerically as at the beginning of the campaign. Nevertheless, this was by far the most effective Union force ever assembled in the Valley, and, in addition, Averell's division and Duffié's command of West Virginia cavalry, and Wilson's division of Army of the Potomac cavalry, were on the way, besides the remainder of the Nineteenth Corps under Grover. The cavalry amounted to a full corps, and needed a commander. Sheridan naturally desired for this important post one of his old subordinates. "Do not hesitate," wrote Grant, "to give command to officers in whom you repose confidence, without regard to claims of others on account of rank. If you deem Torbert the best man to command the cavalry, place him in command, and give Averell some other command, or relieve him from the expedition, and order him to report to General Hunter. What we want is prompt and active movements after the enemy, in accordance with the instructions you already have. I feel every confidence that you will do the very best, and will leave you, as far as possible, to act on your own judgment, and not embarrass you with orders and instructions." [1] Torbert was made Chief of Cavalry, and Merritt received Torbert's division.

---

[1] The portion of the Nineteenth Corps at Halltown, August 6th, consisted of Emory's (First) division, under command of General Dwight, and also eight regiments, 2,750 strong, from Grover's (Second) division, temporarily organized into two brigades under command of General Molineux. Additions to Crook's command from what had been the Eighth Corps, caused it usually to be called by the latter name, to avoid the cumbrous term, "The Army of West Virginia," which was a more exact designation.

Torbert described Sheridan's cavalry force at this time as consisting of three divisions, Merritt's, Averell's, and Duffié's, besides Lowell's brigade, afterward assigned as Merritt's third brigade. But Averell was in West Virginia or at Cumberland, and Duffié's so-called division, at Hancock, was only about 1,000 effective; August 27th, a part of it was given to Averell, a part went to Harper's Ferry, and the rest was sent to Cumberland to remount. The Appendix shows the numerical strength of the army.

Sheridan learned that the enemy had been collecting wheat about Sharpsburg, but "thought it best," he said, "to let them go on until I can get Torbert's division here; then I will strike for Winchester, which is the key, and pick up the parties on the north side of the Potomac." Torbert arriving the 9th, and Grant assuring Sheridan the same day that not one brigade had been sent by Lee to reinforce Early, and that he would "endeavor to hold them and rather create a tendency to draw from your front than allow them to reinforce," Sheridan, the morning of the 10th, marched out from Halltown for Winchester. The movement was divided into two stages, the first being the occupation of a line from Clifton to Berryville. The Sixth Corps moved through Charlestown to Clifton, there occupying the right of the infantry line; the Nineteenth along the Berryville pike, till its right joined the left of the Sixth; the Eighth through Kabletown to Berryville, on the left of the Nineteenth; Torbert, first to Summit Point, where he left Lowell in position, and then along the base of Limestone Ridge, through Berryville to White Post, where he established Merritt on the extreme left.

By this initial step, occupying an easy day's march, the troops were drawn out of Halltown in a method that guaranteed the marching columns against the danger of a flank attack, and were placed in a new position, which, though only preliminary to a second movement framed in the General's mind, was strong in itself, covering Snicker's Gap, through which reinforcements were to come. The position is specially worth noting at the outset, because Sheridan repeatedly returned to it in subsequent movements. The orders for the march were admirably clear and precise.

Next morning, the Sixth Corps was directed to move across the country to the ford of the Opequon on the Berryville pike, and to occupy the crossing; the Nineteenth to move through Berryville on the White Post road for one mile, file to the right, by heads of regiments, at deploying distances, and carry and hold the crossing of Opequon Creek at a ford about three-fourths of a mile from the left of the Sixth; Crook to move on the White Post road a mile and a half beyond Berryville, file to the right, and secure the crossing of Opequon Creek at a ford about a mile to the left of the Nineteenth. The cavalry had equally specific tasks assigned it—Merritt to move along the Millwood pike toward Winchester, while Lowell was to close in from Summit Point on the right of the Sixth Corps.

These well-jointed movements were executed with precision; their purpose was to approach the enemy, and engage him in battle. But Early, observing the manœuvre of the 10th, and divining its aim, marched his troops that day south from Bunker Hill, and at night took up a position covering Winchester, holding the junction of the Millwood and Front Royal roads. Though his formation was line of battle, the Confederate general did not wish to fight there. While his opponent had received large reinforcements, his own, which Lee, accepting Grant's challenge to make the Valley a main scene of military operations, had already despatched, were still on the road, and were to join him by way of Culpepper.[1] His proper move, therefore, was to retreat to

---

[1] "Enemy has detached a division of cavalry with a body of infantry to Washington. General R. H. Anderson, with infantry and cavalry, is in Culpepper to observe their movements" (Lee to Early, August 8th). A day later than this, August 9th, Grant had written Sheridan as follows: " Information derived from deserters, refugees, and a man sent from here to Richmond, all corroborating, locates every division and brigade of Hill's, Longstreet's, and Beauregard's forces. Not one brigade has been sent from here." Grant had sent the best information he had, yet Anderson's force included a division of infantry and one of cavalry. But there was nothing unusual in this ; the field despatches, and even the official reports are crowded with thousands of such instances, relating not only to the

the strong defences in the rear of Strasburg and there effect this junction; and should he be forced beyond that point, the Richmond column could be instructed to cross the Blue Ridge higher up. The first necessity was to escape from his present position. Accordingly, while Sheridan, the morning of the 11th, was moving out to carry the fords of the Opequon, Early was shifting his army above Winchester, toward Cedar Creek and Strasburg.

When Torbert's cavalry discovered this manœuvre, by encountering the enemy on the Millwood pike in a sharp skirmish, Sheridan bent his efforts toward harassing, since he could no longer prevent it. Torbert, riding with Merritt's command, was deflected from the direction of Winchester southward toward Newtown, while Lowell came straight through the former place along the pike. Wright, who had halted some time at the Opequon till the new dispositions could be made, and also Emory, were now ordered to turn to the left, moving up the right bank of the creek. At 5 p.m. the Sixth Corps was halted for the night where the Millwood pike crosses the stream, the Nineteenth being between this and the Front Royal pike, while Crook reached Nineveh, or Stony Point, about five miles east of Middletown. Early marched his forces chiefly between the pike and the Union cavalry, so as to keep the macadamized road open for his trains and artillery; and hence when Merritt moved toward Newtown, he encountered Imboden and

movements but also and especially to the positions and the numbers of the enemy. There were, no doubt, at least as great facilities for getting correct information at City Point as elsewhere, and General Badeau even thinks that, by comparison, "at Grant's headquarters the accumulation of information of this character was reduced to a science;" still, even experienced scouts were often positive on what they knew little about, making themselves the subjects of a coveted attention in one of two ways, either by sensational yarns or else by finding out what color of information their questioner wanted, and then supplying it lavishly.

Vaughan at the toll-gate where the Front Royal pike inter-
sects the White Post and Newtown road. These he drove
toward Newtown, but was there checked by Gordon's infantry,
which had established itself for the night, Early having
gone into camp between that point and Middletown. Sheridan's losses that day were thought by him to be about
125, nearly or quite all in Torbert's cavalry. Colonel Edwards's brigade, of the Sixth Corps, sent back by orders
to Winchester, the next morning, to escort a wagon train
thence, which it did with success, found about 60 Confederate and 70 Union wounded in the hospitals, and others
of both sides were reported to be in the care of private
families.[1]

The next day Early moved on, crossing Cedar Creek and
occupying Hupp's Hill on the southern bank. Toward
evening he withdrew his main body a few miles, to the
stronger position of Fisher's Hill, two miles south of Strasburg, and there establishing himself with his right on the
north fork of the Shenandoah, and his left extending toward
Little North Mountain, awaited signs of his reinforcements.
Sheridan, following, halted on the left bank of Cedar Creek,
with the Sixth Corps on the right of the line, the Nineteenth in the centre, and the Eighth on the left, the latter
east of the pike; the cavalry were of course disposed on
the flanks. A skirmish line from the Sixth and Eighth
Corps crossed the creek at once, on either side of the pike,
and from four to eight o'clock in the evening demonstrated
against the pickets at Hupp's Hill. The next morning the

---

[1] Unlike Martinsburg, on the railroad line, which was largely Union in senti-
ment, Winchester was mostly for secession, so that it is well to quote these words
from Edwards's report: "Too much praise cannot be given to the loyal Union
families of Winchester. They attended our wounded night and day, and hav
used all their tea and coffee, sugar, etc., for sick and prisoners, so much so the
they are in actual want themselves."

cavalry reconnoitred the neighborhood of Strasburg on the
Back road, west of the Valley pike ; and as the enemy was
found to be holding Hupp's Hill with his pickets only,
Wright was directed to occupy this point in force and move
his skirmishers into Strasburg. It was then seen that the
main position of the enemy was at Fisher's Hill, and that he
was intrenching westward across the Valley.

Early was now receiving his expected reinforcements.
First came McCausland's pair of brigades, of Chambersburg
notoriety, or such parts of them as had escaped from Moorefield. Vastly more important were Kershaw's division of
infantry, Fitz Lee's of cavalry, and Cutshaw's battalion of
artillery, all under General Anderson, now commanding the
First (Longstreet's) Corps, Army of Northern Virginia, whom
R. E. Lee, though robbing "the cradle and the grave,"
as Grant phrased it, for his own needs, yet spared for a campaign which, he saw, might have a decisive effect on the
war. Early had sent a despatch to Anderson, explaining the
purpose of his retreat, and asking him to come in through
Chester Gap to Front Royal, so as to guard the Luray Valley—Imboden being meanwhile sent to watch this Valley.
Early also established a signal station on the westerly summit of Three Top, the westernmost of the triple parallel
ridges of the Massanutten Mountains, which here sink abruptly into the plain.

Sheridan learned in season one of the chief objects of
the signalling from this station. At noon of July 11th, while
still near Winchester, Weber had sent him from Harper's
Ferry this important message : " I have information from a
source always found reliable that reinforcements under Hill
and Longstreet are within five days' march of Early's present position, moving up the Valley ; that if attacked Early
proposes to show fight and retire, until a junction can be

formed with the advancing forces." Captain Leets sent a like telegram. Nevertheless, as Grant's message of the 9th had been positive the other way, Sheridan awaited more precise intelligence. "I am exceedingly anxious," he wrote to Halleck, the 12th, "to hear whether Longstreet has left to come here or not;" and he notified Grant, the next day, that "reports from citizens here, Washington, and Harper's Ferry report Longstreet's Corps coming this way from Staunton; but I still rely," he added, "on your telegram that it is not so." However, as measures of precaution, Devin's brigade of Merritt's cavalry division was sent to keep watch at Cedarville, seven miles east, on the Front Royal and Winchester pike, and Wright, who had occupied Strasburg with his skirmishers that morning, was drawn back at night to the north side of Cedar Creek, with his pickets, as during the 12th, on the south side; whereupon the enemy's outposts reoccupied Hupp's Hill.

The morning of July 14th, Colonel N. P. Chipman, of the Adjutant-General's office, rode in hot haste into Sheridan's lines, escorted by a regiment of cavalry, with a despatch which he had brought from Washington through Snicker's Gap—a telegram from Grant to Halleck, written two days before, directing him to inform Sheridan that Lee had sent Early "two divisions of infantry, some cavalry, and twenty pieces of artillery"—for such the report then was, though the real force was soon afterward discovered to be one division of infantry and one of cavalry, with artillery. "He [Sheridan] must be cautious," said General Grant, "and act now on the defensive, until movements here force them to detach to send this way. Early's force with this increase cannot exceed 40,000, but this is too much for Sheridan to attack. Send Sheridan the remaining brigade of the Nineteenth Corps. I have ordered to Washington all the hundred-days men. Their time will soon be out, but for the present they will do to stand in the defences." [1]

On the receipt of this despatch, General Sheridan pre-pared to retreat; for he considered this to be wiser than to remain where he was, in the presence of an enemy of strength as yet unknown. "So far as I have been able to see," he wrote Grant, "there is not a military position in this Valley south of the Potomac. The position here [Cedar Creek] is a very bad one, as I cannot cover the numerous rivers that lead in on both of my flanks to the rear. I am not aware that you knew where my command was when you ordered me to take up the defensive. I should like very much to have your advice." To Halleck he wrote that he had "taken up for the present the line of Cedar Run, but will, at my leisure, take position at Winchester. This line cannot be held, nor can I supply my command beyond that point with the ten days' rations with which I started. I expected to get far enough up the Valley to accomplish my objects, and then quickly return."

During the 15th, Custer's and Gibbs's brigades of Merritt's division were sent to Cedarville and Stony Point, on the Front Royal pike, lest the enemy should turn that flank, and there was sharp skirmishing in the afternoon by the pickets of Wright and Crook beyond Cedar Creek, the Jersey brigade of

---

[1] "The movement to the north side of the James River to-day developed the presence of Field's division of Longstreet's Corps which I supposed had gone to the Valley. Pickett's division is also here. We captured six pieces of artillery and over 100 prisoners. Longstreet's troops were under marching orders, and this move will detain it for the present. I think Sheridan is still superior to Early in numbers, but not sufficiently so to attack fortifications" (Grant to Hal-leck, August 14th). "It is now positive that Kershaw's division has gone, but no other infantry has. This reinforcement to Early will put him nearer on an equality with you in numbers than I want to see, and will make it necessary for you to observe more caution about attacking. I would not, however, change my instructions further than to *enjoin caution*" (Grant to Sheridan, August 14th).

Russell's division supporting Wright's line. Early's pickets resisted with increased pertinacity, at one time driving back the Union skirmishers on both sides of the pike, though the line was afterward re-established. During the night the Nineteenth Corps began the retreat. Its departure was not observed, and the Sixth and Eighth did not follow till 8 P.M. the next day, Wright marching all night and reaching Winchester about five o'clock in the morning; and the whole operation was conducted so secretly in the darkness as not to be discovered.

At daybreak of the 17th the signal station on Three Top, which looked down into both camps, perceived that Sheridan's had been abandoned; and, being notified of this, both Early's forces and those of Anderson pushed forward in pursuit, the former from Strasburg and the latter from Front Royal. A part of Anderson's forces, the day before, crossing the Shenandoah, had encountered at the ford two of Merritt's brigades, Devin and Custer, who drove them across the river with heavy loss, nearly 300 prisoners, mostly of Kershaw's division, and two infantry flags being secured as trophies of this handsome exploit. Merritt, whose loss was but 60 men, afterward withdrew to White Post.

Early moved rapidly in pursuit of his opponent along the Valley pike; but as the rear of Sheridan's infantry was breakfasting at Winchester while Early was still at Strasburg, his speed did not avail him. For Sheridan, though at first intimating to Halleck, as has been seen, that he would "take position at Winchester," had determined, even before leaving Cedar Creek, that Winchester was not a defensible position, and had accordingly notified Halleck that instead he would move back to Berryville, holding Snicker's Gap. Thither he now directed his forces, while Torbert was left at Winchester, the afternoon of the 17th, to cover the withdrawal, Wilson having fortunately reported to him there with his division of cavalry. To Wilson and Lowell, as rear-guard, were added Penrose's Jersey brigade of the first division of the Sixth Corps. Penrose, numbering but eight hundred and fifty muskets in line—the Fourth, Tenth, and Fifteenth regiments, under Colonels Campbell and Tay and Major Boeman—was deployed by Torbert along a small affluent of the Opequon, winding south of Winchester near the town, with McIntosh's brigade of Wilson, dismounted, piecing out the line, and the remainder of the cavalry massed near the town, a cavalry battery aiding with its canister from the heights in the rear. The Jerseymen held Early's horsemen in check all the afternoon, and only when Wharton's division of infantry attacked their right, and Ramseur's division their front, while Gordon's advanced against the cavalry, was the line broken. The Union casualties in this engagement were more than 350, for Penrose had 97 killed and wounded, and lost 200 prisoners, and the cavalry lost about 50 prisoners. The captures were chiefly due to the pertinacity with which the line had been held until late at night.

Meanwhile from Winchester the retrograde of the main army had been continued, with the clockwork precision that had marked the advance, toward the old Clifton-Berryville line, Wright re-occupying the crossing of the Opequon, and Crook and Emory their places near Berryville. Merritt withdrew in like manner to White Post; and when Wilson and Lowell fell back at night from Winchester to Summit Point, the whole army was positioned very nearly as when a week before it had moved to intercept Early.

The considerations that commend Early's retreat from Bunker Hill to Strasburg must also approve Sheridan's from Strasburg to Berryville. Independently of the express in-

structions he had received from General Grant, coupled
with his own judgment that the Clifton-Berryville line was
a better defence than Cedar Creek, the conjunction of Early
and Anderson in the neighborhood of Strasburg might
soon have led to his defeat. And there was still another
justification of this retrograde movement in the reinforcements which he well knew were marching to join him,
through Snicker's Gap, consisting, as has been said, of the
remaining portion of Grover's infantry, and the whole of
Wilson's cavalry; while Averell's division of cavalry had
also two days earlier reported at Martinsburg, and Duffié's
was at Charlestown. With these strong reinforcements, and
with the Opequon between him and the enemy, Sheridan was
much better situated than at Cedar Creek for advantageously
executing the imperative orders he had received to act on
the defensive.

At Berryville, Sheridan set forth more fully to Grant the
reason for his withdrawal from Cedar Creek : "The position
I held in front of Strasburg was a very bad one, from which
I could be forced at any time precipitately. Winchester is
untenable, except as a provisional garrison. I have therefore taken a position near Berryville, which will enable me
to get in their rear, if they should get strong enough to
push north. Winchester is now held by the cavalry, with
one brigade of infantry of the Sixth Corps to act with it."
As, however, the enemy's activity at Winchester showed him
to be in strong force, it was deemed best to move to a more
compact line, and the next day Wright was ordered to draw
back through Clifton to Welch's Spring, two and one-half
miles west of Charlestown on the Smithfield or Middleway
pike, and Emory to the same distance south of Charlestown
on the Berryville pike, Crook, a day or two later, coming
back to the left and rear of Emory. Merritt was then drawn

into Berryville, with his pickets out from Snicker's Ferry, via Stony Church on the Millwood pike, across to the Opequon, while Wilson at Summit Point watched the crossing of the Opequon, the left of his picket line connecting with Merritt's, and scouting the east bank of the creek and the country up to the Valley pike, where Averell, with his main force at Shepherdstown, guarded the region back to the Potomac, his pickets going up to Martinsburg. The infantry line crossed the Charlestown pike at the north fork of Bullskin Run, and extended to Welch's Spring on the Summit Point road.

Although the successive moves from Strasburg to Winchester, Winchester to Berryville, and Berryville to Charlestown, were made with a military judgment fully justified at last, they excited some alarm at first among those ignorant of the reason, who already in imagination saw the enemy moving across the Potomac. The true statement of the case at this time was the one given by Sheridan to Grant. Having explained the manner in which Torbert was compelled to evacuate Winchester, he added these words : " There has been no advance toward Martinsburg. I destroyed all the wheat, hay, and provisions south of Winchester and Berryville, and drove off all the cattle. The enemy is very much chagrined at it. If the enemy should go north of the Potomac I will follow him. There is no occasion for alarm." Before leaving Berryville that morning, Sheridan informed Averell, who was near Martinsburg, that Torbert had fallen back to Summit Point from Winchester, and directed him to move his command " to the north side of the Potomac, if necessary, and cover the country from Williamsport to Sharpsburg."

When Early found that Sheridan had retired from the Clifton-Berryville line, where he would always be threatening Winchester, being within a short march of it, he ventured to move his own forces, the 19th, to Bunker Hill, yet leaving all Anderson's troops to guard Winchester, while Ransom's cavalry, now under Lomax, who at Fisher's Hill had relieved Ransom, made reconnoissances to Martinsburg and Shepherdstown. Sheridan, however, knowing that Averell could easily cross the river and hold the north fords, cared little for these demonstrations. "In fact," said his orders to this officer, the night of the 19th, "the General rather desires that the enemy should cross ; " while to Grant he wrote that he had "left everything in that direction for them, but they have not accepted the invitation as yet." Early contented himself with going just far enough down the Valley to insure keeping the Baltimore and Ohio Railroad broken, and to be where he could get grain and forage ;[1] for Sheridan had burned the Valley above Winchester. Thus three days of comparative quiet passed.

The force which Anderson brought with him consisted, as has been said, of Kershaw's division, Cutshaw's battalion of artillery, and two brigades of cavalry under Fitz Lee. Anderson ranked Early, but declined to take command, not being sent there for the purpose of superseding him. Although Sheridan knew from the prisoners he had taken that these reinforcements had arrived, he could not be sure that others were not on the way, and all his information was to the effect that at least one additional division of Longstreet's old corps was already in the Valley. Indeed, it seemed very improbable that Anderson himself, who now commanded the corps, would accompany a single division of it to the Valley, while the greater part remained at Richmond.

---

[1] " No wheat has been burned in this country, and if we can stay here we can live. I have sent Lomax to Martinsburg. I think Fitz Lee had better try and shove the enemy back on the Berryville road" (Early to Anderson, August 19th).

Grant's scouts, on the other hand, brought him news totally different from Sheridan's reports, and some uncertainty was thus caused. August 16th Grant wrote that " Fitz Lee's division is not in the Valley. We took quite a number of prisoners from it yesterday, north of the James. Kershaw's division has gone to the Valley, and probably two brigades of Wilcox's division. Some cavalry has gone, but I do not know whose. I would not advise an attack on Early in an intrenched position, but would watch him closely with the cavalry, and if he attempts to move north, follow him." Sheridan answered the next day that " Kershaw's division is here, and Wickham's and Lomax's brigades of Fitzhugh Lee's cavalry division ; also another brigade from Ream's Station. One division of A. P. Hill's corps is reported here. My impression is that troops are still arriving." The 17th, Grant wrote that his movement to the north of James River had " undoubtedly prevented sending reinforcements to the Valley," and that a large part of Early's force was likely to be recalled. " Be prepared to move at any moment. If you find Early sending off any of his troops, strike suddenly and hard." Sheridan rejoined that all his reports were that Early was steadily receiving reinforcements ; and the 19th he again wrote as follows : "I receive constant reports of the passage of troops across to this Valley from Culpepper. I have taken the defensive until their strength is more fully developed. I still think that two divisions of infantry have come here, and Fitzhugh Lee's cavalry." The 20th, Grant responded that " As stated in previous despatches, no division or brigade has gone from Lee's army to the Valley except Kershaw's and Fitz Lee's."

While the Confederate strength and purposes thus re-mained obscure, Early and Anderson determined, the 21st, to attack Sheridan in a combined movement, the former proceeding through Smithfield towards Charlestown, while Anderson was to advance by the direct road that runs through Summit Point.   Sheridan's cavalry pickets on the Opequon were so quickly driven in that Early pressed at once against the Sixth Corps, advancing the divisions of Rodes and Ramseur. A sharp engagement ensued. Ricketts was transferred from his position in reserve to the left of the corps line, and the lost position was regained at nightfall, though with the loss of 260 killed and wounded, mainly in Getty's division. The Eighth Corps drew up to co-operate on the left and the Nineteenth on the right. But the attack was over ; for Anderson, moving from Winchester and having a somewhat longer road to travel, did not take part, his advance having been handsomely retarded by Merritt's cavalry division at Berryville and Wilson's at Summit Point. The consequence was that dusk found him still at the latter place, where accordingly he went into camp. At midnight Sheridan drew in Merritt and Wilson, and moved the whole army back to Halltown, which was a far better, and, indeed, an impregnable position. For, with a river on either flank, and a compact line stretching between them, the Sixth Corps on the right, the Nineteenth in the centre, and the Eighth on the left, his fine corps of cavalry watchful, strong intrenchments all along his front, and aided by the heavy guns of the Heights, he had the best defensive position in the Valley.[1]

While Sheridan was at Cedar Creek, Mosby with a few score men made a dash at Berryville upon one of his trains

---

[1] "My position at best being a very bad one, and as there is much depending on this army, I fell back and took a new position in front of Halltown " (Sheridan to Halleck, August 22d). " Some of my scouts report Pickett's and Field's divisions here, and that they will go through Snicker's Gap. I do not believe they are there, but the rebels have been very bold " (Sheridan to Augur, August 23d).

proceeding to the front, dispersed the guard, Kenly's brigade of hundred-days men, ran off three hundred and fifty mules, and burned the wagons with such of their contents as his band and helpful citizens could not carry away. The wagons were chiefly loaded with forage, subsistence, and the officers' baggage and regimental property of Merritt's cavalry division. The 15th, Lieutenant Walker, First United States Cavalry was killed, and Lieutenant Dwyer, Fifth Cavalry, wounded and captured by Mosby's troopers ; and the following day Lieutenant Barry, First Cavalry, was attacked and suffered the loss of 7 men.

Although this primary move of the new campaign had come to naught, yet it was the Lieutenant-General himself who superseded his original instructions by an express order to assume the defensive, until a specific time, namely, when Lee's necessities should weaken Early by the withdrawal of some of his troops to Richmond.

In moving back from Cedar Creek to Winchester, Sheridan had instructed Torbert to burn, as he withdrew, the barns and crops, and to seize all mules, horses, and cattle that might be useful to the Union army. "Loyal citizens," he said, "can bring in their claims against the Government for this necessary destruction. No houses will be burned, and officers in charge of this delicate, but necessary duty, must inform the people that the object is to make this valley untenable for the raiding parties of the rebel army." Sheridan wrote to Grant that he had "destroyed everything eatable south of Winchester, and they will have to haul supplies from well up toward Staunton."

CHAPTER VIII.

THE SHENANDOAH LINES IN SEPTEMBER.

THE Army of the Shenandoah had again fallen back to Harper's Ferry, much as when, on former occasions, it had received the soldiers' nickname of "Harper's Weekly," in allusion to a pretended regularity of arrivals and reissues at this spot. What a story of marchings and countermarchings the soil of the lower Valley might tell! What a history is that of its villages from 1861 to 1865—now in Secession and anon in Union keeping; sometimes sheltering "Yanks" at dawn, swarming with "Rebs" at noon, and again sleeping under the stars and stripes at night! "We have walked the pike-road so often," writes an Alabama officer, "that we know not only every house, fence, spring, and shade-tree, but very many of the citizens, their wives, and children." The Valley turnpike had come to be known as the race-course of armies.

Early occupied three days in demonstrating against Halltown, principally on the fronts of Crook and Emory. Finding the position impregnable, he left Anderson facing the Halltown lines, with Kershaw's division, McCausland's cavalry, and one regiment of Fitz Lee's, and, August 25th, sent the main part of Fitz Lee's force to Williamsport, while he himself moved, with Rodes, Ramseur, Gordon, and Wharton, and their artillery, northward to Shepherdstown, Cutshaw remaining with Anderson. The alleged purpose of this

seemingly imprudent division of his forces was "to keep up
the fear of an invasion of Maryland and Pennsylvania."
Fitz Lee started on his way through Leetown and Martinsburg. Early, following, turned off at Leetown, and between
this place and Kearneysville came upon the greater part of
Merritt's and Wilson's divisions, under Torbert, who, supposing he had only cavalry to deal with, attacked sharply,
driving back Wharton in confusion. That Torbert's troopers were immediately afterward roughly handled is not to
their discredit, since they were confronted by four divisions
of infantry, though Breckenridge's corps was the only force
much engaged. Pressing against the Union cavalry, Early
cut off the brigade of Custer; but this vigorous soldier, by
great exertions, escaped through Shepherdstown across the
Potomac, the Confederate commander fortunately having no
cavalry at hand with which to follow him. Wilson and the
remainder of Merritt found their way back safely, by different roads, to the army. In this affair there were losses on
each side, Colonel Monaghan, Sixth Louisiana, commanding
a brigade, being among the Confederate killed.

When Merritt and Wilson came back to the Union lines
with the account of what had befallen them, preparations
were made for the emergency. "Early and Breckenridge,"
telegraphed Sheridan to Halleck, "moved this morning in
the direction of Shepherdstown. It is possible that I may
have to cross the river to the north side, should the enemy
cross." To Grant he said that there was not much doubt of
the presence of two divisions of Longstreet's corps. "The
cavalry were forced to give up Shepherdstown, all but one
brigade coming back to Halltown. This brigade, it is supposed, crossed at the Shepherdstown ford. I cannot say
whether the enemy will attempt to cross in the morning—
they must be very strong to do so. My information is that

Early marched with that intention. The enemy are in very strong force. I will not give up this place," he added, confidently, "and hope to be able to strike the enemy divided. I hardly think that they will attempt to go to Washington." He hurried Wilson across the Potomac to Boonsboro, to hold the South Mountain gaps, and next day directed Averell to unite with Wilson, should Lee ford at Williamsport. "Wilson," he said, "is at one of the lower crossings of Antietam. You would then be strong enough to take care of the enemy's cavalry until I could get Merritt's division with you."

But Early's project, whatever its real nature may have been, had already come to an end; for Fitzhugh Lee, reaching the Potomac, found Averell's cavalry guarding the fords on the north side, and after a little skirmishing, drew off toward Shepherdstown.

Meanwhile, Anderson had been left in so small force before Halltown, that Crook, reconnoitring, the 26th, with Duval's division and a part of Thoburn's, Lowell's cavalry co-operating, broke the enemy's skirmish line, and reported that he had also driven two brigades from their position behind earthworks. Lowell captured 7 or 8 officers and 69 privates. Crook's infantry loss was 141 killed and wounded.

The Confederate commander had now found it hopeless to attack Sheridan in front at Halltown; impossible to get at his river-protected flanks and rear, with Maryland Heights behind; and perilous to invade the North, with three divisions of cavalry, one of them beyond the Potomac, free to fall on his trains. He resolved to move back to his old position, west of the Opequon. The 26th he marched his infantry from Shepherdstown to Leetown, and the following day from Leetown to Bunker Hill, while Anderson moved back, the night of the 26th, from the Halltown front to Stephenson's Dépôt.

Lest rumor should, as usual, magnify and distort Early's latest demonstration, Sheridan wrote to Halleck that "the movement of the enemy toward Shepherdstown yesterday amounted to nothing. It did not disturb me, nor cause me to make any changes, except to send one division of cavalry to Antietam Creek, on the north side. No attempt was made to cross the ford, although it was left open for the enemy. They must have retired to the vicinity of Charlestown. I think I can manage this affair. I have thought it best to be very prudent, everything considered." The same night Grant informed Sheridan, that, after the great battles just delivered around Petersburg, ending in the seizure of the Weldon Railroad, " all troops will be ordered back from the Valley, except what they believe to be the minimum number to detain you. I think," he added, "I do not overstate the loss of the enemy in the last two weeks at 10,000 killed and wounded. Watch closely, and if you find this thing correct, push with all vigor. Give the enemy no rest, and if it is possible to follow to the Virginia Central Road, follow that far. Do all the damage to railroads and crops you can. Carry off stock of all descriptions and negroes, so as to prevent further planting. If the war is to last another year, we want the Shenandoah Valley to remain a barren waste." These views accorded with Early's latest movements, and Sheridan wrote to Washington that "the indications to-day are that they will fall back out of the Valley."

The main army lay quiet that day, but the morning of the 28th, it moved [1] forward to Charlestown, meeting no

---

[1] General Grant had written to Sheridan as follows : · " If you are so situated as to feel the enemy strongly without compromising the safety of your position, I think it advisable to do so. I do not know positively that any troops have returned yet from the Valley, but think you will find the enemy in your immediate

opposition. Sheridan had apparently fixed upon the Clifton-Berryville line as the true counter-position to occupy,
whenever Early established himself at Bunker Hill; for
there he could strike the turnpike south of Winchester,
should it become advisable to resume the offensive, or could
retire to Halltown should the enemy be found in too great
strength. Toward this line he now moved, yet by gradual
approaches, as the country was very open, and the enemy's
purposes not fully known. While the infantry advanced to
Charlestown, Averell crossed from Hagerstown through
Williamsport to Martinsburg, and Wilson also returned
south of the Potomac at Shepherdstown, and Custer at
Harper's Ferry. Merritt moved forward to Leetown, and
there finding a cavalry force, handsomely defeated it, driving it with the sabre to Smithfield and across the Opequon.
The next day, two of Early's infantry divisions expelled
Merritt from Smithfield and re-established the Confederate
cavalry there; but Ricketts's division of the Sixth Corps
being hurried to Merritt's relief, drove out the enemy's
troopers and definitely secured the position for Merritt.
The loss of Gibbs's brigade, Merritt's division, was 35 killed
and wounded. The following day, August 30th, Lowell's
brigade, which in August had held the right at Smithfield,
now resumed that charge, while the remainder of Merritt's
division and Wilson's were sent, in conformity with the old
dispositions, to Berryville. The enemy making no effort to
impede this change, after a few days the infantry were
moved to the old line, threatening Winchester, the Sixth
Corps on the right at Clifton, next the Nineteenth, and then
the Eighth at Berryville—Merritt's and Wilson's cavalry

---

front weaker than you are." Sheridan's orders, however, to move out of the
Halltown position, had been given and executed before this despatch arrived, the
Sixth Corps marching at 7 A.M., and the Nineteenth Corps connecting on its left.

divisions of course guarding that flank. This positioning was effected September 3d, six days after leaving the Hall-town lines.

A source of annoyance to Sheridan at this time were the calls made upon him to detach troops from his army to repel the enemy's incursions into West Virginia, on the ground that this region belonged to his Military Division. "There is considerable panic in West Virginia," wrote Halleck, August 27th, "from apprehended rebel raids to destroy the Baltimore and Ohio Railroad, while Early is holding you in check at Harper's Ferry. We have no troops to send to that Department, and must leave its protection entirely to your forces." Grant, in a different spirit, wrote to Sheridan, the 29th, as follows: "If it is ascertained certainly that Breckenridge has been detached to go into Western Virginia, attack the remaining force vigorously with every man you have." Sheridan denied this supposition, which was, in fact, groundless, as "a copperhead report," adding the prophetic words, "I believe no troops have yet left the Valley, but I believe they will, and that *it will be their last campaign in the Shenandoah*." Crook notified Kelley to do the best he could for West Virginia, aided by the dismounted men of Duffié's command, whom Sheridan spared to "quiet the fears of the people."

As soon as Early retired to Bunker Hill, Averell, as we have seen, had moved up the pike from Williamsport to Martinsburg. Perceiving that there he could cover the repair of the railroad, Early sent against him Rodes, who drove him back to Falling Waters. But September 2d, Early, breaking up his camp at Bunker Hill, moved with three divisions of infantry and a part of McCausland's cavalry across the country toward Summit Point, on a reconnoissance, while Rodes accompanied the trains to Stephen-

son's. Averell thereupon immediately marched back from
Falling Waters to Martinsburg, and, continuing to Bunker
Hill, found Vaughan's and Johnson's brigades, which he
routed in succession, capturing 55 prisoners, two flags, a
herd of cattle and some loaded wagons. Driving the two
brigades pell-mell before him to Stephenson's, he there
came upon the inevitable Rodes, and at once made off out of
his reach. But the news of the disaster to Johnson and
Vaughan, reaching Early, arrested his movement toward
Summit Point, and recrossing the Opequon he massed at
Stephenson's. The next day Rodes moved down the pike,
and drove Averell from Bunker Hill, establishing himself
there.

In studying this campaign of the lower Valley, nothing is
more noticeable than the singularly different purposes on
which the minds of the two opposing leaders were bent.
Early's attention was much absorbed in breaking and keeping broken the Union line of railroad, not only as a material
damage to the Northern cause, but on account of the moral
effect of this step as an evidence of Confederate strength in
laying hold and keeping control of the chief military line
between Washington and the West. For this reason, the
daily skirmishes and reconnoissances on the Halltown front,
even when favorable to his troops, and his larger success in
pushing Sheridan back from Berryville to Charlestown and
from Charlestown to Halltown, evidently seemed to him of
minor consequence, and caused him little elation; whereas
the occupation of Martinsburg, on the railroad, even by a
handful of Union cavalry, was always enough to affect the
movements of his whole army, if necessary, to dislodge it.
Sheridan, on the contrary, was wholly intent on the problem
of how to make sure of a victory over the enemy in his immediate front, and hence paid comparatively little attention

to what was going on along the railroad. The probable issue of this diversity of aims was that sooner or later Sheridan, by persistency and vigilance, would, unobserved, or at least unmolested, move into a position dangerous to Early, while the Confederate general, too regardless of his immediate opponent's projects, in his warfare against the North as a whole, would sacrifice his own safety.

A new and decisive element was now to enter into the campaign. Four weeks had elapsed since Lee sent Anderson to Early's relief, and he now desired his return. Affairs in the Valley seemed to justify this recall, for Early had been able to maintain himself a long time at Bunker Hill, and to keep his opponent confined within a short radius of Harper's Ferry. On the other hand, the campaign at Petersburg had brought Lee to a desperate need of troops. Since the departure of Kershaw and Fitz Lee, Grant had extended his right to Deep Bottom, north of the James, thus compelling a similar Confederate prolongation to protect Richmond; and he had seized the Weldon road, to regain which his opponents had made desperate assaults, at great cost. Accordingly, Lee informed Early of his need of the troops temporarily lent him, and this notification is the key to Early's moves at this juncture.

The 31st of August, Anderson had withdrawn from Stephenson's to Winchester; thence, three days later, September 3d, he started with his command toward Berryville, to recross the Blue Ridge on the way to Richmond. But it chanced that while, up to this time, the road had been open, this was the very day on which Sheridan was finishing his reoccupation of the Clifton-Berryville line, which, as has been seen, in repeating the original arrangement, positioned Crook at Berryville. Merritt and Wilson had been sent to reconnoitre beyond the new infantry left, moving through Millwood and White Post to Front Royal pike. Accordingly Anderson, marching to Berryville, which he reached an hour before sunset, stumbled upon the Eighth Corps going into camp there—the surprise being mutual; and an engagement resulted between Crook and Kershaw, which only night put an end to. About three score prisoners were captured from Anderson; Crook's total loss was 166. Anderson had his trains with him, homeward-bound to Petersburg; but the darkness which immediately followed favored concealment of this fact, and Early, learning of the unexpected encounter—for Sheridan's reoccupation of the Clifton-Berryville position had not attracted his attention—hurried at dawn of the 4th with three divisions to Anderson's aid, Gordon being left to cover Winchester. He found Kershaw extended in skirmish line, as yet not fully understanding what he had in his front; and fearing that the nature of Anderson's movement might become known, when it would be followed by a cavalry attack on his trains, Early left an infantry division in line on Kershaw's left, and then moved across toward what he had presumed to be Sheridan's right, to withdraw attention from Anderson by demonstrating there. A march along rising ground gave him for the first time a full view of the new Union position, which, by the aid of field-glasses, he could see extending to Summit Point, strengthened by intrenchments, at which the troops were still digging, all along the front. It was decided that Anderson must return to Winchester, and start for the Blue Ridge again by a more southerly road, carrying him past the Union left. Early therefore withdrew his whole army across the Opequon—after a spirited skirmish at Berryville, in which Torbert, returning from the left, was involved—Anderson's trains going first. The Eighth Corps had that

XI.—7

morning been ordered to fall back to Clifton ; and five days after, with Custer's and Lowell's brigades of Merritt's division, it was sent across to Summit Point, to assure the right flank and the communications with Harper's Ferry. Crook's ambulance train, during these operations, was, in Sheridan's language, "attacked and badly stampeded by six of Mosby's men."

Rodes, on the 5th, getting back to Stephenson's Dépôt, found that Averell was again, as usual, driving toward Winchester the Confederate cavalry that had been left on the Martinsburg road, and accordingly, also, as usual, Rodes, in his turn, drove Averell back to Bunker Hill. During ten days thereafter there was manœuvring and skirmishing along the Opequon, without results of special moment to the campaign. The most brilliant of these minor operations was executed by General McIntosh, who, taking his fine brigade, comprising the Second Ohio, Third New Jersey, Fifth and Second New York, and First Connecticut regiments of cavalry, and a section of " M " battery, Second United States Artillery, proceeded, on the 13th, by order of General Wilson, to reconnoitre the Berryville pike. On his way he captured about 30 dismounted cavalry, and then pressing on toward Winchester, caught sight of an infantry line in his front, and charged it. The enemy broke, and made for a piece of woods, which McIntosh surrounded, there capturing the Eighth South Carolina infantry, Colonel Henagan, of Kershaw's command, with its battle-flag. The remainder of Kershaw's division, which was not far away, hurried forward, but McIntosh sounded the recall, and was off in season. He secured 14 officers and 92 men of Henagan's command, being the entire regiment, besides 2 officers and 35 men belonging to no fewer, it was said, than six different Virginia mounted organizations.[1] The Third New Jersey and Second Ohio especially distinguished themselves in this affair.

This same day, the 13th, Lowell captured an officer and 11 men, and Wright made a reconnoissance with the second, Getty's, division of the Sixth Corps, in conjunction with Merritt's cavalry, to Gilbert's ford, on the Opequon, where the enemy was found in force; Getty's losses were only a dozen wounded. The position of the cavalry from the 5th to the 19th of September was substantially as follows : Wilson, from Snicker's Gap to the Opequon Creek on the Berryville pike; Merritt, from the latter point to Smithfield; Averell, from Smithfield to Martinsburg and also along the Potomac.

The 14th of September Anderson again started, with Kershaw's infantry and Cutshaw's artillery, to cross the Blue Ridge, this time taking the precaution to move for Chester Gap, his road bringing him far past the Union left, toward Front Royal. Fitz Lee was to remain with Early. Thus General R. E. Lee had at last drawn away the greater part of the reinforcements sent to Early's relief at a time when the latter's opponent had even two divisions less than he had now. Lee's own forces at Richmond had been so steadily crumbling under Grant's attacks as to require repairing.

At this juncture a figure reappeared upon the scene, whose presence betokened something urgent and decisive. Though the defensive attitude so long maintained by Sheri-

---

[1] Lest it be supposed that this report was exaggerated, it may be noted that Terry's brigade of Gordon's division had an "aggregate present for duty" of 858 officers and men, and an "aggregate present" of 963 ; but it contained the 2d, 4th, 5th, 27th, 33d, 21st, 25th, 42d, 44th, 48th, 50th, 10th, 23d, and 37th Virginia regiments. York's brigade of the same division contained the 1st, 2d, 5th, 6th, 7th, 8th, 9th, 10th, 14th, and 15th Louisiana regiments, and showed an aggregate "present for duty," August 20th, of 614 officers and men, and an "aggregate present" of 803. Thus there is nothing improbable in the assertion that the 37 prisoners captured represented half a dozen different organizations.

dan was adopted at the express orders of General Grant, and
steadily sanctioned by him, yet he had long been hoping
that Lee would weaken Early, in order that the latter might
be attacked, and the lower Valley thus relieved of his annoying and humiliating presence.[1] Holding the line of the
Opequon, Early had for weeks not only kept Maryland and
Pennsylvania quaking with apprehension, but had persist-
ently maintained his grasp on the Baltimore and Ohio Road
and the Chesapeake and Ohio Canal, checking every effort
to repair these conduits to the capital, and greatly impeding their travel and trade.   His own communications,
meanwhile, were not cut, and the Virginia Central Road
behind him was in free operation between Staunton and
Richmond.[2]

Nevertheless, the records very clearly show not only that
Sheridan's defensive attitude was taken up by the orders

---

[1] There is a remarkable despatch fro n Lee to Anderson, showing that, no
sooner had the Confederate Commander-in-Chief withdrawn Kershaw's division,
than he foresaw the probable result, and sought to avert it by countermanding
his instructions: "I have been desirous for some time of recalling you to me.
But my unwillingness to diminish the force in the Valley has prevented. A victory over Sheridan would materially change the aspect of affairs. I fear General
Early's force without Kershaw's division would be insufficient. Upon the receipt
of this, therefore, should circumstances permit, I wish you would with your staff
return here, and take command of the other divisions of your corps, and direct
General Kershaw to report with his division to General Early, for the present.
Should you and General Early agree that the presence of Kershaw's division in
the Valley is unnecessary, you can bring it to Gordonsville with you. Otherwise
let it remain until I can see farther. Let me know what is your determination "
(Lee to Anderson, September 17th). The date of this despatch somewhat suggests that Lee may not have been aware that Kershaw was already on his
way.

[2] The Lieutenant-General, in his report, states the facts clearly. "Defeat to
us," he says, "would open to the enemy the States of Maryland and Pennsylvania
for long distances before another army could be interposed to check him. Under
these circumstanc s I hesitated about allowing the initiative to be taken. Finally,
the use of the Baltimore and Ohio Railroad and the Chesapeake and Ohio Canal,
which were both obstructed by the enemy, became so indispensably necessary to
us, and the importance of relieving Pennsylvania and Maryland from continu

of General Grant, but that it was expressly approved and sustained by him from time to time, and indeed almost constantly day by day; and that there was perfect accord between them. As late as September 8th, he had written to Sheridan as follows: "If you want to attack Early, you might reinforce largely from Washington. Whilst you are close in front of the enemy, there is no necessity for a large force there. This is not intended to urge an attack, because I believe you will allow no chance to escape which promises success." Sheridan's own views were clear and positive. That day he telegraphed Grant a simple and striking statement of them: "I have not deemed it best to attack him, but have watched closely to press him hard *so soon as he commences to detach troops for Richmond.* This was *the tenor of your telegram to me after I took up the defensive.*" The next day brought from Grant a decisive authorization of this very policy: "I would not have you make an attack with the advantage against you, but *would prefer just the course you seem to be pursuing*—that is, pressing closely upon the enemy, and when he moves, follow him up, being ready at all times to pounce upon him if he detaches any considerable force."

Still there was a great pressure on Sheridan to take the offensive, all sorts of stories being constantly sent him in regard to the alleged withdrawal of Kershaw and Fitz Lee and Breckenridge, so that they seemed almost manufactured for the sake of bringing on prematurely the date at which Sheridan was fixed in his determination to offer battle. One report, brought by a scout to Washington, thence forwarded

---

ously threatened invasion so great, that I determined the risk should be taken. But fearing to telegraph the order for an attack without knowing more than I did of General Sheridan's feelings as to what would be the probable result, I left City Point on the 15th of September to visit him at his headquarters, to decide after conference with him what should be done."

to him for his guidance, and vouched for as "reliable," was that Early himself was at Gordonsville, August 28th, looking on while his troops passed through to Richmond. Halleck, alluding to the rumor that Breckenridge was soon to be in Lewisburg and Charlestown, used this language : " The disappearance of Breckenridge from your front gives weight to the rumor that he was expected in the Kanawha Valley in about ten days. If you do not propose engaging the enemy immediately, that Valley should be looked to." Sheridan quietly replied that "it should be remembered that it is three hundred miles from here to Charleston, *via* Lewisburg. This would require a march of not less than twenty days. General Crook says that for one hundred miles of this distance a cricket could not subsist on the country." The 12th of September Grant received from Sheridan another clear statement of his plans. "It is exceedingly difficult to attack him in this position. Opequon Creek is a very formidable barrier. There are various crossings, but all are difficult. The banks are formidable. I have thought it best to remain on the defensive until he detaches, unless the chances are in my favor. The troops here are in fine spirits; some of them, however, have not seen very hard fighting, and some of them are not entirely reliable. There is no interest suffering here except the Baltimore and Ohio Railroad, and I will not divide my force to protect it." Soon after, Grant received another pressing appeal on behalf of the railroad company, sent through Halleck ; [1] and he left City

---

[1] " It is represented to me by reliable business men that the long and continued interruption of the Ohio and Chesapeake and Baltimore and Ohio Railroads is very seriously affecting the supply of provisions and fuel for public and private use in Baltimore, Washington, Georgetown, and Alexandria. Unless the canal can be opened very soon a sufficient supply of winter's coal cannot be procured before the close of navigation. The gas companies are already thinking of stopping their works for want of coal. The canal and railroad have been several

Point the day following to talk over the subject with Sheridan, and get his views.

Just then Sheridan heard of the long-expected withdrawal of Kershaw, and informed Grant, on his arrival at Charlestown, that the desired change had come over the situation. Sheridan proposed at once to move to the pike south of Winchester, Early's line of supply and retreat. As soon as he announced this plan, which would force a battle, Grant sanctioned it, and "asked him if he could get out his teams and supplies in time to make an attack on the ensuing Tuesday morning"—for his trains and provisions were at Harper's Ferry. This question was asked on Friday, "but his reply was," says Grant's report, "that he could before daylight on Monday," thus being ready, with little more than two days' preparation, to resume the aggressive. Grant had taken with him a plan of battle,[1] but Sheridan did not need it. "I saw," says Grant, "there were but two words of instruction necessary—'*Goin!*'" humorously adding that "the result was such that I have never since deemed it necessary to visit General Sheridan before giving him orders."

But was even this visit necessary? Or, rather, would not General Sheridan have resumed the aggressive even had it not been made? We cannot doubt that he would have done

---

times repaired and as often destroyed. They, therefore, urge the great importance of driving Early far enough south to secure these lines of communication from rebel raids, and that if Sheridan is not strong enough to do this he should be reinforced " (Halleck to Grant, September 14th).

Sheridan wrote to Grant, September 15th. " There is as yet no indications of Early's detaching. It seems impossible to get at the enemy's cavalry. It is in poor condition, and is kept in close on their infantry." This despatch was received the 16th, after Grant had started.

[1] " You may recollect that, when I visited Sheridan at Charlestown, I had a plan of battle with me to give him. But I found him so thoroughly ready to move, so confident of success when he did move, and his plan so thoroughly matured, that I did not let him know this, and gave him no order whatever except the authority to move " (Grant to Badeau, June, 1878).

so; for the very contingency on which his proposed ceas-
ing to act on the defensive was based, had just then happened, Anderson being well on his way toward Richmond.
This fact, Sheridan states, had become known to him the
night before Grant arrived at Charlestown; and thus it
was that when the latter reached Sheridan's headquarters,
he found this officer very eager to go forward and take
advantage of the enemy's error. It may also, we think,
fairly be presumed, that had Kershaw's division effected
its withdrawal on September 3d, when its first attempt was
foiled by accident, Sheridan would have moved long before
he did. His report distinctly says that he had "patiently
awaited its withdrawal before attacking, believing the condition of affairs throughout the country required great
prudence on my part, that a defeat of the forces at my
command could be ill afforded." Within a few days his
sound judgment was to be vindicated by a brilliant victory.

The aggressive movement, in short, really did date, as
Sheridan had decided that it ought to date, from the weak-
ening of Early by the departure of a portion of his forces
to Richmond. "Then," says Sheridan, "our time had
come."

CHAPTER IX.

THE BATTLE OF THE OPEQUON.

THE very air seemed laden now with omens of victory. With Kershaw out of the way, had doubts prevailed as to the result of a pitched battle, Early would have removed them by choosing this moment for giving freer rein than ever to his main error in the campaign. Had he not wofully mistaken his young opponent's character, the elder general would at once, on losing Kershaw, have so repositioned his forces as to be able to retire up the Valley to Strasburg, the moment his adversary should give sign of attack. The service rendered him, it is true, by the departing troops, had gone little beyond the immediate purpose for which they had been sent. A singular ill-fortune even had attended whatever movements Anderson's troops had taken part in. On three occasions during his brief stay he had lost infantry prisoners to Union cavalry—once, near Front Royal, on arriving, to Merritt; a second time, near Winchester, to McIntosh; a third, near Halltown, to Lowell. It had not been his luck to strike Sheridan's left and rear at Cedar Creek, and a subsequent attempt at co-operation was also frustrated —the one of August 21st, when Sheridan retired from Charlestown to Halltown. But while Early cannot therefore have felt as if an invaluable source of reliance had been taken away from him, in the departure of Kershaw and Cutshaw for their own corps at Petersburg, yet so serious a sub-

traction of numerical strength should have led him at once
to alter his campaign to suit the new contingency. He had
retreated up the Valley in August the moment his opponent
menaced him from the precise Clifton-Berryville line he now
reoccupied. Yet his own strength was now greater than
then by only a single division of cavalry, while his opponent's was greater by two divisions of cavalry and part of a
division of infantry. If in August it was a sound military
move to seek a more defensible line, it was now a move absolutely necessary. What Early actually did at this juncture was not only to fail to occupy a position that would secure retreat as soon as his enemy should move upon the pike
between Winchester and Strasburg, but to send a large part
of his army to Martinsburg, twenty-two miles north of Winchester.

    This movement was made in the following manner. The
17th of September, hearing that the railroad was again
under repair, he went from Stephenson's with Rodes's and
Gordon's divisions, and Braxton's artillery, to Bunker Hill,
and next day with Gordon, a part of Lomax's cavalry and a
few guns, to Martinsburg. Having driven away Averell,
who was found there, he regained Bunker Hill, where he
left Gordon with orders to return to Stephenson's the next
morning, whither Rodes marched that night. Thus, on the
eve of a day destined to witness a great and decisive battle,
the Confederate forces were strung along the pike—cavalry
at Martinsburg, Gordon at Bunker Hill, Rodes on the
way to Stephenson's, Wharton with King's battery at Stephenson's, Ramseur with Nelson's battery across the Berryville pike. Early's venturesome journey to Martinsburg had
also greatly aided his opponent's plans. For when, the 18th,
Averell sent word that he had been attacked by two infantry
divisions, Sheridan eagerly changed the orders of march he

BATTLE FIELD OF
WINCHESTER, VA.
19 SEPTEMBER 1864.
DRAWN FROM OFFICIAL MAPS BY
J.P. GENTHON.
COMMANDERS:
UNION FORCES: Major Gen'l P.H. SHERIDAN, U.S.V.
CONFEDERATE .: Lieut. Gen'l JUBAL A. EARLY.
Reference:
UNION   CONFEDERATE.
INFANTRY:
CAVALRY:
ARTILLERY:
Scale of Miles:

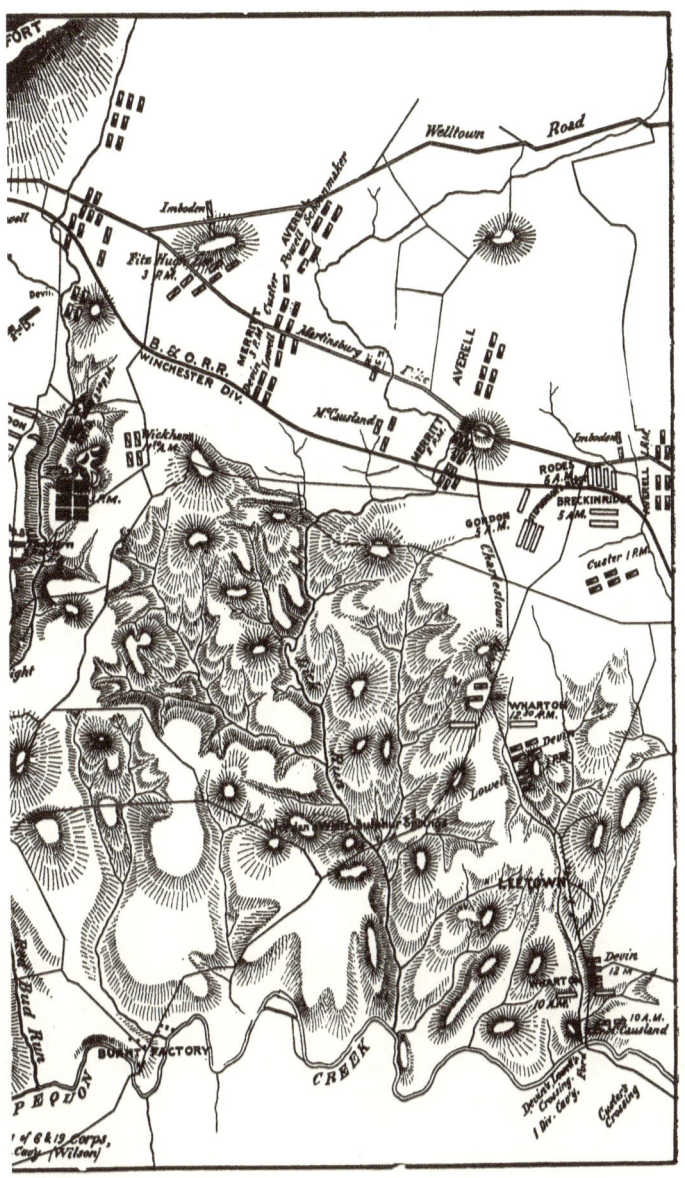

had prepared to issue, and, instead of directing his forces
south of Winchester to Newtown, moved them directly
against the former place, in the hope of striking the two divisions supposed to be there, and thus easily overwhelming
his adversary in detail. It turned out that Rodes and Gordon returned in season to take part in the main action ; but
this fact did not diminish the alacrity and confidence with
which the knowledge of Early's division of his forces had inspired the Union generals. For the new move had dispelled the anxiety always felt in regard to the army's communications in a move to the pike south of Winchester ; and
the battle was to be delivered precisely where at the outset
Sheridan had desired.

The Union commander's plan was to move his infantry,
preceded by a division of cavalry, along the Berryville pike
against Winchester, and the other two divisions of horse to
Stephenson's. His orders were, as usual, clear and precise.
Torbert was to advance across the Opequon from Summit
Point, with Merritt's division, and to form a junction near
Stephenson's with Averell, who was to move up the pike for
this purpose from Darksville. Wilson was to march rapidly
along the Berryville pike, carry the crossing of the Opequon,
and charge through the long ravine beyond, toward Winchester. The Sixth and Nineteenth Corps, the former in
advance, and Emory reporting to Wright on reaching the
Opequon, were to move along the Berryville pike as thus
cleared by Wilson. The Army of West Virginia was to
march across country, taking position in reserve at the crossing of the Opequon.

The *terrain* of the battle now to be fought demands a brief
description. Opequon Creek, rising half a dozen miles
south of Winchester, pursues its course down the Valley

four or five miles to the east of that city, and, continuing in
its general direction parallel to the pike, joins the Potomac
below Falling Waters. The watershed which enables it to
share with the Shenandoah the drainage of the lower Valley
is Limestone Ridge. The turnpike from Berryville to
Winchester, after crossing the Opequon, passes through a
wooded ravine or cañon. Running nearly due east into the
Opequon, and crossing the Valley pike about a mile south of
Winchester, is Abraham's Creek; while a nearly parallel
little affluent, about a mile and a half north of Winchester, is Red Bud Run, the Berryville pike being between
them. The selection by the Confederates of Stephenson's
Dépôt, six miles north of Winchester, as a central point for
massing troops, was obviously due to the convergence there
of four roads that led from positions occupied by Sheridan's forces—from Martinsburg, Charlestown via Smithfield,
Summit, and Berryville via Jordan's Springs. The distance
from Berryville to Winchester is ten and a half miles, the
crossing of the Opequon on the pike being about six from
the former point. Both from Berryville, therefore, on the
Union left, and from Summit Point on the Union right, the
intervals to be passed over before reaching the enemy's
lines were not serious. The region in the suburbs of Winchester was undulating, covered here and there with patches
of woods, but generally high and open, with meadows, cornfields and some houses. Abraham's Creek runs through a
deep hollow, but there is high open ground beyond on the
Front Royal and Millwood roads, while to the north the
country slopes to the Red Bud, which is lower and more
marshy; and north of the Red Bud the country is open, and
excellent for cavalry.

Early's position prior to his movement of two corps to
Martinsburg was this: Ramseur, with Nelson's artillery, a

mile east of Winchester, across the Berryville pike, along an
elevated plateau between Abraham's Creek and Red Bud
Run ; Rodes, Gordon, Wharton, with Braxton's and King's
batteries, at Stephenson's ; one division of cavalry picketing
the Opequon, extending its outpost line northward, and then
crossing the Martinsburg pike westward toward the mountains, to cover the left; the other division picketing the
right along the Millwood and Front Royal roads to the
Shenandoah.

The morning of September 19th broke auspiciously.
Sheridan's army was astir by one or two o'clock, and marching by three, in order to reach the enemy betimes.   Wilson,
galloping through the Berryville gorge, which is two or
three miles long, McIntosh's brigade in advance, at dawn
carried the earthwork at the mouth of the defile, capturing
some of its garrison.   The infantry followed in the path
thus cleared.   The Sixth Corps, Getty's division leading,
crossed the country to a point on the Berryville pike about
two miles from the Opequon.   There the head of the Nineteenth was found, ready to turn in, and was halted by
Wright, to whom Emory had reported, until the Sixth
should pass.   The troops marched on either side of the
pike, the artillery, ambulances, and such of the train as was
carried taking the macadamized road.   Then the column
crossed the Opequon near the junction of Abraham's Creek,
and thence moved through the ravine.   Debouching there,
it found Wilson still in his captured earthwork, unmolested.
Just beyond this work, rolling ground offered sufficient protection for deploying the column ; and the troops that had
been halted in the ravine being gradually drawn up on the
line, the first stage of the enterprise was successfully accomplished.

The position now taken up was two miles from Winchester, but as the enemy was more than a mile in front of the city, the Sixth Corps went into line under a heavy artillery fire, to which the Union guns soon replied. The Third Division, Ricketts, was on the right of the pike, the Second, Getty, on the left; the First, Russell, in reserve. Four batteries, as they came up, were placed on the corps front, under charge of Colonel C. H. Tompkins, Chief of Artillery. The formation was designed to be in two lines, but the Second Division was mostly placed in one line, in order to cover its ground. Wilson took position on the left of the Sixth Corps.

Infantry on marches lasting many days often tire cavalry; but for brief tramps the horsemen have the advantage. It had seemed long from Wilson's attack at 5 o'clock until 9, and it was to seem a delay still more trying before the infantry lines should be fully formed. Marching two corps, one behind the other, fording a stream and moving through a long gorge, a distance of six or eight miles, consumes many hours; and there had been additional distances for subdivisions to make across country before striking the pike.

The Nineteenth Corps had been halted to allow the Sixth to pass, and was further impeded by the guns and wagons of this corps; but Wright, at Emory's request, at length ordered these, except one battery, to the side of the road, so that the Nineteenth might have a better chance.[1] Still it was almost noon before the line was ready to move forward, the

---

[1] Sheridan, with his characteristic study of details and careful preparation, had ordered that only the necessary trains should be taken: "Corps and other independent commanders will have their commands in readiness to march at 9 o'clock P.M.—to-night. All regimental and other wagons that will inconvenience the quick movement of the troops will be parked at Summit Point with the supply train, and sent under guard to Harper's Ferry at 3 o'clock P.M. to-day" (Confidential Circular, September 18th).

which was driven into the woods,[1] broke up the continuity of the Union infantry line. Even before this, Colonel Keifer, commanding the right brigade of Ricketts, which formed the right of the Sixth Corps, had noticed that the turnpike, on which the division was dressing, bore to the left, causing an interval between it and the left of the Nineteenth Corps, and he had pushed three regiments into this space. Lieutenant-Colonel Neafie, commanding the One Hundred and Fifty-sixth New York, of the Third Brigade (Sharpe's) of Grover's division, whose regiment was on the left of that corps, says, "I was ordered to advance and guide on the right of the Sixth Corps, which order I executed, and in order to do so I was obliged to oblique my regiment very much to the left. The advance was made under a very severe fire." Braxton's guns, concentrating against the triumphant Union assailants, soon had a visible effect in checking their advance; and at this moment Battle's brigade of Rodes's division, which had just arrived from Stephenson's, and had formed in the rear of Evans, came through the woods in a charge— fresh troops at a critical hour. They struck the thinly covered junction of the right of the Sixth and the left of the Nineteenth Corps, and quickly supported on their flanks by the remainder of Rodes and all of Gordon, the broken brigade rallying with the rest, they succeeded in driving back Ricketts's division of the Sixth Corps and Grover's of the Nineteenth, while the whole line to some extent felt the effect and came back somewhat toward the position in front

---

[1] "Charged with fixed bayonets at double quick, broke his lines on the active front of the brigade, and drove him through and out of the woods. As the troops entered the woods, I was ordered by General Grover to halt and hold that position, and not to go further into the woods, but the charge was so rapid and impetuous, and the men so much excited by the sight of the enemy in full retreat before them, that it was impossible to execute the order, and the whole line pressed forward to the extreme edge of the timber" (Report of General Birge.)

of the ravine from which it had advanced. This temporary advantage, which caused the chief loss of prisoners suffered by the Union forces, cost Early the life of Rodes, one of the most experienced and skilful of Confederate division commanders.

At this juncture Russell's division of the Sixth Corps splendidly improved a golden opportunity. Ordered at once to move up into the front line, now needing reinforcement, this change brought it into the gap created by the Confederate charge, and continuing its advance it struck the flank of the hostile force which was sweeping away the Union right, and aided by the Fifth Maine battery, which enfiladed the enemy's line with canister, at once turned the tide. The enemy retreated, the line was re-established, the fugitives were gathered from the woods in which they had taken refuge, while the gallant division took position on the right of its corps. But in the hour of his triumph Russell had fallen.[1] "His death," said Sheridan, "brought sadness to every heart in the army." The

---

[1] The report of the operations of the division was made by Major Dalton, A.A.G. "The enemy," he says, "having pushed back the Second Division of the Nineteenth Corps and a portion of the Third Division of this corps, moved down toward the pike, delivering a severe fire of musketry from the woods and cornfields on the right. The Third Brigade (Edwards) was now rapidly moved by the flank to the right of the pike, then forward with the First Brigade (Campbell), under a heavy fire, to a crest commanding the woods and fields through which the enemy moved. This advance was very much assisted by the First New York Battery, commanded by Lieutenant Johnson, which did splendid execution, and was fought with gallantry under a very annoying musketry fire. At this time, General Upton moved his brigade into line to the right of the pike at an oblique angle to it, thence forward into the woods, delivering heavy volleys into masses of the enemy, who were coming up. This fresh fire from the Second Brigade [Upton] soon caused the enemy to fall back, so that the whole line moved forward to a position which was easily held till the latter part of the afternoon, though occasionally sharp musketry fire was interchanged. While personally superintending the advance of the First and Third Brigades to the crest previously referred to, and which he considered of the utmost importance, General Russell was killed by a piece of shell which passed through his heart—he had just before received a

broken portion of Ricketts's line was quickly re-formed behind the First Division, now under Upton, and again moved forward, while Dwight's division having taken the place of Grover's on the right of the line, the latter was promptly rallied and brought up.

It was now long past midday, and after the fierce and continuous struggle which had included Sheridan's initial advance, his recoil under the charge from the Confederate left, and his rally and re-advance toward Early's position in the woods, there was a comparative lull, which the Union commander employed in preparing for a culminating effort with his full strength. The Army of West Virginia, which had been left in reserve, was now moving on the scene. Sheridan's original purpose had been to use it on the left for seizing the Valley pike, when he had supposed that he would have but half the enemy's force to meet at Winchester, and that it would attempt escape to Strasburg ; but the temporary repulse of the Union right, and the strength developed by the enemy there, made it evident that whatever danger was to

---

bullet wound in the left breast, but had not mentioned this to any of his staff, continuing to urge forward his troops."

General Upton's account is as follows : "After marching about half a mile, the troops on the right of the pike gave way ; line was immediately formed, and soon after Lieutenant-Colonel Kent gave me the order to move the brigade to the right. The brigade was faced to the right and marched across the pike into a narrow belt of timber, where the second line was halted and faced to the front. The Second Connecticut continued the march, inclining to the right, making our line oblique to that upon which the enemy was advancing. Bayonets were fixed, and instructions given not to fire till within close range. The enemy's left, extending far beyond our right, advanced till within two hundred yards of our line, when a brisk flank fire was opened by the One Hundred and Twenty-first New York and Sixty-fifth New York, causing him to retire in great disorder. The Second Connecticut immediately moved forward and opened fire. The whole line then advanced, driving the enemy and inflicting a heavy loss in the killed and wounded. The brigade was halted at the edge of the wood, which position it held till the attack was renewed in the afternoon. On the left of the brigade the Thirty-seventh Massachusetts Volunteers rendered invaluable service in supporting Stevens's [Fifth Maine] Battery."

be apprehended would come from that flank—this, indeed, was probable at the outset, since the absent Confederate divisions, hurrying in from Stephenson's and beyond to Ramseur's relief, or driven in by the cavalry there, must necessarily fall upon the Union right.

Leaving a small portion of the corps to guard his trains, Crook was ordered to move the rest rapidly to the front, on the pike. Thoburn, marching forward with the First and Third Brigades of his division, found the ravine "filled with wagons, artillery, ambulances, and stragglers," seriously impeding his progress and that of Duval, commanding the Second Division. Thoburn, under Crook's direction, formed in two lines, Wells the first and Harris the second, on the right of the pike, behind the heavy wood, in front of which Emory was fighting, and then moved forward to Emory's right, connecting closely with it and compactly filling the space to the swampy hollow drained by Red Bud Run. Duval went on the north side of the run, holding Crook's right. Sheridan at that moment arrived, and directed Thoburn, as soon as Duval was up, and connecting with him, to charge directly through the woods in his front. A rousing cheer announced Duval's approach, and both he and Thoburn rushed at the woods with a confident eagerness that broke Gordon's division, which was at that point.

But this was not the only fresh force that now threatened the Confederate left. Torbert, setting out early in the morning with Merritt's division, had crossed the Opequon at Ridgway's and Locke's fords, while Averell had come up the Martinsburg pike. Merritt dispersed the enemy's pickets, but a mile and a half beyond found himself checked by Wharton's division of infantry and King's battery, which were at Stephenson's, and had advanced to meet him. The incident was vexatious; but Averell, driving the enemy in

his own front, comprising Imboden's cavalry, now under
Smith, and McCausland's, now under Ferguson, all the way
up the pike from Darksville to Stephenson's, thus came
into the rear of the infantry facing Merritt, which thereupon
abandoned its position. Only with difficulty and some hard
fighting did Breckenridge succeed in bringing off Wharton
on the pike from Stephenson's, arriving at Winchester about
2 P.M. Patton's brigade was left to help Fitz Lee's cavalry
to withstand Torbert ; but before long the latter was driving
in both Patton and Fitz Lee, "the cavalry," says Early,
" coming back in great confusion, followed by the enemy's."
To add to the stress, Wilson, far on the left, had so threatened the Millwood and Valley pikes, that Early was compelled to weaken Fitz Lee, even in his need, by detaching
Wickham's brigade, so as to secure a route for a retreat,
which was all he could now hope for. He had also at first
moved two of Wharton's three brigades toward his right,
where he feared being cut off; but almost immediately these
were sent back, for by four o'clock Crook and Torbert were
simultaneously attacking Early's left flank—Averell on the
west of the Martinsburg pike, Merritt on the east, and
Crook on Merritt's left.

Crook, on entering the fight along Red Bud Run, had
struck Patton's infantry brigade and Payne's cavalry, which
had been trying to hold back Torbert from coming in on the
rear of Early's left flank. Breckenridge was accordingly
now employing the other two brigades of Wharton and
King's battery in checking Torbert. As Breckenridge's line
was necessarily at right angles with the Martinsburg pike,
its flank was in turn exposed to Crook, who was advancing
between Wharton and Gordon. The latter, therefore, put
in Evans's brigade to fill this gap ; and Thoburn soon received a flank fire. He saw he must change front to the

left, "but the instincts of the soldiers," he says, with a fine frankness, "prompted to the proper movement; before my commands could be conveyed, each man was marching and facing toward the enemy's fire. Colonel Duval's division crossed Red Bud Run or morass at this point, and his command and my own mingled together and acted together until the pursuit was over. 'Tis true our lines were broken and gone; but had we moved in such a manner as to preserve our lines, the enemy would have escaped unhurt, or else driven us back."

While Crook and Torbert were coming in on the right, the Sixth and Nineteenth Corps had been advanced with equal success on their fronts, driving Ramseur and Rodes steadily back to Winchester. For "as soon as the firing was heard in rear of our left flank," says Early, "the infantry commenced falling back along the whole line." A mile of such progress on both flanks brought the Union troops close to the town, where a line of breastworks, constructed early in the war, gave the shattered Confederate forces some refuge, and batteries were planted there and also at the toll-gate and the cemetery. Wickham, hurrying back to Early's left, now took position on Fort Hill, confronting Averell. The remainder of the Confederate line was as before, namely, Fitz Lee, Wharton, Gordon, Rodes, Ramseur, and Lomax, the latter partly opposite the Union left, and partly at the junction of the Millwood and Valley pikes, the former of which Wilson held. The effort to retain this line was fruitless. "The enemy's cavalry," says Early, "again charged around my left flank, and the men began to give way again." As day ended, Early's forces broke through Winchester in complete retreat. "I never saw our troops in such confusion before," wrote a wounded and captured Confederate officer in his diary. "Night found Sheridan's hosts in full and exultant possession of much-abused, beloved Winchester.

The hotel hospital was pretty full of desperately wounded and dying Confederates. The entire building was shrouded in darkness during the dreadful night. Sleep was impossible, as the groans, sighs, shrieks, prayers, and oaths of the wretched sufferers, combined with my own severe pain, banished all thought of rest. . . . Our scattered troops, closely followed by the large army of pursuers, retreated rapidly and in disorder through the city. It was a sad, humiliating sight."

The Sixth Corps, on the left, moved over to the pike south of Winchester, but as it had been a hard and long day of marching and fighting, there was no attempt at infantry pursuit, and probably nothing would have been gained by pushing these tired troops after the flying enemy. The cavalry only followed him up the pike to Kernstown, where Ramseur, by maintaining his organization, effectually covered the retreat, which afterward, under the shelter of the darkness, was continued toward Strasburg. The Union forces were overjoyed at their success, and their enthusiasm became unbounded when General Sheridan, with Generals Wright, Emory, and Crook, rode in front of their lines. The commander-in-chief, elated with his first victory as the leader of an army, hastened to indite a despatch which told the story of the day in the electric phraseology that soon came to be popularly associated with him: "We have just sent them whirling through Winchester, and we are after them to·morrow. This army behaved splendidly." The note of exultation was taken up throughout the North, and the phrase "whirling through Winchester" was on every tongue. Grant ordered each of his two Richmond armies to fire a salute of one hundred guns, and added in his despatch to Sheridan, "If practicable, push your success and make all you can of it," and President Lincoln, on the day after the battle, at the suggestion and urgent wish of Grant, gave the victor the

well-merited appointment of brigadier-general in the regular army, besides the permanent command of the Middle
Division, to which his appointment had till then been but
temporary. Congratulations from all sides poured in, but
none heartier than the following:

"Have just heard of your great victory. God bless you all, officers
and men. Strongly inclined to come up and see you.   A. LINCOLN."

Grant followed his first terse despatch with a longer one:

"I congratulate you and the army serving under you for the great victory just achieved. It has been most opportune in point of time and
effect. It will open again to the Government and to the public the very
important line of road from Baltimore to the Ohio, and also the
Chesapeake Canal. Better still, it wipes out much of the stain upon
our arms by previous disasters in that locality. May your good work
continue is now the prayer of all loyal men."

The conflict had been a bloody one. The Union loss was
from 4,900 to 5,000 men, and of these about 4,300 were killed
or wounded, the killed including Russell, and the wounded
Generals Upton, McIntosh, who lost a leg, and Chapman,
and Colonels Duval, commanding a division, and Sharpe,
commanding a brigade. The exact figures are not ascer-
tainable, since in the following table the losses of Crook's
Army of West Virginia include the very slight casualties
it suffered at Fisher's Hill, while those of the other three
corps embrace only Winchester:

	Killed.	Wounded.	Missing.	Total.
Cavalry Corps	65	267	109	441
Sixth Corps	213	1,424	48	1,685
Nineteenth Corps	275	1,228	453	1,956
Eighth Corps	105	840	8	953
	658	3,759	618	5,035

Early's loss was from 3,900 to 4,000. He officially reported the casualties of the infantry and artillery in this
battle to be 3,611 ;[1] and supposing his cavalry loss to be in
the same ratio as that of the Union cavalry, *i.e.*, about one-
eleventh of the whole, we reach the figures already indicated. Of his casualties nearly 2,000 were prisoners ; and
many of his wounded, also, were left in the Winchester hospitals or elsewhere along the Valley. Among his killed
were Generals Rodes and Godwin and Colonel Patton, a

---

[1] "In this battle the loss in the infantry and artillery was: killed, 226 ;
wounded, 1,567 ; missing, 1,818—total, 3,611. There is no full report of the cavalry, but the total loss in killed and wounded from September 1st to October 1st is :
killed, 60 ; wounded, 288—total, 348 ; but many were captured, though a good many
are missing as stragglers, and a number of them reported missing in the infantry
were not captured, but are stragglers and skulkers" (Early to Lee, October 9th).
Sheridan stated that "most of the enemy's wounded and all of their killed fell
into our hands," and Surgeon Brinton reported to Surgeon-General Barnes, two
or three days after the battle, as follows : "On my arrival here I found about
4,000 Union and 1,200 rebel wounded." On a subsequent day he telegraphed
again : "I sent yesterday (September 22d) 700 wounded to Sandy Hook Hospital.
There are still 3,800 here, including 700 rebels. I learn that more wounded men
are on their way to this place from the front [*i.e.*, Fisher's Hill].
An unsigned memorandum or enclosure, accompanying Early's report of the
battle, gives this statement of the killed and wounded in the artillery :

	Killed.	Wounded.	Total.
Rodes's Division........................... ...	89	597	686
Early's "	42	285	327
Gordon's "	32	364	396
Breckenridge's Division..................	23	194	217
Artillery Corps........	13	68	81
	199	1,508	1,707

Early's report, however, as has been said, gives the number of killed and
wounded as 1,793—the slight discrepancy being not unusual. It will be understood, of course, that Early's old division was commanded by Ramseur, and
Breckenridge's by Wharton.
    In the Nineteenth Corps earlier returns had indicated a greater loss in the bat-
tle of the Opequon. A return of the Second (Grover's) Division, made the next day,

brigade commander; among his severely wounded, Generals Fitz Lee and York. By promptly recognizing his impending defeat, Early was able to save his trains and stores, and the transportable portion of his sick and wounded; but he left as trophies to the victor five pieces of artillery and nine battle-flags, captured on the field.

September 20th, near Strasburg, was, by brigades, as follows, for the ten days preceding.

	Killed.	Wounded.	Missing.	Total.	Strength.
1. Birge..	94	348	271	713	1,495
2. Molineux	58	344	262	664	1,268
3. Sharpe	38	215	74	327	796
4. Shunk	33	141	21	195	1,194
Artillery...............	2	6	0	8	137
	225	1,054	628	1,907	4,890

The last column in this table is the aggregate "effective strength," officers and men, after action, showing also that the division had an effective strength of 6,797 men just before the battle. But the remarks on the original return are that "the lists of killed and wounded are made up from actual knowledge; the missing will be greatly decreased, as men are constantly coming in." This last statement proved to be true, according to the revised table given in the text. A return of the whole Nineteenth Corps by divisions for the ten days preceding September 20th, which is nearly equivalent to the losses at Winchester, since there were not fifty casualties apart from that battle, was as follows:

	KILLED.			WOUNDED.			MISSING.			AGGREGATE CASUALTIES.		
	Officers.	Men.	Total.	Officers.	Men.	Total.	Officers.	Men.	Total.	Officers.	Men.	Total.
1. Dwight	6	65	71	21	414	435	..	60	60	27	539	566
2. Grover.......	19	206	225	77	977	1,054	10	618	628	106	1,801	1,907
	25	271	296	98	1,391	1,489	10	678	688	133	2,340	2,473

These casualties were reduced by the arrival of many who were missing, and perhaps also by the return to duty of some of the wounded before the date of the revised records.

This battle of the Opequon—for so the engagement was styled by General Sheridan, to distinguish it from previous contests around Winchester—restored the lower Valley to Union control, from which it was never again wrested; it permanently relieved Maryland and Pennsylvania from the periodical invasions to which they had been subjected during three years, and the national capital from further humiliations. This result had been accomplished by a battle which, taken with its sequences, inflicted upon the Confederate forces losses in troops nearly as great as those which were sustained by the Union arms—an experience fatal to the fast dwindling forces of the South.

The moral effect of this victory on the North was most wholesome. The discouragement which had prevailed regarding operations in the Shenandoah Valley, over which a sinister fortune had brooded since the year 1861, wholly disappeared. The magnetism the young commander exercised upon his troops spread through the country, and henceforth caused his fortunes in the Valley to be watched with the eager expectation and hearty good-will which fall to the lot of the favorite soldier.

As to his unfortunate antagonist, his chagrin manifested itself in a declaration, more than two years later, that he could only attribute his escape from utter annihilation to the incapacity of his opponent; that "instead of being promoted, Sheridan ought to have been cashiered for this battle;" and that "a skilful and energetic commander of the enemy's forces would have crushed Ramseur before any assistance could have reached him, and thus insured the destruction of my whole force ; and, later in the day, when the battle had turned against us, with the immense superiority in cavalry which Sheridan had, and the advantage of the open country, would have destroyed my whole force, and

captured everything I had." In his ill-concealed vexation,
the Confederate general here passes upon himself as severe
a condemnation as his most bitter detractors could frame;
for the act of leaving Ramseur isolated was his own; and the
great superiority of the Union cavalry was, or should have
been, as well known to him before as after the battle at
Winchester, and should have dissuaded him from risking an
engagement in that open country. Early deserves, nevertheless, the credit of great vigor and skill in fighting
the battle thus forced upon him, and in saving his trains
and his army out of the ruin his opponent had prepared
for him.

The battle of the Opequon was universally accepted as a
vindication of Sheridan's views and policy. His belief that
he ought to wait until Early should be weakened, before assaulting him, had been shown to be one that comported with
extraordinary energy; and a striking feature of the action of
the Opequon had been the personal presence and supervision
of Sheridan at every important point in the front line. If it
be true, as Sheridan's report says, that "at Winchester, for
a moment, the contest was uncertain," might not the presence
of Kershaw at that juncture have turned the scale the other
way? Beyond question, the confidence with which the Union
general that day inspired his troops proved invaluable in the
subsequent stages of the campaign.

CHAPTER X.

AT daylight, September 20th, Sheridan marched up the Valley pike, the Sixth Corps on the left, the Nineteenth on the right, and the Eighth bringing up the rear, in pursuit of the enemy. The cavalry had preceded, Averell on the Back road, Merritt on the Valley pike, and Wilson on the Front Royal pike. Early simultaneously retreated to his old position on Fisher's Hill, two miles south of Strasburg.

Fisher's Hill offers the first strong defensive line to a force advancing from Winchester. Here the main Valley, twenty miles wide below, narrows to four, through the interposition of the isolated Massanutten chain, which rises half way between North Mountain on the west and the Blue Ridge on the east. The westernmost tier of the Massanutten system is composed of Peaked Ridge and Three Top, lying in the same straight line, and substantially a part of the same upheaval. Its western base is washed by the North Fork of the Shenandoah, which turns sharply to the east around the north terminus of Three Top, at Strasburg, and makes a confluence with the South Fork ten miles beyond, near Front Royal. Cedar Creek winds southward into the North Fork just below Strasburg, while to a rivulet which adds its waters to the North Fork, two miles above the town, is given the expressive name of Tumbling Run. West of the North Fork runs the Valley pike from Strasburg

to Staunton, and by its side the then broken and disused
Manassas Gap Railroad. Fisher's Hill is the precipitous
bluff beyond and overhanging Tumbling Run, which at that
point still further narrows the Valley. Here Early halted,
the hill with the Shenandoah beyond protecting his right,
while to seal his left against approach he began to erect additional works across the Valley, westward to the North
Mountain. The pike, which runs over the hill in a depression, was for a long distance under fire from his guns ; and
so secure did he feel, that the ammunition-boxes were taken
from the caissons and placed for convenience behind the
breastworks. His line was substantially the same as when
he had occupied this position in August, Wharton being on
the right, Gordon next, then Pegram (commanding Ramseur's old division), then Ramseur (now transferred to
Rodes's former division), and finally Lomax's cavalry, dismounted, on Ramseur's left. Fitz Lee's cavalry, now under
Wickham, was sent to the right, to prevent the flanking of
Fisher's Hill through the Luray Valley, the chief position
selected for him being at Millford, on the pike, about twelve
miles above Front Royal. Here the South Fork nears the
Blue Ridge, leaving a narrow defensible gorge between.
Early, while at Fisher's Hill, was deprived of the services of
Breckenridge, who received orders from Richmond to return
to Southwest Virginia. With Breckenridge, Rodes, and Fitz
Lee gone, he had fewer lieutenants on whose aid and vig-
ilance to rely.

During the afternoon of the 20th, Wright and Emory arrived at Cedar Creek, and crossing, went into position on the
heights fronting Strasburg, with the Sixth Corps on the
right, and the Nineteenth on the left, the latter extending
nearly to the Front Royal road, which, in fact, was crossed
by a detached subdivision ; while the Eighth, when it came

up, was halted upon the left bank of the stream. By evening the Union pickets occupied the northern part of Strasburg and the Confederate pickets the southern.

Throughout the 21st, Sheridan was occupied in positioning his main infantry line, which, advancing through the town, drove the enemy's skirmishers back to the defences at Fisher's Hill. When the morning mist cleared away, Early was found to have been busy through the night in further strengthening his position with works of earth and stone and in throwing down abatis. Starting out with his staff early in the day, Sheridan rode from one end to the other of the picket line, noting the ground. Accompanied by General Wright, he reconnoitred especially the right flank, and there, well in advance, the chief point to occupy was seen to be the high land on the north of Tumbling Run, confronting the enemy's main position. Wright at once sent three regiments, two from his Third Division and one from the Second, to seize this spot; but the enemy also knew its value, and repulsed the Union forces. The remainder of Warner's brigade of the Second was added, and the position most gallantly carried by Warner. From that time till sundown the axes of the pioneers resounded, making a way for planting the artillery on the important vantage-ground thus secured, while the excellent view now obtainable showed that the enemy had not ceased his defensive labors.

But neither gradual approaches nor experimental assaults on these frowning heights formed the sum of the purposes of the Union commander. He resolved to repeat his tactics of the Opequon by again turning the enemy's left flank with Crook's command, doing this with all secrecy, since the Confederate station on Three Top commanded both camps. At the same time he proposed to move Torbert up the Luray

Valley, there getting past the enemy's right flank, if possible and crossing Massanutten to his rear. The night of the 21st he sent this despatch to Grant : " General Wilson's cavalry division charged the enemy at Front Royal pike this morning, and drove them from Front Royal up the Luray Valley for a distance of six miles. I directed two brigades of the First Cavalry Division, with General Wilson's division, to follow the enemy up that Valley, and to push them vigorously."

The Sixth Corps continued its lodgment on the valuable line it had gained, confronting the enemy along Tumbling Run. The difficult ground, densely wooded, broken by ledges and cut up by ravines, made this an all-night task ; and at daybreak the Nineteenth was shifted to the right and front of its first position, occupying the ground held on the 21st by the Sixth, with which latter its right then connected. The skirmish line of the Nineteenth, extending to the left, and its reserves along the railroad, were not changed, nor the regiment ordered to reconnoitre the extreme left the day before. The troops intrenched, and the artillery was placed in position. Sheridan finding the enemy's right impregnable, and planning to turn his left, had already by degrees moved the two corps well to the right ; but to connect with Crook when the latter should reappear on the scene, besides hiding his movements in the interim, Ricketts's division of the Sixth Corps, which was already on the right, took a desirable position, during the afternoon, still farther to the front, very handsomely driving in the enemy's skirmish line, aided by the three rifle batteries of the Sixth Corps. Averell came up on the right of Ricketts. The Second Division of the corps was then moved to the right and front, connecting with Ricketts, and the First to connect with the Second. It was hardly half a mile from the ridge thus gained to the Fisher's Hill trenches across the ravine.

These movements occupied the day; and Early, fearing rather than hoping attack, thought it had begun with the last movements of Ricketts and Averell. When he saw their advance, "orders were given" he says, "for my troops to retire after dark, as I knew my force was not strong enough to resist a determined assault." Just before sunset, Crook, who, with admirable silence and secrecy, had been all day moving toward and then along Little North Mountain, under the cover of the woods, till he had gained the enemy's left flank and rear, rushed across the intervening space, and, before the enemy could recover from his surprise, was over his intrenchments. "Had the heavens opened," writes one officer, "and we been seen descending from the clouds, no greater consternation would have been created."

More quickly than the story can be told, the divisions of Thoburn and Duval swept along the enemy's left flank, taking his line in reverse, and driving before them the astonished dismounted cavalry of Lomax. In a few minutes Ricketts had joined his right to Crook's left, and the remainder of the Sixth Corps and the Nineteenth, taking up the charge, descended into the ravine of Tumbling Run, with a headlong rush over fields, walls, rocks, and felled trees. Making their way across the brook, they were soon scrambling up heights that it had seemed madness to attack, while Sheridan and his admirable staff were on every part of the line, shouting "Forward! Forward everything!" and to all inquiries for instructions the reply was still, "Go on, don't stop, go on!" Formations were little heeded in the rush: but the whole Confederate line broke from its trenches, Lomax's dismounted cavalry on the left giving way first, whereupon Ramseur and Pegram were routed in turn. "My

8*

whole force retired in considerable confusion," says General Early. In truth, between sundown and dark every portion of the strong position at Fisher's Hill was carried, the action being so rapid that the enemy had not even time to get his guns out of position upon the pike, and sixteen of them were captured by the Union forces.

Early fled in disorder, under cover of the darkness, through Woodstock to a point about four miles beyond, called Narrow Passage, just north of Edenburg. Sheridan pushed after him all night with Devin's brigade of Merritt's cavalry and the Nineteenth and Sixth Corps, both corps reporting to Wright, and the Nineteenth in advance,[1] as far as Woodstock; but the darkness rendered this pursuit unavailing. Devin received instructions from Sheridan himself, Torbert being in Luray Valley, but "found the roads blocked up with our infantry advancing," and only reached the head of the column about ten o'clock. He then got two guns in position, and opened on the enemy's rear, but was afterward sent into the fields on the left of the turnpike, on a line parallel with the head of the infantry. The latter, since the night had been thus employed, were halted from dawn till afternoon of the next day for sleep and food.

Unfortunately Torbert did not succeed in driving Wick-

---

[1] "The advance was made with as much rapidity as the darkness and the nature of the ground would permit. About 9.30 P.M. our skirmish line was fired at, and by some unfortunate mistake, the regiments in the rear, not belonging to my command, opened fire upon my reserves and skirmish line, from which I lost a number of men. Hardly had we advanced a distance of a mile before a brisk fire was again opened upon us from musketry and artillery, and again I sustained a fire from our own troops in the rear. The enemy was evidently prepared to meet us at this point, wire and other obstacles had been placed to delay the skirmish line, and two pieces of artillery were well trained upon the road. After a short delay, the advance was again made, and the enemy driven with but little opposition. The road was found strewn with the remains of burning wagons, and a large number of prisoners was captured by this command and sent to the rear. At 3.30 A.M. we bivouacked on the south side of Woodstock" (Molineux's Report).

ham's cavalry from its strong defensive position at Millford,
and hence the portion of Sheridan's plan which contemplated cutting off the enemy's retreat by seizing the pike
at New Market, was not carried out.   The 21st Torbert had
moved through Front Royal into the Luray Valley, with
the divisions of Merritt and Wilson, excepting Devin's brigade of the former, which was left to guard the rear of the
army at Cedar Creek.   He found Wickham, with his own
and Payne's brigade, posted on the south side of Gooney
Run.   At 2 A.M. of the 22d, Custer's brigade was sent back
across the South Fork, with orders, says Torbert, to march
around the enemy's flank to his rear, as he seemed too
strong to attack in front; but Torbert, on moving forward
at daylight, found that the enemy had retreated to a still
stronger position on the south side of Millford Creek, with
his left on the Shenandoah and his right on a knob of the
Blue Ridge, occupying a short, compact line.   The bank of
the creek seemed to Torbert too precipitous for a direct attack; and "not knowing," he says, "that the army had
made an attack at Fisher's Hill, and thinking that the sacrifice would be too great to attack without that knowledge, I
concluded to withdraw to a point opposite McCoy's Ferry."
The 23d, Wilson crossed McCoy's ford, and Merritt went
back through Front Royal, where he skirmished with
Mosby, driving him off with loss.   During the afternoon
"news was received of the victory at Fisher's Hill, and
directions to make up the Luray Valley."   Both divisions
at once moved forward and bivouacked at Millford Creek,
which the enemy had evacuated.[1]   Had they been able to

---

[1] "Its operations [the cavalry's] up the Luray Valley, on which I calculated so
much, were an entire failure.   They were held at Millford by two small brigades
of Fitz Lee's cavalry, and then fell back toward Front Royal, until after they had
learned of our success at Fisher's Hill" (Sheridan to Grant, September 25th).

move the day before across the South Fork through Massa
nutten Gap, a powerful body of horse would have been in
the rear of the enemy, upon his line of retreat; but Early
was fully alive to this danger, and had guarded against it
with Wickham's force.

Sheridan's loss at the battle of Fisher's Hill was only about
400 men; Early's, between 1,300 and 1,400, the language
of his despatch to Lee being as follows: "The loss in the
infantry and artillery was 30 killed, 210 wounded, and 995
missing; total 1,235.[1] I have been able to get no report of the
loss in the cavalry, but it was slight." As Lomax received
the brunt of Crook's attack, he must have suffered his share of
the loss; and since Sheridan reported that he had 1,100 prisoners, the difference of 105 between Early's and Sheridan's tally
can be safely ascribed to the cavalry, thus making Early's
total loss 1,340, besides some cavalry killed and wounded.

Winchester and Fisher's Hill were really parts of the same
move. If we take the two together, we have a total loss for
Sheridan as follows:

	Killed.	Wounded.	Missing.	Aggregate.
Cavalry Corps................	65	267	109	441
Sixth Corps..................	237	1,634	51	1,922
Nineteenth Corps	286	1,275	455	2,016
Eighth Corps	105	840	8	953
	693	4,016	623	5,332

In the affair of Fisher's Hill the cavalry losses are not included, but they could hardly bring the total up to 5,400.

---

[1] The unsigned memorandum accompanying Early's despatch to Lee, spoken of
on a previous page, gave these details of the killed and wounded: Ramseur, 105,
Pegram, 64; Gordon, 49; Wharton, 14; Artillery, 29; total, 261, 32 being killed
and 229 wounded.

This is almost exactly Early's loss for the two battles—nearly 4,000 at Winchester and over 1,350 at Fisher's Hill. Thus Sheridan's victories had been won with a loss on his part only equal to the enemy's, while the guns, the flags, the military positions, and the moral effect were his prizes. Besides, in ratio to his total strength he had suffered a loss far less than the enemy's, and it was precisely this fact that was to ruin the Confederate campaign in the Valley. He had taken a great number of prisoners—a matter of vital consequence in the waning days of the revolt—while he had lost very few, the highest proportion to the total casualties being in the cavalry.[1]

[1] The returns of Crook's West Virginia army, as has already been noted, lumped its casualties at Winchester and Fisher's Hill, but the other two corps (the cavalry being too little engaged to be included) suffered as follows at the latter point:

	Killed.	Wounded.	Missing.	Aggregate.
Sixth Corps	24	210	3	237
Nineteenth Corps	11	47	2	60

Here, also, some discrepancies occur in earlier reports. A list of casualties for the Nineteenth Corps at Fisher's Hill, made out six days later, September 28th, at Harrisonburg, runs as follows:

Division.	Killed.	Wounded.	Missing.	Total.
First, Dwight	4	29	..	33
Second, Grover................. ...	8	47	2	57
Artillery	..	9	..	9
	12	85	2	99

A list of the killed and wounded in the corps in both battles, made at the same date and place, called "Casualties for the ten days ending September 29th," and there were hardly a score after September 22d, gives those of the First Division, exclusive of the missing, as 83 killed and 474 wounded—total 557; the Second Division, 254 killed and 1,125 wounded—total 1,379; the reserve artillery, 9 wounded. This would make the total of killed and wounded of the corps in both battles 1,945, instead of 1,561, as in the text. But no doubt the revised figures of the text are the more accurate.

Fisher's Hill was the corollary of Winchester. It was a hurricane battle, totally unlike the one delivered three days before; and the Union troops were as palpably inspirited by their previous triumph as the Confederates were unnerved from the same cause. Early expressly attributes the capture of so many of his men to their attempt to "make their way across the North Fork to Massanutten Mountain, under the impression that the enemy had possession of the Valley pike in our rear." The turning of the enemy's left flank at Winchester made the repetition of this manoeuvre at Fisher's Hill the more easy of accomplishment, the fugitives instinctively bolting for the right of their line, even though they scattered among the mountains in so doing. And that the effect of Winchester was not greater on the troops than it was on their commanders, is attested by the promptness and audacity with which Sheridan attacked Fisher's Hill, a position vastly stronger than any his adversary had occupied in the Lower Valley; while Early, who had been underrating his opponent, parading before his fortified front at Halltown, and unhesitatingly scattering his divisions along the pike to Martinsburg, had, just before being attacked at Fisher Hill, given the order to retreat from this stronghold, simply because he observed that an assault on him was contemplated.

Early's second reverse was not due to any mistaken estimate in regard to the natural strength of his position, but to his delay to occupy it until he no longer had men enough to properly cover it. The time to hold Fisher's Hill was when Kershaw's departure had imperilled his communications between that point and Winchester. The first line he took up in the Valley, that of the Opequon, was admirably selected for its purpose. Although it risked a swift advance from Harper's Ferry to Winchester, yet this movement would in turn be exposed to an assault from Bunker Hill

on its rear. Thus Early's Opequon position, differing from
the simpler and more obvious device of a line stretched
across the pike, where the rivers and mountains gave a narrow passage, was really less hazardous than it seemed. In
addition, as his opponent, in proceeding from Halltown to
Winchester, occupied two marches for that purpose, the first
one carrying him to the Clifton-Berryville line, Early had
always ample time to retreat up the Valley, without accepting battle. This line of the Opequon was advantageous in
constantly threatening Maryland, and in keeping the railroad broken. But when the Union commander was found
stationing himself permanently on the Clifton-Berryville
line, and when Early's own army was weakened by the detachment of Kershaw, a few hours' march might at any time
bring Sheridan to the outworks of Winchester; and even
Stephenson's Dépôt as a main camp was too far north to
escape the necessity of accepting battle. In the case of an
attack still farther south, on his communications, Early
might have been in a still worse plight.

Besides, he had remained in the Lower Valley till he
had exhausted his supplies. He had already been receiving
his food from the Upper Valley, on a long line, exposed to
the attacks of cavalry, in which arm his opponent was very
strong. "Nearly the whole of our bread," he says, "was
obtained by threshing the wheat and then having it ground
by details from my command, and it sometimes happened
that while my troops were fighting, the very flour which was
to furnish them with bread for their next meal was being
ground under the protection of their guns.[1] Latterly our

---

[1] "I think now that Sheridan is superior to Early—besides the latter being
where it must take a good part of his force to collect supplies for the balance "
(Grant to Halleck, August 29th). Some of the first prisoners taken in the August
advance from Halltown were Confederate soldiers threshing wheat in barns.

flour had been obtained from the Upper Valley, but also by details sent for that purpose. The horses and mules, including the cavalry horses, were sustained almost entirely by grazing." Why then did he remain, under such circumstances, between Winchester and Martinsburg? We must resort again to his own explanation: "I knew my danger, but I could occupy no other position that would have enabled me to accomplish the desired object. If I had moved up the Valley at all, I could not have stopped short of New Market, for between that place and the country in which I was there was no forage for my horses; and this would have enabled the enemy to resume the use of the railroad and canal, and return all the troops from Grant's army to him."

Still, Early could not forever hold on to the Baltimore and Ohio Railroad, with Sheridan's strong army many miles south of it, threatening his rear. Sooner or later, he must abandon it. The railroad, after all, was but one of several Union lines between East and West, and holding it deprived him of the same opportunity for threatening his immediate adversary's communications that the latter had for molesting his. When at last he went by compulsion to Fisher's Hill, it was with a force too broken and dispirited to hold it.

Writing to Lee from Port Republic, three days after his second discomfiture, Early used the following language:

" The enemy's immense superiority in cavalry and the inefficiency of the greater part of mine has been the cause of all my disasters. In the affair at Fisher's Hill the cavalry gave way, but it was flanked. This would have been remedied if the troops had remained steady, but a panic seized them at the idea of being flanked, and, without being defeated, they broke, many of them fleeing shamefully. The artillery was not captured by the enemy, but abandoned by the infantry. My troops are very much shattered, the men very much exhausted, and many of them without shoes."

Two days later, the 27th, Lee replied from Petersburg as follows :

"As far as I can judge at this distance, you have operated more with divisions than with your concentrated strength. Circumstances may have rendered it necessary, but such a course is to be avoided if possible. It will require the greatest watchfulness, the greatest promptness, and the most untiring energy on your part to arrest the progress of the enemy in his present tide of success. All the reserves in the Valley have been ordered to you. Breckenridge will join you or co-operate, as circumstances will permit, with all his force. Rosser left this morning for Burkesville (intersection of Danville and Southside Railroads), where he will shape his course as you direct. I have given you all I can. You must use the resources you have, so as to gain success. The enemy must be defeated, and I rely upon you to do it. I will endeavor to have shoes, arms, and ammunition supplied you. Set all your officers to work bravely and hopefully, and all will go well."

On the North this second great victory had an effect no less cheering than the first. Grant again ordered a salute of one hundred guns. "Keep on," he said to Sheridan, "and your good work will cause the fall of Richmond." Stanton sent orders for the firing of one hundred guns each to Wallace, Cadwalader, Couch, Heintzelman, Hovey, Burbridge, Rosecrans, Pope, Curtis, Steele, Washburne, Rousseau, Canby, Payne, and Brayman—a salvo of fifteen hundred guns for Fisher's Hill.

CHAPTER XI.

PURSUING EARLY AND LAYING WASTE THE VALLEY.

At 1 P.M. of the 23d, the day following the battle of Fisher's Hill, having rested after the hard night's pursuit, Sheridan's infantry moved up the pike from Woodstock, except Crook's command, which was left to bury the dead and care for the wounded. Early thereupon continued his retreat from the Narrow Passage to Mount Jackson, about half way to New Market. There his main body halted, while his sick and the small part of his wounded [1] which he had brought off with him from his two battles, his hospital stores, and his trains—for these he had managed to save at Fisher's Hill—were carried farther to the rear.

But the Confederates were not to remain long at Mount Jackson ; for that same afternoon, about three o'clock, they were attacked by Averell, aided by Devin, the latter having energetically driven in the Confederate pickets during the morning, and being already engaged when Averell at last came up. Although there was no infantry support, since the Sixth and Nineteenth Corps had been compelled to halt a mile south of Edenburg till their rations could be brought up, Early abandoned Mount Jackson, upon this vigorous demonstration, and retreated across the North Fork of the

---

[1] Sheridan found most of these on his way up the Valley, the greater part at Harrisonburg. Early also abandoned many wagons and four caissons during his retreat.

Shenandoah. His account of the affair is as follows : "In the afternoon, Averell's division of cavalry came up in pursuit, and after some heavy skirmishing was driven back. I then moved to Rude's Hill, between Mount Jackson and New Market."

The morning of the 24th, the Sixth and Nineteenth Corps, with the cavalry, occupied Mt. Jackson, at which point the Eighth, after a long march from Fisher's Hill, arrived at night. Early's skirmishers were driven through the town and across the North Fork to his main position at Rude's Hill on the east side. Devin's brigade was sent to gain his right flank, and Averell's division, now under Powell,[1] to move around his left, while the infantry marched across the North Fork on the bridge. Wright's advance batteries were very soon shelling the enemy's lines ; but when Early, from his post on Rude's Hill, saw these preparations, he retreated. His retrograde was in line of battle, and Sheridan closely followed him, the Sixth Corps on the left of the pike and the Nineteenth on the right, with Devin in advance. The smooth and open country was favorable to rapid marching both by pursuers and pursued ; but Early's advantage at the start was maintained. Desperation lent wings to the heels of the fugitives, and victory lightened the footsteps of those in chase. One stretch of thirteen miles was made without a halt by the infantry, while Taylor's battery, moving with Devin's advance, opened on the enemy whenever he attempted to halt, receiving iron missives in return. The two armies hurried through New Market, near which place

---

[1] "I have relieved Averell from his command. Instead of following the enemy when he was broken at Fisher's Hill so that there was not a company organization left, he went into camp, and let me pursue the enemy for a distance of fifteen miles with infantry during the night" (Sheridan to Grant, from Harrisonburg, September 25th).

Devin was checked for a moment by a hot fire, but soon re-covered and charged through the town.

About half a dozen miles beyond New Market the road forks, the pike keeping on to Harrisonburg, and an earth road leading more to the east through Keezeltown and Cross Keys to Port Republic. Early took the latter, and at sunset halted at this fork in order to protect the transfer of his trains to the Keezeltown road, and formed line of battle, sending out skirmishers, as if to make known his purpose of securing there a night's bivouac. The result was some skir-mishing, with losses on both sides ; but at length Sheridan's leg-weary men went into camp, nearly within range of Early's guns. As soon as the darkness covered his intent, the Con-federate general quietly put five miles between him and his pursuer before re-bivouacking, so as to have a safe start for the next day. Through the night of the 24th Early's army remained at a point about fourteen miles north of Port Re-public. During that day, the Second Cavalry Division, Powell's, holding the Union right, had driven Lomax rap-idly up the Middle and Back roads, west of the Valley pike, towards Harrisonburg, until, says Early, Lomax "retired to the latter place in considerable disorder." Powell regained the pike near Lacy's Springs, capturing there nine wagons and some prisoners.

The morning of the 25th, Early resumed his retreat, and, passing through Keezeltown, marched to Port Republic, on the tongue of land formed at the intersection of South with Middle River, below the junction of the latter with North River, the triple stream there becoming the South Fork of the Shenandoah. But he did not pause here ; for he had had a special purpose in selecting this direction for his re-treat, and a prospect of relief in his trouble. Two days be-fore the battle of the Opequon, as has been noted, Lee, fear-

ing the effect of the withdrawal of Kershaw from Early, had
provided for his return ; accordingly, between the battles at
Winchester and Fisher's Hill, he directed that Kershaw
should join Early from Culpepper, and renewed these instructions immediately after the defeat of Fisher's Hill. This,
then, was the key to Early's selection of the Port Republic
road for retreat, instead of the pike to Harrisonburg, where
he might try to cover Staunton. He needed to bear eastward toward the Blue Ridge, in order to unite with Kershaw.[1] He accordingly made his final halt between Port
Republic and Brown's Gap, in front of and covering the latter. There, the 25th, the cavalry of Lomax, which had been
driven from Mount Jackson to Harrisonburg, and also Fitz
Lee's, now under Wickham, retreating from the Luray Valley, rejoined the infantry. The next day Kershaw came up
from Swift Run Gap.

Meanwhile, the morning of the 25th, when Early withdrew
to Port Republic, Sheridan marched the Sixth and Nineteenth Corps up the Valley pike to Harrisonburg, where
they arrived at 4 P.M., while the Eighth was left temporarily
at the junction of the Keezeltown road and the pike, where
the forces had camped. Torbert, the same evening, came
into Harrisonburg with the divisions of Merritt and Wilson.

---

[1] " Sheridan is in Early's front, fortifying. Wilson is moving up Luray Valley ;
Lee's division is opposed to him, but may be too weak. Move Kershaw to Gor-
donsville or Charlottesville, as occasion requires, or to Swift Run Gap " (Lee to
Anderson, September 22d).

"Early has again met with a reverse, falling back to New Market. Send Kershaw's division, with a battalion of artillery, through Swift Run Gap to report to
him at once. You had best report here in person with your staff, according to
previous orders " (Lee to Anderson, September 23d). That same day, Early,
then at Mount Jackson, had suggested this line of approach : "Kershaw's division
had better be sent to my aid through Swift Run Gap, at once."

" General Early reports enemy advanced against him on 24th at New Market,
when he fell back to Port Republic, to unite with Kershaw. On the 20th, the
enemy advanced toward Harrisonburg " (Lee to Seddon, September 26th).

After the cavalry action at Millford, the 22d, Early had sent
in haste for one brigade of Wickham's force to join him at
New Market, through the Massanutten Gap. Torbert, using
this advantage, fell upon the other brigade, Payne's, drove
it from Millford, and compelled it to retreat again near Luray,
Custer capturing 70 prisoners. Thence, crossing through
Massanutten Gap to New Market, he proceeded up the pike
to Harrisonburg, while Powell had gone forward to Mount
Crawford.

Having all his cavalry with him again, at and near Harrisonburg, Sheridan, the 26th, sent Merritt with a brigade to
strengthen Devin at Port Republic, while he directed Torbert, with Wilson's division and Lowell's brigade, to proceed
through Staunton to Waynesboro, and there destroy the
Virginia Central Railroad bridge over the South River. Each
officer went on his errand, and Merritt, whose demonstrations near Port Republic served to divert attention from
Torbert, after driving back Confederate cavalry, reported
himself checked by infantry—Kershaw's on its way to Brown's
Gap. Some skirmishing near the latter point, in which artillery was used, indicated that Early was disposed to halt
and make a stand.

Here, then, in front of Brown's Gap, with the Union army
at Harrisonburg, the long retreat of Early came to an end.
He had received reinforcements that largely repaired his
losses in battle, and the very morning after their arrival
sought to retrieve his fortunes. His first step was to drive
Merritt across the South Fork at Port Republic, where he
encamped, as if to make this a base of operations ; but there
learning that Torbert was threatening Staunton and Waynesboro, he hastily quitted Port Republic with his whole force,
at dawn of the 28th. Wickham, with his own brigade, was

hurried up South River near the mountain, to endeavor to reach Rockfish Gap before Torbert's arrival; the infantry followed in two columns, one, consisting of Pegram, Wharton, and Ramseur, guarding the trains, while the other, composed of Kershaw, Gordon, and the artillery, moved on the right through Mount Meridian, Piedmont, and New Hope. McCausland's brigade, now under Ferguson, held Brown's Gap, and Lomax, strengthened by Payne, watched the right flank and rear. The reason of this careful adjustment was that Early was moving over an area, in which he had the Blue Ridge on his left, the river on his right, strong hostile cavalry forces in front and rear, and the main army of his antagonist on his right and rear at Harrisonburg.

Torbert, having destroyed at Staunton, arms, ammunition, tents, hay, harness, wagons, and provisions, and captured 57 prisoners, had moved to Waynesboro, destroying the track on the way, and also burning the bridge over Christian's Creek, twelve miles southeast. He found two companies of reserves, from Staunton and Charlottesville, with two guns in position at Rockfish Gap, protecting the railroad tunnel through the Blue Ridge. His working parties were busily engaged in tearing up and throwing into the river the iron railroad bridge—the station with a neighboring tannery and its contents being already burned—when Wickham, hurrying forward, opened on them with his guns from a neighboring ridge. Pegram soon joined Wickham. Early's whole army thus approaching, Torbert withdrew to Spring Hill, on the Back road between Staunton and Harrisonburg, and thence returned, the 29th, to Bridgewater, on the North River.

Sheridan's brilliant successes had made him confident, but not careless. Even before reaching Harrisonburg he had notified the Lieutenant-General of the extreme difficulty of maintaining so long a line of supply. When Grant, after Fisher's Hill, wrote " Keep on and your good work will cause the fall of Richmond," Sheridan answered, from New Market, "I am now eighty miles from Martinsburg, and find it exceedingly difficult to supply this army. The engagements of Winchester and Fisher's Hill broke up my original plan of pushing up the Valley with a certain amount of supplies and then returning. There is not sufficient in the Valley, to live off the country." Grant rejoined, " Your victories have caused the greatest consternation. If you can possibly subsist your army to the front for a few days more, do it, and make a great effort to destroy the roads about Charlottesville, and the canal whenever your cavalry can reach it." He then told Halleck to see that the railroad was repaired toward Sheridan, even if troops were removed from Washington to guard the construction. "After reaching Manassas Junction I would like Sheridan to decide which road should be opened. If he moves—as I expected him— to Charlottesville, the road to Culpepper would be the one to repair." Halleck, accordingly, the 28th, wrote to Sheridan that "General Grant telegraphs that he expects you will be able to push forward to Staunton or Charlottesville;" and the same day Sheridan received Grant's letter.

The night of the 28th, Sheridan sent orders to Merritt— who that morning had been instructed to go to Port Republic and open communication with Torbert—to leave only small forces at Port Republic and Swift Run Gap, and proceed with the rest of his command, then comprising two divisions of cavalry, to Piedmont, and to swing around from that point toward Staunton, "burning forage, mills, and such other property as might be serviceable to the rebel army or Confederacy," and on his return to go into camp on the left of the Sixth and Nineteenth Corps, which were ordered forward from Harrisonburg to Mount Crawford in support of his and Torbert's movements. This instruction was thoroughly executed the next day, and Torbert, who had received like orders, also executed his the same day, starting for Bridgewater. The whole region which, as Sheridan says, had abounded in food and forage as far up as Staunton, and had hitherto enabled Early's army to subsist, from that moment became desolate, and of comparatively little value to Early, should he return to collect supplies there; and he wrote that night in reply to Grant's letter as follows:

"This morning I sent around Merritt's and Custer's divisions, *via* Piedmont, to burn grain, etc., pursuant to your instructions. My impression is that most of the troops which Early had left passed through the mountains to Charlottesville. Kershaw's division came to his assistance, and, I think, passed along the west base of the mountain to Waynesboro. The advance of my infantry is at Mount Crawford, eight miles south of Harrisonburg. I will go on and clear out the Valley. I am getting from 25 to 40 prisoners daily, who come in from the mountains on each side and deliver themselves up. From the most reliable accounts Early's army was completely broken up, and is dispirited. It will be exceedingly difficult for me to carry the infantry column over the mountain and strike at the Central road. I cannot accumulate sufficient rations to do so, and think it best to take some position near Front Royal, and operate with the cavalry and infantry. I will, however, stay here for a few days. . . . The country from here to Staunton was abundantly supplied with forage and grain."

The next day the two infantry corps moved back from Mount Crawford to Harrisonburg, and Merritt, the day following, reoccupied Port Republic; while Early, having remained two days at Waynesboro, guarding the repair of the bridge, which Torbert had very seriously damaged, now, the 1st of October, moved his army across the country to Mount

XI.—9

Sidney, on the Valley pike, and took position between that place and North River, about half way between Staunton and Harrisonburg.[1]

Here the opposing forces remained quiet during four or five days, Early awaiting the arrival of Rosser's brigade of cavalry, which, as Lee had informed him, started from Petersburg September 27th, to reinforce him.

Sheridan, as has been noted, was meanwhile shaping his movements for a return down the Valley; for he was opposed to the march against Charlottesville on military grounds, and had considered it better to put the upper part of the Valley beyond the pale of military occupation. "The difficulty," he wrote to Grant, "of transporting this army through the mountain passes on to the railroad at Charlottesville is such that I regard it as impracticable with my present means of transportation. The rebels have given up the Valley, except Waynesboro, which has been occupied by them since my cavalry was there. I think that the best policy will be to let the burning of the crops of the Valley be the end of this

---

[1] This march from Waynesboro across to the Valley pike below Staunton was one of the grounds assigned by Governor William Smith of Virginia for his request, made through Lee, that Early should be superseded. Smith quoted a letter which he had received from an officer in Early's army, dated from Mount Sidney, October 2d, running as follows: "We left Waynesboro yesterday at 8 A.M. in the rain, and marched all day through the hardest, coldest, and bleakest storm of the season; winter has few more severe days. . . . Unless it was imperative it was cruel and injudicious—cruel, because a great many of the command are shoeless and without blankets, and injudicious, because the Quartermaster states that shoes enough to supply the army were expected at Waynesboro. . . . The army once believed him a safe commander, and felt that they could trust to his caution, but unfortunately this has been proven to be a delusion." Smith alleged various other grounds of complaint against Early, asking that Breckenridge should be appointed to succeed him. Lee answered, "As far as I have been able to judge at this distance, he [Early] has conducted the military operations of the Valley well." Smith rejoined, reiterating his complaints, but Lee again said, "So far as my information extends, General Early has conducted his operations with judgment, and, until his late reverses, rendered very valuable services considering the means at his disposal."

campaign, and let some of this army go somewhere else."
This despatch was written the morning of October 1st, when
Early's troops were still at Waynesboro, as it stated. The
evening of the same day, when also Early's new position had
not been made known, Sheridan wrote again :

" My judgment is that it would be best to terminate this campaign
by the destruction of the crops, etc., in this Valley, and the transfer of
the troops to the armies operating against Richmond. If the Orange
and Alexandria Railroad is opened it will take an army corps to protect
it, as there is no enemy in the Valley to operate against. Early is without doubt fortifying at Charlottesville, holding Rockfish Gap. It is
no easy matter to pass through mountain gaps and attack Charlottesville, hauling supplies through difficult passes fourteen miles in length,
and with a line of communication from one hundred and thirty-five to
one hundred and forty-five miles in length, without the organization of
supply trains and all the appointments of an army making a permanent
advance. At present we are organized for a raid up the Valley, with
no trains except the corps trains. All the regimental trains had to be
used as supply wagons to subsist us as far as this place, and can't do it
at that. I am ready and willing to cross the Blue Ridge, but know,
from present indications, that the enemy will strongly fortify at Charlottesville and Gordonsville, and that these places cannot be taken
without the expenditure of a largely superior force to keep open the
line of communication. With my present means I cannot accumulate
supplies enough to carry me through to the Orange and Alexandria
Railroad."

This letter was received by Grant the 3d of October, and
he immediately replied as follows : " You may take up such
position in the Valley as you think can and ought to be held,
and send all the force not required for this immediately
here. Leave nothing for the subsistence of an army on any
ground you abandon to the enemy. I will direct the railroad to be pushed toward Front Royal, so that you may send
your troops back that way. Keep all of Crook's forces and

the new troops that have been sent to you." [1]   This acquies-
cence in the wishes of Sheridan indicated a cordial appre-
ciation of services which entitled him, in a case fairly ad-
mitting of doubt and an intelligent difference of opinion, to
choose his own way for ending his campaign.

Up to that time exertions had been made both to forward
supplies to Sheridan for the proposed march to Charlottesville, and to repair the Orange and Alexandria Railroad
toward Culpepper, so that he might use and hold it. By the
1st of October, a long wagon train, loaded with supplies, was
close upon him and within reach; the same day a train of
over two hundred additional wagons left Martinsburg, and
was shortly after sent with a guard of 1,500 men from Edwards' post at Winchester; and a third train, still larger, was
ordered to go to the front two days later. Meanwhile, Edwards wrote to Stevenson that he learned from General
Wilson,[2] who left Sheridan's front the 1st, that the army was
well supplied. But, despite these preparations, in reality
the Shenandoah Valley was at this time swarming with
men of Mosby's stamp, who were cutting off small parties
of troops and threatening trains; and it was perfectly obvious that, whatever quantities of supplies were sent forward to Sheridan, it would be very difficult to maintain so
long a line. A picket post of 150 cavalry at Mount Jackson
about this time was captured and sent back to Winchester,
some or all of them paroled by the Seventh Virginia cav-

---

[1] Another despatch of Grant's, of this same date, has the same bearing: "A
despatch is just received from Sheridan up to the 1st instant. The enemy have
entirely left his front and gone to Charlottesville or Gordonsville. He cannot
reach them there, so that we may now confidently expect the return here of at
least Kershaw's division and Rosser's cavalry It will require very close watching to prevent being surprised by the reinforcement."

[2] This officer was on his way to Tennessee, having been selected as chief of
Gen. Thomas's cavalry in the Nashville campaign. General Custer then received
General Wilson's division.

alry. Stevenson wrote to Stanton that one train of five hundred and sixty-one wagons, which was to go to Sheridan,
would have a guard of 2,000 men, "unless this should be
too few."

Meanwhile the work on the railroad toward Charlottesville had of course been abandoned. Halleck, writing to
Grant the 2d of October, that he inferred, from Sheridan's
despatch of three days before, that he would not go to Charlottesville, reported that the construction party on the
Orange road was between Manassas Junction and the Rap-
pahannock, and asked whether it would not be better to
change it over to the Manassas Gap Railroad, leading by Piedmont to Front Royal. This Grant at once approved. The
next day Halleck received a despatch from Sheridan, dated the
1st, giving the situation of affairs as then reported to him :

"All the crops, mills, etc., have been destroyed from Staunton to
Mount Crawford, which is my present front. I will make another raid
with cavalry and infantry to Staunton and Lexington. Early was
driven out of the Valley, and only saved himself by getting through
Brown's Gap in the night, and has probably taken position at Charlottesville, and will fortify, holding Waynesboro and Rockfish Gap."

Sheridan added that he had advised Grant to end the campaign with his destruction of the crops, and the transfer of the
Sixth and Nineteenth Corps to Richmond : "With Crook's
force the Valley can be held. If this course is not deemed
best, then the Orange and Alexandria should be opened ; if it
is, it will require an army corps to protect it. This force
cannot be furnished from this army, and wherever the troops
come from, it will be a loss of that number of men from the
fighting force. There is no objective point, except Lynchburg, and it cannot be invested on the line of this Valley,
and the investing army supported." Halleck answered that

Grant had now changed the workmen to the Manassas Gap road for Front Royal.[1] Thornton's and Chester Gaps," continued Halleck, " should therefore be occupied, so as to cover that place."

But this, also, did not exactly meet the judgment of Sheridan, who wrote to Grant as follows :

" I would have preferred sending troops to you by the Baltimore and Ohio Railroad. It would have been the quickest and most concealed way of sending them. The keeping open of the road to Front Royal will require large guards to protect it against a very small number of partisan troops ; it also obliges me to have a pontoon train, if it is to be kept open, to bridge the Shenandoah, to keep up communication with Winchester ; however, in a day or two I can tell better. I sent a party of cavalry through Thornton Gap, and directed the balance of the division of cavalry which I have in the Luray Valley to take post at Millwood, occupying Chester Gap and Front Royal. Thornton Gap I have given up as of no value. With this disposition of forces I will move infantry round the mountains, *via* Strasburg, as soon as possible."

Grant's consent to Sheridan's plan of ending the campaign reached him October 5th, and the next morning the columns were in motion down the Valley. Following in the rear of the infantry, the cavalry stretched across from the

---

[1] " My intelligence from telegraphic operators is that the Front Royal road is very little broken, and might be put in running order before Sheridan could get his Sixth and Nineteenth there, say in three days. With a rapid accumulation of rolling stock of the Government and Baltimore road they could be moved at once to Alexandria, and with an adequate supply of water transportation reach you by Saturday morning, if you conclude to adopt Sheridan's suggestion of sending them to you " (Stanton to Grant, October 3d).

" I will follow General Sheridan's suggestion of bringing the Sixth and Nineteenth corps here, and yours as to bringing them by rail from Front Royal " (Grant to Halleck, October 3d, 7 P.M.). Stanton also informed Sheridan that the railroad was within sixteen miles of Front Royal, and would be at Piedmont, only fourteen miles distant, by Wednesday noon, with transportation enough there for the two corps to go directly to Alexandria, should he choose that route and march them to Piedmont.

Blue Ridge to the North Mountain, and burned the mills,
barns, and crops, sparing, however, the dwellings, except in
one section, as explained in the following despatch sent from
Woodstock by Sheridan to Grant :

"I commenced moving back from Port Republic, Mount Crawford,
Bridgewater, and Harrisonburg, yesterday morning. The grain and
forage in advance of these points had previously been destroyed. In
moving back to this point the whole country, from the Blue Ridge to
the North Mountain, has been made entirely untenable for a rebel
army. I have destroyed over 2,000 barns filled with wheat, hay, and
farming implements ; over 70 mills filled with flour and wheat ; have
driven in front of the army over four herd of stock, and have killed
and issued to the troops not less than 3,000 sheep. This destruction
embraces the Luray Valley and Little Fort Valley, as well as the main
Valley. A large number of horses have been obtained, a proper estimate of which I cannot now make.

"Lieutenant John R. Meigs, my engineer officer, was murdered [1] beyond Harrisonburg, near Dayton. For this atrocious act all the houses
within an area of five miles were burned. Since I came into the Valley from Harper's Ferry, every train, every small party, and every
straggler has been bushwhacked by people, many of whom have protection papers from commanders who have been hitherto in that Valley.

"From the vicinity of Harrisonburg over four hundred wagon-loads of
refugees have been sent back to Martinsburg. Most of the people were
Dunkers, and had been conscripted. The people here are getting sick
of the war. Heretofore they have had no reason to complain, because
they have been living in great abundance.

"I have not been followed by the enemy to this point, with the exception of a small force of the rebel cavalry that showed themselves
some distance behind my rear-guard to-day.

"A party of one hundred of the Eighth Ohio Cavalry, which I had
stationed at the bridge over the North Shenandoah, near Mount Jack-

---

[1] It was ascertained after the war that this gallant youth, a soldier of brilliant
gifts and promise, the son of the Quartermaster-General, fell at the hands of an
enlisted Confederate soldier, of Wickham's brigade, engaged in scouting ; but the
belief at the time was the one stated in Sheridan's telegram.

son, was attacked by McNeil, with seventeen men, while they were
asleep, and the whole party dispersed or captured. I think that they
will all turn up. I learn that fifty-six of them had reached Winchester. McNeil was mortally wounded, and fell into our hands. This
was fortunate, as he was the most daring and dangerous of all the
bushwhackers in this section of the country. . . ."

Huge clouds of smoke, filling the Valley from one mountain wall to the other, and following down the army, attested
the thoroughness with which this work was done. Its first
effect was soon visible in the lack of subsistence for Early's
army; but there was another important effect, not immediately obvious. This devastation of the crops reduced the
strength of the Confederate forces by giving to some whose
families were in want a plausible ground for deserting the
service. There was an urgent appeal from the Harrisonburg region for exemption from conscription on the ground
of Sheridan's ravages. "Many who are liable," wrote Mr.
Wartmann, presiding justice of Rockingham County, "are
without a pound of meat, bread, or anything to live on, to
say nothing of fire-wood. It will require the daily and
hourly exertions of the poor and those who have been burnt
out to procure a scanty subsistence to sustain life during the
winter. When the soldier now in the army learns that his
neighbor, on whom his family have leaned for support during all this war, is himself called into service, and his family (his wife and little children at home) are sure to suffer,
he will become uneasy in his place, and will weigh the duty he
owes his family; and what the promptings of nature would
be is not difficult to determine. . . . We have no slave
labor, and this call taxes our principal working force.
What is to become of a corn crop? What is to become of
any spring crop?"

CHAPTER XII.

THE BATTLE OF TOM'S BROOK.

As soon as Early found that Sheridan was moving down the Valley, he pushed his forces in pursuit.[1]

The positions of the two armies during the four days previous had been as follows : Sheridan's infantry at Harrisonburg, and his cavalry, except Powell, seven miles beyond, at Mount Crawford ; Early's infantry at Mount Sidney, seven miles above Mount Crawford, with his cavalry close to Torbert's.[2] There had been skirmishing along the North River, both at Mount Crawford and at Bridgewater; while the 2d of October a Confederate reconnoissance had been repulsed. Powell, moving back to Luray, had thence sent Major Farabee, First Virginia Cavalry, to destroy the railroad bridge at the Rapidan, from which exploit he returned by way of Culpepper and Sperryville. It was the morning of October 6th when Sheridan left Harrisonburg, and that night he camped at Rude's Hill.

Reinforced by Kershaw, Early was already stronger than at any time since his defeat at Winchester, and his aggressive

---

[1] "General Early reports Sheridan's whole force commenced retiring down the Valley the night of the 5th. Our troops followed them through Harrisonburg the next day" (Lee to Seddon, October 7th).

[2] "General Early moved to the vicinity of Mount Crawford on the 1st instant. The enemy is north of North River, his cavalry occupying the north banks of that stream" (Lee to Seddon, October 4th).

instincts were again alert.[1]   But he had learned the need of circumspection, and patiently awaited the arrival of Rosser, who, besides bringing his brigade from Petersburg, was to take command of Fitz Lee's division, in place of Wickham. Rosser drew up October 5th, and Early had prepared to move out toward Sheridan at Harrisonburg, when the next morning his pickets brought him word that the Union army was retiring.

Rosser came to his task with fresh energy. His brigade, it is true, had been worn down by a hard march from Richmond, during which the men got little to eat, and the horses needed rest ; but at least it was full of confidence. Eager to redeem the cavalry mishaps in the Valley, he instantly pressed Custer on the Back and Middle roads, attacking him at Brock's Gap, through which Dry River enters the North Fork, about twenty-seven miles from Woodstock ; and Lomax moved down the Valley pike against Merritt. This officer camped the following day within two miles of Woodstock, and Custer near Columbia Furnace ; "the rear-guard of this column," says Torbert, referring to Custer's, " was fighting all day." Powell in the Luray Valley kept his relative position with the other forces by moving down to Millford. Early's infantry arrived that night, the 7th, at New Market, and Sheridan's the next day at Strasburg, while Merritt, covering the rear, reached Tom's Brook, which crosses the Valley pike, three miles south of the town, at the foot of Round Top. Thence Torbert hurried him back to the aid of Custer, whose rear-guard had been harassed throughout the march.

Sheridan, resenting this boldness of an enemy so lately

---

[1] Sheridan also had received some reinforcements, but of much less consequence : " About 5,000 men leave here to day for General Sheridan. Send them forward with trains " (Halleck to Stevenson, September 23d).

routed, directed Torbert to start out at daylight and " whip the rebel cavalry or get whipped himself." Torbert was in the saddle at dawn of the 9th, and, continuing the dispositions of the day before, Merritt was to move Lowell up the pike, the Second Brigade on his right, and the First on the right of the Second, connecting with Custer. A spirited fight of two hours ended in the rout both of Lomax and Rosser, Merritt chasing the former twenty miles up the pike to Mount Jackson, and Custer driving Rosser on the Back road to Columbia Furnace. Merritt captured five cavalry guns and Custer six—as fair a division of spoils as was possible with an odd number of pieces to share. About 330 prisoners fell into the hands of the victors, together with ambulances, caissons, a battery forge, the headquarters wagons of Rosser, Lomax, Wickham, and Pollard, and other wagons, forty-seven in number—in brief, almost "everything on wheels."

Of this engagement Torbert enthusiastically reported that " the cavalry totally covered themselves with glory, and added to their long list of victories the most brilliant one of them all, and the most decisive the country has ever witnessed." Sheridan promptly sent the tidings to Grant : " I directed Torbert to attack at daylight this morning, and finish this ' savior of the Valley.' . . . The enemy, after being charged by our gallant cavalry, were broken and ran. They were followed by our men on the jump, twenty-six miles, through Mount Jackson and across North Fork of the Shenandoah. I deemed it best to make this delay of one day here and settle this new cavalry general." The engagement at Tom's Brook was a fine offset to the check received by Torbert at Millford, for the same two Union divisions had now routed the combined divisions of Lomax and Rosser, inflicting a loss of about 400 men, while Torbert had but 9 killed and 48 wounded. Some of the captured artillery was fresh from the "Tredegar Works"; and with the five guns taken at Winchester, the sixteen at Fisher's Hill, and the eleven at Tom's Brook, point was given to the jest that cannon sent from Richmond to the Valley were marked "P. H. Sheridan, care of General Early."

The moral effect of Sheridan's victory at Tom's Brook was very great. The Confederate cavalry in the Shenandoah Valley had been feeble, compared with the infantry, and Sheridan, while at Charlestown, had remarked that it was "in poor condition" and was kept so close to the infantry that his own large and well-appointed corps of horsemen could not get at it. Fitz Lee's contingent had strengthened it, but the battle at Winchester and the subsequent defeat at Fisher's Hill, in both of which the cavalry held the flank that was turned by Crook, had again greatly dispirited it. The arrival of Rosser had revived the hope of restoring the cavalry to passable efficiency; for though this officer possessed more dash than discretion, he had gained a success in this region early in the year,[1] and had been so fortunate at Richmond that his men returned to the Valley confident of victory there. The assurance with which Rosser challenged Custer all the way down from Harrisonburg showed that he had no conception of Sheridan's mounted strength, though his fatal zeal was probably due in part to the excitement of his men at seeing their farms and houses in flames; for many of Early's cavalrymen were from this region. Their eagerness to exact retribution brought upon them double mortification and suffering, and the disaster of Tom's Brook

---

[1] Toward the end of January Rosser had captured at Moorefield a train of ninety-five wagons, with valuable subsistence stores, had destroyed the railroad property at Patterson's Creek, with the bridges over the Potomac and the canal, and had brought off 1,200 cattle, 500 sheep, and 80 prisoners.

crushed all hope of effecting anything with the Confederate
cavalry, and almost dazed Rosser's immediate command.
The chief value of Sheridan's victory was not made evident
until ten days later, at Cedar Creek, where the Union cavalry, flushed with success, developed great staunchness,
while Early's horsemen proved fatally weak.

The luckless Confederate commander, from his headquarters at New Market, reported to Lee that night his latest
reverse:

"This is very distressing to me, and God knows I have done all in
my power to avert the disasters which have befallen this command;
but the fact is that the enemy's cavalry is so much superior to ours,
both in numbers and equipment, and the country is so favorable to the
operations of cavalry that it is impossible for ours to compete with
his. Lomax's cavalry is armed entirely with rifles, and has no sabres,
and the consequence is that they cannot fight on horseback, and, in
this open country, they cannot successfully fight on foot against large
bodies of cavalry; besides, the command is and has been demoralized
all the time. It would be better if they could all be put into the infantry; but, if that were tried, I am afraid they would all run off.

"Sheridan's infantry moved off from Fisher's Hill this morning, and
I am satisfied that he does not intend moving this way again, as he
burned all the bridges in his rear as he went down, and the question
now is what he intends doing—whether he will move across the Ridge,
send a part of his force to Grant, or content himself with protecting
the Baltimore and Ohio Railroad. . . . He has laid waste nearly
all of Rockingham and Shenandoah, and I will have to rely on Augusta
for my supplies, and they are not abundant there. Sheridan's purpose,
under Grant's orders, has been to render the Valley untenable by our
troops by destroying the supplies. My infantry is now in good heart
and condition, and I have sent a special messenger to you to get your
views."

The day after the action at Tom's Brook, Sheridan moved
his army across Cedar Creek, and there occupied the heights,
with the Nineteenth Corps on the west side of the pike and

the Eighth on the east, Merritt and Custer taking post respectively on the left and right flank. The Sixth Corps was
sent to Front Royal, on its way to Washington. Lomax
followed Powell down the Luray Valley as far as Millford,
while Rosser in the main valley took up the line of Stony
Creek, from Columbia Furnace to Edenburg.

Grant now directed that Sheridan should retain the Nineteenth Corps, and should only send him the Sixth and a
division of cavalry when he thought it advisable; accordingly Wright's command was detained a day or two at Front
Royal. Finding that the Manassas Gap Railroad was repaired only as far as Piedmont, Sheridan ordered the corps
to march to Alexandria through Ashby's Gap, instead of proceeding to Piedmont, fifteen miles distant, and thence by
rail; while he directed Augur, whose troops were at Rectortown, guarding the road, to move back to Manassas Junction
or Bull Run. "He could not complete the railroad to
Front Royal," explained Sheridan to Halleck, "without additional force from me, and to give him that force to do the
work and transport the troops by railroad to Alexandria
would require more time than to march across, *via* Ashby's
Gap." The truth was that Sheridan's judgment could not
approve the opening of this railroad at this time; he regarded the project as premature, as unquestionably it was;
he had counselled the stopping of repairs, and his orders
to Augur, by withdrawing the guard, would practically
put an end to them. These instructions, a copy of which
Augur transmitted to Halleck, led to an issue between the
opposing opinions; for Stanton and Halleck were bent on
this scheme, which superficially seemed a repossession of
Northern Virginia. "The Secretary," wrote Halleck to
Sheridan, the 13th, "wishes you to come to Washington for
consultation, if you can safely leave your command. Gen-

eral Grant's wishes about holding a position up the Valley
as a basis against Gordonsville, etc., and the difficulty of
wagoning supplies in the winter, may change your views
about the Manassas Gap road;" while Stanton the same
day wrote to the same effect: "If you can come here, a consultation on several points is extremely desirable. I propose
to visit General Grant, and would like to see you first."
Stanton meanwhile directed Augur to remain where he was,
at Rectortown, until Sheridan should meet him, and then
act according to the latter's instructions.

It was a characteristic of Grant that when a military project once clearly presented itself to him as desirable, his
mind was sure to revert to it, even when, in consequence of
temporary obstacles, he seemed to have abandoned it.
Though accepting, to a limited extent, his lieutenant's
advice in regard to transferring the Shenandoah troops to
Petersburg, permitting the return of one corps of infantry
and one division of cavalry, he soon returned to his original
plan of an advance on Charlottesville and Gordonsville. He
had distinctly told Sheridan, the 3d, yielding to the latter's
earnest argument, " You may take up such position in the
Valley as you think can and ought˙ to be held, and send all
the force not required for this immediately here." But
eight days later, on reflection, and in view of the military
situation in Virginia as a whole, he told Halleck that Sheridan should " keep up as advanced a position as possible
toward the Virginia Central road, and be prepared to advance on that road at Gordonsville and Charlottesville at
any time the enemy weakens himself sufficiently to admit of
it. The cutting of that road and of the canal would be of
vast importance to us." The substance of this despatch was
sent by Halleck to General Sheridan, with these additional
suggestions : " It [the position] must be strongly fortified

and provisioned. Some point in the vicinity of Manassas
Gap would seem best suited to all purposes. Colonel Alexander, of the Engineers, will be sent to consult with you, as
soon as you connect with General Augur." Sheridan had
just ordered Wright to start for Alexandria, and had also
written Halleck as follows :

"Information received from Colonel Powell, at Sperryville, reports
Early (or Longstreet, I do not yet know which is in command, but think
Early is) with the bulk of his force at Craig's Creek, between Brown's
Gap and Waynesboro. I object to the opening of the railroad and an
advance on the old Rapidan line, on account of the waste of fighting
force to protect railroads, and the additional waste of force, as some
would have to be left in this valley. You see how many troops might
then be rendered unavailable. I believe concentrating at vital points
and the destruction of subsistence resources to be everything ; but do
not let my views influence your better judgment. I believe that a rebel
advance down this valley will not take place."

But on receiving Halleck's despatch, he promptly acceded
to the Gordonsville scheme, although against his judgment,
saying, " If any advance is to be made on Gordonsville and
Charlottesville, it is not best to send troops away from my
command, and I have therefore countermanded the order
directing the Sixth Corps to march to Alexandria. I will go
over and see General Augur and Colonel Alexander, and
communicate with you from Rectortown." Halleck now
directed Augur to continue repairing the railroad till further orders.

Sheridan, however, did not go to Rectortown, for the
campaign suddenly developed an unexpected phase. Early,
who was conjectured to be either " at Gordonsville or at
Charlottesville," as Sheridan had just written Augur, or else
around Brown's Gap and Waynesboro, as Powell's scouts
reported, having learned that his opponent was preparing

to send troops to Petersburg, now moved forward his infantry from its camp at New Market, and the 13th reoccupied Fisher's Hill, pushing his advance, without pausing,
through Strasburg to Hupp's Hill, for the purpose of re
connoitring. While thus engaged, he observed a body of
infantry on Sheridan's left that had " stacked arms in an
open field," and ran out a battery to fire upon it. Thoburn's division, of Crook's command, the one thus visited,
had the day before sent a reconnoissance toward Strasburg
without discovering any signs of the enemy, and the cavalry
had also failed to find him ;[1] so that a big shell, suddenly
dropped near an officers' mess-table just after dinner-call
from the bugles, made a startling addition to the feast.
Another followed, and another ; and now the assembly was
sounding, and Thoburn's men, driven from their meal, were
forming in line, with Wells's brigade on the left and Harris's
on the right. Between the knoll upon which their camp
was placed and the creek in front extended a piece of low,
open ground, which the battery on Hupp's Hill swept with
its fire ; but the two brigades quickly descended the slope,
crossed the interval, forded the creek, and began to toil up
the elevations that lie between the stream and Strasburg.

It happened that a timbered ridge presented itself to the
advancing troops, and, as they moved along either side of it,
Wells and Harris were thrown a little apart. It became
equally obvious to both, however, that Early was in force ;
yet the rage for capturing guns had seized Sheridan's army,
and Thoburn's men went forward through the plunging fire
from the brow of Hupp's Hill, until Early was forced to
throw out Kershaw's infantry, Conner's brigade leading, to

---

[1] " October 12th. I sent reconnoissances from the First and Third Divisions up
the Valley pike and the Back road for ten or twelve miles, but could find no signs
of the enemy " (Torbert's Report).

check them. Harris was driven back, but this Wells did not see till Conner had gained his right flank, and then his own retreat was hurriedly ordered. The casualties of this engagement, thought to be between 200 and 300, were chiefly in the First Brigade, whose right regiment, the Thirty-fourth Massachusetts, alone lost about a hundred men, Wells, the gallant brigade commander, being among those that fell, mortally wounded, into the enemy's hands. On the Confederate side Conner lost a leg from the fire of the Union batteries across the creek, and the casualties were unofficially reported as between 50 and 75. Early, having completed his reconnoissance, withdrew to Fisher's Hill, by no means pleased with the appearance of the position in which he had found his opponent.

During the affair on Hupp's Hill Early's cavalry forded the creek on the Back road, and attacked Custer, who drove them back, while Merritt put his division in the saddle, and by Torbert's order, moved it west of the pike, to Custer's left, ready to aid him. This march brought both divisions together on the right of the infantry ; and, as it was an audacious and unexpected stroke for the enemy to cross the creek and attack, Merritt was retained there.[1]

The ulterior importance of battles is not measured by the

---

[1] "They succeeded in driving part of the cavalry pickets across Cedar Creek, and advanced about a mile. Brigadier-General Custer moved out promptly, and drove the enemy back across the creek, and held that line. When the attack commenced, Brigadier-General Merritt put his division (First) in the saddle, and late in the afternoon the First Division (Brigadier-General Merritt) was moved on the right of the army and to the left of the Third Division (Brigadier-General Custer).

"October 14th. The First and Third Divisions (Brigadier-Generals Merritt and Custer) were in camp on the right of the army, covering the country for five or six miles to the right of the infantry. Brigadier-General Custer sent reconnoissances out on the Back road, and found the enemy had retired to the line of Fisher's Hill.

"October 15th. Remained in camp. All quiet " (Torbert's Report).

number of men engaged, nor always by the magnitude of the slaughter. Thoburn's combat at Stickley's Farm, which even lacks an official name, brought on momentous sequences; for when Early's presence in force was disclosed by this encounter, a courier hastened to Wright with orders to return to Sheridan's army. The messenger found the Sixth Corps on the banks of the Shenandoah, opposite Ashby's Gap, whither it had marched that day from Front Royal.[1] The corps, which was just about fording the river, was at once faced about, and at noon of the 14th, arrived at Cedar Creek. As the Eighth Corps was on the left of the pike, and the Nineteenth on the right, Sheridan put the Sixth on the right and rear of the Nineteenth, ready to support either of the others; from this point he could easily despatch it again to Grant, without disturbing his main defensive line. Merritt and Custer were on the right of the position assigned to the Sixth.

If it be admitted that one of Lee's objects at this time was to aid in prolonging the defence of Petersburg through the winter by detaining in the Valley all the Union forces, Early's clamorous announcement of his presence in the reconnoissance of the 13th may be regarded as successful, since it was followed by the return of the Sixth Corps to the Cedar Creek lines; but, in a broader view, the shelling of Thoburn's camp proved a misfortune to Early, since, save for that, a few days later the Sixth Corps might have been beyond timely recall, and Early might have fallen upon and crushed the remainder of the army. In point of fact, he had heard that his opponent was preparing to send away troops, but did not know that any had actually started.

Sheridan warned his subordinates the night of the 13th to

---

[1] " On the same day, in consequence of the advance of the enemy to Fisher's Hill, it was recalled " (Sheridan's Report).

be ready to give battle the next morning; but Early made
no further demonstrations, and reconnoissances on the 14th,
both by a brigade of the Eighth Corps, on the pike, and by
the cavalry, showed, after some skirmishing, that he was at
Fisher's Hill; still, his strength could not be determined.

The following day, the 15th, Sheridan received from Grant
important instructions. "What I want," said Grant, "is for
you to threaten the Virginia Central Railroad and canal in
the manner your judgment tells you is best, holding yourself ready to advance if the enemy draw off their forces. If
you make the enemy hold a force equal to your own for the
protection of these thoroughfares, it will accomplish nearly
as much as their destruction. If you cannot do this, then
the next best thing to do is to send here all the force you
can. I deem a good cavalry force necessary for your offensive as well as defensive operations. You will not, therefore, send here more than a division of cavalry." Sheridan
directed Torbert to move Merritt's division to Front Royal,
that same night, with a view of sending it through Chester
Gap toward the Virginia Central Railroad, and of reinforcing
the expedition with Powell's division. He accompanied
Merritt's command in person as far as Front Royal, intend-
ing to pay his postponed visit to Augur at Rectortown, and
thence, by the repaired road, to proceed to Washington, according to Stanton's request.

But when he had reached Front Royal, just before the
cavalry was setting out on its errand, he received a startling
message from Wright, who, as senior officer, had been left
in charge of the troops at Cedar Creek : " General, I en-
close you despatch which explains itself. If the enemy
should be strongly reinforced in cavalry, he might, by turning our right, give us a great deal of trouble. I shall hold
on here until the enemy's movements are developed, and

shall only fear an attack on my right, which I shall make
every preparation for guarding against and resisting." The
following was the despatch enclosed :

" *To* LIEUTENANT-GENERAL EARLY :

" *Be ready to move as soon as my forces join you, and we will crush
Sheridan.*

"LONGSTREET, *Lieutenant-General.*"

This message had been taken from the signal flag at the
Confederate station on Three Top. There was something
very strange about it, and, as far as the present writer is
aware, no complete solution of the mystery has ever been
given—although now that its fictitious character is known,
it would be easy to offer several conjectural clues, of vary-
ing degrees of value. But it was of great worth to Sheridan. For, although he was naturally inclined to consider it
a *ruse,* yet, as Wright's language implied, one of the divisions of cavalry had been taken away from the position at
Cedar Creek ; and in any possibility of attack Sheridan did
not wish his subordinates there to want for any troops
that he could give them. Hence, with his habitual prudence, which in this instance was to prove of great value,
he put off the cavalry expedition, and gave Torbert directions to return to the lines at Cedar Creek.

But should Sheridan himself also return, or should he
continue his journey to Washington? There had been recent reconnoissances and skirmishes, which indicated that
Early was at Fisher's Hill in some force, and an attack by
him, with the aid of Longstreet's troops, would be no trifling
affair. On the other hand, the intercepted despatch was
very obscure, false alarms about Longstreet had been
sounded ever since Sheridan came to the Valley, and the
settlement of the disputed policy affecting the Manassas
Gap Railroad, the operations against Gordonsville, and the

despatch of troops to Petersburg, had become urgent and imperative. Besides, the Secretary himself had already— three days before—requested his presence at Washington. Sheridan was entitled to presume that his four lieutenants would be specially watchful over their commands during his absence. He sent to Wright the following note :

"MAJOR-GENERAL H. G. WRIGHT, Commanding Sixth Army Corps :
   " *General*—The cavalry is all ordered back to you. Make your posi- tion strong. If Longstreet's despatch is true, he is under the impres- sion that we have largely detached. I will go over to Augur, and may get additional news. Close in Colonel Powell, who will be at this point. If the enemy should make an advance, I know you will defeat him. Look well to your ground, and be well prepared. Get up everything that can be spared. I will bring up all I can, and will be up on Tues- day, if not sooner."

Sheridan then rode on the same morning to Rectortown, where he took the precaution to telegraph to Halleck, be- fore two o'clock, that an intercepted despatch " would indi- cate that Longstreet was marching to join Early with con- siderable force, and was not far off ; " and he inquired whether he had heard of any such movement. Several hours passed without an answer. Sheridan still waited, for the matter was important. At length, at 5 o'clock, he again telegraphed to Halleck, repeating the exact words of the in- tercepted message. "Wright, in command," he added, " has made every preparation to meet the threat of Long- street, if the despatch should be true, and I feel confident of good results. I would like to see you. Is it best for me to go to see you?" A reply at last answered both despatches, indicating that in the meantime Halleck had consulted the Lieutenant-General at City Point : " General Grant says that Longstreet brought with him no troops from Richmond, but I have very little confidence in the information collected at his headquarters. If you can leave your command with safety, come to Washington, as I wish to give you the views of the authorities here." Then Sheridan went forward to Alexandria.

One sign of aggressiveness on the part of the enemy's cavalry attracted Torbert's attention immediately on his return to Cedar Creek. Merritt had resumed at noon of the 16th the position on the right and rear of the Sixth Corps, from which he had set out the evening before,[1] and Custer had remained where he could watch the fords near the Back road. That night Rosser, whose scouts had reported that one of Custer's brigades was apparently detached from the main body, was allowed by Early to undertake its capture with a brigade of infantry mounted behind the same number of cavalry ; and the whole of the Confederate army was moved out at dawn, to cover Rosser's return. However, he found only a picket of three officers and two score men of the First Connecticut Cavalry, instead of a brigade, and these he captured.

Perceiving that the left of the line needed cavalry, Sheridan had directed Wright to " close in Colonel Powell ; " accordingly, Moore's brigade of Powell's division was moved in several miles to Buckton ford, on the Shenandoah, so

---

[1] " October 15th. After dark, the First Division (Brigadier-General Merritt) was ordered to move to Front Royal. The Second Division (Colonel Powell) was ordered to concentrate at the same point. Both of these divisions being designed for a raid on Charlottesville and Gordonsville, I moved to the Shenandoah near Front Royal in the afternoon, to go in command of the expedition, which was to start on the morning of the 16th. . . .

" October 16th. The First Division (Brigadier-General Merritt) was ordered back to the army, and took position on the right of the infantry. The Second Division was ordered to resume its old position, and I returned to the army on Cedar Creek. Brigadier-General Custer made a reconnoissance in his front, but could find no enemy outside of their lines on Fisher's Hill " (Torbert's Report).

" At 12 M. the brigade returned to camp, near Middletown " (Devin's Report).

that its pickets might connect with Crook's on the infantry left.[1] The other two brigades remained posted near Front Royal, to prevent Lomax from coming down through Luray Valley past the Union left, so striking the pike in the rear. Crook's command worked at prolonging the line of intrenchments in its front.

In Early's camp, meanwhile, there was busy study. Sheridan's torches had laid waste the Valley, the provisions and forage which the Confederate general had brought from New Market were nearly exhausted, and he was forced either to attack or retreat. He chose the former alternative. For not only would attack, he thought, delay that meditated transfer of forces to Grant's army, whose importance Sheridan had been so quick to see, but in addition Early had some ground for hoping to win at least a partial success, since he had received heavy reinforcements, amounting, exclusive of the Valley reserves that may have joined him, to nearly 5,000 men.

Having reached this determination, he set about planning an attack. Gordon, taking a brigade, went forward to Hupp's Hill, to find whether Sheridan's position was fortified, and reported that it was; Early, therefore, resolved to take the intrenchments in reverse. Pegram was sent to reconnoitre the Union right, but the project of turning that flank was abandoned, "because," as Early wrote to Lee two days later, "the greater part of the enemy's cavalry was on his right, and Rosser's attempt had caused that flank to be closely picketed." There, also, the banks of Cedar Creek were found to be high and precipitous. Yet, on the other

---

[1] "October 17th. The same day, one brigade of Second Division (Colonel Powell) was moved nearer the infantry, and posted at Buckton's ford, on the Shenandoah River, connecting their pickets with the left of the infantry" (Torbert's Report).

hand, "to get around the enemy's left was a difficult undertaking, as the river had to be crossed twice, and between the mountain and river, where the troops had to pass to the lower ford, there was only a rugged pathway." Early, however, upon the whole, decided that the chances of success would be greater here, "from the fact that the enemy would not expect a move in that direction, on account of the difficulties attending it, and the great strength of their position on that flank." Careful examination by Gordon and by Captain Hotchkiss, of Early's staff, from the signal station on Three Top, also showed that Sheridan's left flank "was lightly picketed, and that there was but a small cavalry picket on the North Fork of the Shenandoah, below the mouth of the creek."

From Three Top Gordon and Hotchkiss could look down into both camps—rivers, hills, roads, fords, woods, and clearings all spread out before them, and not less clearly the troops and the tents, the guns and the parapets. Not only did they discover the positions of Sheridan's forces, but they had found that it was possible to move infantry along the base of Three Top, on the edge of the river, so as to cross below Cedar Creek. The North Fork makes a bend in front of Fisher's Hill, by Strasburg, enclosing there several farms, which were occupied by Payne's brigade of cavalry. The proposed flanking route first forded the Shenandoah from the right of the position at Fisher's Hill, then traversed this bend and crossed again at McInturff's and Bowman's fords, the former being a few hundred feet below the mouth of Cedar Creek, and the latter half a mile below. Moving thence through the dense woods, a column of infantry could be secretly placed less than half a mile from Crook's camp, taking it in reverse. The ground fronting Cooley's house was seen to be favorable for forming the

XI.—10

troops in the attack.   We can hardly exaggerate the advan·
tage of the bird's-eye view from Three Top.

For this turning movement were set apart the divisions of
Gordon, Ramseur, and Pegram, all under Gordon, with Payne's
brigade of cavalry, the latter being directed to try to capture
Sheridan at the Belle Grove House, for his absence was not
known.   Early was to manage the divisions of Kershaw and
Wharton, and all the artillery, since this could not be moved
on the blind path taken by Gordon.   The cavalry were to
co-operate—Rosser to move with two brigades, his own and
Wickham's, on the Back road across Cedar Creek, and attack
Custer at 5 A.M., while Lomax was to come down through
the Luray Valley, cross the river, and strike the Valley pike
wherever he might find the battle going on.

The execution of the plan followed hard on its conception.
Immediately after dark of the 18th, Gordon, crossing the
North Fork, proceeded to the foot of Three Top, and there
halted to give the troops a few hours' sleep.   An additional
intrenchment being reported by Pegram as thrown up on
Crook's lines since Gordon and Hotchkiss made their examination, Early, lest this work should in any way interfere
with Gordon's plan, at a late hour altered the line of
march of the force under his immediate command, allowing
Wharton to proceed, as before, over Hupp's Hill, but de-
flecting Kershaw to the right near Strasburg, so as to strike
Cedar Creek at the left of Sheridan's line, a short distance
above the mouth of the creek.

Stealthily, an hour after midnight, the Confederate columns moved forward.   Since silence was essential to success, swords and canteens were left in camp, lest their
clinking should betray the march; while the artillery was
massed on the pike at Fisher's Hill, there to wait until the
hour set for the infantry attack, when it was to move at a

gallop through the town to Hupp's Hill—for an earlier advance might betray the secret by the rumbling of the heavy wheels, in the dead of night, over the macadamized road. Early accompanied Kershaw, his centre column, and "came in sight of the Union fires at 3.30 o'clock; the moon," he adds, "was now shining, and we could see the camps." Kershaw was halted under cover, and while his men shivered in the chill night air, Early, during the hour that followed, pointed out precisely how and when this part of the attack should be made. Kershaw was to "cross his division over the creek as quietly as possible, and to form it into column of brigades as he did so, and advance in that manner against the enemy's left breastwork."

The scene was memorable. The Union camps on the hills beyond the creek wrapped in slumber; a corps of infantry, Jackson's old corps, and a brigade of cavalry, stealing along the base of Massanutten, to gain the rear of its unsuspecting foes; in the background forty guns and more, awaiting the signal to rush down the pike; an infantry division creeping over Hupp's, and another crouching yonder nearer the creek. Before five o'clock, Early ordered Kershaw forward again, and after a time came the welcome sound of a light crackle of musketry on the Confederate right, where Union picket stations had been set near the fords at which Gordon was crossing. This petty sound did not disturb the dreaming camps, but to the attent ears of Kershaw and Wharton it was the signal of attack. Kershaw quickly moved down to the creek; and meanwhile, as if nature had enlisted to aid in this enterprise, the moon had vanished, and a thick fog, clouding the landscape, now hid from sight the Confederate march.

CHAPTER XIII.

THE BATTLE OF CEDAR CREEK.

THE morning of October 19th brought to the Union camps little presage of the approaching peril. The enemy's cavalry dashes and his disclosure of infantry on Hupp's Hill had been looked upon by many as bravado, the prevailing belief being that Early's army could not risk serious attack. The plans for sending away the Sixth Corps and a division of cavalry had additionally lulled the troops into a certain sense of security, not wholly disturbed by the temporary recall of the Sixth. The daily reconnoissances from both flanks had confirmed this prevailing impression; while those of Tuesday, October.18th, had been specially reassuring.[1] A reconnoitring brigade, Colonel Harris's, of General Crook's command, even reported that night that the enemy had apparently retreated up the Valley. As the destruction of the crops and forage made it necessary for Early, while keeping troops at Fisher's Hill, to haul supplies from Staunton in wagons, the Union commanders had been expecting for some days that he would either attack or retreat; hence

---

[1] "October 18th. All quiet, and cavalry in same position. Reconnoissances showed no enemy in their immediate front" (Torbert's Report).

"About 9 o'clock of that evening [the 18th] I was called upon by Major-General Crook, commanding the Army of West Virginia, who reported that the re-connoissance of a brigade sent out by him that day to ascertain the position of the enemy, had returned to camp and reported that nothing was to be found in his old camp, and that he had doubtless retreated up the Valley" (Wright's Report).

the report that he had chosen the latter course occasioned
no surprise. The probability is that the reconnoitring officer, in reporting that nothing was to be found in the enemy's old camp, referred to the position temporarily occupied on Hupp's Hill, from which, five days before, Early had
shelled the lines of this very command; and this position
the enemy had certainly abandoned. The further belief
that he had retreated up the Valley was of course erroneous;
yet the very part of the army destined for attack by the enemy that same night was unfortunately the one most likely
to be influenced by this error. If the reconnoitring party,
returning through its own lines, spread amongst its comrades [1] its news of the enemy's departure, a movement de-
signèd for precaution may have tended to lessen vigilance
where it chanced to be specially needed. Wright, at all
events, immediately ordered two more reconnoissances, and
since the evening was already misty, after a fine autumn
day, the time of their departure was expressed in the instructions as "at daylight in the morning, or as soon thereafter as the fog will permit of objects being clearly distinguished"—one from the Nineteenth Corps, up the pike to
Strasburg, and the other by the cavalry on the Back road.
The object is, said the orders, "to ascertain if the enemy is
still on the line of Fisher's Hill in force, and the General
desires the troops pushed far enough to the front to accomplish this object."

The army of Sheridan was camped on the left bank of
Cedar Creek, just above its junction with the Shenandoah.
Such are the bends of the creek that at that point the three
infantry corps, in facing it, fronted somewhat southerly, so

---

[1] "Relying upon the report of our reconnoitring party, all slept in confidence
and security. But. notwithstanding that report, Early was near at hand" (History of the Thirty-fourth Massachusetts, of Thoburn's Division).

that although its general direction is by no means east and
west, the army was yet usually spoken of as being on the
"north," instead of the east bank of the creek. Owing to
these same bends, in taking advantage of the ground, the
three corps were positioned, as we have seen, partly *en
échelon*—the Eighth near the junction of the creek and the
river; the Nineteenth, at the right and rear of the Eighth;
the Sixth, at the right and rear of the Nineteenth. The
creek could be waded everywhere, as could also, for that
matter, the Shenandoah itself in that season and in that
neighborhood, the main value of the fords here as elsewhere
in the Valley, during the summer and autumn of 1864, being
that at them the high banks fall away or are cut down, so
that easy access is given to wagons that may desire to cross;
and this advantage was equally needful for the orderly passage of troops and trains. The steep banks of the creek
were in themselves defences along a large part of the line,
and far beyond the extreme right of the infantry.

Crook's corps, the Army of West Virginia, on the left of
the pike, was encamped in two portions. The First Division,
Thoburn, in front, and on the extreme left of the infantry
line, occupied a round hill or high mound, and was intrenched, with the line of works facing in general toward
the junction of the creek and the river. This knoll with its
guns commanded two fords of the creek, one on the right,
near by, connecting with the pike just beyond the bridge, and
the other several hundred yards distant, in front, leading by
a dirt road to Strasburg. There were woods to the left, extending part way across Thoburn's front. The Second Division, Duval's, now under Colonel R. B. Hayes, and Kitching's provisional division, were in rear or north of Thoburn,
on another hill, or another part of this same hill, close upon
the pike. This second elevation was the highest on the

Back Road

CROOK
4 P.M.

GETZ 9.A.M

PEGRAM

FISHER'S
HILL

WHARTON

STRASBURG

Fort Banks

WHARTON

HUPP'S
HILL

CROOK
5 A.M. Sep.22nd

Ford

Ford

Ford

NORTH BRANCH

Enemy's signal stat

MASSANUTTEN

THE TOP MOUNTAIN

MANASSAS GAP R.R.

BATTLE FIELDS OF
FISHER'S HILL (Sep.22nd 1864)
AND
CEDAR CREEK (Oct.19th 1864).
DRAWN FROM OFFICIAL MAPS BY
J. P. GENTMON.
— References: —
UNION. CONFEDERATE.

INFANTRY ,
CAVALRY ,
ARTILLERY ,
Scale of Miles.

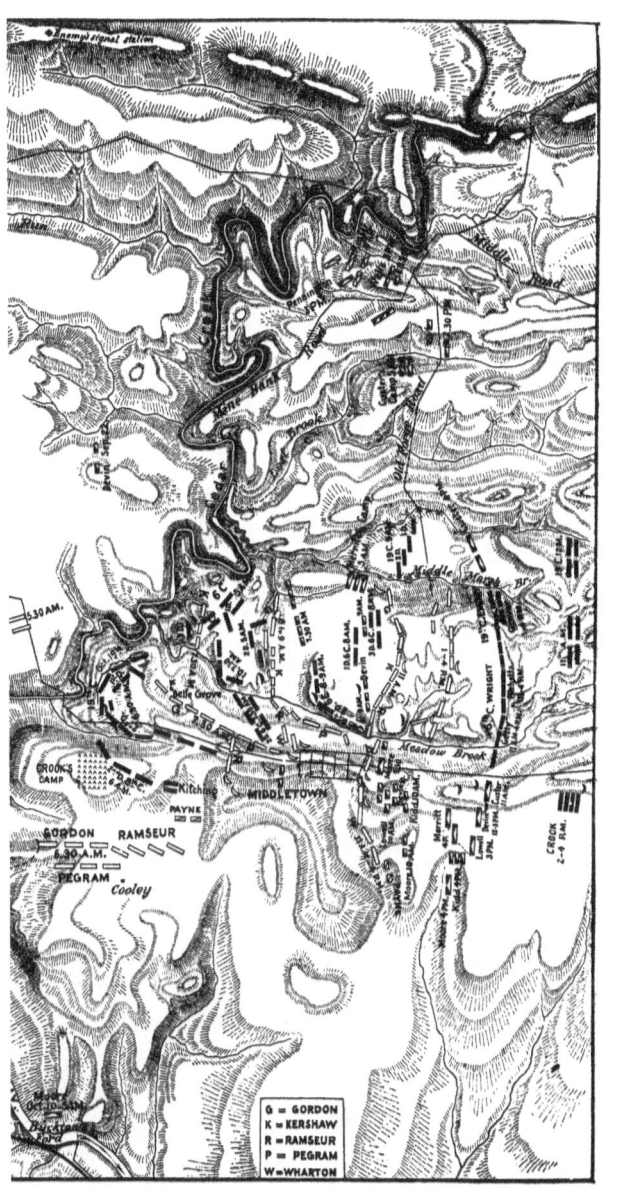

G = GORDON
K = KERSHAW
R = RAMSEUR
P = PEGRAM
W = WHARTON

Union line, thirty feet higher even than the highest part of the ridge across the pike, on which the Nineteenth Corps was encamped, and at its treeless summit one hundred and ninety feet higher than the level of the creek. The position was not intrenched, but Hayes and Kitching could either reinforce Thoburn, from whom a wooded hollow separated them, or, facing to the left, could defend the pike from an enemy coming in there.

The Nineteenth Corps, at the right of the Eighth, and west of the pike, was encamped on an elevated plain, being separated from the Sixth Corps by Meadow Brook, a rivulet feeding Cedar Creek in a direction generally like that of the pike. The corps was compactly established and intrenched in a space of three-fourths of a mile, the creek in its front, the right of its First Division on Meadow Brook, and the left of its Second on the pike. On this left was the greater part of its artillery, which commanded the road and the bridge across the creek. The line of intrenchment was nearly one hundred and twenty feet above the creek, to which the ridge fell off somewhat abruptly; and the plain rose gradually in the rear of the intrenchment. Back of this camp, on elevated ground, was Belle Grove House, the headquarters of Sheridan and also of Crook, the portion of the Commanding General's staff that had not gone to Washington with him continuing to occupy it during his temporary absence.

The Sixth Corps, beyond Meadow Brook, was not intrenched. Its position was a supplementary one, in reserve, and it was intended that the corps should be foot-loose for use anywhere on the main line, which had been formed with the expectation of sending the Sixth to City Point. The cavalry were in the positions before indicated—Merritt's camp near that of the Sixth Corps, on the right of the in-

fantry line, at Middle Marsh Brook ; Custer's about one mile
and a half beyond Merritt's, watching the fords where the
Back and Mine Bank roads cross the creek, and the neighborhood of Kupp's Mill ; Moore's brigade, two miles or
more beyond Crook's left, at Buckton's ford, where the
Front Royal road leads to Middletown ; the rest of Powell's
division at or near Front Royal. As events turned out, it
might have been much better to transfer Merritt again to
the left of Crook. For though this change would not necessarily have prevented Kershaw's advance directly on Crook's
front, it would, of course, have prevented Gordon's corps from
being formed unperceived in front of Cooley's. Possibly
such a change might have forced Early to choose a different
form of surprise and attack—putting his main column on
Kershaw's path, for example, or even assailing the other
flank. Suppositions apart, Wright, save for drawing in
Moore, seems to have retained the line as he found it when
his corps entered it the 14th of October.

Long before sunrise, a ringing volley of musketry startled
the men of Thoburn's division from their sleep ; and as
they came bewildered from their tents to learn the cause,
over every part of their parapets, through the darkness and
the fog, rushed Kershaw's infantry.[1] The position was
swept in an instant, with its seven guns, from which not a
shot had been fired. Such of Thoburn's men as escaped
capture fled to the rear, which was the only thing left for

---

[1] A battalion of the Fifth New York Heavy Artillery was on picket from Thoburn's division, and the Thirty-fourth Ohio from Hayes's. "The evening before the battle the regiment [Thirty-fourth Ohio], under command of Lieutenant-
Colonel L. Furney, was sent on picket. In the morning, before dawn, when the
surprise occurred, the colonel and 18 of his men were taken prisoners. The
colonel escaped at Mount Jackson, and joined his command a few days thereafter. The loss of the Thirty-fourth in this affair was 2 killed, 12 wounded, and
18 prisoners " (Ohio in the War).

them to do. Kershaw turned the guns on the retreating troops, since he had no artillery of his own; and leaving him to advance against Hayes's camp on the further knob of the ridge, at the pike, Early rode back to Hupp's Hill, to urge forward Wharton's division and Carter's artillery.[1]

Roused by the noise of the firing, Emory was quickly at the pike, followed by Crook from Belle Grove and Wright from his headquarters, the latter having simultaneously heard Kershaw's volley firing on the Union left, and Rosser's lighter rattle on the Union right. They all exerted themselves at once to form a line for the defence of the road, with Crook's Second Division (Hayes) and Kitching's provisional command as a basis, the Nineteenth Corps aiding, while Wright sent to Ricketts, commanding the Sixth Corps (Colonel Keifer being in charge of the Third, Ricketts's, division), to hurry two divisions forward to the pike. Happily the orders given for a reconnoissance from Emory's front at daylight had caused Grover's Second Brigade, Molineux, to be standing ready to move; and this brigade was immediately available, a part of it being sent by Emory to the new pike line, and the rest holding the trenches in the proper front of the Nineteenth Corps.[2]

---

[1] The point where Kershaw crossed the creek is given on the official map, and hence in the map of the present volume, as near the house of J. Roberts. It may be well to note that Roberts did not live there at the time of the battle, nor during the summer of 1882, when the writer was examining the region, so that it might be misleading to speak of this important point in the opening scene as Roberts's ford, he being only a temporary resident there at the time of the military survey made ten years ago.

[2] "I caused breakfast to be prepared for the men at an early hour, and at the appointed time we were in line awaiting orders. At about 5.40 A.M. I heard the sound of heavy firing in the direction of the position of the Eighth Corps, and apprehending an attack, immediately ordered my command into the rifle-pits, turning out a few sharpshooters to give me early intimation should an attack be made in my front. Shortly afterward I received orders to detach two regiments to my left to support the battery which commanded the pike and ground about the main bridge, and accordingly I sent the Twenty-second Iowa and Third Mas-

10*

Under ordinary circumstances this effort to form a line at the pike would have been entirely effective against the force which had destroyed Thoburn, while at the same time enough of the Nineteenth Corps could have been left to guard its trenches facing the creek,[1] to hold off the advance of Wharton—for the latter had now come nearly to the creek, capturing a few pickets on that side of the stream, and Early's artillery was exchanging shots with the Union guns. But at this moment, while the Union troops were intent on the approach of Kershaw, who was already firing upon Hayes's camp with the artillery captured in Thoburn's, a second and no less startling surprise fell upon them. Sheltered by the fog till close at hand, and also greatly aided by the clamor that had gone on since the beginning of Kershaw's

---

sachusetts dismounted cavalry. By this time a battery of the enemy, directly in my front, on the other side of the creek, opened a fire of shell upon us, and the mist, breaking from the Valley, discovered a line apparently prepared to attack us. It was not long before a fire of shell, enfilading our line from the left, with another directly in my rear, and a sharp musketry fire from the same direction (the position occupied by the Eighth Corps), showed me that the enemy had outflanked us; I sheltered my men as much as possible in the rifle-pits, and awaited orders. In the meantime the troops on my left and the batteries passed me, together with the two regiments of this brigade which had been sent in support of the batteries, all apparently striving toward the pike (these two regiments mentioned rejoined me subsequently); and finding that we were completely outflanked, that the retreat was general, and that my men were rapidly falling from a fire they could not return, and that a line of battle was being formed in the rear by the Sixth Corps, I moved out by the flank, in good order, detaching the Eleventh Indiana, by order of Brevet-Major-General Emory, to hold the hollow stone wall near the headquarters of the Second Division " (Molineux's Report).

[1] Brigadier-General McMillan, in temporary command of the First Division, Nineteenth Corps, says he was directed by Emory to put the Second Brigade on Grover's left, nearly perpendicular to the intrenchments, to resist the enemy then coming in from the rear. " I put the Second Brigade, Colonel Thomas, in the position indicated, occupying a deep ravine and thick copse of wood, from which it was soon driven by overwhelming force, but not until completely flanked, and nearly one-third of its members were killed, wounded, or captured." McMillan meanwhile had ordered his First Brigade, Colonel Davis, to hold the hill as long as possible with the Thirtieth Massachusetts and One Hundred and Fourteenth and Ninetieth New York. These troops gallantly obeyed their orders.

attack, Gordon came through the woods in a direction nearly perpendicular to the pike, and suddenly burst upon the left flank of the divisions of Kitching and Hayes, which had no intrenchments. Already shaken by the disaster of their comrades, who were streaming through their camp to the rear, the remainder of Crook's corps broke under this formidable onslaught from a wholly unexpected quarter, and thereby uncovered the position of the Nineteenth Corps, which was immediately brought under a concentrated fire that enfiladed and took in reverse its entire line of works. It being impossible to maintain the original position, Wright commanded this corps to fall back.[1]

Conjectural comparisons in regard to the behavior of different commands were never more out of place than as applied to this morning's calamity. An attack like Kershaw's, successfully initiated at that hour, against a single unarmed division, as thoroughly surprised as if it had had no pickets out, could not have resulted otherwise than it did, no matter what troops might have been thus assaulted. Nor was it remarkable that the remainder of Crook's bewildered forces, and the portion of the two divisions of the Nineteenth Corps that had joined them, should have been unable to withstand a quickly following combined assault of Ramseur, Pegram, Gordon, Kershaw, and Wharton, the greater part of it coming in upon the rear. It is even probable that had the attack of Kershaw not been delivered at all, and the surprise been wholly left to Gordon, the same or a greater success would have been achieved, and Thoburn's division captured as a body, instead of largely dispersed. It should

---

[1] " Seeing that no part of the original line could be held, as the enemy was already on the left flank of the Nineteenth Corps, I at once sent orders to the Sixth Corps to fall back to some tenable position in rear ; and to General Emory, commanding the Nineteenth Corps, that as his left was turned, he should fall back and take position on the right of the Sixth " (Wright's Report).

further be observed that though Early's army was smaller than Sheridan's, he was able, by concentrating first against the Eighth Corps, then against the Nineteenth, and then against the Sixth, to have the more powerful force at the actual points of conflict. It must not be supposed that Crook's command had broken to the rear with no attempt whatever to show fight; its loss that day was 46 killed and 268 wounded, as well as 533 missing. From it had been captured seven guns, ten caissons, and sundry wagons; the Ohio battery escaped, and fired its guns during the retreat. The Nineteenth Corps lost eleven guns, through being unable to get them away from the crest of the hill when Gordon crossed the pike in rear of the intrenchments; and even the Sixth Corps afterward lost six, so that twenty-four pieces in all fell into Early's hands. Most of Crook's ambulance train, many army wagons, much camp equipage, and more than 1,300 prisoners were also captured during this disastrous morning. As for the gallant Thoburn, he had yielded his life in breasting the tide of his ill-fortune.

The Sixth Corps was now coming on the scene, halting first on a wooded knoll not far from the pike, and holding off the enemy there. Emory was directed to place his corps on the right of the Sixth,[1] which immediately began to receive the combined assault of Gordon's corps and Kershaw's division. Ricketts was soon wounded, and the management of the corps thereafter devolved on Getty, while the senior officer of Getty's division was Grant, of the Vermont brigade. Fog and smoke still shrouded both the combatant forces, but Early soon learned that the Sixth Corps had been able to " take position so as to arrest our progress." The first

---

[1] " The Sixth Corps, of which two divisions were on the march to the support of the left, at once moved to the rear, on receiving instructions to that effect, as did the Nineteenth Corps " (Wright's Report).

stand of much consequence beyond the wooded knoll first occupied was near Middletown,[1] about a mile to the rear of the camp of the Second Division of the corps. This division,[2] in the hard task of retiring slowly and checking the enemy at every available point, performed superb service, whose importance to the fortunes of the day cannot be exaggerated ; for, being on the extreme left of the infantry, near the pike, it bore the brunt of the attacks.

In the position taken up on the ridge west of Middletown, the Sixth Corps batteries were in or near the cemetery. The enemy was forced by this halt to consolidate and strengthen his own line, and Ramseur and Pegram, who confronted the Union left, reported that they must have assistance, as they could not break through ; accordingly Wharton, some of whose men, after crossing Cedar Creek on the pike bridge, had rushed from their ranks to plunder the Nineteenth Corps camps, was ordered forward to their aid. Getty's own division, now under Grant, was posted with Bidwell's brigade on the left, nearest the pike, the Vermonters in the

---

[1] " It [the Sixth Corps] was found posted," says Early, " on a ridge on the west of the pike and parallel to it, and this corps offered considerable resistance. The artillery was brought up and opened upon it, when it fell back to the north of Middletown, and made a stand on a commanding ridge running across the pike."

Although the lines of the elaborate official map are reproduced, as the best attainable authority, in the one which accompanies the present volume, they are to be regarded as only approximating the actual lines of the battle. There is considerable evidence to show that a temporary stand was made by a portion of the Nineteenth Corps immediately on the arrival of the Sixth, not far from the Belle Grove House, where some of the regiments could see their own camps plundered by the Confederate soldiers ; still, temporary halts, which did not affect the course of the battle, are naturally not represented on the map.

Wright's report indicates but *two* lines as undertaken by him, apparently viewing any intermediate ones as temporary halts to check the enemy. The first of these was the one broken by Gordon's onset before the Sixth Corps came up, "on a ridge to the eastward of and nearly parallel to the pike," that is, at the camps of Hayes and Kitching. The second was the one north of Middletown.

[2] " A portion of the First Division, under Generals Wheaton and Mackenzie, and a part of the artillery of the corps, also behaved admirably " (Wright's Report).

centre, and Warner on the right. A fresh attacking division, thrown in at such a juncture, not seldom carries all
before it; but Wharton's was greeted with a tremendous fire,
under which his whole line recoiled. Rushing forth from
their places in the cemetery and the adjoining grove, Grant's
command drove Wharton down the hill; but Early's artillery, which had followed close, checked the gallant counter-
charge with a withering fire from eighteen or twenty guns,
and the division fell back, Bidwell being among the mortally wounded.[1]

Three hours had now elapsed since the opening of the
battle. It was between eight and nine o'clock, and the sun
had dispelled the fog, allowing the Union generals to see
what there was in their front, and how best to meet it. From
causes which soon became better understood, the vigor of
the enemy's attack was slackening. The peculiar character
of the engagement thus far was explicable. The position *en
échelon* of the Union corps had caused each to be farther
north than the one on its left; hence, when Early turned the
left of the Cedar Creek line, the successive marching across
of the Union forces to confront him, brought them farther
and farther down the pike. Thus the Second Division of the
Sixth Corps, if it marched by the shortest cut to the main
road, would already be two and a quarter miles in rear of

---

[1] " While I was endeavoring," says Early, " to discover the enemy's line through
the obscurity, Wharton's division came back in some confusion, and General
Wharton informed me that, in advancing to the position pointed out to him by
Generals Ramseur and Pegram, his division had been driven back by the Sixth
Corps, which he said was advancing. He pointed out the direction from which
he said the enemy was advancing, and some pieces of artillery which had come
up were brought into action. The fog soon rose sufficiently for us to see the enemy's position on a ridge to the west of Middletown, and it was discovered to be
a strong one. After driving back Wharton's division he had not advanced, but
opened on us with artillery, and orders were given for concentrating all our guns
on him."

Thoburn's camp, and fully a mile below the point where Gordon's column first struck the pike; while if Merritt's men should ride from their camp by the shortest straight line to the pike, they would come upon it at Middletown. Again, the very success of the morning attacks of Gordon and Kershaw had caused them to pursue their retreating enemy across and west of the turnpike; so that the Sixth Corps, when encountered, was well over to the Confederate right. These two elements in the situation forced the victorious assailants to laborious changes of position before they could secure a line that would properly confront the two corps not surprised and now getting into supporting position, namely, the Sixth and Torbert's. The attack of Early's reserve division, Wharton, on the Union left, was repulsed, as has been seen; but when repetitions of Wharton's attempt and a concentration of Early's artillery threatened to once more turn that flank, the Union troops withdrew north of Middletown, fully two miles to the rear of Getty's camp. After Early had brought up his fagged lines to this new position, he found his task increasing in difficulty, for the Union cavalry now extended beyond the pike. The manner in which this force had entered into the main battle requires an explanation.

When, before daylight, firing had broken out simultaneously on the right and left, Torbert's first effort was to check Rosser, who appeared on the Back road and attacked Custer. Hardly were adequate arrangements made for this purpose, before a rush of stragglers came through the cavalry lines, going to the right and rear. "I deployed my escort, First Rhode Island Cavalry," says Torbert, "as did Brigadier-General Merritt his, the Fifth United States Cavalry. After an hour or two's work it proved to be a fruitless effort. The escorts were drawn in, and officers sent farther to the rear, to form the men. By this time the enemy had come near enough for the cavalry batteries to open on them, which they did. The enemy did not bring their lines in the open country between them and the cavalry, but kept them under cover of the woods. Between nine and ten o'clock I was ordered by Major-General Wright, commanding the army temporarily, Major-General Sheridan being temporarily absent, to move my whole cavalry force on the left of the army." Torbert promptly made this transfer, which occupied but a short time ; and he left three regiments to picket the right and to hold Rosser from the pike on that flank, while a horse battery also remained there until the infantry line at that point was ordered back, when it rejoined Devin's brigade on the left. Moore's command, which had been stationed at Buckton's ford picketing the left flank, after being cut off from the main army by Gordon's movement, had promptly regained it at Middletown.

While the Union generals had thus secured the valuable assistance of the greater part of the cavalry in the main stress of battle, Early was little aided by this arm. Payne's brigade was all the mounted force he had at the pike. A piece of good fortune, among much ill-luck for the Union forces, was this collapse of the Confederate cavalry. Neither Rosser nor Lomax was able to strike the pike, although Early's surprise of the infantry camps had filled it with fugitives. Rosser had indeed promptly attacked Custer, on the Back road, at Kupp's Mill, but there, as in Emory's front, a reconnoissance had been ordered for daybreak ; and besides, Rosser's minor attempt, two days before, put the Union horsemen on their guard against surprise. Lomax had crossed the river at Front Royal, after much delay from Powell's force, which fortunately was there confronting him, and his whole division was occupied all day in pressing back Powell's two brigades to Stony Point and Newtown,[1] so that he did not reach the main battle-field, but returned to Luray Valley the way he came. The feebleness of Rosser's efforts can be best judged from the fact that the entire loss of Custer's division in the all-day battle, ending in a pursuit which yielded scores of cannons, caissons, and wagons, was 2 killed and 22 wounded. Indeed, the greater part of the Union mounted forces had been left free to aid in holding the pike; while the inestimable value of this service is attested by Early's haunting anxiety lest the cavalry should flank him there. The best fruit of Tom's Brook was plucked at Cedar Creek.

The Union line, then, as has been said, was at length drawn or driven back a mile and a quarter northeast of Middletown, and four miles in rear of Thoburn's camp. Yet Early was no nearer his goal; for, after having reckoned as one advantage of attacking the Union left the massing of the cavalry on the other flank, he found this powerful force threatening to envelop his own right. He therefore crowded his troops further to the east. Pegram, moving through Middletown, took position across the pike; Kershaw was put into the gap left by Pegram; Wharton, reformed, was, with Wofford's brigade, which had become separated from Kershaw's division, put east of the pike, to check Torbert.

But discouraged, at length, by the presence of the Union cavalry, and by Getty's gallant resistance, Early determined

---

[1] " During this time the Second Brigade, Second Division (Colonel Powell commanding division), fell back slowly by order on the Front Royal and Winchester pike to Stony Point, and then to a point near Newtown, followed by the rebel General Lomax's division of cavalry, where they remained a greater part of the day. Colonel Powell thus prevented the enemy's cavalry from getting on the pike to attack our trains and rear " (Torbert's Report).

to essay an attack from his other flank,[1] and sent an aid to direct an immediate advance there. This officer, says Early, returned with the report "that he delivered my order to General Kershaw, but the latter informed him that his division was not in a condition to make the attack, as it was very much scattered, and there was a cavalry force threatening him in front. Lieutenant Page also stated that he had seen Gordon's division in Kershaw's rear re-forming, and that it was also much scattered, and that he had not delivered the order to General Gordon because he saw that neither his division nor Kershaw's was in a condition to execute it!" The discreditable fact was that not only had the enforced lull occurred which is so familiar where troops have been marching and fighting since midnight, but in addition Early's organization was broken by the absence of men plundering the captured camps.[2]

Meanwhile had occurred the most dramatic incident in the annals of the Valley. Journeying from Rectortown to

---

[1] " Discovering that the Sixth Corps could not be attacked with advantage on its left flank, because the approach in that direction was through an open flat and across a boggy stream with deep banks, I directed Captain Powell, serving on General Gordon's staff, who rode up to me while the artillery was being placed in position, to tell the general to advance against the enemy's right flank, and attack it in conjunction with Kershaw, while a heavy fire of artillery was opened from our right " (Early's Memoir).

[2] Early's official report to Lee the day after the battle, confesses this fact: " So many of our men had stopped in the camp to plunder (in which I am sorry to say that officers participated), the country was so open and the enemy's cavalry so strong, that I did not deem it prudent to press further, especially as Lomax had not come up. I determined, therefore, to content myself with trying to hold the advantages I had gained, until all my troops had come up, and the captured property was secured." In the same report he spoke of the extraordinary inability of his left to advance, when ordered to do so : " Word was sent to Gordon, who had got on the left with his division, and Kershaw, who were then also to swing around and advance with their divisions; but they stated in reply that a heavy force of cavalry had got in their front, and that their ranks were so depleted (by the number of men who had stopped in the camps to plunder) that they could not advance them."

Washington the night of the 16th, Sheridan had completed his business there the next morning, the 17th, and had hurried by the noon train to Martinsburg.[1] Finding himself again in the Valley, with no apparent urgency for his presence at Cedar Creek, he deemed it expedient to remain and finish the business on which Colonels Alexander and Thom had accompanied him. The morning of the 19th found him at Winchester; and when, about 7 o'clock, an officer on picket reported the sounds of artillery, he gave no special heed to the matter, supposing that this firing resulted from a reconnoissance. However, about two hours later, mounting his horse, he rode through Winchester, and then the sound of the artillery made a battle unmistakable; while at Mill Creek, half a mile beyond the town, he found trains and troops already there from the broken line.

Hastily giving orders to park the retreating trains, and to use the spare brigade at Winchester to form a cordon across the pike and fields, so as to stop the stragglers, Sheridan dashed up the pike, with an escort of twenty men. He called to the fugitives to turn about and face the enemy; and, as he well phrases it, "hundreds of the men who, on reflection, found they had not done themselves justice, came back with cheers." On reaching the army, then eleven and a half miles from Winchester, he was received with a tempest of joy and enthusiasm.[2]

---

[1] "General Sheridan has just been here. He has not yet fully decided about the Manassas road, but will do so in a day or two. He has gone back with Colonels Alexander and Thom, to make a fuller reconnoissance" (Halleck to Grant, October 17th, 12.30 P.M.).

[2] "Far away in the rear was heard cheer after cheer. What was the cause? Were reinforcements coming? Yes, Phil. Sheridan was coming, and he was a host. . . . Dashing along the pike, he came upon the line of battle, 'What troops are those?' shouted Sheridan. 'The Sixth Corps,' was the response from a hundred voices. 'We are all right,' said Sheridan, as he swung his old

When Sheridan arrived, the enemy had just been forced
to relinquish his latest attempts to seize the pike, yet had
not completed his arrangements for attacking the Union
right; and the only parts of the army which Sheridan
found engaged were the Second Division of the Sixth Corps
and the cavalry, while even these were comparatively little
engaged. Affairs at the pike, therefore, being no longer
urgent, he proceeded at once to the most important task now
demanding attention, namely, that of securing a strong formation of his line.[1] For, in the concentration of exertions
on the one side to carry, and on the other to hold the turnpike as the key-point of the battle, both the Union and the
Confederate lines, as a whole, were much broken; and moving and fighting across several miles of uneven ground had
left divisions disjointed, and some in rear of others. Sheridan, therefore, rode off to personally aid his staff in bringing up all his available troops on a line about perpendicular
to the pike, extending Getty's line, while, as the left was
now more than adequately guarded, he caused all of Custer's

---

hat and dashed along the line toward the right. 'Never mind, boys, we'll whip
them yet, we'll whip them yet! We shall sleep in our old quarters to-night!'
were the encouraging words of the chief as he rode along, while the men threw
their hats high in air, leaped and danced and cheered in wildest joy " (Three
Years in the Sixth Corps).

[1] "One thing at once struck me as curious—that the stream of men was now
going toward Middletown. Astonished, I left Wheaton and galloped over to the
pike, where I learned that Sheridan had just passed up—as well as can be ascertained, it was half-past eleven o'clock—and directly after, meeting General Forsyth,
chief of staff, I received orders to go to Newtown, form a guard, and collect all
the stragglers I could, and bring them up to the front. This I proceeded to do,
and finally collected about two thousand men of all corps, and brought them up
and turned them over to the command of General Crook, then on our extreme
left and rear. From the time the Sixth Corps became engaged, at about nine A.M.,
until Sheridan came up, about noon, the attacks of the enemy were on the whole
feeble and ineffective. . . . Sheridan rode along his line, seeing for himself
all his troops, and saying a word or two as he went along to encourage them, to
which they responded with cheers " (Colonel B. W. Crowninshield's Cedar
Creek).

cavalry to be brought together on the right.[1] From the moment that he saw the situation of the battle, he had determined not to allow the enemy to remain in possession of the field, but to recover it as soon as all should be ready for attack. This assurance he gave to the troops as he rode along the lines, and the splendid inspiration of his presence was the best omen of coming victory.

We must now turn again to the lines of the assailants. Astonished at the reports brought him from his left, Early had proceeded thither to direct an attack. About one o'clock he succeeded in getting some of his troops ready, and the Nineteenth Corps and Wheaton's division of the Sixth were assaulted; but the enemy was easily repulsed. The affair might have proved, however, very serious, had not the Union right been strengthened by Sheridan, and made ready to receive the onset, a temporary breastwork of rails and logs having been hastily thrown up.

The repulse of Early's left told him that fortune had quitted his standards. He thenceforth contented himself with the endeavor to get his prisoners and his captured guns and wagons back to Fisher's Hill. But at four o'clock Sheridan ordered an advance, and the whole Union line gallantly responded. Wright was on the left, Emory on the right, Crook in column in reserve, Merritt and Custer on the left and right flanks. The enemy had improved the two or three hours that had elapsed since he ceased his aggression to establish himself behind stone walls, and to make other defensive preparations. But his dread of being flanked by the cavalry caused him to so extend his lines as to make them

---

[1] " I hastened from Winchester, where I was on my return from Washington, and found the armies between Middletown and Newtown, having been driven back four miles. I here took the affair in hand, and quickly united the corps—formed a compact line of battle just in time to repulse an attack of the enemy " (Sheridan to Grant, October 19th, 10 P.M.).

unduly thin. Still, in Emory's front the advance was stoutly
contested, until a spirited dash of a portion of Dwight's
division, under the personal direction [1] of Sheridan, put the
enemy to flight at that point. The tactical movement selected had been a left half-wheel—the same that Sheridan
had employed at Winchester and Fisher's Hill; and Dwight's
division, which was cn the wheeling flank, made such progress that a portion of it came under the fire of a Sixth
Corps battery, which was nearer the pivot. Grover, of the
Nineteenth Corps, and Wheaton, of the Sixth, on their fronts
handsomely broke the enemy's line; while of the infantry
and cavalry at the pike it is enough to say that they fought
with the vigor they had exhibited throughout the battle.
Custer, on the right, charged with his usual spirit.

Now consternation spread along the Confederate ranks,
until division after division gave way, and the army that had
swept over the field in triumph at dawn was a mass of fugitives at night. Though Sheridan's opponents were among the
choice troops of the South, who, up to a month before, had
considered themselves invincible, at least in the Valley, yet
never was greater rout seen on a battle-field since Bull Run. [2]

---

[1] General Dwight now resuming charge of the division, McMillan had returned
to his brigade. "The Second Brigade," says McMillan, "encountered a most
murderous fire from a hidden enemy on the right and rear. At this critical moment I wheeled the Second Brigade, and, by Colonel Davis's assistance, two of
his regiments to the right forming a line perpendicular to the one of direct attack, in a few moments drove the enemy flying from his cover. After moving to
the right a short distance, I began to get my command in its former position
to the left and front, when Major-General Sheridan rode up and told me to move to
the left, so as to complete the line as when it first advanced. So rapidly had we
driven the enemy that horsemen could with difficulty get through the woods as
rapidly. After changing the direction of the troops by direction of Major Forsyth,
of Major-General Sheridan's staff, 1 halted my command to wait for General Custer to get into position to protect my right."

[2] Early's own language sustains the truth of the assertion in the text: "A portion of the enemy had penetrated an interval which was between Evans's brigade,
on the extreme left, and the rest of the line, when that brigade gave way, and

The Union line, hurrying over the field, captured fugitives by scores. At Cedar Creek the infantry pursuit stopped, but the cavalry kept on. A bridge across a little brook between Strasburg and Fisher's Hill broke down, and at once the road became blocked with a mass of guns, caissons, ambulances and wagons. Custer and Devin, swooping upon these, gathered them up; for the disorganized mob took to the fields, neither attempting to check the pursuit nor to save anything. During the evening Dwight's division crossed the creek, and camped at Hupp's Hill.

Early's loss in this engagement seems to have been about 3,100—1,860 killed and wounded, and "something over 1,000 prisoners," according to his own account; but about 1,200 had fallen into the hands of Sheridan. Twenty-four Confederate guns were captured; the twenty-four lost by the Union troops in the morning were all retaken, with all the captured ambulances, and fifty-six of Early's ; and a number of battle-flags were among the spoils. The cavalry also set fire to scores of abandoned wagons and ambulances. The only trophies retained by Early were 1,429 prisoners, whom he had taken the precaution to send betimes to the rear, and to forward to Richmond, where they arrived a few days later.

The Union loss in killed, wounded, and missing was 5,764, distributed as follows :

Gordon's other brigades soon followed. . . . Every effort was made to stop and rally Kershaw's and Ramseur's men, but the mass of them resisted all appeals and continued to go to the rear." He adds that Ramseur only succeeded in retaining with him 200 or 300 men out of his whole division, and Major Goggin, of Kershaw's staff, about the same number of Conner's brigade ; and when these troops were overwhelmed, and Ramseur was mortally wounded, Pegram alone got "a portion of his command" across Cedar Creek in an organized condition ; "but this small force soon dissolved." A part of Evans's brigade had been rallied in the rear, and held a ford above the bridge for a short time, "but it followed the example of the rest."

	Killed.	Wounded.	Missing.	Aggregate
Cavalry Corps	25	139	50	214
Sixth Corps	255	1,666	294	2,215
Nineteenth Corps	243	1,352	893	2,488
Eighth Corps	46	268	533	847
	569	3,425	1,770	5,764

In the morning Colonel Thoburn and General Bidwell
were killed, and Colonel Kitching fatally wounded ; Generals
Wright, Grover, and Ricketts were also wounded, and Colonels Mackenzie and Penrose, commanding brigades. In
Merritt's final charge at Middletown fell the accomplished
and chivalric Lowell, commanding the Reserve or Regular
Brigade, whose commission as brigadier-general had been
signed that day. His command had performed admirable
service, having held, during the morning, an advanced position, dismounted, behind a stone wall, from which the enemy
could not drive it. "I do not think there was a quality,"
said Sheridan, "which I could have added to Lowell. He
was the perfection of a man and a soldier."

When it became known throughout the North how glory
had been plucked out of calamity in this memorable battle
at Cedar Creek, the country rang with praises of Sheridan.
Grant caused a salute of one hundred guns to be fired from
each of his armies at City Point, in honor of the achieve-
ment. "Turning what had bid fair to be a disaster into
glorious victory," he wrote to Stanton, "stamped Sheridan
what I have always thought him, one of the ablest of generals." Meade, on receiving the news, wrote to Grant that
"to achieve such results, after having met the reverse he
describes, is one of the most brilliant feats of the war."
Congress, a few months later, passed a resolution tendering

its thanks to "Major-General Philip H. Sheridan, and to the officers and men under his command, for the gallantry, military skill, and courage displayed in the brilliant series of victories achieved by them in the Valley of the Shenandoah, and especially for their services at Cedar Run, on the 19th day of October, 1864, which retrieved the fortunes of the day, and thus averted a great disaster." State Legislatures passed resolutions of eulogy. President Lincoln, on receiving news of the battle, sent to General Sheridan the following message :

" With great pleasure I tender to you and your brave army the thanks of the nation, and my own personal admiration and gratitude for the month's operations in the Shenandoah Valley, and especially for the splendid work of October 19, 1864."

When, a few weeks later, the President appointed Sheridan a Major-General in the army, the appointment was expressed to be "for the personal gallantry, military skill, and just confidence in the courage and patriotism of your troops, displayed by you on the 19th day of October, at Cedar Run, whereby, under the blessing of Providence, your routed army was reorganized, a great national disaster averted, and a brilliant victory achieved over the rebels for the third time in pitched battle within thirty days." These words were dictated by Abraham Lincoln.

Cedar Creek, the crown of Sheridan's campaign in the Valley, presents an illustration of the part which the unexpected often plays in war. This engagement was the sequel of a retrograde from Harrisonburg which had been undertaken with no prevision that such a combat could occur. Grant and Sheridan, under the impression that the enemy's army in the Valley was hopelessly dispirited and nearly destroyed, were arranging new combinations of much importance. These included the transfer of an infantry corps and

XI.—11

a division of cavalry to Petersburg, and the beginning of operations east of the Blue Ridge by a portion of the forces. Only the chance discovery of an obscure and even fictitious warning, taken from a Confederate signal station, gave to the Union army the services of the two cavalry divisions that were just departing on an expedition to the Virginia Central Railroad. Only a needless display of a portion of Early's infantry in a reconnoissance caused Wright's command to be hurried back from Ashby's Gap ; and no seer would have been needed to foretell the result of the battle at Cedar Creek, with the part played by the Sixth Corps left out. But Early also had his share of good fortune in the timely fog that screened his attack, and favored a surprise which alone could warrant a reasonable hope of success ; above all, he was, without suspecting it, greatly aided in his initial stroke by the temporary absence of the leader of the Union forces. This latter piece of luck, again, was more than counterbalanced by the return of Sheridan at the very moment when his presence was most potent to turn the wavering scale ; for the Union army received an inestimable reinforcement in regaining its commander.

Yet, strange as was the entrance of fortuitous elements into this battle, they cannot be said to have controlled its issue ; for the inspiration and strength which Sheridan's personality lent to his forces that day were the fruit of a thorough confidence in him, which had been steadily growing ever since he had taken command, and which, at his sudden and unexpected appearance on this field, burst forth in an enthusiasm unexampled in the war. " The accident of the morning," declared Sheridan, in his despatch to Grant, " turned to our advantage as much as though the whole movement had been planned." Certainly no train of events could well have been framed to bring into a more vivid and dramatic light his qualities as a leader of men.

CHAPTER XIV.

WAYNESBORO.

THE battle of Cedar Creek put an end, for a time, to the project of transferring a part of the Army of the Shenandoah to City Point. For, though utterly routed, Early's plight was apparently no worse then than it had been after the action of Fisher's Hill ;[1] and his resumption of a dangerous aggressive after that overthrow, clearly suggested that, if again reinforced, and the Union army should be diminished, he might repeat the attempt which had just come so perilously near success. Besides, he was now numerically stronger than after his September defeats. "These reinforcements," he says, speaking of Kershaw's and Rosser's troops, "about made up my losses at Winchester and Fisher's Hill ;" hence as his casualties at Cedar Creek were a third less than in the two former battles combined, he must have brought more troops out of that encounter than out of the two preceding ones. Finally, the burning of the Valley all the way down from Staunton, which had made it impracticable for the Confederate army to sustain itself save for a few days at Fisher's Hill, also rendered difficult any serious pursuit.

During the night after its defeat at Cedar Creek, the Southern army rested in its intrenchments on Fisher's Hill,

---

[1] "I feel certain that its rout from Fisher's Hill was such that there was scarcely a company organization held together" (Sheridan's Report, February 3, 1866).

but long before dawn retreated to New Market. Rosser remained some hours as rear-guard at Fisher's Hill, but in
his turn soon retreated, sharply pursued by the Union cavalry to or beyond Woodstock. He then established his line
on Stony Creek, from Columbia Furnace to Edenburg, about
half-way between Woodstock and Mount Jackson. Lomax
drew back through the Luray Valley, and took post in the
narrow gorge at Millford, which he successfully held against
Powell, covering Early's right flank beyond the Massanutten.

At New Market Early remained three weeks, and there
received many convalescents and hundreds of conscripts, who
had been absent on details ; and to these was now added Crosby's brigade from Breckenridge's Department of Southwestern
Virginia. Despite these reinforcements, he contented himself with remaining on the defensive. The 24th of October,
Powell made a reconnoissance of Lomax's position in the
Luray Valley, and two days later attacked in force ; he was
compelled, however, to withdraw, since the Millford defenses
were too strong to carry. The principal other operation
in the Military Division, during October, was the repulse
of Moss Hill and 360 men, by the garrison of Beverly, consisting of the Eighth Ohio cavalry. In this affair Hill was
said to have lost 140 men.

Sheridan's success in the Valley had been too marked for
his opinions to fail of receiving great consideration, both at
Washington and City Point. Grant wrote to him : " If it is
possible to follow up your great victory until you can reach
the Central road, do it, even if you have to live on half rations. I say nothing about reaching Lynchburg with a portion of your force, because I doubt the practicability of
it." Sheridan, however, was tenacious in his opinion. " I
have found it," he wrote, October 25th, "impossible to
move on the Central Railroad as you desire. If I do so, it

must be up the Valley, *via* Swift Run Gap or Brown's Gap,
or across, *via* Front Royal and Chester Gap. To move up the
Valley *via* the routes designated would be exceedingly difficult, on account of supplies and forage, and would demoralize
the troops, now in magnificent trim. To move by Chester Gap
I would have to leave at least 5,000 (the whole of Crook) in
the Valley. To open the Orange and Alexandria Railroad
would require a corps on it to protect it, which would leave
me very little to operate with successfully. To advance
against Gordonsville and Charlottesville with a line of communication up this Valley and through the Blue Ridge, is
impracticable. I have been meditating cavalry operations
against the Central Railroad as soon as the necessary preparations can be made." Soon after, the Winchester and Potomac Railroad was rebuilt, and the relaid road, from Piedmont back to Manassas, taken up. Thus both the railroad
question and the proposed Charlottesville campaign were
settled as Sheridan advised and desired.[1]

November 9th, Sheridan withdrew his army to Kernstown, where it would find better quarters in the waning
season, and a shorter line of supply. Informed by his
scouts of this movement, and thinking it might mean the
detachment of troops to Petersburg, Early the next morning hurried his whole army from New Market, and, crossing Cedar Creek, advanced down the pike to Middletown.
Sheridan soon had his army in readiness to deliver battle,
and directed Torbert, about noon of the 12th, to move

---

[1] "Colonel Mosby, under date of the 6th instant, reports that the enemy are
taking up the rails of the Manassas Gap Railroad, and using them to repair the
Winchester and Potomac road, which has been completed as far as Charlestown.
From the time the enemy occupied the Manassas road until its abandonment,
Colonel Mosby states that his command killed and captured about 600 men, an
equal number of horses, ten wagons, etc. " (R. E. Lee to Seddon, November
11th).

out the cavalry corps—Merritt's and Custer's divisions to the right, on the Back and Middle roads, against Rosser, and Powell to the left, on the Front Royal pike, against Lomax.

Rosser was speedily driven across Cedar Creek by the Union horsemen, with Pennington in advance, being so hotly pressed that Lomax was moved over to his assistance. Thereupon Powell, falling upon McCausland's brigade at Stony Point, routed it, driving it completely across the Shenandoah and through Front Royal up the Luray Valley, capturing its two guns and several caissons and ammunition wagons, besides 20 officers and 225 men, with two battle-flags. Dudley's brigade of the Nineteenth Corps and a skir-mish line of the Sixth moved out in support of the cavalry, advancing three miles from the intrenchments; and the whole army was ordered to be on the alert for the 13th.

But Early had withdrawn under cover of the night, his rear-guard of infantry being slightly harassed by Merritt. He returned to his camp at New Market the 14th. " Citi-zens report," wrote Sheridan to Grant, the following day, " Early's army very much increased in numbers ; " and cer-tainly his inspection reports indicated a comparatively large infantry force. But he had withdrawn from Middletown without venturing an attack.

Kershaw's division was now returned to its proper corps at Petersburg, and Crosby's brigade to Southwest Virginia, where important operations were at hand. These move-ments caused the rumor to reach City Point that Early's whole army had been recalled from the Valley, and Grant thereupon directed Sheridan, if he was satisfied that this was the fact, to send him the Sixth Corps without delay. " If your cavalry," he added, " can cut the Virginia Central road, now is the time to do it." To Halleck he said, the next day, that one division of cavalry ought also to be sent to City Point, "unless they can get through to cut the Central road and canal." Sheridan at once ordered his cavalry up the Valley to determine whether it would be best to detach these forces.

Torbert marched his Second and Third Divisions up the Valley to Mount Jackson, driving in Early's cavalry pickets from the Stony Creek line, and crossing the North Fork into Meem's Bottom, at the foot of Rude's Hill. He caused the enemy, as he reported, "to develop about 10,000 infantry and artillery, and one division of cavalry." Torbert's loss was only about 30, and prisoners were captured, from whom it was learned that Kershaw's was the only division that had left the Valley.

Sheridan, accordingly, the 25th, notified Halleck that "there are still here four divisions of infantry and seven brigades of cavalry. . . . Unless there is some great necessity for sending off the Sixth Corps immediately, I deem it best to wait until the season is a little further advanced."

Throughout Sheridan's campaign the Confederate trooper Mosby had continued the peculiar system of warfare for which long before he had become noted. As his headquarters were in Loudoun County, he moved now across the Potomac into Maryland, and now through the Blue Ridge into the Valley, surprising pickets at the fords, bushwhacking stray soldiers, burning supply trains, and surrounding and paroling small detachments. The restless activity of men like Mosby, White, and McNeil kept many regiments of Union troops engaged in hunting them down.

August 16th Grant had written to Sheridan : " If you can possibly spare a division of cavalry, send them through Loudoun County to destroy and carry off the crops, animals, negroes, and all men under fifty years of age capable of bearing arms. In this way you will get many of Mosby's men. All male citizens under fifty can fairly be held as prisoners of war, and not as citizen prisoners. If not already soldiers, they will be made so the moment the rebel army gets hold of them." An exemption was soon made in favor of "all loyal persons;" however, Sheridan could not then carry out this plan.

Toward the end of November Sheridan sent a division of cavalry, under Merritt, into Loudoun County to "consume and destroy all forage and subsistence, burn all barns and mills and their contents, and drive off all stock." The movement was described to be " in retaliation for the assistance and sympathy given them [Mosby and his men] by the inhabitants of Loudoun Valley," and the orders were executed, Merritt bringing off among his spoils between three thousand and four thousand sheep, nearly one thousand hogs, several hundred cattle, and over five hundred horses. Few of Mosby's men, however, could be found.

While these operations were starting in Loudoun County, Early again attacked the Baltimore and Ohio road. Rosser crossed the Great North Mountain with two brigades, his own and Payne's, marched to New Creek on the railroad, and surprised that fortified post, commanded by Colonel Latham, capturing about 500 of its garrison, with their arms and colors, and its seven guns; four of these being heavy pieces, were spiked and left, the carriages being burned. All the Government buildings and the supplies in them were soon aflame, and Rosser carried off about two hundred and fifty horses.

At the beginning of December Lee called for the return of his entire Second Corps to Petersburg; for infantry campaigning in the Valley was ended, whereas it was still possi-

ble around Richmond.   Almost simultaneously Grant called
for the Sixth Corps ; and both bodies started, a division at
a time.   Not long after, Early broke up his camp at New
Market, leaving cavalry pickets there and a signal party on
Three Top, and moved his remaining infantry, Wharton's
division, with the artillery and cavalry, back to Staunton for
winter quarters.   The 9th of December, two brigades of the
last division of the Sixth Corps left Kernstown, and Warner's
quitted Monocacy the 12th, so that by the middle of the
month the whole corps was again with the Army of the Potomac.   Crook's command next departed, one division to
City Point and the other afterward to West Virginia, to
check the enemy's operations there.   At the close of the
year, Sheridan had left of infantry only the Nineteenth
Corps, and early in 1865 one of its divisions went South.

Meanwhile the cavalry had proved, by a rough experience,
the futility of further operations until Spring.   December 19th, in conformity with Grant's urgent desire,[1] Sheri-

---

[1] On December 4th Grant had asked Sheridan if he thought it possible to
send cavalry through to break the Central road, as he conceived such an enterprise to be very desirable. Sheridan replied that he had contemplated the move,
but had "not estimated the breaking of the road as very important.   I am satisfied," he said, "that no supplies go over the road toward Richmond from any
point north of the road or from the Shenandoah Valley.   On the contrary, rebel
forces here in the Valley have drawn supplies from the direction of Richmond.
To break the road [at] Charlottesville and up to Gordonsville would only be
breaking the circuit.   The supplies south of the road and between it and the
James could be hauled on straight lines to the road, and run in both directions
via Louisa and via Lynchburg to Richmond.   I have the best of evidence to
show that there is no depot at Gordonsville or Charlottesville, and that the trains
passing through these places are only burdened by necessities of Early's army.   I
think that the rebels have looked at this matter about as I do, and they have not
been at all fearful of my going in that direction, as the temporary destruction
would only inconvenience them, and would be of no great value to me."   Grant,
however, the 12th, answered that "the inhabitants of Richmond are supplied ex-
clusively on the road north of James River.   If it is possible to destroy the Virginia Central road, it will go far toward starving out the garrison of Richmond.
If the enemy are known to have retired to Staunton, you will either be able to

11*

dan despatched Torbert, with 8,000 cavalry, encumbered by neither guns nor wagons, to strike, if possible, the Virginia Central Railroad. The divisions of Merritt and Powell, under Torbert's own command, were to move through Chester Gap toward Gordonsville, while Custer was to march against Staunton.

Early, who had shortly before reached Staunton for winter quarters, having been informed of both marches by his signal on Three Top and his pickets at New Market, moved Lomax to Gordonsville and Rosser below Harrisonburg, sending Wharton also to the latter point. Torbert drove Jackson's brigade, the 22d, from Madison to Liberty Mill, where it joined McCausland, blew up the bridge at the river, and planted two guns there. Crossing his divisions, one on each flank, by a wide detour, Torbert brought them together beyond the stream, and captured the guns, with several of the gunners. At Gordonsville, the next day, he demonstrated strongly, but finding that infantry had succored the place, desisted. His withdrawal was not molested, and he brought off about two hundred cattle.

Custer, the evening of the 20th, had reached Lacy's Springs, nine miles north of Harrisonburg, and there bivouacked. Before daylight Rosser, with his own and Payne's brigade, dashed in among the slumberers. Custer withdrew down the Valley, with a loss of 22 killed and wounded. He reported the capture of 27 prisoners, and the enemy that of 40 prisoners. Wharton's infantry had been

make a dash on the communications north of the James or spare a part of your command. Let me know your views as to the best course—to make a dash on the Central road and canal, or to detach from your command." Sheridan in answer strongly advised the withdrawal of infantry, saying that " one division can now be spared and perhaps two in a very short time." As to the railroad, he said he would try to break it as soon as the weather would permit ; but there was then snow on the ground, and the weather was wintry.

sent forward to check Custer; but on the latter's retreat was moved back through Staunton to Charlottesville, to aid Lomax in checking Torbert. This officer, however, had also withdrawn, the infantry that caused his retreat having been a force despatched from Richmond. The cavalry suffered greatly from the intense cold, while the roads were slippery with ice, and during the march there was a furious hail-storm. The expedition proved that the campaigning season in the Valley was ended for the year.

Before winter was over, Grant began to desire the repetition of the attempt to reach Staunton and Gordonsville, which had been thwarted in December. February 8th he wrote to Sheridan that he believed "there is no enemy now to prevent you from reaching the Virginia Central Railroad, and possibly the canal, when the weather will permit you to move," and the 20th he added: "As soon as it is possible to travel, I think you will have no difficulty about reaching Lynchburg with a cavalry force alone. From there you could destroy the railroad and canal in every direction."

Before Sheridan started on this expedition one or two minor exploits had attracted attention. February 4th, Lieutenant-Colonel Whitaker, First Connecticut Cavalry, with 300 picked men, was piloted by Colonel Young, Sheridan's valuable chief of scouts, on a difficult march of seventy miles across the mountains into Hardy County, and captured Major Harry Gilmor. A few weeks later, McNeil's and Woodson's men, under the command of Jesse McNeil, dashed into Cumberland at night, and captured and brought off Generals Crook and Kelley. Rosser crossing the mountains in the snow, January 11th, surprised the post of Beverly, garrisoned by the Thirty-fourth Ohio and the dismounted portion of the Eighth Ohio cavalry.   Over 500 prisoners were taken and sundry stores.

After this affair Rosser's brigade was temporarily disbanded, most of the men taking their horses to their homes, subject to call, as Early could not obtain winter forage for them.   Fitz Lee's two brigades were sent to Petersburg, Lomax's cavalry to West Virginia, most of the artillery horses in various directions, and one brigade of Wharton's division to Southwestern Virginia.   Wharton's two remaining brigades, with a portion of the artillery, were now the sole relics of Early's army.

The 27th of February Sheridan moved up the Valley from Winchester with a superb column of 10,000 sabres—the Third Division, Custer's, 4,840 aggregate effective, and the First, Devin's, 5,047, with two sections of artillery, 100, all under the immediate command of General Merritt, now Chief of Cavalry.   Sheridan's orders were to destroy the Central Railroad and the canal, to capture Lynchburg, if practicable, and then to either join Sherman in North Carolina, or return to Winchester, as might seem best.   Transportation was reduced to a minimum.

The spring thaws had come on, with hard rains; the roads were heavy, and the streams swollen.   Rosser, ordered to collect his men in the Valley, with a few hundred of these attempted to resist Sheridan's march at Mount Crawford, but was swept away, and thirty of his troopers, with a score of ambulances and wagons, captured.   The next morning Sheridan entered Staunton, and found that Early had taken post at Waynesboro.   He at once sent forward his troops to attack this position, Custer, with Wells's, Pennington's, and Capehart's brigades, in advance, followed closely by Devin, with Gibbs's, Fitzhugh's, and Stagg's brigades.   The morning of March 2d, Early was found posted on a ridge west of

Waynesboro, with Wharton's two brigades of infantry, Nelson's battalion of six guns, and Rosser's cavalry. Custer at once sent three regiments around the enemy's left flank, while at the same time charging in front with the other two brigades. The position was carried in an instant, with little, if any, loss on either side, and almost the entire force captured—all Early's wagons and subsistence, tents, ammunition, seventeen flags, eleven guns (including five found in the town), and, first and last, about 1,600 officers and men. The prisoners were sent back to Winchester under a strong guard, commanded by Colonel Thompson, First New Hampshire, who was attacked by Rosser, near Mount Jackson; but Thompson drove off his assailants with loss. As for Early, Long, Wharton, and the other Confederate generals, they fled into the woods, and Early himself soon after barely escaped capture by Sheridan's cavalry, while making his way to Richmond.

The victory at Waynesboro left Sheridan complete master of the Valley. His lieutenants now began the destruction of the railroad and canal. The iron bridge over the South Fork of the Shenandoah was wrecked, and the troops entered Charlottesville. From that point the railroad was thoroughly broken, both toward Gordonsville and toward Lynchburg. Delays to the trains caused by the incessant rains forced the Union commander to abandon the project of capturing Lynchburg, since sufficient time elapsed for succor to reach it. The 6th of March, Merritt set out, with Devin's division, along the canal, and destroyed every lock from Scottsville to New Market, and from New Market to Duguidsville, besides burning flour-mills and factories. Meanwhile Sheridan, with Custer's division, broke the Lynchburg Railroad as far as Amherst.

The events of the expedition had made it impracticable

to reach Sherman, and Sheridan therefore determined to make
his way through to Grant, and to utterly ruin the canal as
he went on. The 10th of March he reached Columbia,
where he was joined by Fitzhugh's brigade, which had destroyed the canal for a distance of about eight miles east of
Goochland. Thence he notified Grant of his successes, and
asked that supplies might be forwarded to White House,
at which point he arrived the 19th. "There perhaps never,"
says Sheridan, in his picturesque language, "was a march
where nature offered such impediments, and shrouded herself
in such gloom, as upon this. Incessant rain, deep and almost
impassable streams, swamps, and mud, were overcome with
constant cheerfulness on the part of the troops that was
truly admirable. Both officers and men appeared buoyed
up by the thought that we had completed our work in the
Valley of the Shenandoah, and that we were on our way to
help our brothers in arms in front of Petersburg, in the final
struggle."

The war in the Valley was now ended, the purpose for
which Sheridan was sent there having been completely ful-
filled. During its progress his sound military judgment
and tactical skill had shown him to be one of the ablest and
surest of the great Union soldiers; while his fiery energy
on the field of battle had secured him imperishable renown
as a popular hero of the War. When he entered the Valley,
it was wholly under Confederate control; he left it with
Confederate power there wholly broken.

APPENDIX A.

OPPOSING FORCES IN THE SHENANDOAH VALLEY.

I.—*Organization of the Army of the Shenandoah, in the Middle Military Division, commanded by* MAJOR-GENERAL PHILIP H. SHERIDAN, *date August* 31, 1864.

(General Headquarters Escort, Sixth U. S. Cavalry.)

CAVALRY FORCES.[1]

BRIGADIER-GENERAL ALFRED T. A. TORBERT, COMMANDING.

FIRST DIVISION (A. P. C.).

BRIGADIER-GENERAL WESLEY MERRITT.

First Brigade.	*Second Brigade.*
Brig.-Gen. GEORGE A. CUSTER.	Colonel THOMAS C. DEVIN.
1st Michigan.	4th New York.
5th Michigan.	6th New York.
6th Michigan.	9th New York.
7th Michigan.	17th Pennsylvania.
	1st U. S. Art., Batteries K and L.

Third Brigade.	*Reserve Brigade.*
Colonel CHARLES R. LOWELL, JR.	Colonel ALFRED GIBBS.
1st Maryland (P. H. B.).	1st New York Dragoons.
2d Massachusetts.	6th Pennsylvania.
25th New York.	1st United States.
	2d United States.
	5th United States.
	2d U. S. Artillery, Battery D.

THIRD DIVISION (A. P. C.).

BRIGADIER-GENERAL JAMES H. WILSON.

First Brigade.	*Second Brigade.*	*Reserve Horse Art. Brigade.*
Brig.-Gen. J. B. McINTOSH.	Brig.-Gen. G. H. CHAPMAN.	Capt. LA RHETT L. LIVINGSTON.
1st Connecticut.	3 1 Indiana (det.).	1st U. S. Art., Battery I.
3d New Jersey.	1st New Hampshire.	2d U. S. Art., Battery A.
2d New York.	8th New York.	2d U. S. Art., Batteries B and C.
5th New York.	22d New York.	2d U. S. Art., Battery M.
2d Ohio.	1st Vermont.	3d U. S. Art., Battery C.
18th Pennsylvania.		4th U. S. Art., Batteries C and E.

[1] The cavalry divisions of Averell and Duffié are transferred to this head from the roster of the West Virginia troops, on which they are borne, inasmuch as they were under Torbert's orders. Of Duffié's division, four days prior to August 31st, some troops had been given to Averell, others to the post at Harper's Ferry, and the remainder were sent to Cumberland to remount. Custer afterward received Wilson's division; Powell, Averell's; and Lowell, the reserve brigade.

FIRST DIVISION (W. Va. C.).

BRIGADIER-GENERAL ALFRED N. DUFFIÉ.

First Brigade.

Colonel WILLIAM B. TIBBETS.
2d Maryland, P. H. B. (Co, F).
1st New York (Lincoln).
1st New York (Veteran).
21st New York.
14th Pennsylvania.

Second Brigade.

Colonel JOHN E. WYNKOOP.
15th New York.
20th Pennsylvania.
22d Pennsylvania.

SECOND DIVISION [1] (W. Va. C.).

BRIGADIER-GENERAL WILLIAM W. AVERELL.

8th Ohio.
1st West Virginia.

2d West Virginia.
3d West Virginia.

5th West Virginia.
5th U. S. Art., Battery L.

SIXTH ARMY CORPS.

MAJOR-GENERAL HORATIO G. WRIGHT, COMMANDING.

FIRST DIVISION.

BRIGADIER-GENERAL DAVID A. RUSSELL.

First Brigade.

Col. W. H. PENROSE.
4th New Jersey.
10th New Jersey.
15th New Jersey.

Second Brigade.

Brig.-Gen. EMORY UPTON.
2d Connecticut Heavy Art.
65th New York.
67th New York (det.).
121st New York.
95th Pennsylvania.
96th Pennsylvania.

Third Brigade.

Col. OLIVER EDWARDS.
7th Massachusetts (det.).
10th Massachusetts (det.).
37th Massachusetts.
23d Pennsylvania (det.).
49th Pennsylvania.
82d Pennsylvania.
119th Pennsylvania.
2d Rhode Island Battalion.
Wisconsin Battalion.

SECOND DIVISION.

BRIGADIER-GENERAL GEORGE W. GETTY.

First Brigade.

Brig.-Gen. FRANK WHEATON.
62d New York.
93d Pennsylvania.
98th Pennsylvania.
102d Pennsylvania.
139th Pennsylvania.

Second Brigade.

Brig.-Gen. LEWIS A. GRANT.
2d Vermont (det.).
3d Vermont (det.).
4th Vermont.
5th Vermont.
6th Vermont.
11th Vermont.

Third Brigade.

Brig.-Gen. DANIEL D. BIDWELL.
7th Maine.
43d New York.
49th New York.
77th New York.
122d New York.
61st Pennsylvania.

THIRD DIVISION.

BRIGADIER-GENERAL JAMES B. RICKETTS.

First Brigade.

Colonel WILLIAM EMERSON.
14th New Jersey.
106th New York.
151st New York.
87th Pennsylvania.
10th Vermont.

Second Brigade.

Colonel J. WARREN KEIFER.
6th Maryland.
9th New York Heavy Artillery.
110th Ohio.
122d Ohio.
126th Ohio.
67th Pennsylvania.
138th Pennsylvania.

---

[1] The returns for this division are obviously imperfect in the roster from which the foregoing is compiled. Colonel Powell and Major Gibson commanded the brigades, and there was afterward a third brigade.

Artillery Brigade.

Colonel CHARLES H. TOMPKINS.

Maine Light Artillery, 5th Battery.	1st Rhode Island Light Art., Battery C.
1st Massachusetts Light Art., Battery A.	1st Rhode Island Light Art., Battery G.
New York Light Artillery, 1st Battery.	5th United States, Battery M.

NINETEENTH ARMY CORPS.

BRIGADIER-GENERAL WILLIAM H. EMORY.

FIRST DIVISION.

BRIGADIER-GENERAL WILLIAM DWIGHT.

First Brigade.	*Second Brigade.*	*Third Brigade.*
Col. GEORGE L. BEAL.	Brig.-Gen. J. W. McMILLAN.	Col. L. D. H. CURRIE.
29th Maine.	12th Connecticut.	30th Maine.
30th Massachusetts.	13th Maine.	133d New York.
90th New York.	15th Maine.	162d New York.
114th New York.	160th New York.	165th New York.
116th New York.	47th Pennsylvania.	173d New York.
153d New York.	8th Vermont.	

Artillery—New York Light Artillery, 5th Battery.

SECOND DIVISION.

BRIGADIER-GENERAL CUVIER GROVER.

First Brigade.	*Second Brigade.*
Brig.-Gen. HENRY W. BIRGE.	Colonel EDWARD L. MOLINEUX.
9th Connecticut.	13th Connecticut.
12th Maine.	3d Massachusetts Cavalry (dis.).
14th Maine.	11th Indiana.
26th Massachusetts.	22d Iowa.
14th New Hampshire.	131st New York.
75th New York.	159th New York.

Third Brigade.	*Fourth Brigade.*
Colonel JACOB SHARPE.	Colonel DAVID SHUNK.
38th Massachusetts.	8th Indiana.
128th New York.	18th Indiana.
156th New York.	24th Iowa.
175th New York.	28th Iowa.
176th New York.	

Artillery—Maine Light Artillery, 1st Battery.

Reserve Artillery.

1st Rhode Island Light Artillery, Battery D. Indiana Light Artillery, 17th Battery.

ARMY OF WEST VIRGINIA.

BRIGADIER-GENERAL GEORGE CROOK, COMMANDING.

FIRST DIVISION.

COLONEL JOSEPH THOBURN.

First Brigade.	*Second Brigade.*	*Third Brigade.*
Col. GEORGE D. WELLS.	Col. WILLIAM G. ELY.	Col. JACOB M. CAMPBELL.
34th Massachusetts.	18th Connecticut.	23d Illinois.
5th New York Heavy Artil-	2d Eastern Shore, Md.	54th Pennsylvania.
lery (4 Companies).	1st West Virginia.	10th West Virginia.
116th Ohio.	4th West Virginia.	11th West Virginia.
123d Ohio.	12th West Virginia.	15th West Virginia.

SECOND DIVISION.

COLONEL ISAAC H. DUVAL.

First Brigade.

Colonel RUTHERFORD B. HAYES.
23d Ohio.
36th Ohio.
5th West Virginia.
13th West Virginia.

Second Brigade.

Colonel DANIEL D. JOHNSON.
34th Ohio.
91st Ohio.
9th West Virginia.
14th West Virginia.

MILITARY DISTRICT OF HARPER'S FERRY.

BRIGADIER-GENERAL JOHN D. STEVENSON.

Cavalry.

12th Pennsylvania.　　Virginia Rangers.　　Loudoun Independent Co.

Artillery.

Indiana Light Artillery, 17th Battery.
Kentucky Light Artillery, 1st Battery.
Maryland Light Artillery, Battery A.
Maryland Lt. Art., Baltimore Battery.
5th New York Heavy Artillery.
New York Light Art., 30th Battery.

New York Light Artillery, 32d Battery.
Ohio Light Artillery, 1st Battery.
1st Ohio Light Artillery, Battery L.
1st Pennsylvania Light Art., Battery G.
1st West Virginia Light Art., Battery A.
1st West Virginia Light Art., Battery F.

Infantry.

1st Maryland P. H. B.
2d Maryland P. H. B.

135th Ohio.
160th Ohio.

161st Ohio.

FORCES WEST OF SLEEPY CREEK.

BRIGADIER-GENERAL BENJAMIN F. KELLEY.

Cavalry.

Ohio 3d Independent Company.　　　　6th West Virginia.

Artillery.

1st Illinois, Battery L.　　1st W. Virginia, Battery H.　　1st Maryland, Battery B.

Infantry.

122d Ohio.　　　　6th West Virginia.　　　　165th Ohio.

KANAWHA VALLEY FORCES.

BRIGADIER-GENERAL JEREMIAH C. SULLIVAN.

7th West Virginia Cavalry.

1st Pennsylvania Light Art., Battery D.
Pennsylvania Acting Engineers, Independent Company.
Virginia Exempts, Independent Co. A.

Veteran Reserve Corps, 132d Co., 2d Bat'y.
1st West Virginia Light Art., Battery D.
1st West Virginia Light Art., Battery E.
5th United States Artillery, Battery B.

II.—*Organization of the Army of the Valley District, commanded by* LIEUTENANT-GENERAL JUBAL A. EARLY, *date September 30, 1864.*

RODES'S DIVISION.[1]

MAJOR GENERAL S. D. RAMSEUR, COMMANDING.

Grimes's Brigade.

Brig.-Gen. BRYAN GRIMES.
32d North Carolina, Col. D. G. Cowand.
43d North Carolina, Col. J. R. Winston.
45th North Carolina, Col. J. R. Winston.
53d North Carolina, Col. D. G. Cowand.
2d North Carolina Battalion, Col. D. G. Cowand.

Cook's Brigade

Brig.-Gen. PHIL. COOK.
4th Georgia, Lt.-Col. W. H. Willis.
12th Georgia, Capt. James Everett.
21st Georgia, Capt. H. J. Battle.
44th Georgia, Lt.-Col. J. W. Beck.

Cox's Brigade.

Brig.-Gen. W. R. COX.
1st N. Carolina, Capt. W. H. Thompson.
2d North Carolina, Capt. T. B. Beall.
3d N. Carolina, Capt. W. H. Thompson.
4th North Carolina, Col. Ed. A. Osborn.
14th North Carolina, Capt. Jos. Jones.
30th N. Carolina, Capt. J. C. McMillan.

Battle's Brigade.

Brig.-Gen. C. A. BATTLE.
3d Alabama, Col. Chas. Forsyth.
5th Alabama, Lt.-Col. E. L. Hobson.
6th Alabama. Capt. J. Green.
12th Alabama, Capt. P. D. Rose.
61st Alabama, Maj. W. E. Pinckard.

GORDON'S DIVISION.[2]

MAJOR-GENERAL JOHN B. GORDON, COMMANDING.

Hays's Brigade.[3]

Colonel WM. MONAGHAN.
5th Louisiana, Major A, Hart.
6th Louisiana, Lt.-Colonel J. Hanlon.
7th Louisiana, Lt. Colonel T. M. Terry.
8th Louisiana, Capt. L. Prados.
9th Louisiana, Col. Wm. R. Peck.

Stafford's Brigade.[3]

Colonel EUGENE WAGGAMAN.
1st Louisiana, Capt. Joseph Taylor.
2d Louisiana, Lt.-Col. M. A. Grogan.
10th Louisiana, Lt.-Col. H. D Monier.
14th Louisiana, Lt.-Col. David Zable.
15th Louisiana, Capt. H. J. Egan.

Evans's Brigade.

Colonel E. N. ATKINSON.
(October 30th, Brig.-Gen. C. A. EVANS.)
13th Georgia, Col. John H. Baker.
26th Georgia, Lt.-Col. James S. Blain.
31st Georgia, Col. John H. Lowe.
38th Georgia, Major Thos. H. Bomar.
60th Georgia, Capt. Milton Russell.
61st Georgia, Capt. E. F. Sharpe.
12th Georgia Battalion, Capt. J. W. Anderson.

---

[1] "I would call attention to the great scarcity of officers in the entire command. The best and most efficient officers in nearly every brigade have for the most part been either killed or wounded during this campaign. . . . Cox's brigade had not a single field officer present, and the Fourth Regiment in it is commanded by a second lieutenant" (from Inspection Report of Rodes's Division, September 30th).

[2] From Inspection Returns of August.

[3] These brigades were united under General Zebulon York, succeeded by Lieut.-Colonel D. Zable.

Terry's Brigade.[1]

Brig.-Gen. WM. TERRY.

2d Virginia.		21st Virginia.	
4th Virginia.	(Stonewall Brigade.)	25th Virginia.	(J. M. Jones's Brigade.)
5th Virginia.	Col. J. H. S. Funk;	42d Virginia.	Col. R. H. Dungan;
27th Virginia.	Oct. 30th, Col. A.	44th Virginia.	Oct. 30th, Col. W. A.
33d Virginia.	Spangler.	48th Virginia.	Witcher.
		50th Virginia.	

10th Virginia,) (G. H. Steuart's Brigade.)
23d Virginia, } Lt.-Col S. H.Saunders;
37th Virginia.) Oct. 30th, Lt.-Col. Martz.

EARLY'S DIVISION.[2]

BRIGADIER-GENERAL JOHN PEGRAM, COMMANDING.

Pegram's Brigade.	*Johnston's Brigade.*
Colonel JOHN S. HOFFMAN.	Brig.-Gen. ROBERT D. JOHNSTON.
13th Virginia, Capt. Felix Heiskell.	5th North Carolina, Col. John W. Lea.[3]
31st Virginia, Lt. Col. J. S. K. McCutchen.	12th North Carolina, Col. Henry E. Cole-
49th Virginia, Capt. John G. Lobban.	man.[3]
52d Virginia, Capt. J. M, Humphreys.	20th North Carolina, Col. T. F. Toon.
58th Virginia, Capt. L. C. James.	23d North Carolina, Col. C. C. Blacknall.[3]

Godwin's Brigade.

Lieut.-Colonel W. T. DAVIS.

6th N. Carolina, Lt. Col. S. McD. Tate.	57th North Carolina, Capt M.H. Hunter.
21st North Carolina, Maj. W. I. Pfohl.	1st N. Carolina Battalion, Capt. R. E.
54th North Carolina, Capt. A. H. Martin.	Wilson.

WHARTON'S DIVISION.

BRIGADIER-GENERAL G. C. WHARTON, COMMANDING.

Echols's Brigade.	*Wharton's Brigade.*
Captain EDMUND S. READ.	Captain R. H. LOGAN.
22d Virginia, Capt. Henry S. Dickerson.	45th Virginia, Maj. Alex. M Davis.
23d Virginia, Capt. John M. Pratt.	51st Virginia, Col. August Fosberg.[4]
26th Virginia, Capt. Frank S. Burdett.	30th Virginia Battalion, Lt.-Col. J. Lyle
	Clarke.[4]

---

[1] Composed of the "fragmentary remains of fourteen of the regiments of John-son's division, most of which was captured by the enemy, May 12, 1864." The inspection report of August 21st says that the fusing of Hays's and Stafford's brigades into one, under York, and the consolidation of three brigades, "the re-mains of fourteen regiments," into one, under Terry, produced a bad effect on the discipline of the troops, who lost their chance of perpetuating their brigade history; and that Evans's brigade had lost by casualty so many valuable officers as to interfere seriously with its good management.

[2] Commanded by Ramseur, until he took Rodes's division, after the battle of the Opequon.

[3] These officers absent and actual commanders not indicated. October 31st, after the battle of Cedar Creek, the officers in place of Lea, Coleman, and Black-nall, respectively, were Captains E. M. Duguid, Kemp Plummer, and Abner D. Peace.

[4] These officers absent and actual commanders not indicated. The Fifteenth Virginia, Vanderventer's, is ascribed to this brigade in a roster of October 31st.

Smith's Brigade.

Colonel THOMAS SMITH.

36th Virginia, Lieut. Jackson Vin.	45th Virginia Battal'n, Capt. W. B. Hensly
60th Virginia, Capt. A. G. P. George.	Thomas Legion, Lt.-Col. J. R. Love.

KERSHAW'S DIVISION.

MAJOR-GENERAL J. B. KERSHAW, COMMANDING.

Wofford's Brigade.

Col. C. C. SANDERS.
16th Georgia, Major J. S. Gholston.
18th Georgia, Col. Joseph Armstrong.
24th Georgia, Col. C. C. Sanders.
3d Georgia Battalion, Lt.-Col. N. L. Hutchins.
Cobb's Legion, Lt.-Col. L. J. Glenn.
Phillips's Legion, Lt.-Col. J. Hamilton.

Kershaw's Brigade.

Brig.-Gen. CONNER.
2d S. Carolina, Col. J. D. Kennedy.
3d S. Carolina, Col. W. D. Rutherford.
7th S. Carolina, Capt. E. J. Goggans.
8 h S. Carolina, Col. J. W. Henagan.
15th S. Carolina, Col. J. B. Davis.
20th S. Carolina, Col. S. M. Boykin.
3d S. Carolina Battalion, Lieut. [Col.]
W. G. Rice.

Humphreys's Brigade.

Brig.-Gen. B. G. HUMPHREYS
13th Mississippi, Lt.-Col. A. G. O'Brien.
17th Mississippi, Capt. J. C. Cochran.
18th Mississippi, Colonel T. M. Griffin.
21st Mississippi, Col. D N. Moody.

Bryan's Brigade.

Brig.-Gen. GOODE BRYAN.
10th Georgia, Col. W. C. Holt.
50th Georgia, Col. P. McGloshan.[1]
51st Georgia, Col. E. Ball.[1]
53d Georgia, Col. J. P. Simms.

ARTILLERY DIVISION.

COLONEL T. H. CARTER, COMMANDING.

Braxton's Battalion.

Lieut.-Col. C. M. BRAXTON.
Alleghany Artillery, Va., Capt. J. C. Carpenter.
Stafford Artillery, Va., Capt. W. P. Cooper.
Lee Battery, Va., Lieut. W. W. Hardwick.

Cutshaw's Battalion.[2]

Major W. E. CUTSHAW.
Orange Artillery, Va., Capt. C. W. Fry.
Staunton Artillery, Va., Capt. A. W. Garber.
Courtney Battery, Va., —— L. F. Jones.

McLaughlin's Battalion.

Major WM. McLAUGHLIN.
Bryan's Virginia Battery.
Chapman's Virginia Battery.
Lowry's Virginia Battery.

Nelson's Battalion.

Lieut.-Col. WM. NELSON.
Amherst Artillery, Va., Capt. T. J. Kirkpatrick.
Fluvanna Artillery, Va., Capt. J. L. Massie.
Milledge's Artillery, Ga., Capt. John Milledge.

---

[1] Absent wounded, and actual commanders of these regiments not stated. The foregoing organization is for August, when Kershaw arrived in the Valley.

[2] In an earlier roster Fry's Orange Battery is ascribed to Carter's battalion, and in its place appears the Charlottesville Artillery, Captain J. M. Carrington.

CAVALRY FORCES.[1]

LOMAX'S DIVISION.

MAJOR-GENERAL J. J. LOMAX.

McCausland's Brigade.	*Johnson's Brigade.*	*Jackson's Brigade.*
Brig.-Gen. J. McCAUSLAND.	Brig.-Gen. B. T. JOHNSON.	Brig.-Gen. H. B. DAVIDSON
14th Virginia.	8th Virginia.	1st Maryland.
16th Virginia.	21st Virginia.	19th Virginia.
17th Virginia.	22d Virginia.	20th Virginia.
25th Virginia.	34th Virginia Battery.	46th Virginia Battalion.
37th Virginia Battalion.	36th Virginia Battery.	47th Virginia Battalion.

Imboden's Brigade.

Colonel GEORGE H. SMITH.

18th Virginia.	23d Virginia.	62d Mounted Infantry.

LEE'S DIVISION.

MAJOR-GENERAL FITZHUGH LEE.

Wickham's Brigade.	*Lomax's Brigade.*
Brig.-Gen. W. C. WICKHAM.	Brig.-Gen. L. L. LOMAX.
1st Virginia, Col. Carter.	5th Virginia, Col. H. Clay Pate.
2d Virginia, Col. Munford.	6th Virginia, Col. Julien Harrison.
3d Virginia, Col. Owen.	15th Virginia, Col. C. R. Collins.
4th Virginia, Col. Payne.	

Rosser's Brigade.

Brig.-Gen. THOMAS L. ROSSER.

7th Virginia, Col. R. H. Dulany.	12th Virginia, Col. A. W. Harman.
11th Virginia, Col. O. R. Funsten.	35th Virginia Batt'n, Lt.-Col. E. V. White.

---

[1] These forces are, for convenience, here grouped together, although the reader of the text will observe that they were not all present September 30th in this exact form. Rosser's brigade, for example, was at that time only on its way to the Valley; and when it arrived Rosser received command of the division. The organization of Lomax's cavalry is from the roster of October 30th, after the battle of Cedar Creek.

[NOTE.—For the foregoing rosters and for the statistics of numerical strength in Appendix B, the writer is indebted to the War Records Office. In the original returns the Union regimental commanders were not indicated. The troops of Generals Stevenson, Kelley, and Sullivan, though reckoned on the official Department Returns, were in garrison, not in the marching army.

It must be carefully noted that Sheridan's line-of-battle strength was, from several causes, at all times far below the totals of these official returns, which, in addition, take in the Department; and also that Early's Valley reserves, with which, in part, he repaired his heavy losses, do not appear, as such, on his inspection reports.]

APPENDIX B.

TABLES INDICATING NUMERICAL STRENGTH.

I.—*Abstract from Tri-monthly Return of the Department of West Virginia,* MAJOR-GENERAL FRANZ SIGEL, *Commanding, for April* 30, 1864.

STATION.	COMMANDING OFFICER.	COMMAND.	PRESENT FOR DUTY.		Aggregate present.
			Officers.	Men.	
Martinsburg ..	Major-Gen. Franz Sigel..	General and Staff.	10	....	10
Webster	Bg.-Gen. J. C. Sullivan..	First Division	208	4,597	5,435
Charleston....	Brig.-Gen. Geo. Crook ..	Third Division....	145	3,331	4,359
Harper's Ferry	Brig.-Gen. Max Weber ..	Separate Brigade..	114	3,612	4,177
New Creek ...	Col. N. Wilkinson.......	Separate Brigade..	108	2,545	2,968
Wheeling.....	Capt. Ewald Over	Independent Co...	3	71	82
		Total Infantry..	578	14,156	17,021
Cumberland ..	Major-Gen Jul. Stahel..	General and Staff.	3	....	3
Charleston....	Brig.-Gen.W. W. Averell.	Second Division...	139	3,355	4,392
Charleston....	Brig.-Gen. A. N. Duffié..	Brigade..........	97	2,747	3,343
Cumberland ..	Col. J. E. Wynkoop.....	Brigade	65	1,676	2,008
Burlington ...	Col. R. M. Richardson ..	15th New York....	28	730	1,067
Cumberland ..	Capt. Frank Smith......	3d Ind. Co. Ohio..	1	48	68
Cumberland ..	Capt. Wm. King........	Co. M, 4th Va	2	51	56
Webster	Capt. J. Jaehne........	Co. C, 16th Illinois	3	40	56
		Total Cavalry...	338	8,647	10,933
Webster	Bg.-Gen. J. C. Sullivan..	....	8	361	384
Charleston ...	Bg.-Gen. W. W. Averell..	....	3	76	79
Charleston ...	Brig.-Gen. Geo. Crook...	....	7	248	283
Harper's Ferry	Brig.-Gen. Max Weber ..	....	48	2,075	2,539
New Creek ...	Col. N. Wilkinson......	....	14	531	570
Wheeling.....	Capt. Ewald Over......	....	3	29	35
		Total Artillery[1].	83	3,320	3,890
Frederick	Lieut. James Drysdale ..	132d Co. V. R. C...	1	18	54
Cumberland ..	Lieut. V. N. Higgins....	147th Co. V. R.C...	1	40	41
Cumberland ..	Capt. F. E. Town	Det. Signal Corps .	13	96	112
		Total...........	1,024	26,277	32,061

[1] Eighty-six pieces of artillery.

II.—*Abstract from Return of the Army of Western Virginia,* MAJ.·
GEN. JOHN C. BRECKINRIDGE, *C. S. Army, Commanding, for
the month of April,* 1864.

COMMANDS.	PRESENT FOR DUTY.		Effective total present.	Aggregate present.	Aggregate present and absent.
	Officers.	Men.			
General Staff	21	....	....	21	21
Echols's Brigade 1	107	1,139	1,339	1,615	2,182
McCausland's Brigade	99	1,548	1,548	1,774	2,257
Wharton's Brigade 2	....	....	....	....	....
Forty-fifth Virginia Regiment	42	749	749	840	971
Bosang's Company	....	41	39	48	96
Total Infantry	248	3,677	3,675	4,277	5,506
Jackson's Brigade	89	810	810	1,010	1,994
Jenkins's Brigade (collecting)	115	1,315	1,332	1,616	3,008
Thirty-seventh Virginia Bat'n, Co H.	4	67	67	71	99
Total Cavalry	208	2,192	2,209	2,697	5,101
Artillery (7 batteries)	30	642	597	675	822
Engineer Troops (1 Co.)	3	57	57	61	73
Grand total	510	6,568	6,538	7,731	11,523

III.—*Strength of the Infantry of the Army of the Valley District,
August* 20, 1864, *as shown by Inspection Report of this date.*

TROOPS.	Aggregate present for duty.	Aggregate present.	Aggregate present and absent.
Gordon's Division	7	7	8
York's Brigade	614	803	3,708
Terry's Brigade	858	963	6,042
Evans's Brigade	1,344	1,597	4,254
Total	2,823	3,370	14,012
Rodes's Division			
Battle's Brigade	966	1,154	3,271
Grimes's Brigade	918	1,113	3,317
Cook's Brigade	699	902	2,447
Cox's Brigade	803	991	4,085
Total	3,386	4,160	13,120
Ramseur's Division	11	11	12
Pegram's Brigade	595	831	2,334
Johnston's Brigade	600	742	2,410
Godwin's Brigade	854	928	2,627
Total	2,060	2,512	7,383
Grand total	8,269	10,042	31,515

1 " This brigade, under the command of Major-General John Echols, entered upon
the campaign of 1864 with 2,150 men and a full complement of officers on May 6, 1864.
The brigade was then well armed, equipped, and provided with a full supply of clothing, and in a thorough state of discipline and efficiency. . . . The military bearing
and appearance of the brigade was soldierly and inspiring. In this thorough state of
organization and discipline the brigade opened its campaigning with the battle of New
Market " (abstract from Inspection Report of Col. G. S. Patton's brigade. Sept. 29th).
  "The brigade entered the present campaign with an aggregate effective of 2,100
men. It now numbers but little over 400 aggregate effective. . . . At Cloyd's Farm,
May 9, 1864, it fought the Eighth Corps, and June 5th, at Piedmont, in conjunction
with a small force of dismounted cavalry and the forty-fifth regiment of infantry, it
fought the command of General Hunter " (abstract from Inspection Report of Smith ·
brigade, Wharton's division, September 29th).
  2 Not reported, the returns being delayed.

IV.—*Abstract from the R turn of the Middle Military Division*, MAJOR-GENERAL P. H. SHERIDAN, *Commanding, for August*, 1864.

COMMAND.	PRESENT FOR DUTY.		Aggreg'te present.	Ag'gate present and abs't.	Field pieces.
	Officers.	Men.			
General Headquarters........	24	120	216	389	
Department of West Virginia—					
Staff and Infantry........	538	11,898	14,032	23,443	
Cavalry..................	241	6,231	8,457	14,722	
Artillery.................	83	2,877	3,521	4,478	
Total Dept. West Virginia...	862	21,006	26,010	42,643	
Sixth Army Corps—					
Staff and Infantry........	635	11,333	15,717	29,599	
Artillery	24	623	697	812	24
Total Sixth Army Corps.....	659	11,956	16,414	30,411	24
Det. Nineteenth Army Corps—					
Staff and Infantry........	657	12,068	14,187	21,081	
Artillery...............	15	436	458	559	20
Total Nineteenth Army Corps	672	12,504	14,645	21,640	20
Cavalry Forces—					
Cavalry and Staff.........	371	7,891	10,347	20,028	32
Artillery.................	22	611	701	979	24
Total Cavalry forces	393	8,502	11,048	21,007	56
Grand total...............	2,610	54,008	68,333	116,090	100

V.—*Strength of* EARLY'S *Infantry, August* 31, 1864, *as shown by Abstract from Monthly Returns.*

TROOPS.	PRESENT FOR DUTY.		Aggregate present for duty.	Aggregate present.	Aggregate present and absent.
	Officers.	Men.			
Staff........................	17	....	17	17	19
Breckenridge's Division [1]..........	243	2,104	2,347	2,832	6,860
Rodes's Division..................	323	3,013	3,336	4,185	16,109
Gordon's Division................	300	2,544	2,844	3,339	14,208
Ramseur's Division	210	1,909	2,119	2,571	7,363
Total, exclusive of Kershaw....	1,093	9,570	10,663	12,924	44,559
Kershaw's Division [2].............	377	3,445	3,822	4,769	11,390
Total	1,470	13,015	14,485	17,693	55,949

[1] Commanded by Wharton when a corps command of this division and Gordon's was given t Breckenridge.

[2] Present at this time with Early's army; not present in battles of Opequon and Fisher's Hill, but present at Cedar Creek.

Ten days later than the foregoing, September 10, the figures of "present for duty" were:

COMMANDS, ETC.	Officers.	Men.	Aggregate.
Breckenridge's Division........................	194	2,172	2,366
Rodes's Division	307	3,244	3,551
Gordon's Division.............................	271	2,690	2,961
Ramseur's Division	182	2,010	2,192
Carter's (Artillery) Division	39	818	857
Lomax's (Cavalry) Division	353	3,215	3,568
	1,346	14,149	15,495

The Inspection Reports of June 30th gave Fitz Lee's division 130 officers and 1,553 men—aggregate, 1,683 ; those of July 10th, 115 officers and 1,591 men—aggregate, 1,706 ; those of November 30th, "total effective," 1,455. If 1,700, for Fitz Lee, should be added to the figures already given, the total, without Kershaw, would be 17,195 ; with Kershaw, about September 10th, the total would be, in round numbers, about 21,000.

VI.—SHERIDAN'S *Strength, September* 10, 1864.

HEADQUARTERS MIDDLE MILITARY DIVISION,
September 13, 1864.

GENERAL—I have the honor to forward as complete a field return as is possible at the present time. The most strenuous exertions are being made by me to obtain a full return, but the difficulty in obtaining such from the commanding officer Department of West Virginia, because of his command covering so great an extent of country, has so far prevented.

The enclosed return does not include the cavalry under Averell, about 2,500, or the troops of the Departments of Washington, Susquehanna, or Middle.

I simply forward it you as a statement showing the number of men for duty south of the Potomac. Hoping soon to furnish complete all reports required,

Very respectfully, your obedient servant,

P. H. SHERIDAN,
Major-General.

Brigadier-General L. THOMAS,
Adjutant General, United States Army.

Field Return of Troops in the Field, belonging to the Middle Military Division, September 10, 1864.

TROOPS.	PRESENT FOR DUTY.		
	Officers.	Men.	Aggreg'te.
Sixth Army Corps, Infantry.....................	668	12,028	12,696
" " Artillery......................	22	626	648
Nineteenth Army Corps, Infantry	660	12,150	12,810
" " Artillery	7	208	215
Army of West Virginia, Infantry......	306	6,834	7,140
" " Artillery	12	355	367
Cavalry (Torbert's).............................	339	6,126	6,465
Artillery	7	346	353
Military District, Harper's Ferry................	204	4,611	4,815
	2,203[1]	43,284	45,487[1]

[1] A clerical error in casting up the first column of the foregoing table, which is taken from Badeau's Military History of U. S. Grant, makes it read 2,203 instead of 2,225 ; and the aggregate, in like manner, should be 45,509.

VII.—*Abstract from Return of the Middle Military Division*, MAJOR-GENERAL P. H. SHERIDAN, *Commanding, for September*, 1864.

COMMANDS.	PRESENT FOR DUTY.		Aggregate present.	Aggregate present and absent.	Field pieces.
	Officers.	Men.			
General Headquarters..................	22	66	145	281	
Department of West Virginia:					
Staff and Infantry................	380	9,917	11,077	19,475	
Cavalry	167	4,591	6,537	14,833	
Artillery	88	3,006	3,661	4,502	
Total Department West Virginia.	635	17,514	21,275	38,810	
Sixth Army Corps:					
Staff and Infantry..	419	9.648	13,068	28,690	
Artillery.........................	24	576	662	776	24
Total Sixth Army Corps.........	443	10,224	13,730	29,466	24
Detachment Nineteenth Army Corps:					
Staff and Infantry................	502	10,360	12,244	21,134	
Artillery...	12	405	438	527	20
Total Nineteenth Army Corps....	514	10,765	12,682	21,661	20
Cavalry Forces:					
Cavalry and Staff................	267	6,076	8,318	19,785	
Artillery................	22	520	614	858	24
Total Cavalry Forces..	289	6,596	8,932	20,643	24
Grand total........	1,903	45,165	56,764	110,861	68

VIII.—*Partial Strength of* EARLY'S *Army, September* 30, 1864, *as shown by Inspection Reports.*

TROOPS.	Aggregate present for duty.	Aggregate present.	Aggregate present and absent.
Rodes's Division (Ramseur com'd'g), Gen'l Staff.	17	17	19
Battle's Brigade, Brig.-Gen. C. A. Battle.....	743	973	2,952
Grimes's Brigade, Brig.-Gen. Bryan Grimes...	795	1,018	3,310
Cox's Brigade, Brig.-Gen. W. R. Cox.........	579	800	3,889
Cook's Brigade, Brig.-Gen. Phil. Cook........	442	663	2,359
Total.................................	2,576	3,471	12,509

VIII.—*Partial Strength of* EARLY'S *Army, September* 30, 1864, *as shown by Inspection Reports—*Continued.

TROOPS.	Aggregate present for duty.	Aggregate present.	Aggregate present and absent.
Early's Division (Pegram com'd'g), Gen'l Staff..	12	12	12
Pegram's Brigade, Col. John S. Hoffman.....	437	663	2,308
Johnston's Brigade. Brig.-Gen. R. D. Johnston.	456	627	2,438
Gordon's Brigade, Lt.-Col. Wm. T. Davis	712	843	2,984
Total..................................	1,617	2,145	7,742
Wharton's Div. (Wharton com'd'g), Gen'l Staff.	11	12	14
Patton's Brigade, Capt. E. S. Read	286	416	1,092
Forsbey's Brigade, Capt. R. H Logan........	417	578	2,131
Smith's Brigade, Col. Thos. Smith...........	457	632	1,494
Total.................................	1,171	1,638	4,731
Carter's Artillery [1] (Carter commanding).......			
Braxton's Battalion (6 guns)............	222	259	420
Cutshaw's Battalion (12 guns)	381	460	1,188
McLaughlin's Battalion (8 guns)............	239	286	457
Nelson's Battalion (9 guns).................	259	305	419
Total.................................	1,101	1,310	2,404

IX.—*Strength of the Army of the Valley District, December* 31, 1864, *as shown by Inspection Reports.*

TROOPS.	Aggregate present for duty.	Aggregate Present.	Aggregate Present and absent	Pieces of artillery.
General Staff.................	7	7	10	
Wharton's Division—Staff ...	12	12	13	
Echols's Brigade..	570	663	1,981	
Wharton's Brigade...........	809	1,043	2,607	
Smith's Brigade	592	733	1,993	
Artillery...	942	1,153	2,391	28
Cavalry (not reported)	.....	....	....	
Total Infantry and Artillery.	2,932	3,611	9,085	28

"The camps of the artillery and infantry of the army are located near Fisherville, Augusta County, Va., about seven miles south of Staunton, on the Virginia Central Railroad. Major-General Lomax's cavalry division is cantoned from Swift Run Gap, in Rockingham County, Va., across the Blue Ridge to Madison Court House, and Major-General Rosser's is collected near Swoop's Depôt, nine miles south of Staunton, on the Central Railroad."

[1] Thirty-five guns and 499 serviceable horses.

APPENDIX C.

LIST OF CASUALTIES AND CAPTURES.

I.—*Casualties in the Shenandoah Valley Forces of* GENERAL SHERIDAN, 1864.

COMMAND.	BATTLE.	Killed.	Wounded.	Missing.	Aggregate.
Sixth Army Corps.......	Opequon	213	1.424	48	1,685
	Fisher's Hill	24	210	3	237
	Cedar Creek	255	1,666	294	2,215
	Reconnoissances and minor engagements.	86	665	11	762
Total......		578	3,965	356	4,899
Nineteenth Army Corps .	Opequon	275	1,228	453	1,956
	Fisher's Hill.........	11	47	2	60
	Cedar Creek	243	1,352	893	2,488
	Reconnoissances and minor engagements.	57	446	13	516
Total.............		586	3,073	1,361	5,020
Army of West Virginia..	Opequon and Fisher's Hill	105	840	8	953
	Cedar Creek	46	268	523	8.7
	Reconnoissances and minor engagements.	150	839	96	1,085
Total.............		301	1,947	637	2,885
Provisional Division	Cedar Creek	19	91	121	231
Cavalry	Opequon	65	267	109	441
	Tom's Brook.........	9	48	...	57
	Cedar Creek.........	15	139	50	214
	Twenty six (26) other engagements	355	2,363	487	3,205
Total.............		451	2,817	646	3,917
Grand total........		1,938	11,893	3,121	16,952

II.—*Official Report of Prisoners Received in the Military Division.*

HEADQUARTERS MILITARY DIVISION OF THE GULF,
NEW ORLEANS, November 18, 1865.

GENERAL—I have the honor to report that the number of Confederate prisoners received by the forces under your command, from August 1, 1864, to March 1, 1865, was about thirteen thousand (13,000).[1] The names of nearly that number are recorded on the books recently used in the office of the Provost-Marshal-General Middle Military Division.

Respectfully submitted,

E. B. PARSONS,
Late Provost-Marshal-General Middle Military Division.
Maj.-Gen. P. H. SHERIDAN, *United States Army.*

III.—*Summary of* GENERAL SHERIDAN'S *Official Statement of Captures and Destructions in the Middle Military Division, from August* 8, 1864, *to January* 1, 1865.

One hundred and one pieces of artillery, 83 artillery carriages and limbers, 35 caissons, 128 double sets of artillery harness, 2 anvils, 5,067 small arms; in addition, 23,000 rounds of artillery ammunition, 131 wagons, 137 ambulances, 7 medical wagons, 1,006 sets of harness, 1,040 sets of horse equipments, 49 battle-flags, 14,163 small arms, 1,061,000 rounds of small-arm ammunition, 4,240 horses, 553 mules, 120 flour-mills, 1 woollen mill, 8 saw-mills, 1 powder-mill, 3 saltpetre works, 2,300 barns, 7 furnaces, 1 railroad depot, 1 locomotive, 6 distilleries, 3 box-cars. 4 tanneries, 460,072 bushels of wheat, 22,000 bushels of oats, 157.076 bushels of corn, 874 barrels of flour, 51,380 tons of hay, 500 tons of fodder, 450 tons of straw, 16,438 beef cattle, 17,837 sheep, 16,141 swine, 250 calves, 12,000 pounds of bacon and ham, 10,000 pounds of tobacco, 947 miles of rails, 2,500 bushels of potatoes, 1,865 pounds of cotton yarn, 3 factories.

IV.—*Summary of* GENERAL SHERIDAN'S *Official Statement of Captures and Destructions in Expedition from Winchester to Petersburg, March,* 1865.

Three breaches in James River canal, 60 canal locks, 5 aqueducts, 40 bridges, 2 naval repair-shops, 2 dredges, 1 machine shop, 1 forge, 9 portable forges, 1 lumber-yard, 1 foundry, 21 warehouses, 6 government warehouses, 606 hogsheads, 500 kegs, 58 boxes, and 3,000 pounds of tobacco; 1 tobacco factory valued at $200,000, 336 sacks and 500 bushels of salt, 12 barrels of potash, 29 canal boats and 6 flat boats loaded with stores and ammunition, 41 miles of railroad and 27 of telegraph, 10 depots, 400 feet of trestle work, 4 cars, 22 bridges and 6 culverts, 400 cords of wood, 3,000 pairs of trousers, 2,000 shirts and drawers, 50 kegs of powder, 500,000 pounds of rifle ammunition, 1 barrel of oil, 400 gross of buckles and rings, 3 saw-mills, 7 flour- and grist-mills, 1 cloth-mill with manufactured gray cloth, 3 cotton-mills, 1,500 pounds of wool, 35 bales of cotton, 1 candle manufactory, 1,000 pounds of candles, 3 tanneries, 1,500 bushels of wheat, 1,000 grain sacks, 600 barrels of flour, 18 wagon loads of grain and stores, 1 military jail at Goochland, 225 ambulances and wagons, 93 wagons loaded with ammunition and stores, 75 beef cattle, 100,000 feet of bridge timber, 1,500 cotton quilts, 1,000 pounds of bacon, 7 water-tanks, 3,000 pounds of fixed ammunition, 2,000 tents, 500 saddles, 110 sides of leather, 904 sets of harness, 1,600 prisoners. 17 pieces of artillery, 6 caissons, 1,900 small arms, 60 carbines, a quantity of shells and small arms, 16 battle-flags, 2 United States guidons, 2,143 horses and mules.

---

[1] "Altogether, during the campaign, I had on the Provost-Marshal's books record of 7,000 unwounded prisoners, who were soldiers, besides which there were a large number of civil prisoners sent to the rear. Colonel E. B. Parsons, who succeeded me as Provost-Marshal-General, in an official communication, puts the actual number of prisoners on the books at 13,000; and this from August, 1864, to March, 1865" (Colonel B. W. Crowninshield's Cedar Creek).

APPENDIX D.

CONFEDERATE ACCOUNTS OF EVENTS.

I.—*Action at New Market, May* 15, 1864.

Colonel J. Stoddard Johnston, of Breckenridge's staff ("Southern Hist. Soc. Papers," June, 1879), says that in May, 1864, Breckenridge's entire infantry was ready to prevent Crook's march against Newbern when Lee directed him to march at once, with all his available force, to the defence of Staunton, news being received of Sigel's advance from Martinsburg, and his occupation of New Market with a part of his column. "Breckenridge marched at one o'clock the morning of May 15th, and by daylight was in line of battle two miles south of New Market, his front being covered by Imboden's cavalry, Harmon's command being left as rear-guard to the trains, a mile farther in the rear. . . . To accomplish the defeat of Sigel's advance he had but a meagre force—the aggregate of infantry muskets being but thirty one hundred. With this command, as the morning opened, he advanced in line of battle; the cavalry of Imboden giving way to our infantry skirmishers and going to the right, with instructions to operate during the day as a cover to our right flank, and to endeavor, as the battle progressed, to gain the rear of Sigel, and to burn the bridge across the Shenandoah near Mount Jackson, four miles from New Market. . . .

"General Breckenridge formed his line of battle with the right resting on the turnpike, and his left on the summit of the ridge, placing the cadets in the centre between the two brigades. He had but one line of battle in two ranks, with no reserves. It was not long before the skirmish line of the opposing forces became engaged, and after sharp firing the enemy fell back beyond New Market. Then ensued heavy artillery firing, which occupied the greater part of the morning. A reconnoissance showed that Sigel, finding he was opposed by infantry instead of cavalry, had abandoned the offensive and assumed the defensive. To this end he had retired with his main force to the crest of the hill about a mile north of New Market, where, with open ground in his front and his flanks well covered by the topography already described, he occupied an exceedingly strong defensive position. The rain was almost continuous during the day, and Breckenridge's forces had operated in wheat-fields, which made it very laborious, particularly in handling artillery. . . .

"When his line had reached within two hundred yards of that of the enemy, the position was very critical, and for a time it seemed doubtful as to which would be the first to give way. At this juncture Sigel's cavalry, on his left, were seen deploying for a charge down the pike. Breckenridge, with his keen eye, detected the manœuvre and ordered the guns to be double-shotted with canister. It had scarcely been done before they were seen advancing in squadron front, when, coming in range, the artillery opened and the charge was repulsed disastrously—not more than a score reaching our lines, and they as prisoners, lying on the necks of their horses. This seemed to turn the tide of battle, for in a few moments Sigel's line gave way and our troops pressed to the crest, only to see the enemy in full retreat. Pursuit was given as soon as our line could be reformed. Sigel made a brief stand at Rood's Hill to cover his retreat, which he effected beyond the Shenandoah, burning the bridge as his rear-guard passed over. Had Imbo den succeeded in carrying out his instructions, the whole of Sigel's command would have been captured. As it was, Breckenridge captured five pieces of artillery, which were abandoned on the field, besides five or six hundred prisoners, exclusive of the wounded left on the field. His own loss, though not nearly so large as Sigel's, was several hundred killed and wounded."

II.—GENERAL GORDON'S *Report of the Battle of the Monocacy.*

"About 2.30 P.M., July 9th, I was ordered by Major-General Breckenridge, commanding corps, to move my division to the right and cross the Monocacy about one mile below the bridge and ford. . . . I ordered the command to advance *en échelon* by brigades from the right. The troops emerged from the woods seven hundred yards in front of the enemy's left, under heavy fire from infantry and artillery. . . . This battle, though short, was severe. I desire, in this connection, to state a fact of which I was an eye-witness, and which, for its rare occurrence and the evidence it affords of the sanguinary character of this struggle, I consider worthy of official mention. One portion of the enemy's second line extended along a branch from which he was driven, leaving many dead and wounded in the water and upon its banks. This position was in turn occupied by a portion of Evans's brigade in the attack on the enemy's third line. So profuse was the flow of blood from the killed and wounded of both these forces that it reddened the stream for more than a hundred yards below. It has not been my fortune to witness on any battlefield a more commendable spirit. . . . I regret to state that my loss was heavy in both officers and men, amounting in the aggregate, as shown by tabular report of brigade commanders, to 698."

III.—SHERIDAN'S *Pursuit of Early, August,* 1864.

" It was on this retreat [from Winchester to Strasburg, August 11th] that General Breckenridge and General Early were riding along together very moodily at the prospect, both of the Valley campaign and the general course of Southern independence, when General Early spoke up quizzically and said : ' Well, Breckenridge, what do you think of our rights in the territories now ? ' The inquiry was so humorous, and in a vein so much in contrast with the gloomy feelings of the company, that General Breckenridge and all present were thrown into good spirits at once. Early was an old Whig, and up to the breaking out of the war a violent Union man, always the antipodes of Breckenridge in politics " (Col. J. S. Johnston, as above).

IV.—*Early's Menace of Washington.*

In a comparatively recent statement, regarding his march to Washington, Early says : " My advance, a small body of cavalry, arrived for the first time in front of the defences about noon of the 11th, and I followed this advance in person, arriving in sight of the defences a little after noon. The main body of my command did not get up until some two or three hours later." Speaking of the skirmish at 1.30 P.M. that day, he says that his cavalry only was then engaged : " At that time the leading brigade of my command had not come up, but soon after came up, formed line, and sent forward skirmishers, who drove those of the enemy back to the cover of his works. It took some time to get the remainder of the leading division into line, and it was much later when the rest of my command was brought up. . . . My troops did not all get up and into line before four o'clock, and my leading brigade was not in line before two o'clock." While, therefore, General Badeau's statement that " Washington had really been in very little danger, for the works were so admirable that the merest handful of men could hold off an army until reinforcements arrived " may be a somewhat extreme assertion, General Grant's official report that adequate reinforcements arrived before Early's troops did seems to be within bounds.

Colonel Johnston, of Breckenridge's staff, in the article already cited, speaks of Early's command as including, July 3d, Breckenridge's corps, two divisions, Early's corps, also two divisions, and " a corps of cavalry, commanded by General Ransom. . . . the whole being about 3,000 cavalry, most of it being known as wild cavalry—of the inefficiency of which there was constant complaint and almost daily exhibition."

As to Early's numbers, in marching from Staunton, if to the 10,663 aggregate infantry present for duty, exclusive of Kershaw's, on his inspection reports of August 31st, be added the 3,000 cavalry spoken of in round numbers, by Colonel Johnston, or rather the aggregate of 3,568 of Lomax's (previously Ransom's) cavalry, command, present for duty September 10th, we get a force of over 14,000 infantry and cavalry. The artillery must have brought the total to 15,000, inasmuch as, September 30th, after a hard campaign, the three battalions that went to Washington still numbered, aggregate present for duty, 820. Early could hardly have lost fewer than 2,000 men prior to the inspection returns of August 31st, since Gordon reports that his division alone suffered 698 casualties at Monocacy, where McCausland was also heavily engaged ; and Ramseur is known to have lost about 400, perhaps more, at Carter's Farm, August 20th. In addition there were the losses at Leetown, Maryland Heights, Fort Stevens, and Snicker's Ferry, and McCausland's cavalry loss of 75 at Cumberland, and of fully 400 at Moorefield. Early also speaks of hundreds of stragglers. Making allowance for the very few reinforcements received on returning to the Valley, we reach the approximate estimate of 17,000 given in the text. Of course Early had no such force with which to attack Fort Stevens, as several thousand must be deducted for the losses then already suffered in battle and hard marching, and for the part of his cavalry absent around Baltimore; and his artillerymen and train guards would also have to be deducted from a possible storming column,

V.—*Official Diary of First Corps, A. N. V.*[1] (*Extracts*).

"August 7th.—Leave Richmond at 7.30 A.M. by rail, and arrive at Mitchell's Station at dark.

"August 8th.—Last of Kershaw's division arrives to-day.

"August 11th.—Cutshaw's artillery horses and Fitz Lee's cavalry division arrive. Hear of Early at Bunker Hill.

"With Kershaw's division and Cutshaw's battalion of artillery, we move from Mitchell's Station soon after sunrise, and halt at Culpeper at midday.

"August 16th.—To hold Guard Hill and cover the passage of the Shenandoah, Wofford's brigade of infantry and Wickham's of cavalry are sent to seize the position, which is done with the loss of but eight or ten men. Wofford, however, moves off to the right to attack the enemy's cavalry, and the enemy, just at that moment, having charged and driven back our own cavalry, pitches into Wofford and drives him back in confusion and with loss.

"August 25th.—Kershaw moves at daylight with Cutshaw to relieve Rodes and Ramseur. Early's force moves to threaten Martinsburg, and Fitz Lee (who has resumed command of all the cavalry) toward Williamsport.

"August 20th.—Enemy in position, and quiet until afternoon about five o'clock, when he advances four or five regiments of infantry and one of cavalry to feel our lines. The picket line of the 15th South Carolina Regiment, Kershaw's brigade, breaks, and about 100 men of it are captured. The enemy soon retires. During the night we hear from Early, who is at Leetown.

"September 3d.—Move at 12 M. from Winchester for Berryville, by the pike. Strike the enemy about four miles from Berryville.

"September 15th.—Move at sunrise with Kershaw and Cutshaw up the Valley pike, and camp on North Fork of Shenandoah."

---

[1] From Southern Hist. Soc. Papers.

INDEX.

NOTE.—*Regiments, batteries, etc., are indexed under the names of their States, excepting batteries called by their captain's or by some other special name. These are indexed under* BATTERIES.